Kandy Shepherd swapped her career as a magazine editor for a life writing romance. She lives on a small farm in the Blue Mountains near Sydney, Australia, with her husband, daughter, and lots of pets. She believes in love at first sight and real-life romance—they worked for her! Kandy loves to hear from her readers. Visit her at kandyshepherd.com

Christy Jeffries graduated from the University of California, Irvine, with a degree in criminology, and received her Juris Doctor from California Western School of Law. But drafting court documents and working in law enforcement was merely an apprenticeship for her current career in the dynamic field of mummyhood and romance writing. She lives in Southern California with her patient husband, two energetic sons and one sassy grandmother. Follow her online at christyjeffries.com

D1354715

THEIR ROYAL BABY GIFT

KANDY SHEPHERD

HIS CHRISTMAS CINDERELLA

CHRISTY JEFFRIES

MILLS & BOON

First Published in Great Britain 2020
by Mills & Boon, an imprint of HarperCollinsPublishers,
1 London Bridge Street, London, SE1 9GF

Their Royal Baby Gift © 2020 Harlequin Books S.A.
His Christmas Cinderella © 2020 Harlequin Books S.A.

Special thanks and acknowledgement are given to Kandy Shepherd for her contribution to the *Christmas at the Harrington Park Hotel* collection

Special thanks and acknowledgement are given to Christy Jeffries for her contribution to the *Montana Mavericks: What Happened to Beatrix?* series.

ISBN: 978-0-263-27902-3

1120

THEIR ROYAL
BABY GIFT

KANDY SHEPHERD

To Deanna Lang, with many thanks.
Not just for your ongoing friendship but
for your help in creating my hero Edward's character
and background.

CHAPTER ONE

SALLY HARRINGTON WAS having fun pretending to be an awestruck tourist as she gawked at the rooftop garden with its towering palm trees, lush tropical plants and enormous infinity swimming pool, all poised a breathtaking sixty storeys high above the city of Singapore. The resort in the sky exceeded all her expectations—it was nothing short of spectacular. No wonder a well-heeled international crowd made it their playground. She snapped photo after photo on her phone's camera, even taking a few selfies in pursuit of authenticity.

She was playing Sally the tourist because she wanted to keep her real interest in the roof garden secret. Truth was, she was in Singapore on a confidential research mission on behalf of the iconic Harrington Park Hotel in London that had recently come back into her family's hands.

She wasn't here as a holidaymaker but as a professional designer. Some might say she was conducting a little industrial espionage—whatever you called it, she didn't want to be caught out. The aesthetics of the roof garden interested her, but also the logistics of how it had been created. Structural support for the weight of the pool and the plantings? Materials brought in by helicopter or crane? Details were vital—she only had seven weeks to create a fabulous roof garden of her own for the splashy, invitation-only Christmas Eve relaunch of the Harrington Park.

'Hotel royalty' *Celebrity* magazine called the Harringtons. It was impossible for Sally and her two brothers to fly under the radar in London but here, so far from home, it was easier to be anonymous as she sought inspiration for her ambitious project. And, she had to admit, she'd jumped at the chance to take a break from the total upheaval of the ordered life she had fought so hard to achieve.

First had been the decision by her and her twin brother James—Jay to family and friends—to use a substantial inheritance from their grandmother to bid for the Harrington Park when it suddenly came onto the market. The luxury hotel on Regent's Park had been in their family for more than one hundred years until their unscrupulous stepfather had taken it over and run it down. She and Jay had been thwarted in their purchase by a mystery buyer who had turned out to be their estranged older brother, Hugo. Sally hadn't seen Hugo for seventeen years since he'd left their family when she'd been ten years old and he seventeen. Now he expected her to forgive all and work with him to restore both the hotel and their family's pride.

Jay, a top chef with his own award-winning restaurant, had found it easier than she to fall in with Hugo's plans to bring the hotel back to its former glory. Sally had agreed to oversee the refurbishment of the interiors because she couldn't bear to see how shabby they had become. She'd said yes to the urban roof garden too, in spite of her initial protests that there simply wasn't time to undertake such an ambitious project.

But that didn't mean she'd thawed towards Hugo. She still remembered her distress when she'd woken up on Christmas morning all those years ago to find her beloved older brother had run away without so much as a goodbye. On top of her father's death and her mother's marriage to a man Sally had despised and distrusted, Hugo's betrayal had been too much to forgive. And now he was back and flinging olive branches at her. A break away in tropical Singapore from both her older brother and chilly London had seemed like a very good idea indeed.

With the pool behind her, Sally edged back to get a final shot that would encompass the plantings of glorious pink and purple orchids around the restaurant. The tropical afternoon sun beat down on her arms, bare in her sleeveless white linen dress. She thought vaguely about applying more sun cream. Then, distracted, she tripped. In a split second of panicked disbelief and horror she realised she was about to topple backwards, arms windmilling, into the swimming pool.

She was aware of a collective gasp from the onlookers around the other side of the pool. Then she lost control of her balance and fell, hitting the water on her back. She tried to scream but all she managed was a splutter as the cold water engulfed her and she went under. Her long hair floated over her face, her wedge-heeled sandals made it difficult to kick, her dress tangled around her legs and dragged her down as she struggled. She choked on her terror.

She couldn't swim.

Edward Chen was striding past the pool, intent on the agenda of his next meeting for the afternoon, when he saw the woman with the long chestnut hair fall in the water with a splash. Heard the gasps and laughter from the people seated around the other side of the pool. Like him, they no doubt expected her to surface straight away and swim to the edge. But she didn't. The woman momentarily broke the surface of the water, panic and terror etched on her face, then went under again, leaving only a few bubbles floating on the surface.

With no thought to his Italian tailor-made linen suit or his handmade leather shoes, Edward dived in. Just a few strong strokes and he was with her. He grabbed her under her arms and kicked hard to take them both to the surface.

Once clear, he trod water to keep them both afloat. The woman blinked the water from her eyes, coughed and spluttered, took in deep gulps of air, gripped his shoulders hard. She tried to say something, but the words were lost in another fit of coughing. Edward realised she was trying to thank him.

'Don't say anything—just catch your breath,' he said.

He steered her towards the shallow steps that led out of the pool. As she shakily emerged from the water, still clinging tightly to him, there was muted applause from the people who had only minutes before laughed at the sight of a fully dressed woman toppling into the pool. Edward cursed under his breath in his own language. Anyone with a cell phone was a potential paparazzo.

Did they know who he was?

The woman's eyes widened in alarm. 'Please,' she managed to choke out, 'get me away from here. I… I…don't want to draw attention to myself.'

Edward had every reason not to want to draw attention to himself either. Especially in the company of an attractive young Englishwoman. Even drenched and dripping she was lovely: heart-shaped face, grey eyes, tall and slender. Under the water, with her dark chestnut hair waving around her, she'd looked like a mermaid.

She was shivering, whether chilled from the cold water of the pool or from shock he couldn't be sure. Edward was wet through himself and his shoes squelched with each step.

He couldn't be seen like this.

He came from a family that had been rocked to its foundations by scandal. It was vital for his family's future that he stayed free of it. He dreaded the innuendo and speculation the media would build around his good deed if they got wind of it. The woman's wet dress clung to her body, making no secret of her curves. She was a scandal in the making.

He grabbed a striped towel from a stack on a nearby lounger and threw it around her shoulders, another one around himself. 'Keep your head down and walk as quickly as you can,' he said.

She attempted a faster pace but stumbled and he had to put his arm around her to keep her upright. He scarcely broke his stride to pick up the phone she'd dropped when she'd fallen.

'Are you hurt?'

'Only…only my pride.'

'Are you staying at this hotel?'

She shook her head and wet strands flew around her face, sending droplets of water onto him. 'I… I only came here for lunch. My hotel is in the older part of town.'

'I'm in the penthouse here. There's a private elevator down to my suite. I'll take you there.'

'Please.' She was still shivering, and her eyes didn't look quite focused.

He had to get her—and himself—out of here. Edward kept his arm around Ms Mermaid as he ushered her to the discreet private elevator. If people didn't recognise him, a scandal could be averted.

Within minutes they were in the expansive suite where he was living while his Singapore house was being gutted and refurbished. He slammed the door behind them and slumped in relief. No one with a camera could follow him here. He turned back into the room. Then realised he had swapped one problem for another. Standing opposite him, dripping water on the marble floor of his hotel suite, was a beautiful stranger—and her presence here could so easily be misconstrued.

'Thank you,' she said. 'I could have drowned.' Her eyes were huge, her lush mouth trembled. Hair wet and dripping, make-up smudged around her eyes, she was breathtakingly lovely. A red-blooded male, no matter how chivalrous, could not fail to feel a stirring of attraction. 'I… I can't swim, not enough to save myself. But you… you saved me.'

'It was the right thing to do,' Edward said gruffly. He had been brought up to follow a strict code of duty and honour. To help a person in danger was second nature. And there'd been something so desperate in her expression when she'd gone under for the second time. He could not have denied her silent cry for help.

'You were a gentleman. No one else came to my rescue. I've never been so frightened in my life. I really thought… I thought it was the end.'

She started to shake and shiver, her teeth chattering. Edward thought back to his first aid training. His family's country compound back home was on a private beach. There he'd learned to swim and to keep both himself and others safe in the water. She didn't appear injured. She didn't need CPR. What this woman needed was warmth and comfort. He hesitated for only a second before he pulled her into his arms. And was shocked by how good she felt there, her curves pressed to him, how instantly his body reacted to her.

Sally's thoughts raced. She must be in shock. Why else would she unquestioningly follow an unknown man to his hotel room? Why would she press her body so close to a total stranger? And welcome his comforting hug? His warmth and strength seemed to infuse her, calm her, bring her breathing back to normal. Her reaction could only be from shock. Or some kind of insanity. How else could she explain how much she was enjoying his embrace, the feel of his hard chest, his strong arms around her?

She'd been too long without the intimate touch of a man.

'I can't thank you enough.' Her voice was muffled against his shoulder.

'There's no need to thank me again,' he said. His deep, resonant voice with a blur of an American accent to his impeccable English, sent shivers up her spine. Luckily, she'd only just stopped shivering from shock so hoped he wouldn't notice.

This was crazy.

There was something deeply disconcerting about how readily she had relaxed into the embrace of a stranger in that unguarded moment between panic and the relief of rescue. She pulled away from her rescuer, stuttered her thanks. Without his warmth it was chilly in the air-conditioned room. She wrapped her arms around herself, but it was no consolation for the loss of his hug.

Under the water, Sally's only thought had been how grateful she was for the man's help. As he'd guided her out of the pool she'd realised he was very strong and very competent. Now she looked—really looked—up at him. At five foot ten she was tall, but her rescuer was so much taller. Just as she was getting her voice back, she lost it again. The man was catch-your-breath handsome. So good-looking all she could do was stare. Young—older perhaps than her twenty-seven, but not by much—black hair, slashed cheekbones, *hot*. Although his clothes were dripping all over the floor, his linen suit was obviously well cut and stylish, his watch worth a small fortune. She hoped it was waterproof.

'I… I…tripped,' she stuttered.

'I saw,' he said seriously, so seriously she suspected he was trying not to smile.

'The strap on my sandal, it…er…it's a bit loose.' Why

did she feel she had to explain? she thought, cross at herself for losing her cool. Her heart pounded, not with residual panic but with awareness of how close she stood to this gorgeous, gorgeous man.

'You don't need to explain,' he said. 'It was obviously an accident.'

'It was so sudden. I... I...' In contrast to the intense heat and humidity outside, the air-conditioning in his suite was icy and she was very wet. She sneezed. 'Sorry.' She sneezed again.

'We need to get you out of those wet clothes,' her rescuer said.

Sally stilled. Fought a crazy, unbidden thrill at his words which she again blamed on shock. She backed towards the door. 'I don't think so,' she said.

He frowned. 'I didn't mean *that*. I need to get out of mine too.'

What had she got herself into? She gauged the distance between herself, him and the door.

Her rescuer slammed his hand against his forehead. 'That's not at all what I meant.'

'What do you mean? Because I'm thinking I need to get the heck out of here.'

He shrugged. 'You're welcome to do that. It would be easier for me. But you did say you didn't want to draw attention to yourself. Traipsing out of the hotel and hailing a cab with your clothes dripping wet might just—'

'I get it,' she said.

She needed to stay incognito. The media had long tentacles.

Harrington heiress seen escaping hotel in Singapore!

The speculation would blow her cover. The drama surrounding the return of Hugo had focused new attention on the 'photogenic Harrington twins' and their older brother. There were other spectacular roof gardens she wanted to inspect while she was in Singapore—the city was famous for them. That was her mission. The reopening of the Harrington Park was a big deal. She didn't want to be the one to take the surprise out of the relaunch. As well, deep down, she had to admit she wanted to impress Hugo with her talent and skill. Drawing unwelcome media attention was not the way to go.

'There are four bathrooms in this suite,' her rescuer said. 'I suggest you take the nearest one and I'll take the furthest one. You can lock the door. We can reconvene in the living room when you're done.'

'I'm not sure…' This whole scenario seemed somehow too intimate, too laced with the threat of danger.

'You don't know me, but I assure you that you can trust me,' he said. She saw only sincerity in his narrowed eyes. He was powerfully masculine but there was nothing threatening in his stance. His tone was commanding without being overbearing, which would have sent her running a mile, wet clothes or not.

Sally was not a person to act on impulse. She liked to plan, consider, have everything in its place before she made a decision. Yet somehow she felt she could trust the man who had saved her from the pool. Her late mother's words came back to her: *'Darling, most people are basically good and would help you rather than hurt you.'* Of course that hadn't applied to her stepfather.

'Okay,' she said, surprising herself at her willingness to take such a risk.

Her rescuer showed Sally to a bathroom, being careful, she noticed, to maintain a respectful distance from her. He didn't linger but turned on his heel and strode away. He appeared sophisticated, urbane, but the effect was somewhat ruined by the rather rude squelching noises his waterlogged shoes made on the marble floor. Sally unsuccessfully tried to smother a laugh.

He turned around to face her and he shrugged self-deprecatingly. 'I know,' he said with a half-smile.

'The leather will be ruined,' she said.

'I have other shoes,' he said.

He set off again and she swore he stepped harder to exaggerate the noise made by his wet shoes. She laughed, this time making no effort to conceal it. He laughed too as he left a trail of wet footsteps behind him, then taking his shoes off before he entered what she assumed must be the living area.

With a smile still on her face, Sally slipped into the bathroom. Locked the door. Noted—just in case—there was a phone on the wall. Handsome and charming he might be, but her rescuer was still a total stranger.

Her cell phone had suffered a cracked screen from its drop to the tiled surrounds of the pool but seemed otherwise intact. To keep it from further damage, she tucked it into the tiny travel shoulder bag she had worn slung across her body. Thankfully the bag had lived up to its claim of being impenetrable.

As she stripped off her wet clothes, she couldn't help but admire the bathroom with a professional eye, noting the top-grade marble, the expensive fittings, the unstinting luxury. She wanted a more traditional, very English look for the Harrington Park but there was a lesson to be learned from this hotel's devotion to guest comfort.

Could she ever allow herself to switch off from work?

The Ice Queen, she knew people called her. Nicknamed for both her ruthless devotion to her business and her reputation for never letting relationships get deeper than dating. The name hurt, but she never let anyone see that. It wasn't that she wanted to be on her own. She needed love and intimacy as much as anyone else. But she always seemed to go for men who were unattainable.

Her first major crush at boarding school had been on

a darkly handsome Spanish boy—until he'd told her he wanted to be a priest and needed to remain celibate. She had shared her first kisses with another schoolmate—then he'd confessed he was experimenting but was pretty sure he was gay. They'd become good friends instead of lovers, although it had taken a long time for her not to be half in love with him. Her most recent Mr Out-of-Reach had been a quite well-known actor, recently divorced and determined to avoid commitment—he'd made that very clear when she'd met him. His ruthless dumping of her had been more than a year ago. The press coverage had not been kind. She'd been too wounded to bother with dating since. Work had become her refuge from romance.

She showered and shampooed her hair with the expensive toiletries supplied, revelling in being warm and safe. Then towelled herself dry in a decadently fluffy towel—they must have only this quality of towel for the Harrington Park. She dried her hair into its usual sleek lines, taking particular care with the styling. Call it vanity, or something more deeply instinctive, but she had an urge to look better than the drowned rat her handsome rescuer had pulled out of the pool. She couldn't do much for the smeared makeup but tidy it up with a tissue.

No way could she get back into her sodden clothes that she had thrown into the bathtub. In fact, she didn't ever want to wear that dress again. She shuddered at the memory of how the midi-length skirt had tangled itself around her legs, hindering her attempts to swim. Her sandals appeared to be a lost cause. Still, she did her best to squeeze the water out of her dress and underwear. Perhaps there was a tumble dryer somewhere in this suite, but she doubted it. People who could afford to stay in luxury penthouses didn't do their own laundry.

Unless she intended to stay in the bathroom until her clothes dripped dry, she had no choice but to slip, naked, into the hotel's thick, velvety black bathrobe. She wrapped it right around her waist for total coverage and belted it tightly. Feeling somewhat revived, she opened the door and padded barefoot on the marble floor towards the living room of the suite.

CHAPTER TWO

THE ENORMOUS LIVING room of her rescuer's suite opened to a balcony with a view to the Gardens by the Bay and out to Marina Bay and the ships waiting in the harbour. The amazing futuristic tree-like structures of the Super-tree Grove and the adjacent Flower Dome and Cloud Forest conservatories were on her to-do list for the next day.

Her Sir Galahad was fixing drinks at the full-sized bar. He was dressed casually in wheat-coloured linen trousers and a white silk knit T-shirt. Sally could not help but appreciate his back view, broad shoulders tapering to a very appealing butt.

At her entry to the room, he turned. She had to swallow hard at how good he looked. Dry, his hair was spiky and black, and the T-shirt showed sculpted muscles, smooth brown skin. For a long moment their gazes met. A current of curiosity and speculation seemed to crackle between them.

He was seriously hot.

She was the first to drop her eyes.

'I could do with a drink—how about you?' he said. He smiled. Sally didn't think he could get any better-looking, but the smile did it—perfect white teeth and eyes that smiled too.

All caution about accepting drinks from a stranger fled

her mind. She had nearly drowned; a drink was very much in order. 'A Singapore Sling?'

He smiled again. 'I'm no barman. But I can order one from room service.'

The hotel where she was staying was home to the iconic cocktail. She'd try one later. 'Dry white wine then, please,' she said.

When he handed her the wine, she noticed the absence of a wedding band. He was very careful to avoid any accidental touching of fingers, but even so they brushed. Just that slightest of touches sent a shiver of awareness through her.

Did he notice?

He was drinking black label whisky, no ice. She took a sip from her wine and willed herself to relax.

'Your wet clothes,' he said.

'The hotel laundry. I thought…'

'Do you have time to wait for that?'

Sally had lost all track of time. She glanced at her watch—thankfully waterproof. It was already past five p.m. 'No,' she said. But would she be happy travelling back to her hotel in a bathrobe? Perhaps she had no choice.

He cleared his throat. 'I've taken the liberty of ordering you a new dress from one of the hotel boutiques.'

'You *what*?' Oddly, she didn't call him out on his high-handed action—which it most certainly was—but rather blurted, 'How did you know my size?' He was exceedingly handsome, obviously wealthy; perhaps he often bought clothes for women.

'My sister is about your size, although she isn't as tall. She often shops there on her visits to Singapore. I asked the manager to find something that would fit her. They'll send it up to the room soon.'

'My wallet survived its plunge in the pool. My credit cards should be okay. I'll call down—'

'No need. It's already paid for.'

'But I can't possibly accept that. I must repay you.'

He made a dismissive gesture that had a certain arrogance. 'Too difficult. I don't take credit cards. It's nothing. Please accept the dress as a souvenir of your visit to Singapore.'

Sally was too flabbergasted for coherent speech. 'But I… No.' It was out of the question to accept such a gift from a stranger. She knew his room number. The boutique's details would no doubt be on their shopping bag. She would phone through a payment from her and a refund for him after she got back to her hotel.

'I've also ordered some food from room service,' he said.

'But I… I'm not hungry.'

'You can take the meal or leave it. However, you've had quite a shock. You might find you need some food.' The door buzzer sounded. 'That's either room service or your dress.'

An obsequious waiter wheeled in a trolley and placed silver trays on the glass-topped dining table. Delicious smells of spicy food wafted upwards and Sally's appetite suddenly revived. But it was a stretch from being rescued by a stranger to sharing a meal with him.

A meal made it feel more like a date.

The waiter lifted the silver domes from the trays to reveal a *dim sum* feast—small plates and bamboo steamers of bite-sized snacks. Some Sally recognised, others she did not.

'A taste of Singapore,' said her rescuer—or was he now her host? 'Like the city itself, the flavours are Chinese, Malaysian, Indian and Western.'

The waiter briefly described each of the dishes. They included fluffy steamed savoury buns, dumplings full of spicy broth, pan-fried oysters, tiny western-style sliders, vegetables she didn't recognise as well as the more familiar spring rolls and samosas. The waiter was deferential in the extreme; he couldn't have used the term 'sir' more often and he bowed deeply before he left the room. Her host must be a generous tipper.

Sally looked longingly at the *dim sum*. 'I... I'm not sure it's appropriate to...to linger here.'

But she was still in the hotel bathrobe, her clothes too wet to wear. She was trapped...although she didn't feel in danger. Call it instinct or hunch but she didn't think her rescuer meant her harm. Quite the opposite—she had felt so safe and comforted in his arms. Safe and something so much more—a stirring of a long subdued sensual interest, an undefined longing for something that had always remained out of her reach.

'If you don't want to eat, I'll have the food taken away.' He motioned to call the waiter back.

'Yes. I mean *no*. Don't have it taken away. It looks too good to resist.'

He smiled that very appealing smile. 'You've had a big shock. The food at this hotel is good. You might find a snack is just what you need.'

'Thank you. I... I appreciate your thoughtfulness.' The *dim sum* was making her mouth water.

He waved away her thanks. 'It's nothing.'

It was actually extraordinarily generous and hospitable of him. A different kind of man might have pulled her from the pool and sent her on her way. Or ignored her plight and left her to flounder.

'Where do I start?' Sally said, once she was seated at one of the dining chairs opposite her host.

Just like on a date.

'Wherever you like.' He poured her hot Chinese tea in a small porcelain cup without handles. Sally took the cup with thanks and sipped, looking over its edge at him. It was a long time since she had been in the company of a man as strikingly attractive as this one.

She was dressed in a bathrobe and sharing a meal with a handsome stranger. All in all, it was a slightly bizarre situation she found herself in. Bizarre but, in its own way, exciting.

She tried to keep her eyes on the food but was unable to stop herself from darting glances at him. Every time she found something new. A sexy cleft in his chin. A full, sensuous mouth. Smooth skin she wanted to reach out and touch.

'Can you use chopsticks?' he asked.

'Not very skilfully, but yes.' She deftly picked up a prawn roll and transferred it to her bowl.

'I see you need no tuition at all,' he said, amused.

'I have a favourite Chinese restaurant in London,' she said. 'So I get some practice.'

He put down his own chopsticks on a silver rest. 'You're from London. Are you on vacation in Singapore?'

She nodded. A working holiday—but he didn't need to know that.

'Is it your first visit?'

'Yes,' she said. 'I only arrived here this morning.'

Several of the wealthy foreign clients of her high-end interior design business had been so pleased with her work on their residences in the UK, they had invited her to work for them in their home countries. She flew frequently to Dubai and Mumbai in particular. But never before to Singapore.

'There's a lot to see in Singapore,' her rescuer said.

She'd like to see more of him.

His comment seemed somewhat trite—but what else did she expect from a conversation with a stranger? Especially a stranger she had met in such an extraordinary circumstance. As far as she could tell on such brief acquaintance, they had no common ground. But wasn't that the point of such conversations—to establish common ground?

This is not a date, she had to remind herself again.

She answered in kind. 'I'm only here for a few days and I'm determined to see as much as I can.'

He paused. 'Just before you fell in the pool I noticed you taking photographs of the rooftop garden.'

Sally's heart stopped. Was the game up? Had he picked her for an industrial spy? Did he have a connection to the hotel? She rushed a reply. 'It's impressive, isn't it? Especially those towering palm trees and the exquisite orchids. I… I probably took way too many snaps. Gardening is somewhat of a hobby.'

'Really?'

His obvious scepticism was no surprise. No one else in her social set shared her interest in gardening. That was a pastime for parents, grandparents even. But she had been deeply unhappy at her prestigious boarding school and the garden had become her refuge. The head gardener had taken her under her wing and Sally's interest had developed from there. After she'd left school, she had even started an apprenticeship in garden design until she'd realised interior design was her overwhelming passion. Since she'd had her own business, she'd been able to combine both her interests.

'I'm fascinated by the challenges of planting such a large garden on a rooftop,' she said.

'There are many such gardens in Singapore.'

'So I believe. This morning I saw a flourishing garden on top of a bus. I couldn't believe it. You should have seen how many photos I took of that.'

He smiled. 'I haven't seen such a bus myself. I'll take your word for it.'

She indicated with a wave the view of Supertree Grove below. 'I'm heading down there tomorrow; those gardens look amazing.'

Was that too much information? Did he believe her? Did it matter if he did or he didn't?

For a long moment their eyes again met in a gaze too

long and too intent for strangers. Her spine tingled with awareness of just how attractive she found him. Was that an answering interest in his dark eyes? How would she know? She was notorious for misreading men. And when it came to flirting, the Ice Queen didn't have a clue.

She tore her gaze away, reached with her chopsticks for an oyster. Her hand wasn't steady and she missed the first time, the chopsticks clicking against each other. *Flirting.* No way should she even be entertaining that thought. But where was the harm in finding out a little more about him?

Her words came out in a rush. 'You're visiting Singapore too? I mean, you're staying in a hotel, so I assume—'

'I'm here on business. I fly out tomorrow.'

There was no reason she should feel so disappointed.

'What line of business?'

'Telecommunications. And you?'

'Interior design.'

'Commercial or residential?'

'Mainly residential,' she said.

The exception being the urgent refurbishment of an iconic hotel that bore her family name.

'In Singapore?'

Was that a trick question?

'Not right now. I'm enjoying being a tourist. Exploring. Seeing the gardens. As I...er...said.' She was annoyed at herself for the nervous edge to her voice. She prided herself on being in control, not letting anything get to her. Let alone a man.

'You did,' he said. He certainly wasn't a person to rush into mindless conversation. Her rescuer had a calm way of speaking that might have, in different circumstances, evoked more of a sensible response from her. But she found him so darn desirable she found it difficult to concentrate on anything else but imagining what it might be like to kiss him.

She picked up a dumpling with her chopsticks and popped it into her mouth, savoured it, gave a sigh of appreciation. 'Delicious—everything is delicious.' She put down her chopsticks, looked up at him. 'You were right about me needing food.'

'I'm glad you're feeling better.' He sounded genuinely pleased he had met her needs. It wasn't something she was used to. The men in her world were not the kind, caring type—with the exception of her brother Jay. This man was considerate, caring and hot. It was a dizzying combination.

She needed to make her gratitude clear. 'Thank you. For rescuing me. For making me feel less embarrassed about making such a fool of myself. For all of this.' With the wave of her chopsticks, she encompassed the meal, the room. 'You've been such a gentleman.'

Hidden beneath her polite words was an urgent subtext she would never allow to be voiced. What she'd appreciated the most was the pleasure of being held in his arms. The intimacy of his hug. Even the memory of it sent arousal tingling through her body.

She wanted more.

Edward gritted his teeth. If only Ms Mermaid knew just how very ungentlemanly he was feeling. His unexpected guest made a hotel dressing gown look like the sexiest of evening gowns—and he'd become obsessed with the desire to slide it off her.

His heart had started to pound as she'd made her way from the bathroom to the living room. The black velvet had swished around her legs, highlighting the alluring sway of her hips, giving him enticing glimpses of slender pale legs. He strongly suspected she was naked under the gown. The hotel tried to anticipate a guest's every need, but underwear for a woman whose clothes had suffered a plunge in the swimming pool was almost certainly not stocked in the bathroom.

Now, as she sat opposite him, the lapels of the dressing gown had fallen open just enough to reveal a tantalising hint of cleavage. Her hair swung sleek over her shoulders, reddish glints caught by the late afternoon sunlight filtering through the glass doors that led to the balcony.

She was beautiful.

His heart pounded harder just looking at her.

More than just beautiful.

He wasn't a man prey to instant infatuation. Such madness was not to be tolerated in the life that had been mapped out for him. Yet he was utterly fascinated by this woman who he had, on an uncharacteristic impulse, pulled to safety from the pool.

The intense attraction wasn't just about her good looks. It wasn't just sexual—although that was certainly there. *Man, was it there.* There was something about the light in her eyes, her generous smile, the musical tone of her voice. It was an indefinable pull towards this woman that was impossible to explain or analyse because he had never before felt anything like it.

He wanted to lean across the table, take her hand in his, make an amusing comment about what an unusual way it was to meet. Tell her he was glad that he had happened to be walking by as she tripped. Confess he was a great believer in fate and that fate had brought her to him. Ask her if she was married, engaged, promised—she wore no rings on either hand. Suggest that the *dim sum* could be followed by dinner in the private dining room of the most fashionable club in Singapore.

But the reality of Edward's situation punched into him to deflate every such fantasy. He could take none of those actions. He was thirty-one years old and under pressure from his father to make a politically advantageous marriage. An arranged marriage, with a bride chosen for him by his parents, the King and Queen. As Crown Prince of the south-east Asian kingdom of Tianlipin, Edward was duty-bound to do what was best not for him but for his country.

His father's dissolute older twin brothers had brought disgrace to the kingdom. The corrupt former King—older than his identical twin by ten minutes—had died in dubious circumstances. His twin and heir had been arrested for embezzlement on a grand scale, forced to relinquish his claim to the throne and live in exile. Edward's father—the youngest brother—had had to step up to the throne, clear up the mess his brothers had made and regain the trust of their people.

The current King's rule was a very different one, based on a strong moral code, honour, service and above all duty. That had been drummed into Edward ever since his father had ascended the throne when Edward had been ten years old. He'd gone from carefree son of a third son to Crown Prince. That was when the choice of how he, as heir to the throne, might live his life had been taken away from him.

Edward's future wife had been chosen for him, although they were not as yet engaged. She was ten years younger than him. There had been one awkward meeting between them. Sparks had not flown. Certainly not on his side and not, Edward suspected, on her side either. In fact, he wasn't sure he'd even liked the young Princess.

But his rogue uncles had not only put a dent in his country's treasury with their decadent excesses but also soured relations with neighbouring kingdoms with which Tianlipin had formed alliances centuries ago. Marriage to the Princess, daughter of their closest ally and trading partner would, according to Edward's parents, go a long way to righting the lingering wrongs of his uncles. Bound by duty and honour, he had had little choice but to agree.

Edward had had girlfriends. There had been a certain amount of freedom when he had studied for post-graduate degrees in England and America as plain Edward Chen instead of Chen Wangzi—wangzi meaning prince in his language—Prince Chen of Tianlipin. To English speakers he was Prince Edward. However, because he was unlikely to be able to choose his own bride, he had always held back on his emotions. Only once had he allowed himself to fall in love, with disastrous consequences for both himself and his 'unsuitable' girlfriend.

But now he was about to become engaged, girlfriends were off the table. He would never be allowed to follow his heart. Or ask a beautiful stranger he had rescued from a swimming pool on a date.

He realised he had not acknowledged her thanks, had probably been looking at her for longer than politeness dictated. 'I'm happy I was able to help you,' he said stiffly.

Conversation had flowed easily but now it appeared she was as lost for words as he was. He found himself unable to tear his gaze from her and she flushed high on her cheekbones. But she didn't drop her eyes. If he was mesmerised so, it seemed, was she.

The buzzer to the suite sounded. The dress he had ordered for her, no doubt. He swallowed a swear word. While she'd been in the bathroom, he'd decided he wanted more than a few minutes with her. He'd arranged for a delayed delivery for the dress, ordered the meal, cancelled his plans for the late afternoon and evening. Now his snatched time with her had run out. Fantasies of spending more minutes, more hours with her clamoured at him. But the reality of his situation dictated he had to usher her out of his hotel room with no further delay.

'Aren't you going to let them in?' she said, still holding his gaze. 'It might be the dress you ordered for me.'

He wanted to send the delivery person away. Keep her

here with him, alluring in the black velvet dressing gown. But she had to leave, and she needed the dress before she could do so. 'Of course,' he said and reluctantly rose to accept the delivery.

He returned with a boutique bag that bore an exclusive, instantly recognisable label.

Ms Mermaid's eyebrows rose. 'You chose well,' she said.

'My sister has good taste,' he said.

His guest got up from the table and stepped away from it to meet him in the open space of the living room. He held out the boutique's bag to her. But she made no move to take it from his hands.

Instead she looked up at him and took a deep breath that made the lapels of her gown part further to reveal more than a glimpse of the curves of her breasts. He had to force himself not to let his gaze drift in that direction.

'I don't want to take the dress,' she said. 'If I do, I have to go. And I don't want to go. Not…not yet.' The stumble over her final words made Edward see she wasn't as boldly confident as she seemed. So she felt it too—this inexplicable connection. Elation surged through him.

'I don't want you to go,' he said, speaking the unvarnished truth. But what he wanted wasn't always possible. His royal birth had brought with it incredible privilege but also responsibility and duty.

She took a step closer. 'Then…then should I not stay?'

The air between them hummed with anticipation and shimmered with unspoken words. Her lovely mouth parted and she swayed towards him in an invitation that was impossible to resist. With a groan, Edward stepped closer. His eyes stayed locked with hers as his mouth came down on hers. Her lips were soft and warm and sweet under his and, as he pulled her to him, he pushed aside every reason why he should not be kissing her.

* * *

Sally didn't know what she'd been expecting when she'd invited his kiss, but it wasn't this instant ignition of long dormant passion. Desire flamed through her, urgent and demanding, as his lips possessed hers, his tongue tangled with hers in intimate exploration. She trembled from the overwhelming force of her reaction, pressed her body closer to his, strained to be closer to hard muscular chest, strong thighs.

At this moment he was everything she wanted, everything she *needed*. She wound her arms around his neck as she kissed him back, demanding more. He deepened the kiss, hard and hungry.

Her wants, her needs had been put on hold for so achingly long. There had been no hugs, no kisses, no *intimacy* in her life even before she finished with the actor. And it would be the same when she got back to London. Running her business, with its demanding clients and team of creatives, always looking for the next innovation that would keep Sally Harrington Interiors on top, used up every scrap of energy and drive. But then she'd had to dig deep to find even more of herself to deal with the new demands on top of her business, brought about by her older brother's sudden return. The refurbishing of the Harrington Park was a full-time job in itself, the roof garden another. Something had to give. And her needs had been pushed right to the back of the line. Until now. Now her body was clamouring for its turn.

As she revelled in the sensations of the moment, Sally blocked everything else but this gorgeous man and how he made her feel. Her family tragedies, her conflict about her older brother's return, the pressure of the deadline to restore the hotel, her empty, lonely personal life were shoved firmly to the back of her mind. All she wanted was the pleasure of his kiss, the aching anticipation of more. She needed this escape from the reality of her Ice Queen life. She *deserved* it. He slid his hands down her back. She gasped at the intense sensation of his touch, her awareness she was wearing nothing at all under the robe.

She would take the escape he was offering.

At her gasp, he stilled and broke the kiss. She gave an unintelligible whimper of distress at the withdrawal of his warmth—she had no breath for anything more.

He tilted her chin upward with his fingers, so she looked up into his face. His gaze was intent, his voice unsteady. 'Is this what you want?'

She didn't need him to explain what *this* meant. Wordlessly, she nodded.

'Because if it isn't you need to go. Now.'

She replied without hesitation. 'I want this. I want *you.*' This was pure, primal need.

'I want you too. But…but this is all it can be.'

She took a deep breath to steady herself. 'Are you married? Because, if so, I can't—' Despite her past with unattainable men, married men were strictly out of bounds.

'I'm not married,' he said. 'But there are…other reasons why I can't give you anything more than one night.'

Sally felt swept by a glorious sense of freedom, of chains falling away—the self-imposed constrictions on her tightly controlled life. *A one-night stand.* She had never done anything remotely like it. But she had never wanted a man like she wanted this man.

She could pick up the dress, go change in the bathroom, walk out—and always wonder what it would have been like to be with him. Or she could take what he offered—and gift him the same. No past. No future. No strings.

And no regrets.

'One night it is,' she said with a shiver of exhilaration and anticipation.

There would be no anxiety about tomorrow. No possibility of an ill-fated relationship spluttering to an acrimonious end.

Just one night.

All she had to do was release her inhibitions and heed the reckless call to sensual adventure.

He looked serious. 'So long as you're sure. I don't want to take advantage of your near drowning, your shock—'

'You're not taking advantage of me.' She stepped closer to him, rested her hands on his shoulders, looked up at him with a slow smile. 'Perhaps I'm taking advantage of you.'

He smiled back and she was struck again how much she liked that smile. How much she liked *him*.

'I hadn't thought of it in those terms.'

That voice!

'So…let's not waste one second of our one night together,' she murmured.

His eyes searched her face. 'I wasn't expecting this,' he said slowly.

'Neither was I. But…but I'm glad it's happening.'

'Me too.'

He laughed and pulled her close. She pressed her lips to his. Ice Queen? *Huh.* She was melting with need. For him.

He kissed her back. This time she sensed he held nothing back, his lips urgent and demanding.

Heaven.

Very soon kissing was no longer enough. She craved so much more. With impatient fingers, she tugged his shirt from his trousers, slid her hands to his back—smooth, warm skin over rippling muscle—as he groaned his appreciation. She broke their kiss just long enough to push his shirt up and over his head.

'We need to even the score here,' he said, his voice husky. He kissed a trail from the corner of her mouth, down the column of her throat to the curve of her breast, meanwhile undoing the sash of her robe. 'I'm wondering what underwear you have on under there.'

'Wh-why not find out?' she managed to stutter.

He pushed the velvet robe off her shoulders. Her nipples tightened and tingled under his appreciative gaze. 'No bra. As I thought.' She wondered when he had actually thought that but was too caught up in the sensation of his hands on her bare skin to actually ask. When he caressed her breasts she could think of nothing else and could only gasp when he followed his hands with his mouth, licking and teasing her nipples. Desire pooled deep in her belly.

The front of her robe slid further open to reveal her bare thighs. 'Aren't you going to check if I'm wearing panties?'

He cleared his throat. 'I think we should take this to the bedroom.'

Effortlessly, he picked her up. 'You're very strong,' she gasped as she looped her arms around his neck and pressed into his hard chest. She was five foot ten and it would be no mean feat to lift her. Normally she would bridle at such a masterful tactic, but she loved the way he took charge. His strength made her feel feminine and desired. It wouldn't be something she'd care for in real life, but this wasn't real life. This was more akin to fantasy.

'Fastest way to get you to the bed,' he said in a voice that set her senses rioting.

There seemed to be a number of bedrooms in the suite but he carried her to what must be his; she recognised the spicy scent of his soap from the adjoining bathroom. An enormous bed loomed ahead of her, piled with silk cushions. But her hotelier's eye was switched off. She didn't give a toss about the furnishings. Only him and the sensual intent in his dark eyes.

He pushed the robe right off her shoulders. There was a moment's awkwardness as her elbow got stuck and he had to help her extract her arms from the sleeves. Laughter bubbled from them both at her predicament. Laughing with him was almost as arousing as anything he did with his clever mouth and fingers. The velvet fell off her body in a silky slide and pooled at her feet. As she stepped out of it, she felt self-conscious about her nakedness. But then came the liberating thought that it didn't matter. She wouldn't see him again. Wasn't that part of the fantasy? She straightened her shoulders and let herself bask in the sensual caress of his eyes.

They tumbled together onto the bed to land facing each other, kissing distance apart. Her breath quickened, as did his. She took a few heartbeats to admire him, the defined muscles of his chest and arms, his six-pack. He was the most gorgeous man she'd ever seen. And there was so much more for her to admire. She reached to undo his belt. 'Now it's my turn to even the score,' she murmured.

More laughter ensued as he helped her remove his remaining clothes and toss them on the floor. Then the laughter stilled as she faced him with no barriers whatsoever between them. Her heart was beating so loud she felt sure he could hear it. He reached out for her and traced the contours of her face in gentle exploration. She trembled at his touch. Tentatively, she did the same, his skin smooth under her exploring fingers as she traced along his high cheekbones, his straight, narrow nose, his full, sexy mouth. His expression was a mix of puzzlement and awe, as if he couldn't believe she was here in his bed with him. Something made her wonder if he were as unfamiliar with the code for a no-strings fling as she was.

They spent a long time exploring each other's bodies. He learned just what it took to please her and arouse her to the point where she couldn't wait a second longer for him to enter her. She whimpered as she strained her body towards him.

He pulled her close so they were skin to skin, feminine

curves against male hardness. She bucked her hips towards him, letting him know how ready she was for him. But, as he positioned himself, she put her hand on his cheek to stay him. There was something she felt compelled to say before the ultimate intimacy. 'My name is Sally,' she whispered.

'Edward,' he said, his voice hoarse.

After that, she didn't think of anything else but the intensity of their lovemaking. She was so aroused she climaxed almost as soon as he entered her. The world shrank to just him and her in the luxurious bedroom high above the city of Singapore. Nothing had prepared her for the storm of pleasure as they concentrated on discovering what pleased each other. There was no more laughter, just murmurs of pleasure, sighs and cries of fulfilment. On her third climax she couldn't help a tear from escaping the corner of her eye. He frowned and tenderly wiped it away. 'It's nothing,' she whispered. 'Don't stop.'

Her tears were for the realisation that she would never again have the chance to experience this intense fulfilment with him.

No regrets, she fiercely reminded herself. Perhaps it was so perfect *because* it was only for the one night.

Insomnia had plagued her since her older brother's return. She was too wired from worry about whether the tattered remnants of their once happy family could be woven into something new and strong. But now, replete, she drifted towards a deep sleep with her rescuer's—*Edward's*—arm slung across her.

When she awoke it was well past midnight, according to the clock glowing on the nightstand. The myriad lights of Singapore twinkled through the floor-to-ceiling windows. For a moment she didn't know where she was and looked around the room in momentary panic. Then she remembered and smiled. A beautiful man slept next to her on his back, the linen sheet rumpled over his hips. Edward—if that was indeed his name. His breathing was deep and even, his face heartbreakingly handsome in repose, dark stubble shadowing his jaw. She ached to kiss him lightly on his lips, thank him, whisper her goodbye.

But she couldn't risk waking him. The awkwardness that would surely follow would be unbearable. She'd never done this before. Perhaps there was an etiquette to be followed after a one-night stand with a stranger. If so, she hadn't read the rule book. The best thing she could think of to do was to leave without any fuss. They'd agreed on one night. He'd had his reasons for setting the limit; she'd had hers for accepting it. It had been the most glorious one night. In fact, every moment with him had been memorable, from when he'd fished her out of the pool, to eating *dim sum,* to sharing passion like she'd never known existed.

The thawing of the Ice Queen.

She was grateful to him more than he could know. *No regrets.*

She slid as silently as she could to the edge of the bed. He murmured something in his sleep, in a language she didn't understand. She froze. But then his breathing returned to the steady rhythm of a deep sleep.

She stepped over the discarded velvet robe, his clothes tossed nearby. Then tiptoed to the door of his bedroom. She turned back just the once to blow him the most silent of kisses. Then crept away.

Hastily, as silently as she could, she opened the boutique bag to find an elegant straw-coloured linen dress that bore the label of a famous Italian designer. It was a perfect fit and fell modestly below the knee, which was a good thing as she was without underwear. There was a pair of designer open-back sandals in the bag too. They were a little on the small side, but she was grateful for them. She would slip them on once she was out of the suite and headed down to the hotel lobby. Then she'd catch a taxi back to her own hotel.

Sally found the bathroom and stuffed her own wet clothes and shoes into a hotel laundry bag to take with her. Inside her small handbag, she heard her phone ping with a message. She stilled, fearful the sound would wake her lover. But there was no sound from Edward's bedroom.

Carefully, she reached for the phone and found several missed messages from her twin, Jay. She would call him later, when she could speak coherently. The unanswered calls could be blamed on the time zones. Jay would understand. She and her twin were opposites in personality, he the outgoing one people flocked to, she the more introverted one who found it difficult to trust people enough to open up to them. Jay was the sunshine to her shadow. But they'd always been on the same wavelength in that special way that twins, even fraternal ones, could be.

But she wouldn't tell anyone, even Jay, about Edward. Or indeed anything that had happened after she'd fallen into the pool. Edward would remain her private secret to hug to herself. No one would ever know about the night where she had scaled the peaks of sensual ecstasy with a handsome stranger.

Edward awoke at dawn to a cold, empty bed. Immediately he realised he was alone and was overwhelmed by a deep sense of loss. He reached out a hand to find sheets still with a hint of her warmth, her scent.

Sally.

He suspected she was long gone. But he threw himself out of bed to check the rest of the suite. The only trace of her ever having been there was the carefully folded tissue paper sitting next to the empty boutique bag. Nothing in her bathroom save the lingering scent of the body wash she'd used. He breathed it in, but it did nothing to ease his sense of loss. He cradled his head in his hands and groaned.

Why had he let her go?

The answer came to him with stark clarity, almost as if it were his father the King intoning the words.

Because of your duty to the throne and your people.

She had done him a favour by slipping away in the dark. Her actions had spared him—and her—the awkwardness of a morning-after encounter. He could give no glib promises that he could keep in touch or they would meet again. The truth was he was destined to marry in a loveless political union.

He had only the memories of an amazing woman with whom he'd shared unforgettable lovemaking and a connection that went so much deeper than the sexual. That kind of connection was rare. Instinct told him that, if nurtured, what he had shared with her could grow into something profound. But he could never see that connection flourish. The one night was all he could ever have with her.

Sally. It was a common enough English name. He could track her down if he was so inclined. Access to the hotel's CCTV cameras would be easy—after all his family owned this hotel. He could note the licence plate of the taxi she would no doubt have taken. Then trace it to her hotel. But that would put him in no less of an untenable position. He should be grateful for that brief time he had shared with her.

Still, he was haunted by the melancholic thought that he had let go something—*someone*—more precious than the egg-sized rubies and emeralds in the ceremonial crown that would one day be placed on his head when he was crowned King.

CHAPTER THREE

Five weeks later

SALLY HAD FLOWN to Mumbai last week, Dubai the week before and before that made a quick trip to Tokyo for a briefing on the restoration of a small but significant castle. In between trips she'd been flat out working in London. Jet lag was piling up on jet lag with never a chance to get over it. Now early December saw her in Singapore again, five weeks after her first visit, having flown eight hours direct from Japan's Narita Airport after a brief site visit to the castle. She'd arrived very late the previous night and hadn't been able to sleep either on the plane or at her destination. No wonder she was so exhausted.

The fatigue was overwhelming, bringing with it nausea and insomnia worse than she had ever suffered. She threw herself back on her hotel bed in a desperate effort to get some rest before her lunchtime meeting. It wasn't the historic hotel she'd stayed in last visit. Nor was it the sky-high hotel with the rooftop garden where she had spent the most memorable night of her life. Memorable in the true sense of the word—she had been unable to forget the man who'd called himself Edward.

It hadn't been as easy as she'd so blithely anticipated to put that night behind her. Not just the sensational lovemaking but also how much she'd enjoyed his company—in and out of bed. A day didn't go by that she didn't think about him. She couldn't count the number of times her heart had jolted when she'd seen a tall Asian man on the streets of London, only to find up close he looked nothing like her one-time lover.

She'd felt a connection with Edward like she'd never felt before and couldn't help but wish she'd been able to explore it. But she'd gone into their encounter with eyes open. *One night*. That was the agreement. And she didn't regret it, not for a moment. Letting go of her strict self-control, unleashing her inhibitions, learning what intense pleasure lovemaking could bring when you were with the right person, had done her good. Now she knew to what heights the Ice Queen could soar.

Trouble was, how could another man ever live up to him? No wonder she couldn't forget him.

She adjusted the pillow and forced herself to focus on work, the reason she was here again in Singapore. When she'd got home from her first trip to Singapore, she'd asked for a meeting in the boardroom with her brothers Jay and Hugo. The idea for the urban roof garden had been Hugo's. In a spirited discussion, Sally had expressed her concerns about the practicality of such a venture. 'Lush green outdoor roof gardens are all very well in a tropical climate like Singapore,' she'd said. 'But how successful would something on that scale be in the middle of an English winter? I know there are such gardens in London, but we want something unique. Palm trees and exotic blooms simply don't feel right for the Harrington brand and our relaunch. I propose something different.'

Hugo had protested. She'd learned her older brother had strong views; he was now the owner of a very successful chain of boutique hotels in the United States. He was used to his opinions being taken as law.

'Let me outline my alternative,' she'd said, using every

skill she'd learned in dealing with difficult clients in her own business. 'I didn't just visit rooftop gardens when I was in Singapore. I also saw the most amazing climate-controlled indoor gardens. The Changi Airport has an indoor forest complete with indoor waterfall. Wouldn't an enclosed garden be a better option in our climate? Why not an indoor winter wonderland? A splendid mini forest with fir trees, winter berry shrubs, snow and a skating rink that looks like a frozen lake. It would be perfect for an English Christmas. And what an incredible space to hold our Christmas Eve launch party for the restored Harrington Park.'

Hugo had frowned while Jay had given her an encouraging thumbs-up from behind his brother's back. 'Where would you put such a garden?' Hugo had said.

'The hotel roof would need an incredible amount of reinforcement that's simply not possible in our timeframe. The large covered courtyard to the north of the entrance foyer is essentially unused, and the gardens have been neglected. Our winter wonderland, enclosed with glass walls and roof, could rejuvenate that under-utilised space. After the holiday season we could convert it to a beautiful conservatory with glamorous outdoor furniture and potted plants appropriate to the season. Then bring back the winter garden the following year as a highlight of the Harrington Park holiday calendar.'

She'd paused, out of breath from the effort of injecting a high level of enthusiasm to her proposal.

'It's worth considering,' Hugo had said slowly.

'Oh, and another thing,' she'd said, her voice breaking a little. 'The winter garden could be a memorial to our parents. Daddy loved Christmas and, if you remember, winter was Mummy's favourite season.'

'Great idea,' Jay had said.

Hugo had blanched and Sally had clenched her fists under the table. Had she gone too far with her idea for the memorial? All those years ago, Hugo had taken off to America and abandoned his mother and siblings. However, Hugo seemed to believe *they* had abandoned *him*. He was bitter about their mother; Sally couldn't help but be defensive on her behalf. Yet in Sally's dealings so far with her newfound brother she'd found him to be scrupulously fair.

On that first visit to Singapore she'd met with a leading Singapore landscape architect, Oscar Yeo, responsible for some of the indoor gardens that had so impressed her. He had referred her to his associated London office, who also had expertise in working with artificial snow. With their expert input she had come up with a detailed timeline for the winter wonderland and had been able to slide it across the table to Hugo.

Her computer-assisted drawings had shown him exactly how it would look. Hugo had almost immediately approved her plan. The landscape architects had been engaged and a project manager appointed. Now, five weeks later, thanks to a team of experienced professionals who'd pulled out all the stops, work was well under way on the winter garden.

But there had been a few hiccups that threatened to delay completion by Christmas Eve. They *had* to meet that deadline. She'd always found it better to deal face to face with such problems rather than relying on phone calls and emails. Hence her flight to Singapore and her scheduled lunchtime meeting with Oscar Yeo. There was also something nagging at her about the plan, a detail that she had perhaps overlooked, but she couldn't think quite what it might be.

Her exhaustion was bone-deep. But, her mind racing, Sally found it impossible to rest. She got up from the bed, too quickly it seemed, as she suddenly felt overwhelmed by dizziness. She clutched onto the bedhead for support and waited until the room stopped spinning around her.

As she took a deep breath to steady herself, she was hit by a sudden rush of nausea so urgent she barely made it to the bathroom on time. The bout left her feeling weak and shaky. Food poisoning. Was it something she'd eaten on the plane? Or maybe she'd caught a horrid stomach flu? Great. Just what she didn't need right now with such a busy schedule. She was booked to fly home to London the following day.

After a long shower, she felt a little better. The hotel was on Orchard Road, Singapore's famous shopping strip. There was an underground mall beneath the hotel. She'd head down and get some anti-nausea medication from the pharmacy. It was important to be on top of things for the meeting with the landscape architect.

From her suitcase she pulled out a full-skirted sundress she hadn't worn since her last trip here in early November. Surprisingly, it was too tight across the bust. It must have shrunk, although it had been carefully laundered. She tried a button-through shirt and a skirt. Again, too tight. She swore under her breath. How had this happened? It wasn't the clothes; it was her. She didn't have large breasts but suddenly they seemed a size larger. How could that be?

She sat down rather too quickly in the hotel armchair. Swollen, tender breasts. Nausea and fatigue. It couldn't be. No. *She couldn't possibly be pregnant.* Impossible. There had only been that time with Edward. She wiped her hand across her suddenly damp forehead. Just one time was enough to get pregnant—and there had been more than one time. She was on the pill. She'd told him that when he'd mentioned protection. But the pill she was on had to be taken at the same time every day and never missed. With her erratic timetable, regularly crossing time zones and out of routine, it would be easy enough to miss a pill or two.

With hands that weren't steady she threw on a light embroidered kaftan—at least that fitted—and headed down to the pharmacy. Her thoughts were running away too fast. Methodical as she was, she bought three different types of pregnancy testing kit. They would prove she wasn't pregnant.

All three of the testers indicated that she was, indeed, pregnant. She stared, stunned, at the results. The testers could be faulty. Did the pharmacist have any other brands she could try? But deep in her heart she knew three testers were a good enough sample.

She was pregnant.

About five weeks pregnant, she thought as she frantically counted back to the glorious night with Edward. So much for a fling without consequences.

She paced up and down the room until she got dizzy again.

How could she have let this happen?

Her first urge was to call Jay; at one time he had always been the first person with whom she shared momentous news or asked for advice. But she resisted. She had to handle this on her own. Besides, Jay had his own issues with Chloe, his teenage love with whom he had recently reconnected. She hoped all was well; she'd liked his schoolmate. But Chloe had broken her brother's heart the first time around. She would have to contend with Sally if she broke it again.

Panic paralysed her. She couldn't have a baby on her own. Children had been on the distant agenda for when she got married. *If* she got married, that was. Her lack of luck with men had made her begin to think she wasn't the marrying kind.

She wasn't exactly surrounded by happy marriages. She'd been bridesmaid to her two closest friends from school. They were both already divorced. Her parents' marriage had been happy although, as her father had died suddenly of a heart attack when she'd been only six years old, she would hardly have noticed if it hadn't been. Just a year after being widowed, her mother had married Nick Wolfe, an American businessman who had been a regular visitor to the hotel. Nick had been all sunshine and unicorns until he'd got a ring on her mother's finger. Things hadn't been so romantic when the honeymoon was over. Sally suspected her mother's second marriage had been anything but perfect. As well, it had ushered in the decline of the Harrington Park Hotel.

She was almost glad her mother wasn't here to see the predicament her daughter had got herself into. Pregnant to a stranger after a one-night stand. She didn't know the father's surname, or even if his first name was real. How irresponsible did that sound? She shut her eyes tight at the thought of what her brothers would think. And yet…this baby had been conceived in joy, no matter how temporary. The father was considerate and kind and had made her laugh as well as shared with her the best sex of her life. She could only think well of him.

She didn't need to be married to be a mother. Twenty-seven was biologically an excellent age to have a baby. She owned a successful, profitable business and her own home. Her spacious period apartment in South Kensington had been bought with the first part of her inheritance from her maternal grandmother when she was twenty-one. The second part of the substantial inheritance had kicked in when she was twenty-five. She could afford the best for her baby.

Her baby.

She placed her hand on her still flat tummy. Such a new thought and already not such a terrifying one.

She could do this.

But she had to push her pregnancy worries aside—she was good at suppressing inconvenient emotion—and concentrate on her meeting with the landscape architect. Fortunately, the linen shift dress she'd brought with her for the

meeting was loosely cut across the bust and still fitted. So
did the matching lightweight jacket. She'd learned from
her last visit to Singapore that while it might be sweltering
outside, air conditioning inside could be chilly.

She'd chosen her hotel because it was only a block from
the office tower where Oscar Yeo's company had its headquarters. The heat and humidity hit her as she stepped out
of the hotel onto the busy street. She halted, stunned.

So many Christmas decorations.

If she'd thought she could escape Christmas while in
Singapore she'd been mistaken. Orchard Road was known
as the Oxford Street of Singapore and the spectacular festive decorations rivalled anything she might see in London.
To see Christmas cheer in a hot, sunny December was dis-
orientating. It was so different from seeing decorations in
gloomy, wintry London when it got dark by four p.m. and
showed the illuminations to their best advantage.

However, none of the Christmas bling impressed her.
Buskers playing Christmas carols grated on her ears. She'd
become very bah humbug about Christmas.

It hadn't always been that way. When she was a child,
with both adored parents alive, they'd lived in their beautiful family home in the grounds of the Harrington Park
Hotel. It had been the estate manager's house in the days
the hotel was a grand private home. Christmas Eve had
been the major celebration for the hotel, but her parents
had made it about family too. Her memories were childish
ones, her impressions of love and magic and the fabulous
Christmas tree in the hotel lobby that had towered above
her. Each year, she and her two brothers would be allowed
to buy a special ornament each to hang on the tree, and
their parents hung one too.

One of her clearest memories was of her father, jovial
and kind, lifting her up in his arms to hang her ornament
as high on the tree as she could reach. She had felt safe,

secure, loved. That had been the last Christmas her father had been alive. She had never felt that loved again. And Christmas had lost its sparkle. Their mother had done her best to maintain the festive traditions, but her heart hadn't been in it.

When her mother had married Nick she'd handed over the reins of the Harrington Park to her new husband so she could spend more time with her children. He had immediately made drastic changes and had set about chipping away at the Harrington traditions, including those long-standing Christmas customs that he had deemed a waste of money. First to go had been the Christmas Eve party. An enormous tree, decorated with the family heirlooms, had never gone up in the lobby again.

Sally had been too young to be aware of all that, just that her life had changed irrevocably. Hugo, however, seven years older than Sally, had grown up with the expectation that he would one day run the family hotel. He was only too aware of what had happened. When she and Jay had met their older brother again after seventeen years' absence, he'd told them that it was Nick Wolfe who had forced him out of the hotel and their lives. Nick, thief of their legacy, who had mismanaged the hotel so badly that he'd had to declare bankruptcy and sell.

Hugo was determined to reverse that. One of the first things her older brother had done when he'd corralled her and Jay into working with him on the restoration of the hotel was to go through the meticulously kept archives of the hotel. The idea had been to show them what a grand hotel the Harrington Park had been before its decline and to inspire them to do even better.

All three had delighted at the images of the splendid balls, the many famous celebrities and dignitaries who had stayed in the hotel in its heyday. There were also priceless records of the practical running of the hotel, although no such records had been kept under their step-father's management.

Jay, an award-winning chef with his own Michelin starred restaurant, had been excited about the old menus from days gone by and had decided to recreate some of them, while adding his own twist. He'd employed his friend, Louis Joubert, from Paris as head chef to work with him.

Sally's particular interest was the décor of both the guestrooms and the public spaces. A real find had been invoices from years ago for the traditional porcelain bath-tubs and basins in the bathrooms, and the subsequent dis-covery that the firm was still in business. That kind of hardware was as important as the luxurious furnishings and fabrics she was splashing out on. Her attention to such practical details as well as the wow of the decorating was part of her success as a designer.

Then there had been the photos of the Christmas Eve party for family, guests and staff—dating right back to the nineteen-twenties. She and her brothers had fallen silent, each swamped by their own memories. Sally could barely bring herself to look at the images for that last Christmas when her father had been alive. When they'd been a happy, united family.

Christmas celebrations after Hugo left had comprised just Sally, Jay and her mother. Not even Nick Wolfe, who'd had no time for family celebrations. Her grandmother had refused to come anywhere near the hotel once Nick had come on the scene. After their mother had died in a car accident when Sally was thirteen, she'd stopped celebrat-ing Christmas at all.

Now Hugo was determined to restore the Christmas Eve traditions in all their grandeur with a spectacular re-opening party. And time was running out to get the winter wonderland finished.

Sally walked as quickly as she could in the heat and humidity of Singapore to her destination, shunning the gigantic Christmas tree that was the centrepiece of the Orchard Road decorations. As she passed a newsstand a magazine poster caught her eye. It featured a strikingly handsome black-haired man who looked very much like Edward. Her heart jolted and she stopped in her tracks to stare at it, then made herself move on before she even read the coverlines. When would she ever stop thinking she saw the man at every turn? She would *never* be able to forget him, that was for sure. Always, she would wonder about the father of her child.

Her meeting with Oscar Yeo went well. She hadn't dared eat lunch; even to push food around her plate made her feel queasy. The technical and production issues were solved to her satisfaction. Now she had every confidence her winter wonderland would come in on time and under budget. The trip to Singapore had been worth it; she could confidently fly back to London tomorrow and report to Hugo on a successful trip.

As she made her farewells to Oscar, who was both professional and courteous, he asked whether he and his wife could include her in their evening's entertainment and show her more of Singapore. Although she appreciated the gesture, Sally politely declined. She was desperate to get back to the hotel. She'd planned to use her afternoon to revisit some of the indoor gardens but that had to be put on hold. Much as she loved the design for the winter wonderland, there was something missing that continued to elude her and she'd hoped to find further inspiration. But she badly needed rest and time to give more thought to how she would manage the changes her unexpected pregnancy would bring to her life.

On the way back to her hotel, however, she couldn't resist popping into an upscale baby store, just one of the many glitzy shops on Orchard Road, to buy a darling little baby cardigan that cost an inordinate amount of Singapore dollars. Holding it, she felt stirrings of excitement and wonder.

She was going to have a baby.

Her other shopping expedition was to a convenience store to buy a packet of dry crackers. Once back in the hotel, she lay back on the bed in the blissful air conditioning, nibbled on the crackers and sipped fizzy mineral water until her tummy settled. She used the remote to turn on the television.

It opened to an English-speaking news service. Singapore was a vibrant, progressive city state, one of the leading financial centres of the world. Sally had seen it described as an alpha-plus global city, and the local news issues interested her. It was an excellent place for her to do business as English seemed to be the first language. One news item ended and another began. An image of yet another Edward lookalike appeared on the screen. Having just discovered she was pregnant with his baby was making her think way too much about him without all these lookalike reminders. She went to flick the television off but then suddenly jerked forward, her mineral water splashing on the bedcover without her even noticing.

She stared, mesmerised, as a different newsreader chattered on.

'Rumours are growing that Asia's most eligible—and hottest!—bachelor, thirty-one-year-old Prince Edward of Tianlipin, is about to announce his long-awaited engagement. The Crown Prince of the wealthy island kingdom has been tantalising us with his tight-lipped "No comment". Yet his Singapore house has been completely refurbished. Getting it ready for his future bride? Could it be the lucky lady is from Singapore?'

The TV showed a montage of pictures of the Prince: serious in a business suit, elegant in a tuxedo, smiling in white shorts on the deck of a yacht and, most mindboggling of all, solemn in the ceremonial national dress of his country, heavily encrusted with gold and precious stones.

Sally froze as she stared at the screen. In one film clip he held up his hand as if to say *No comment*. The voice was immediately recognisable. So was that devastating smile. She reeled at the revelation, her heart pounding so hard she shook, and her breath came in short, panicky gasps. She put her hand to her heart to steady herself. There could be no doubt. It was him. Edward. *Prince* Edward.

Suddenly the father of her baby had a name and identity. Sally uttered a strangled, mirthless laugh. When it came to unattainable men, she sure knew how to pick them. A prince. An about-to-be-engaged prince. A celebrity prince, no less.

But she had been attracted to him as just a regular businessman, she thought wistfully. He'd seemed her equal.

The newsreader continued. 'Prince Edward will be attending the charity gala at the Beauville Hotel this evening. Rumour informs us he will be attending solo. There's no doubt about it—Prince Edward is holding his romance cards very close to his chest.'

That news segment finished; Sally switched off the television. Immediately, with hands that weren't steady, she turned on her laptop to research Crown Prince Edward of Tianlipin.

She discovered his home was a substantial island in the South China sea, north-east of Singapore and south of Vietnam. Tianlipin was a hereditary monarchy and, while staggeringly rich in oil and gas, in modern times its fastest growing export was telecommunications. Billionaire Crown Prince Edward had been educated in both his home country and Singapore, with postgraduate studies at Cambridge and Harvard. He was CEO of the family owned telecommunications company and spent considerable time in Singapore. His sister Princess Jennifer ran the family's international hotel portfolio, which included the Singapore hotel with the rooftop resort.

Slowly Sally closed her laptop. No wonder his sister was so familiar with the hotel boutique. And that was why Edward had occupied what had seemed to be the presidential suite. Looking back, she realised he had been as keen to keep away from unwanted attention as she had been. After all, he was considered to be *Asia's hottest bachelor*.

He must have women by the thousands flinging themselves at him. She'd been just one more, she thought a little bitterly. One more before he got engaged. But she refused to let her thoughts go in that direction. He had not set out to seduce her; she had made the first move. He had been at pains to ensure he wasn't taking advantage of her shocked state after her near drowning. Their lovemaking had been completely consensual, and he had treated her with respect and consideration. Would she have gone ahead if he had told her the truth about his identity? Most likely not. Firstly, she probably wouldn't have believed him, and secondly, if she had, she would have been too intimidated by his royal status to let him kiss her, let alone undo the tie of her robe.

Then she wouldn't have had that memorable night with him. Then she wouldn't be pregnant with his child. She sighed a long, heartfelt sigh. The revelation of his true identity made her predicament so much more complicated. And completely smashed any lingering hope that she might bump into him somewhere in Singapore and discover he missed her as much as she missed him. Because wasn't it the truth that, deep down in the frozen heart she had allowed him to warm for just one night, that hope was the real reason she had jumped at the chance to return to Singapore?

Now she knew who he really was, it would be possible to get in touch with him. But she cringed at the thought. How would he see such contact? An anonymous one-night stand showing up in Singapore, pregnant and demanding money from a prince? Sally shuddered at what she imagined his reaction might be. She didn't need his millions—no, it was billions. She certainly didn't need the humiliation. But did he deserve to know he was going to be a father?

She was more than capable of bringing up her baby on her own and she intended to do just that. Her child would have the security of one loving parent who would put him or her first. Boy or girl? She hadn't yet thought about it, but the image of an adorable little black-haired, brown-eyed boy looking very like his father flashed into her thoughts. A little boy—or a little black-haired girl—who would one day ask questions about his or her father. And if she hadn't told Edward about the child's existence she would have to lie.

All of a sudden, her situation seemed utterly overwhelming. She prided herself on keeping control of her emotions, locking down weakness and acting the Ice Queen when it came to revealing hurt. She'd learned those survival techniques when, at the age of thirteen, grieving for her mother, her stepfather had dropped all pretence of caring for his stepchildren. He'd made her and Jay full boarders at their school, effectively keeping them away from everything and everyone they'd known for weeks at a time. And left them to fend for themselves.

Now she was feeling more vulnerable than she had ever imagined she could feel. With brutal honesty, she forced herself to face the truth. Edward, the man she had thought she would never see again, was in Singapore—and she desperately wanted to see him. Not force a meeting. Not tell him she was carrying his baby. Just see him, even from afar. Perhaps just to prove to herself he was real.

While she was guilty of prevaricating on emotion, Sally was good at making snap decisions. She picked up her phone and dialled Oscar Yeo's number. She asked him if it would be possible for him to get her a ticket for the charity gala event being held at the Beauville Hotel that night.

He did better than that. He and his wife were attending the gala themselves. They already had a ticket for their daughter, but she'd cried off. Sally would be more than welcome to come with him and his wife. She could sit at their table. They would pick her up from her hotel.

Sally spluttered her thanks. Then got herself in a totally uncharacteristic tizz. What on earth would she wear?

CHAPTER FOUR

A KNOT OF tension settled in Sally's chest the moment she entered the ornate ballroom of the Beauville Hotel with Oscar Yeo and his delightful lawyer wife Iris. *Where was Edward?* She had to force herself to act composed and not peer around the crowded room, anxiously seeking a glimpse of the Prince. She was on a razor-edge of anticipation and dread—what if he was not as she remembered? That edge was only too close to leading to a plummet of despair—what if he wasn't there at all? The thought she might come close to him and he wouldn't recognise her didn't bear thinking about.

The other women at the gala were dressed to the hilt in formal gowns and an abundance of jewellery. Thank heaven she had decided against the simple black cocktail dress she kept packed to cover any social occasions she might encounter on her frequent business trips. Instead, after her phone call with Oscar, she'd ventured out again to Orchard Road and found something more glamorous in one of the designer boutiques.

Disconcertingly, the assistant at the store had known immediately she was pregnant but had thought her further along than five weeks. However, there could be no mistake about the timing of conception. There had been no one else but Edward. When she'd asked the assistant how she knew, the woman had replied that years of observing female bodies in changing rooms meant she could just tell.

Did that mean others could tell? For how long could she conceal her pregnancy? When would she tell Jay and Hugo they were going to be uncles? What would she say about the father of her baby? Her doubts and fears strangled rational thought. She couldn't consider all that just now. The possibility of seeing Edward was the only thought she wanted to occupy her mind.

If she did see him—and he saw her—she felt confident in the elegantly cut long gown in midnight-blue silk, embellished with swirls of beading in shades of indigo through violet. She'd bought new sky-high heels in a toning dark shade of blue, deciding she might as well enjoy heels while she still could, before her pregnancy meant she had to graduate to flats. Luckily, she'd snagged the last appointment of the afternoon with the hairdresser in the hotel, who'd put up her hair in a stylish knot. She thought back to when all she had to wear was a black velvet dressing gown, and still she'd wanted to look her best for Edward.

She went to accept a cocktail from a waiter passing drinks around on a silver tray, then remembered she now shouldn't be drinking alcohol and swapped it for a soft drink. Feeling more on edge by the second, she stuck close by her hosts as she didn't know one other person. Except Edward, of course. And could she say she really knew him at all?

She followed Oscar and Iris to their table, set about a third of the way down the expansive room. Thankfully, the other people on the table were from Oscar's company, and they were all intrigued by the winter wonderland garden at the Harrington Park. Social chit-chat wasn't Sally's strength, especially when her mind was elsewhere with a tall, black-haired prince, but she could always talk fluently and happily about work.

Of course, she didn't indicate to any of her table companions that she had any interest whatsoever in Crown Prince Edward of Tianlipin. But he was an almost immediate topic of conversation. The Prince was guest of honour at the gala in aid of a cancer research institute—an important donor, it seemed. But it wasn't his philanthropy that had Iris Yeo agog with interest; rather it was the rumour and speculation about his impending engagement.

It took a mammoth effort for Sally to appear impartial, to express interest in the Prince without going overboard—even though she was dying to find out everything she possibly could about him. Especially his engagement, the thought of which made her feel the ache of a deep, stabbing envy.

Singapore was one of the world's most expensive cities, with many ultra-wealthy people, Iris explained, but this man was a real-life *prince.* His kingdom was extremely wealthy and who knew what splendours he would endow on the lucky woman he made his Princess. Not to mention a splendid home in Singapore, where he spent a lot of time.

That lucky woman would be married to the most wonderful man, Sally thought. Her envy of his unknown fiancée was not over the riches, but over *him.* He was the prize, not his wealth. She had to shake that thought out of her head. The Edward she'd known could be very different from his princely self.

'Do you know who his fiancée might be?' she asked tentatively.

'Not a clue,' said Iris, who confessed to an avid interest in celebrity gossip. 'His private life is kept private. No scandals that we know of. Which is why we're agog about his engagement. It's like the story of Cinderella—who is the lucky girl whose foot fits the glass slipper?'

'You've got me curious about the Prince,' Sally ventured, proud of how steady she kept her voice. 'You must point him out to me.'

Iris scanned the room. 'Prince Edward is at the VIP table, up front, closest to the stage,' Iris said. 'He's standing up, talking to the chairman of the governing board, I believe. Yes, I can see the chairman, but the Prince has his back to us.'

Sally's heart caught in her throat. *He was here.*

Frustratingly, all Sally could see of the man who towered over his companion were his black hair and broad shoulders in a dark tuxedo. She fought the urge to stand up so she could see better. 'I can only see his back,' she said, keeping the frustration from her voice. From this distance he could be any tall man.

'Shame,' said Iris. 'He is extraordinarily good-looking. That's why there's all the fuss. He's also smart and of course so very, very rich.'

'I hope he turns around soon,' Sally said lightly. 'He seems to be wearing a tuxedo. I thought he might be wearing something more elaborate.'

'You mean royal regalia? He might wear traditional clothes in his home country, but when he's here in Singapore he's low-key in the way he presents.'

Low-key. That perfectly described the Edward she had known. Maybe there wasn't such a difference between his two personas.

She was getting increasingly desperate to see his face. And yet she was beginning to get cold feet at the thought of an encounter. Could she really pluck up the courage to approach him—a *prince*—if she got the chance? Would it be wise to do so? She had cherished the memories of that night with him for five long weeks. Yet it appeared he'd been cheating on his soon-to-be fiancée. What kind of man did that make him? A liar and manipulator like

Nick Wolfe? Or an arrogant playboy prince used to taking what he wanted and intent on one last fling?

Edward was at the gala dinner with great reluctance. Undoubtedly the cancer research institute was a very worthy cause. His family-owned telco company, which he headed, was responsible for the institute's telecommunications, and he was a generous donor. But not only was the event more than a touch tedious, and the speeches interminable, he knew that there was an undercurrent of interest about his marital status buzzing through the ballroom. He hated being the focus of such attention.

Media speculation on his impending engagement was becoming frenzied. Not that he or his family had given even a hint of any such action to be taken. But a snippet had been leaked from somewhere, perhaps from his prospective fiancée's side. When he found out where it had come from, there would be trouble.

Perhaps the leak had been intended to hasten his proposal. Because he was certainly guilty of delaying, of putting every obstacle he could legitimately find in the way of a commitment. His father had expressed ill-concealed annoyance. His mother had gently reminded him of his duty—his duty to make a loveless marriage. The more he thought about it, the more his inner despair grew. Yet he had grown up knowing that duty always came before personal desires. His uncles' decadent defiling of the age-old traditions had proved what happened when they were reversed.

He had had another meeting with Princess Mai, and it had gone no better than the first. She was undoubtedly very pretty, but the ten-year age gap between them might as well have been one hundred years for all they had in common. Conversation had been stilted on both sides. Marriage was beginning to look like a life sentence rather than something to anticipate.

Trouble was, he was unable to get out of his mind the night with Sally, the beautiful English stranger. Even a pretty princess could come nowhere near Sally, if indeed that had been her name. He had felt more excitement and emotion in one night with her than he believed he ever would with Mai in a lifetime. No matter how many times he told himself his time with Sally had been a steamy casual encounter, he knew it had been something so much more. He had felt something for her he had never felt before. Something indefinable he wanted to find again—and he knew he wouldn't find it with Mai.

Even with a different choice of bride, he would never feel again what he'd felt for Sally in the brief magical interlude when he had been just Edward, with none of the expectations that came with his royal status. She hadn't known him as a crown prince but as a man. He had been himself with her—and she had come to his bed purely to be with him, not for what she could get from him or to solve a political impasse.

The meal and the speeches over, he signalled to his bodyguards—always a presence when he was in public—that he intended to make an exit before dessert was served. He could have left discreetly via a backstage door. Instead he chose to walk down the centre of the ballroom. While he despised publicity, he knew any mention of him in the media would also mean a mention for the cancer research institute. Besides, there were people in the room he had to acknowledge with a brief greeting or even just a nod.

He was part way down the room when he saw her.

Sally.

He broke step, froze, then quickly recovered himself.

Could it be true?

His heart thudded and his mouth went dry. He looked again.

She was here.

His one-night lover was sitting at one of the tables, her head turned towards him as if, perhaps, someone had pointed him out to her.

He recognised her immediately, even though she looked very different to when he had last seen her. Now she wore a formal dress; then she'd worn nothing at all. Now her hair was swept up off her face; then it had been spread across his pillow and he had fisted it in his hands as he had kissed her. If he'd had any doubt it was Sally, and not someone with a strong resemblance to her, it dissipated at the flash of recognition in her eyes. Recognition and a fleeting glimpse of panic. Something in her expression told him that his anonymous Edward cover had been completely blown.

What was she doing here?

His first impulse was to head straight for her, to exclaim his surprise at her presence, and express his pleasure at seeing her again. But common sense restrained him. The rumours of his impending engagement were rippling through the room. He reminded himself again that anyone with a camera phone was a potential paparazzo. There were a lot of curious eyes on him. He could not be seen singling out this woman any more than on the day he had rescued her from the swimming pool.

But nothing could make him walk past her without stopping.

Thankfully, he recognised the man seated near her as Oscar Yeo, the eminent landscape architect, who had worked with his sister Jennifer on several occasions. What was Sally doing at Yeo's table?

Edward stopped as he reached the table. Oscar and his wife rose to greet him with expressions of surprised pleasure. Sally was sitting next to Yeo's wife. She was even lovelier than he remembered, elegant, sophisticated, regal even. The colour drained from her face as she slowly rose too. He noticed she had to clutch the back of her chair for support. Was she, like him, remembering that the last time she had seen him she had fallen asleep in his arms, both of them spent from the passion they had shared? Everything he'd felt that night came flooding back.

He still wanted her more than any other woman.

It took formidable restraint not to ignore his surroundings and sweep her into his arms. Instead he had to make sure his eyes didn't stray to Sally instead of the Yeos.

'Mr Yeo,' Edward said. 'My sister was full of praise for the last hotel landscape design you did for her.' He shook the landscape architect's hand.

'Thank you,' Yeo said. 'As always, it was a pleasure to work with Princess Jennifer.'

Edward liked that the older man didn't appear overawed at his royal status. The way Edward saw it, he would like to be Edward Chen when he was living and working in Singapore, the Crown Prince when he was in his own country. Although others didn't see it that way—his royal status was the first thing people recognised him by and judged him on. Only that night with Sally, in the privacy of the hotel room, had he been able to be himself. Secure in his anonymity, he had relaxed. She too had been free from expectations, uninhibited and delightful.

'My wife, Iris,' said Yeo, by way of introduction.

Flustered, Mrs Yeo bobbed a quick curtsy.

Edward allowed himself a slight inclination of his head towards Sally, as was the polite thing to do to another member of Yeo's party. She kept her eyes downcast. He suspected she, like him, was terrified of letting slip any prior knowledge of each other by the merest change in her expression.

'May I introduce Sally Harrington,' said Yeo.

She was real.

Sally was a genuine first name. Now she also had a genuine surname. She hadn't lied to him by inventing a fake identity and that pleased him.

'Edward Chen,' he said. She looked up to him and their eyes met. He saw not just recognition but also a fleeting flash of joy. Royal protocol dictated that he be always the first to offer his hand to shake. She took his hand in a firm businesslike grip, but he was aware of her pulse fluttering. Her touch triggered a flood of sensual memories. But he was careful not to hold her hand for a second longer than politeness dictated. Too many interested eyes were on him. He could not risk revealing how affected he was by this unexpected reunion.

He doubted there was a woman in the room more beautiful than Sally Harrington in a shimmering gown that hinted at her curves rather than flaunted them. High heels brought her eyes so much closer to his than when she'd been barefoot in that black velvet robe.

Did she remember?

He wanted to ask her that, ask her so much more. He gritted his teeth against his frustration that he couldn't acknowledge her. He wanted to ignore everyone else at the table. Instead he had to continue the charade that they were strangers to each other.

Oscar Yeo continued the introduction. 'Ms Harrington is an important client of mine, here from London.'

Edward found it difficult to school his expression to hide his surprise. Who was she? Not just a tourist in Singapore, it seemed. He fought his inclination to issue a string of commands for her to answer about who she was and why she was here.

'Indeed,' he said instead.

'She is from the Harrington Hotel family and we are working with her on a project through our London office.'

A tightening of her lips let him know she didn't want Yeo to spill any further details of that project. He found that intriguing. Or was she just nervous about encountering him?

'I stayed at the Harrington Park in Regent's Park with my family many years ago,' he said. From his memory, it had been a very grand hotel indeed.

'The Harrington Park is our flagship,' she said without elaborating further.

These days, the royal family stayed only at their family-owned hotels. Under his sister's management the portfolio had expanded considerably. However, when in London they stayed at their apartment in Mayfair. He'd had cause to use it when he was studying at Cambridge and went down to London. He vaguely remembered his sister saying that the Harrington Park had changed hands quite recently. She'd considered making an offer, but it had sold immediately to an unknown buyer for an undisclosed sum. How could that be if it was a family enterprise?

'My sister Jennifer is a hotelier,' he said, deliberately downplaying her role as CEO across a vast portfolio.

'How interesting,' Sally said. He saw the cool, self-possessed businesswoman. But the tension hunching her shoulders betrayed her discomfort. No wonder, as the other women at the table were agog even at this businesslike conversation between them. He was very conscious of eyes that went from him to Sally and back again—not just at this table but what felt like the entire ballroom.

'I believe my sister would be interested in meeting another woman in the same business as her.'

'I would like to meet her too. It does tend to be a male-dominated industry.' She spoke with just the right amount of professional interest and courtesy. How did she really feel about seeing him again? He ached to find out.

'Are you in Singapore for long?'

'I fly out tomorrow afternoon,' she said.

'Perhaps you have a business card I could pass on to my sister?'

'Er…certainly,' she said, with the first break in her composure. She reached down to the table to a small beaded purse in the same colour as her dress, fumbled for a moment and pulled out a very smart business card. Her tension was palpable, not perhaps to the others at the table, but he had spent an evening learning her body.

'Thank you,' he said. He slid her card into his inside jacket pocket without looking at it; that would only cause speculation. He felt a rush of exultation.

He had her phone number.

But he schooled his voice to be businesslike. 'I'm sure you'll hear from Jen, if not while you are in Singapore, the next time she is in London.'

'I'll look forward to that,' Sally said.

He ached to pull her into his arms and rush her with him out of the hotel and somewhere private. But cameras would flash if he did so. He tried to express all that in a glance he held for a second too long for a businesslike exchange. But she did not drop her cool façade and her eyes told him nothing.

As he walked away from the table he was aware of her gaze following him. He felt more alive, more invigorated than he had since he'd awoken to that empty bed five weeks ago.

No matter the risk, he had to see her again.

With an inestimable feeling of loss, Sally watched Edward walk away from the table. Two burly bodyguards followed at a distance. There was still time for her to make her excuses to the Yeos, pick up her skirts and rush after Edward, barrelling her way past the bodyguards. But she would only make an utter fool of herself.

There had been a glimmer of recognition in his eyes, for

sure, but that was all. However, as soon as she'd seen his face, all the attraction, the excitement, the intense feelings he'd aroused on that day five weeks ago had come rushing back. She'd wanted to drink in his features, touch him, re-assure herself he was very real. Hold him. Kiss him.

The father of her baby.

But his princely status put an unscalable barrier between them. The fact he was about to get engaged made the bar-rier even higher, put barbed wire and shards of glass on top.

As soon as he was out of sight, she had to field ques-tions from Iris. 'Prince Edward asked for your card! What could that mean?'

Sally had to force herself to smile at the buzz of excite-ment from Iris and the others at the table. Left to herself, she would weep.

'He wanted my card for his sister, not him,' she said, trying to sound light-hearted and as if their meeting had no significance.

'I wonder if Princess Jennifer will get in touch,' Iris persisted.

'It would be nice if she did, but I very much doubt it,' Sally said. 'My brother often thinks he's found someone or something that would interest me. I just humour him and never follow it up. The Prince's sister might be the same.'

Did she protest too much? Or not show enough ex-citement at the honour of having been singled out by a prince? Trouble was, she wanted him as much as she had back in his hotel room all those weeks ago, wanted him so much she ached to be with him. It was an effort to feign indifference.

Coming here had been a hideous mistake. It was so much worse to see him and know she could never again be with him. It would have been better if he had remained in the realm of her dreams and fantasies.

'He's so handsome, don't you think?'

'He most certainly is,' Sally said lightly, while fending off a stab of pain at Iris's words. 'I was so glad to have got a good look at him. Now I see what the fuss is all about. His fiancée is a lucky lady.' Not so lucky that her fiancé had cheated on her. For the first time? For the umpteenth time? Again, she wondered what kind of a man Edward really was.

'She certainly is,' sighed Iris.

'I suppose you see royals all the time in London,' said one of the other women.

'Not really,' she said. 'Although I don't live far from Kensington Palace so I'm always hoping to catch sight of Prince William or Catherine.'

She'd gone to school with a minor royal but didn't think that was worth mentioning. Nor did she see fit to mention that she was related to a duke way back on her mother's side of the family tree. And that her great-great-great-something grandfather, the founder of the Harrington Park, was the youngest son of an earl. He'd had no chance of inheriting the title and had gone very successfully into commerce. The fact that blue blood—somewhat diluted—ran in her and her brothers' veins wasn't something they had been brought up to trade on. In fact, she wondered if her brothers had even listened to their grandmother's stories about their titled ancestors. They were Harringtons; that was enough. Jay wouldn't give a toss and Hugo…well, Hugo was a stranger to her now and she had little idea of what was important to him.

'How exciting. London must be a fabulous place to live,' said the same woman.

'I could say the same about Singapore,' Sally said. 'I love it here.'

While she kept on top of the conversation, underneath all she could think about was Edward, the touch of his hand on hers, how incredibly good he looked in a perfectly tailored tuxedo, how he was a *prince* and utterly and totally out of her reach.

She managed to get through the rest of the evening. Back in her hotel room, she stood looking in the mirror, fighting back tears of despair, overwhelmed by an uncharacteristic self-doubt. What had he seen in her? Not enough to be interested, that was for sure. But why should he show interest? The man was about to get engaged.

Sally heaved a great sigh of regret, consigning Edward—*Prince Edward*—to the past. She slipped off her new shoes with some relief. She slid out of her beautiful new dress with a pang; she wouldn't be able to fit into it for much longer.

She started to take off her make-up in the bathroom when her phone pinged a text message. Singapore was eight hours ahead of London. At this time of night, it was probably her brother Jay. Or even Hugo. Hugo would certainly be interested in the results of her meeting with Oscar. She hadn't had time to contact either of them, being way too busy getting sorted for the gala. She wasn't really in the mood to talk about the winter garden, but she'd better check the text in case it was something important.

The text wasn't from either of her brothers. Rather it was from an unknown number. She opened it anyway.

I have to see you. Edward.

Sally stared at the words on the screen, scarcely able to believe them. Disbelief and excitement made her tremble all over. With hands that shook, she tried to text back, but she fumbled the screen and dropped the phone. Finally, she managed to get her thumbs working enough to text a reply.

Yes.

I will send a car to your hotel.

Now?

Be in the foyer in five minutes.

Nothing would stop her from being in that foyer. Her heart was racing. What did he want with her? To warn her to keep their tryst of five weeks ago secret? Was there even a slight chance he was as filled with anticipation as she was? Heaven knew where he intended taking her. He could drive her up and down Orchard Road for all she cared. She ached with a painful intensity to see him. *Just see him.* She would have to wait to see his reaction to her before she considered anything as bold as telling him she was pregnant.

She touched up the make-up she'd been about to remove. Then slipped into narrow black trousers—which now fitted a little more snugly at the waist—black stilettoes and a sleeveless black silk top, layered and trimmed with silk fringing. She left on her grandmother's diamond earrings and bracelet she'd worn to the dinner.

She was going to meet a prince.

Sally silently cursed the slow elevator. Seconds wasted on stabbing the down button were seconds taken from seeing Edward. It was probably six minutes by the time she got to the foyer.

Was he waiting for her?

The concierge approached her and told her that her car was there. He indicated a man dressed in a chauffeur's uniform. Sally fought a sharp pang of disappointment that Edward hadn't come to meet her himself but dismissed the thought immediately. The driver no doubt had his instructions of where to take her. The speculation about Edward's impending engagement had reached fever-pitch after he'd left the Yeo table at the gala. Under that kind of fierce spotlight, he couldn't be seen with her—or any other woman who wasn't his fiancée. Her excitement dimmed a little—she was, when it came down to it, his scandalous little secret.

CHAPTER FIVE

THE CHAUFFEUR OPENED the back door of a sleek black limousine with dark tinted windows and politely ushered Sally towards it. About to climb inside, she paused momentarily. Trust didn't come easily to her, and she was taking a lot on trust, but in that heartbeat of hesitation she decided she had nothing to fear. Or lose.

Edward.

She sensed his presence before she saw him on the other side of the wide seat. Yet so close she could reach out and touch him, if she dared. She turned to face this man she knew so intimately and yet did not know at all.

Why had he cheated on his soon-to-be fiancée?

'Sally,' he said slowly, his eyes intent on her.

Her heart jolted into an erratic rhythm that stole her breath. Back in her hotel room, in those few minutes between getting his text and heading out of the door, she'd practised over and over in her head what she'd say to him— this man she had been unable to forget, who had made love to her and made her laugh, whose baby she carried. But, faced with the regal presence of Crown Prince Edward of Tianlipin, she felt paralysed by nerves, her words frozen on the tip of her tongue. Was she expected to address him as *Your Highness*?

All she could manage was a croaky and totally inadequate, 'Hi.'

He had taken off his tuxedo jacket and rid himself of his bow tie. In white shirt and black trousers, he seemed more like her Edward, where no formalities were required. *Her* Edward? *Huh.* She had no claim whatsoever on this royal personage. Some poor cheated-on woman did. She kept a careful distance from him, at the same time aching to slide across the seat to be nearer.

Edward acknowledged her single word of greeting with a nod. He seemed tense, his face set in rigid lines. But surely not as nervous as Sally, alone with him in the darkened back seat of the car.

Once the driver was settled behind the wheel, Edward reached out to close the communication panel between driver and passengers. 'That's better,' he said as he turned back to face her.

She noted in his dark eyes a shadow of the same uncertainty that choked her words and made her clutch tight the strap of her handbag. But there was nothing to clarify what she was doing there alone with him on the night he'd been expected to announce his engagement. Or to justify the violent whirlpool of her senses that was shaking her off her balance simply by being near him.

'Thank you for agreeing to meet with me,' he said finally, very formally.

She had a polite response ready but other words overwhelmed it and tumbled out of her mouth. 'You're a prince,' she blurted out. 'A real, honest-to-goodness prince. Of all the things I imagined you might be, I never thought of a prince.'

'From a dynasty dating back many hundreds of years.' He paused. 'And I believe you're "hotel royalty".' He made quote marks with his fingers. Long, elegant fingers that had played her body so intimately. She was glad for the darkened interior of the car to hide her blush.

'A tag invented by the media. Not quite the same thing

as your brand of royalty,' she said, a smile tugging at the corners of her mouth.

'Perhaps not,' he said, with an answering lightening of his features.

'You were quick to research me,' she said.

'As soon as I could look at your business card without causing a media meltdown.' The remembered edge of humour to his voice did much to ease her nerves.

'Online there was a lot more about you than you would have found about me,' she said.

Her grip tightened on her handbag with the hope he hadn't read the rundown of her disastrous break-up with the actor in *Celebrity* magazine. Her Ice Queen moniker had got quite an outing in that article.

'I discovered you're a very successful businesswoman, boss of your own company, Sally Harrington Interiors, with clients all around the world. A winner of prestigious design awards. The *London Evening Post* filled me in on the background of your stepfather's bankruptcy and your older brother's subsequent purchase of the Harrington Park Hotel.'

'All correct,' she said. As far as her business success went, she was proud of what she'd achieved, fired by the determination to succeed on her own terms, to never be reliant on a man the way her mother had been.

'For so long, all I knew was your first name, that you were an interior designer and that you liked gardening.'

'I knew even less about you.' But she knew the important, secret things—the way he used his tongue when he kissed; the warm, salty taste of his skin; his moans when she'd discovered his most sensitive spots; how he was ticklish in the crook of his elbow. A shiver of desire rippled through her at the memory, tightening her nipples, making her press her thighs together.

'When did you discover my identity?' he asked.

'Just this afternoon.'

'Only then?'

'I saw you on television. The programme I was watching in my hotel room segued from a report on the admirable health of the Singapore economy to the current status of Asia's most eligible bachelor. I was surprised to find I recognised him.' Surely that day would go down as the most momentous of her life for unexpected discoveries.

'I'm sorry you had to find out that way. You must have been shocked.'

'*Shocked* is probably too mild a word for it.' She couldn't keep the quiver from her voice.

He paused. 'Were you angry I didn't tell you the truth about who I was the last time we met?'

Sally girded herself to provide the nonchalant answers required by the one-night stand rules.

'No. It was only one night. A game. A fantasy.'

He frowned. 'If you put it like that.'

She added some Ice Queen cool to her words. 'That's what we agreed. One time was all we had to offer. No regrets.'

'Do you regret that night?'

She couldn't help the slow smile that curved her lips at the memories of their lovemaking. 'Not for a moment. It was...you were...extraordinary.'

She couldn't mention the unintended and life-changing result of their time together. Not now. Not yet. Maybe never.

He was a prince.

'And you?'

'I regret it was only the one night,' he said hoarsely. He angled his body so he narrowed the gap on the leather seat between them. 'I haven't been able to stop thinking about you.'

Sally stared at him in disbelief and a bubbling of unexpected joy. 'Me too. Stop thinking about you, I mean.'

She would be too embarrassed to admit just how much she had thought about him, even dreamed about him—erotic dreams from which she awoke overwhelmed by an aching sense of frustration and loss.

'I tried to find you. By the time I got back from my business trip to Bangkok, you'd checked out of your hotel and flown back to London.'

'How did you know where I was staying?' She paused. 'Never mind. I guess princes have ways of finding out things ordinary people can't.'

He smiled. 'Simple, everyday detection work, I can assure you. But a good hotel doesn't give out names and personal details of its guests, even to royalty. Yours stuck to the rules.'

'Quite rightly,' she said. 'We would do the same at the Harrington Park.' She didn't know whether to be grateful or cranky at her Singapore hotel for its discretion.

He had tried to find her.

And she, in spite of all her fervent self-lectures that it had been *just one night*, had tried to find him. After four days of sleepless nights and distracted days, she'd called his hotel, only to be told there was no Edward staying in that room. No surprises there. Even less surprising now she knew his family owned the hotel.

Her emotions were flip-flopping all over the place. To know he felt in some way the same about their encounter made her spirits soar, and she allowed herself a flash of crazy, one-night stand rule-breaking hope.

But then reality intruded. 'That night. Back then. I asked you if you were married. You said you weren't. But it appears you were about to get engaged. You cheated on your girlfriend. I would *never* date another woman's man. Let alone…let alone sleep with him. You were not honest with me.'

Edward pushed his hands through his hair and uttered

a low groan that sounded a mix of frustration and despair. 'She was not my girlfriend. I was not her man. I did not cheat on her with you.'

She frowned. 'So why—?'

'My situation is impossible. I am about to become en-gaged to the Princess of a neighbouring kingdom.'

Sally's emotions plummeted to painful depths.

How could she compete with a princess?

'Congratulations. That…that's lovely for you.'

'No, it's not.' He thumped his fist on the car seat in an action that made Sally start. 'I finally agreed to a marriage made purely for political and dynastic reasons. I don't even like my future bride, let alone love her. I've only met her twice.'

'You…you don't love her?'

'No.'

'Then why—?'

'Duty. Obligation. The honour of my country.'

She drew back a little. 'So why am I here, alone with you, when you're about to get engaged?'

Not for a booty call, she thought, the words ugly in her mind. That wasn't going to happen. Not when he was about to get engaged. Not when, seeing him again, she wanted him as much as she had five weeks ago and couldn't bear to have him again and lose him again.

'At the gala it seemed unbelievable you were here in Singapore. Despite the risk, I had to stop at your table. But that wasn't enough. I had to see you alone.'

Sally swallowed hard. 'If you're worried I've told any-one about our time together, don't be. I haven't told a soul that I met you, let alone that I…that we—'

He made a dismissive gesture. 'It's not that. I didn't ex-pect anything less of you than discretion. I still don't or you wouldn't be here. But our last meeting had left so much unsaid. I had to talk with you away from the scrutiny of a ballroom full of onlookers. Find out who the real Sally is—obviously more than the mermaid of my memories.'

'You thought of me as a *mermaid*?'

'That's how you looked under the water—your pale skin, your long hair floating around you. You enchanted me.'

'And you were my…my Sir Galahad. But if I was a mermaid I'd be able to swim properly,' she said. 'I still feel embarrassed about that.'

'No need to be. Pulling you from the pool gave me the opportunity to get close to you, a woman I might never have met otherwise.'

'Because you're having an arranged marriage?' The idea seemed so old-fashioned. But she knew different countries had different customs.

'I am Crown Prince of my country.' Both arrogance and pride underscored his words. 'It is expected of me. Marriage for senior members of the royal family is about more than personal desire.'

'I understand,' she said.

But did she really? In her experience, people chose who they wanted to marry. That the choice was always a good one could be debated—look at her mother choosing to marry a horrible man like Nick Wolfe. That choice had caused a wave of repercussions. The splintering of her family. Loss of livelihoods for Harrington employees. A damaged reputation for the Harrington Park that she and her brothers were now trying to claw back.

'My family is complicated,' Edward said.

'So is mine,' Sally said, rather too wholeheartedly.

'In what way?'

'It would take all night to explain,' she said. 'I'd much rather hear about your family—and why you're going to marry someone you don't even like, let alone love.'

'I'd prefer not talk about it here,' he said.

'Then where?'

'The only place we can talk with any real privacy is my place.'

'You mean your palace?'

He laughed. 'I don't have a palace in Singapore.'

'But you do in your home country?'

'A very splendid palace where I have my own apartment.'

I'd like to see that.

The words hung unspoken between them. They both knew she would never see his palace. He was going to marry a princess.

'So you have an apartment here too? Wait. Do you live in that penthouse where we met?'

He shook his head. 'That was temporary while my Singapore home was being remodelled and refurbished.'

'For your future bride?'

'For myself. The interiors were dated and needed refurbishing more to my taste.'

'Is your home far?'

'Not far. Tanglin. Near the Botanic Gardens. You may have visited the gardens on your last trip.'

One of the most exclusive, desirable places to live in Singapore, so Iris had told her in a general discussion about Singapore real estate. Home to multi-million Singapore dollar 'landed houses', increasingly rare in a city of soaring skyscrapers.

'Do you live alone?' She couldn't—*wouldn't*—go there if she were to be judged and scrutinised.

'My sister also shares the house. We have separate residences under the same roof. I live upstairs; she lives downstairs. We're good friends as well as siblings.'

'Is your sister there now?'

'Jen's in Australia. She's acquired a historic building in the heart of the city of Sydney and is repurposing it into a boutique hotel.'

'Can I mention that project if she calls me? You know, to kickstart the conversation?'

He paused for a beat too long. 'Sure. It's no secret.'

Sally narrowed her eyes. 'Will your sister actually call me? Or—'

'She might do. If and when I pass on your card.'

'You asked for my card so you—?'

'Could get your contact details. It was a ploy.' At last a return of his wonderful smile. 'Did you know I would be at the gala?'

Sally didn't want to admit she had been at the gala purely in the hope of seeing him. 'Oscar invited me. Once I knew you would be there, of course I wanted to see you.'

'Would you have sought me out if I hadn't approached you?'

'Unlikely.'

'Why not?'

'You're a prince. I'm, to all intents, a stranger. I had no idea of what my reception might be. Your bodyguards would probably have stopped any approach from me.'

'My bodyguards do as I instruct them.'

'Which is probably to protect you from over-enthusiastic fans. You have many fans. Entire websites and blogs devoted to you.'

'I know,' he said tersely. 'I choose to ignore them.'

'You're a celebrity.'

'Not on my terms. I'm the member of an ancient royal family fulfilling my duties.'

'Who just happens to be movie-star-handsome.'

He growled his very negative response, which made her laugh.

'Well, you are. But even if you were simply Edward, the businessman I thought you to be, I still would have hesitated to approach you. I've never done anything so impulsive as our one night together. Besides, I liked you as Edward. Prince Edward was an unknown quantity.'

'I'm the same person. Can you see that now?'

'I'm beginning to…' she said slowly. But how sure could she be?

His brow furrowed. 'That night. It wasn't just about the sex for me. Although we were sensational together.'

She caught her breath. 'Yes, we were.' For a long moment he fell silent and she wondered if he was reliving, as she was, those passionate moments they had shared.

'I felt something more,' he said. 'A different level of connection.'

She paused, wanting to be sure she used the right words. 'I'm usually cautious when I meet someone new. But I liked you immediately. As well as fancying you.'

'You were a person I wanted to get to know if—'

'Circumstances were different.' This finishing off of each other's sentences didn't seem out of place. In bed they'd each seemed to know instinctively what the other had wanted.

'Our coming together felt like something inevitable,' he said.

'Inevitable but—'

'Impossible,' he said heavily.

He went to take her hand, but Sally gently released it from his clasp. 'You're right; it's impossible. Utterly impossible.' And her pregnancy took it to an entirely new level of impossibility. 'We can talk but we really mustn't touch.'

No touching.

Edward knew she was right. But he was having immense trouble keeping his thoughts on an even keel. In terms of royal protocol—especially at this time of his impending engagement—his impulsive decision to ask Sally to join him at his house would not be seen as wise or advisable. Even more so than before, she was a scandal in the making. But he would regret it for the rest of his life if he had passed on the chance to see her again.

If he were indeed Mr Edward Chen he would have a lot more to say to her about how he'd felt that night five weeks ago, how important and special he'd believed she could have become to him. But he was heir to the throne of the country he loved, who honoured and respected his parents, and a future crown weighed heavily on his head. As Prince Edward he had no choice but to keep her at arm's length.

Common sense dictated he tell the driver to turn around and return his guest to her hotel. But he made no such order. Sally was *real*, more beautiful even than he had remembered. He had slipped so easily back into conversation with her. And he wanted her.

He could not deny himself further time with Sally, stealing every possible second before he had to say goodbye to her—this time for ever.

CHAPTER SIX

SALLY FOLLOWED EDWARD into his house via a dimly lit back entrance to avoid, he said, any possible unwanted media attention. She was aware of palm trees and shrubs and the heady scents of a warm, humid tropical night. Once inside, they shot up in an elevator to his quarters and inside to a blast of air conditioning. It was the upper half of an elegant converted colonial mansion and retained mansion-like proportions as, no doubt, did his sister's floor below.

Edward told her there was separate staff accommodation and he had dismissed the staff for the night, so their privacy was assured. 'You'll have to manage with me looking after you,' he said with a grin.

Sally suppressed a shiver of desire at the thought of the exciting ways he could look after her but forced them to the back of her mind. She'd meant what she said about no touching. It was the only way she knew to keep her equilibrium.

Pregnant by a prince.

Although that didn't stop her from aching to pull him down with her to one of the oriental day beds in the loggia that seemed placed for their sensual comfort.

'Can a prince operate without staff?' she asked, confident enough now in his company to risk a little teasing. 'The Harrington Park's lore includes tales of a royal personage who demanded staff dip his teabag in his cup for him because he didn't know how.' Sally always wondered why a porcelain teapot wouldn't have been in service for such an esteemed guest but didn't want to ruin the story.

Edward laughed.

She loved his laughter.

'I studied in both the UK and the US. I had bodyguards but their duties didn't include waiting on me. I enjoyed being independent when I got the chance. You can trust me to get you a drink or something to eat.'

Sally realised the risk he took in bringing her alone to his house amid the media frenzy focused on his personal life and she appreciated it. She would have been heartbroken if he'd dropped her back at her hotel. These bonus moments with him were to be cherished. They were all she would have with him before she flew back to London the next day. Memories stored up from this night and hugged close would have to last a long, long time.

He ushered her through to the living area. She didn't have to feign enthusiasm for his Singapore home. Usually Sally examined interior design with a silent conviction she could do better. In this case she wasn't sure she could. His house was superbly designed and decorated, with dark floors and white walls, contemporary furniture and antique dark carved pieces set off by a perfectly placed collection of Asian and western artworks. She particularly liked the ceramics, which Edward told her were a speciality of Tianlipin.

'My Chinese ancestors brought the skills with them when, many centuries ago, they invaded and conquered the indigenous people living on the island. They had their own skills in wood carving, which became part of our cultural heritage.'

Sally admired an outsize jar that seemed a museum piece yet sat unprotected on its own pedestal.

Not a house for children.

The thought flashed from nowhere. When she told Edward about her pregnancy it would be his choice if he wanted to have anything to do with the baby's London upbringing. She certainly wouldn't expect or demand it.

'Your ancestors were fierce invaders,' she said.

'Fierce defenders too. Our island has never again been invaded or colonised and our people from different ethnic backgrounds live harmoniously.'

'No uprisings?'

His black brows rose. Again, Sally reminded herself that different places had different cultures and customs. 'I'm not being critical. Remember I live under a monarchy myself.'

'The British monarchy is not quite the same as ours,' he said very seriously. 'We have an elected advisory council, but we are not a democracy. However, my father's rule is, thankfully, a benevolent one.'

'The rulers weren't always benevolent?' Sally was interested in his home country, not so much the politics of it but to extend her knowledge of both him and the heritage of her baby. It was also a relief to talk about something other than their one night together. And to delay the time when she had to confess that she was pregnant. She wanted to enjoy Edward's company a while longer before she faced his reaction to her news. Truth be told, she was still coming to terms with it herself.

Edward heaved a sigh. 'That's where I told you my family was complicated. Let me get drinks and I'll explain.'

He led her to an elegant sofa with dark carved wooden arms, upholstered in cream silk and adorned with vibrantly coloured silk cushions. It was a very fine piece indeed. An identical sofa sat opposite, separated by a marble coffee table.

'White wine?' he asked.

Sally shook her head, searching for an excuse. 'Mineral water with a slice of lemon, please. I've had enough to drink tonight.' He didn't question her choice, although she could tell he was surprised after her enjoyment of the same drink on their first meeting. In fact, she hadn't touched alcohol at all at the gala. Or eaten much food. It was only the excitement of being with Edward that was staving off exhaustion and an underlying nausea that came and went.

'A snack?'

'No, thank you.' Her stomach roiled at the thought. She was too wary to tempt fate by eating.

Edward returned with drinks, whisky for him and her mineral water in a tall frosted glass. He took his place across from her on the opposite sofa with athletic grace. He looked so at home, so unbelievably handsome. She couldn't help but speculate that her child would be good-looking with such a man as their father.

'I noticed in my research into you that you're a twin,' he said.

'Yes, my brother Jay is my twin, the older by just a few minutes.'

Edward held his whisky glass and swirled its contents around without drinking from it. 'Traditionally, in my country, twins are considered to be bad luck and bearers of ill fortune.'

Sally stared at him and felt the colour leach from her face. 'Why would you tell me that when you know I'm a twin?'

'Because, awful as it is, it directly relates to the story of my family. I don't believe such ignorant superstition, of course. Not for a moment.'

'I should hope not,' she said, affronted. Whether by accident or design, she was grateful for the distance the coffee table put between her and Edward on their opposing sofas.

'Being a twin has only ever been good for me. When you're a twin you're never alone. Jay is my closest friend.' Or he had been until, halfway through the sixth form, he'd upped and left school to work in a restaurant kitchen in Paris. Finishing that last year at St Mary's without him had been difficult. Jay's popularity had shielded his quieter, more aloof sister and she'd been left vulnerable. Sally wasn't sure their close relationship had ever quite recovered from his departure, or whether twins by nature grew apart as they grew up.

'I didn't mean to offend you. I'm sharing this story to help you understand why duty and honour are so important to my family and my country,' he said. 'We have a scandal-ridden past to overcome.'

Sally leaned towards him. 'Sounds intriguing.' The internet had hinted at some old scandal but all she'd been interested in reading about was him, not his ancestors.

'My father was the youngest of three brothers; the oldest were identical twins. They were born five minutes each side of midnight, so the firstborn was theoretically a day older than his twin. My grandfather, then the King, died relatively young when his car went off the road in the mountains. There were suspicions that it hadn't been an accident. Nothing was ever proven, although persistent rumours circulated that his heir, the older twin, burdened by gambling debts the King had refused to cover, had hastened his father's demise to accelerate his accession to the throne.'

Sally's eyes widened. 'That's quite a story.'

'It gets worse. I was only a baby when this all happened, but my father made sure I knew the history so as to understand how it affected us as a family.'

'I can relate to the family history thing,' Sally said. She recalled her mother trying to keep memories of her father and the glory days of the Harrington Park alive for her children. Although never in the presence of Nick Wolfe. Weren't she and her brothers, by the restoration of the hotel, trying to bring back those good times to somehow heal the wounds the loss of their family unit had brought all three?

Edward continued. 'The country was in mourning for their loved and respected King, but his son demanded an inappropriately lavish coronation. He started his reign the way he meant to continue, by draining the country's coffers. He and his twin funded an extraordinarily decadent lifestyle of astonishing excesses. The world's most expensive yachts, cars, jets, racehorses—every overpriced plaything you can think of—this corrupt ruler grabbed in multiples. Women too, to the extent he kept a modern-day harem, some of whom later claimed to have been kidnapped. He and his twin spent large parts of the year in Europe with their international so-called friends, who sponged ruthlessly off them.'

'When did the King find time to rule the country?'

'In our ancient tradition, the King was a man of virtue who appointed other men of virtue as magisterial officers to help him govern.'

'Your uncle turned this on its head?'

'His officials were as corrupt as he was. Taxes were raised to burdensome levels. Bribery became endemic. And still more money left the country to fund the twins' dissolute lifestyles.'

'Sounds the perfect set-up for a revolution,' she said slowly.

'Dangerously so, my father tells me.'

'So what happened?'

'Fate intervened. My uncle, the King of our proud country, died in compromising circumstances in a brothel.'

Sally gasped. 'Murdered?'

'An undiagnosed heart condition accelerated by a cocktail of recreational drugs.'

'So the other twin took over?'

'The weaker twin didn't dare come home without the protection of his brother. He abdicated, put himself into voluntary exile and died not long after. Neither brother had ever married.'

'So they left no heirs?'

'My father, the third son, became King.'

'I don't know a lot about dynasties, but I guess a third son—'

'Hadn't been prepared for it from birth like his brothers had. My father was a scholar—somewhat of a nerd in fact—happy to live his life on the sidelines of the court. But, when duty called, he jumped right in and did his best to repair the damage his brother had done to his beloved country.' Edward's obvious respect for his father shone through his words.

'And you?'

'At the age of ten I became Crown Prince.'

'Your life must have changed.'

'Completely. That's why I'm telling you all this. Duty and honour became all-important. From the time I was ten years old my destiny was drummed into me. It took some years for my father to turn both the finances and the reputation of the royal family around. He did that by reinstating traditional values and a strong moral code of behaviour, but within a modern context.'

'An admirable man, your father.'

'My mother, also. She worked alongside him to regain the respect and love of our people, although she'd never wanted the attention the role of Queen brought with it.'

'Your family history sounds like the plot of a movie. It's a lot to take in.' These people were her baby's ancestors, she reminded herself. Both the good and the bad. As there was in any family.

Edward took a slug of whisky. 'After the precedent set by my corrupt uncles, avoiding scandal became a priority. Their behaviour put the international spotlight on our country and not in a good way. My father has spent more than twenty years trying to subdue it.'

The intensity of his expression tore at Sally's heart. Who knew he had the weight of all this responsibility on his shoulders? 'So now there's that movie-star-handsome Crown Prince doing his best to avoid scandal.'

'Scandal of the rescuing of mermaids kind,' he said wryly.

Sally laughed. But there was an edge to her laughter. Every word he spoke distanced him further and further from her.

'Not that you and I did anything wrong back then,' he said. 'Not that we're doing anything wrong by being alone together now.'

'But not when you're about to get engaged.'

'Correct.' He sighed, loud and heartfelt. 'Then it becomes a betrayal of my father's moral code.'

'But not yours. If you feel so unhappy about your engagement, why go through with it?'

'My uncles did more damage to the country than merely raiding the treasury. They also alienated long-time allies. Our nearest neighbour has, for political reasons of its own, delayed a full resumption of relations with us. Diplomatic and trade efforts can only go so far. A marriage uniting the royal families could do much to cement new bonds.'

Sally had to swallow hard against a sudden lump of hopelessness. 'That's where your Princess is from?'

'Yes.'

Sally could not help but be gratified to see he showed none of the anticipation one would expect of a man in love with a princess.

'Is she crazy about you?'

'She's twenty-one. I'm thirty-one.'

'When I was twenty-one I would have thought you were from a different generation.'

He grimaced. 'Let's just say I don't think she belongs to one of my fan clubs.'

Sally frowned. 'Are you telling me she's reluctantly doing her duty too?' How could any woman not leap at the chance to have him in her bed?

'I would suggest so. We've met twice and it was awkward.'

Sally took a deep steadying breath. How she hated the pretence of this cool conversation about a woman this man, the father of her baby, was going to marry. Marry after having met her just twice. It hurt. Not that she wanted to marry him—even if it had been possible. For all their talk of feeling a special kind of emotional connection, they hardly knew each other. Marriage was something to be slowly weighed and deliberated and never undertaken on impulse. Look at the ongoing damage her mother's ill-considered marriage had brought to her family.

But, ever since Edward had approached her at the gala, the truth had been slowly percolating through the turbulence of her thoughts.

She could so easily fall in love with him.

Prince Edward of Tianlipin was the only man she'd met, since her gay high school friend, who made her spirit truly sing. Her habit of falling for unattainable men had reached its apex.

A persistent inner voice reminded her that this mad spark of attraction had been ignited before she knew he was royalty. But what difference could that possibly make?

'Is she…is she pretty?' Sally hated herself for asking the question, but she couldn't seem to help it.

'Yes. She's pretty,' he said.

His words felt like tiny but deadly stabs from a poisoned stiletto. 'Oh,' she managed to choke out.

Edward got up and in a few steps was beside Sally on

her sofa. He looked deep into her eyes. 'But nowhere near as beautiful as you.' He reached out to cradle her face in his hands, warm and strong and possessive. 'There is no woman more beautiful than you, Sally Harrington.'

As she breathed in his scent, lemongrass and sandalwood—already heart-stoppingly familiar—she had to momentarily close her eyes at the ecstasy of his closeness. She reached up to place her hands over his. Her *no touching* embargo crumbled.

'That's very kind of you to say but—'

'Please. No self-deprecating remark of the kind you English are so good at. Even half drowned, your face pale with panic, you were beautiful. In a hotel dressing gown you were beautiful. When I saw you at the gala tonight you took my breath away. All you needed was a tiara to look more of a princess than a princess born to it.' His voice was thick with emotion.

Sally turned her head away from him, caught her breath on a barely suppressed sob. 'Please don't talk like that when we both know there's no future possible for us.' A *future* for them? How had she let herself voice the word? There could perhaps be some contact for their child if Edward wanted it, but not for her.

She knew now was the time to tell him about the baby, but she couldn't bear to ruin the moment. She had no idea how he would react, but a pregnancy wasn't the news he'd be welcoming from a one-night stand, even if he wasn't a prince.

'I know very well I shouldn't be saying it but it's difficult not to,' he said. 'Nobody and nothing have ever made me feel the way you do.'

'Same…same for me,' she managed to choke out.

She sat very still as he traced her features with his fingers as if learning her face, as if *memorising* her for a time he would no longer see her. He continued to lightly stroke down her cheekbones, her nose and then feather across her lips in the most subtle of caresses.

Her body felt hyper-sensitive to his touch, delight and arousal thrumming through every nerve-ending. She was tired, emotional, surging with pregnancy hormones. But her overriding feeling was an overwhelming need to be close to him All reason, all common sense was pushed away. She wanted him so badly she ached.

For just one more night.

Her lips parted as invitation to his kiss and she held her breath until he took it. His mouth was tender, undemanding and as she kissed him back she felt the rest of the world fade away until he became her world.

Edward.

He pulled back from the kiss and looked deep into her eyes. Words became superfluous as they exchanged unspoken messages. Assent was asked, consent given. When his mouth came down on hers, passionate and demanding, she responded with a heartfelt whimper of need as she pressed her body close to his. The rights and wrongs of them being together, the *impossibility* of it, were subsumed in a rush of heat and desire.

Edward had never wanted a woman as much as he wanted this one.

Sally Harrington.

Now he had a name for her and a place for her in the wider world. But she had occupied a prominent place in his thoughts for the past five weeks. He could scarcely believe she was now again in his arms. Lovely, sexy, smart Sally. Sally who'd listened so sensitively to the story of his family's recent ugly past. Who had shown nothing but non-judgmental support for him. And who, sensual and responsive, seemed to want him as much as he wanted her.

It felt so right to have her in his house—but wrong to

have to hide her away. He wanted more time with her—proudly and out in the open. And yet that decision wasn't his to make. He had no right to date her. Once he became engaged he would become a pawn in a game of politics. Sally would fly back to England the next day to resume her life independently of him.

For the first time, he truly resented the crown's control over his life.

He did not want to marry Princess Mai.

At the age of ten he had been tipped out of a more normal life—or as normal as any members of the royal family were able to live—and thrust into the role of Crown Prince. In the pressure cooker atmosphere of a new royal family intent on righting festering wrongs in as short a time period as possible, he had been forced to grow up quickly. Because he was intelligent, personable and tall for his age, he had become rather more involved in the ins and outs of his father's new role than perhaps had been appropriate for a young boy. He'd seen the harm caused by his uncles' misdemeanours, been horrified by things he hadn't really understood at the time. He'd readily taken on board his father's edict of putting honour and duty above all—after all, his father was now also his ruler.

There'd been some teenage rebellion, but very minor. He genuinely hadn't wanted to disappoint his parents. In his sophomore year at university in Singapore he'd fallen in love. Lim Shu had been clever, vivacious and sweet. She had been deemed unsuitable in that she'd been of low birth and social status. Her family had been paid off and Lim Shu had disappeared from campus without him even getting to say goodbye. He'd been gutted—but eventually resigned to a future that had been predetermined for him. When doing postgraduate study at Harvard he'd met another serious contender for his heart. That time he'd ended it before the blossoming relationship could result in heartache for both of them. He hadn't told his father but had later discovered the King had put eyes on his girlfriend from their first date. He continued to date but was careful to guard his heart.

In spite of all this, Edward had never been roused to seriously fight against the many things forbidden to him. He hadn't wanted something enough to battle for it.

Until now. Her. Sally.

He could not imagine anything he wanted more than to be with this woman, and not just for another stolen night.

She could be important to him.

They needed time together to get to know each other. But tonight was all he had been granted. He would have to do something about that.

Sally's kisses were fierce and demanding in response to his possession of her lovely mouth. She opened up to him and moaned a sweet sound of deep need as she snuggled closer to him on the sofa. Man, she was hot in subtle, sexy black, the trousers hugging the curves of her hips and those long, long legs. Since she'd got in the car, the layers of fringing on her top had driven him crazy—the way they accentuated the swell of her breasts.

At last he slid his hands under her top and cupped her breasts in his hands. He loved her murmurs of pleasure as he pushed the lacy top of her bra aside and played with her nipples to bring them to tight peaks.

Her pleasure gave him pleasure.

Was his memory playing tricks on him, but did her breasts feel fuller than when he'd last had the pleasure of caressing them?

His hands slid to her waist as he lowered her to the sofa. She squirmed with anticipation as he ran his fingers around the waist of her trousers, looking for the fastening. In turn, she tugged his shirt free of his trousers, grappled impatiently with studs and buttons so she could slide her hands across his back and chest, on a path of exploration and discovering. He took a sharp, deep intake of breath at the intensity of pleasure when she headed with unerring accuracy to his most sensitive spots. Not the least of his delight was that she had remembered what pleased him most.

It took a huge effort of will for him to put a halt to such intoxicating exploration. He didn't want to waste even a minute of his precious time with her. But since the media interest in his engagement had intensified he had become even more protective of his privacy.

He hugged Sally tight and then pulled back to break the kiss, well aware they were about to spontaneously make love on his sofa. Sally murmured her protest, her eyes dazed and unfocused. Her mouth was pouting and swollen from his kisses, her hair falling loose from the knot at her neck. He reached out and undid the pins so her hair tumbled down her shoulders, gloriously glossy and untamed. Had a more magnificent woman ever been born?

'Those large windows are at the front of the house,' he said. 'There are gardens and high walls between us and the street. But the media can be cunning. Who knows where they could gain access with their lenses?'

Her lips pursed into a tiny moue of displeasure which he found very cute. 'So you're saying we should stop? Because I don't want to stop. Not for a moment do I want to—'

'Hell, no. I'm saying I take you to the bedroom, which has blackout curtains and total privacy. There we can be as uninhibited as we want.'

She smiled, a slow seductive smile that sent his blood racing. 'Is that a promise?'

'You can count on it,' he said hoarsely, transfixed by that smile.

'Better get on with it then,' she said, stretching her arms above her head indolently, sensually, her top rucked up to reveal the underside of her breasts, her trouser zip half undone.

Edward needed no further invitation. He stood up from the sofa, reluctant to let go of her in case she disappeared, a fantasy woman he'd conjured up from the intensity of his longing for her. He leaned down and effortlessly swept her into his arms. She felt very, very real.

'Just like last time,' she murmured as she looped her arms around his neck. 'This is getting to be a habit—one I like a lot.'

Once in the seclusion of his bedroom, despite his high level of excitement, he forced himself to take his time, to tease her with a slow stripping of her clothes, a sensual exploration of her body, to take her to the peaks, prolong her pleasure, watch her face as she came. But she was too impatient for him to enter her so they could come together. Who was he to argue? After all, they had hours left to experiment with further ways to please each other.

When they were finally both sated, he lay on his back with her head resting on his chest, her glorious hair spilling across him. The ceiling fan flicked languorously overhead as he drifted into drowsiness. He noticed a tiny translucent gecko resting high on the wall and wondered if Sally was the type to freak out over such realities of living in the tropics. Life both in Singapore and in Tianlipin was very different to life in London.

He knew he should wake her and take her back to the hotel, but he simply couldn't bring himself to do it. Rather, he shifted a little to readjust her weight on his shoulder.

She stirred. 'There's something I really have to tell you,' she murmured, barely audible, without opening her eyes.

'It can wait until later,' he whispered as he drifted into sleep.

CHAPTER SEVEN

SALLY AWOKE IN Edward's bedroom, the early morning sun filtering through the blinds. She was disappointed to find she was alone in the enormous bed. Where was he? For a moment she luxuriated in the pale linen sheets, stretching, recalling the ecstasy of their lovemaking of the night before. Was there time for another—?

With the soft chiming of a clock from somewhere in the house, reality hit.

What was she doing still here?

She sat up abruptly. Edward had agreed that it wouldn't be wise for her to stay. But neither of them had been able to say goodbye and they'd fallen asleep in each other's arms.

On a surge of panic, she checked her watch. Her flight home was scheduled for two p.m. She had to get back to her hotel, pack and be at Changi Airport in plenty of time for her international flight back to London. The taxi to the airport had been booked well in advance. She liked to leave as little as possible to chance. Chance had never served her well. But she still had time. There wasn't much to pack. The ride to the airport only took twenty minutes.

She wouldn't have missed her *just one night more* with Edward for anything. But she was running out of time to tell him she was pregnant. It might be better to do it this way. If things got awkward there would be little time for recriminations.

The uncomfortable stirrings of nausea made her lie back against the pillows and take deep breaths to try and fight it. There were dry crackers in her handbag but where was it? In Edward's living room. Where was Edward? Where, in fact, was the living room? She could remember being carried from the living room by that gorgeous man in a fever of urgency and arousal, but that wasn't useful for directions. This could get awkward.

She was preparing to slide out of bed and retrieve some clothes from where they'd been tossed randomly around the room when Edward came in. He wore white boxers, a smile, and carried a large bamboo tray. Her heart seemed to miss a beat. He was, quite simply, the most wonderful man she'd ever known. Even in the midst of her battle against nausea she took a moment to appreciate her lover's splendid body. He was an athlete in bed, but she knew so little about him she didn't even know what sports he played to achieve his honed athletic shape. The thought made her immeasurably sad. How likely was it that she would ever know?

She pulled the linen sheet up over her breasts, false modesty, she knew, when they had bared everything to each other the night before. But that had been in the heat of passion. This was the reality of the morning after for lovers who scarcely knew each other. However, last night she thought she had known everything she needed to know about Edward.

How could she bear to say goodbye?

'You've made breakfast?' she asked in amused disbelief.

'I dismissed the staff, if you remember. We still have the house to ourselves.'

'Being served breakfast by a prince—now that's a first,' she said.

Even the word 'breakfast' made her feel nauseous. She tried to force anticipation and appetite into her voice. But, as he came closer, so did the smells from the tray and its bounty of tropical fruits.

'Fresh fruit to start,' he said.

He indicated slices of pineapple; starfruit; mango cut into cubes; dragon fruit with its seed-flecked white flesh and hot pink skin; purple passionfruit sliced in half to reveal golden flesh and dark seeds; tiny plump bananas in blemish-free yellow skins. Oh, for such bounty in a cold, grey London winter. On her travels she always took the opportunity to savour exotic fruits. But there was papaya on the tray too, and she'd never liked the smell of that particular tropical fruit. It rose up into her nostrils and made her gag.

'S-sorry.' Sally clamped her hand over her mouth against the overwhelming wave of nausea and leapt out of the bed. She made it to his en suite bathroom just in time, slamming the door shut behind her. The episode was more dry retching than anything, but it left her shaken and weak. She leaned against the cool tiles of the bathroom wall and wished herself anywhere but here. Her body had betrayed her.

She splashed her face with cold water, cleaned her teeth with one of the spare toothbrushes, finger-combed her hair back from her face. When she knew she couldn't stay hiding in there any longer, she wrapped an enormous white bath towel around her, tucking it firmly between her breasts.

On shaky legs, she emerged from the bathroom. Edward had thrown on a wheat-coloured linen robe over his boxers. He stood by the bed, the breakfast tray abandoned on a nearby table. His expression was inscrutable. 'Are you okay?' he asked.

Wordlessly, she nodded.

'Food poisoning?'

She shook her head, summoning the courage to tell him the truth. 'I… I'm pregnant.'

'By me?'

'Yes.'

'When were you going to tell me?'

'I only found out myself yesterday. It…it came from out of the blue.'

'Are you sure?'

'Sure that I'm pregnant or that you're the father?'

His expression didn't change. 'That you're pregnant.'

'I did three different tests from the pharmacy yesterday. All showed a definitive yes. And there are…symptoms.' He started to say something, but she cut across him. 'There has been no other man in my life for a long time. There can be no doubt you're the father.'

'I would not have doubted your word.'

'And another thing. I thought I was protected. After all, I was on the pill. But I travel so frequently across time zones I might have missed one or taken it at the wrong time. It… it was careless of me.'

'The responsibility wasn't all yours,' he said. 'I should also have taken precautions.'

'That night. I'm usually a dot the Is and cross the Ts person, but… I wanted you so much I…didn't think any further than being with you.' She put up her hand in a halt sign. 'Before you say anything further, I want this baby. Very much so. But I don't intend to make any demands on you. I can support him or her perfectly well on my own and—'

He reached out and gripped the top of her arms. 'Stop. Please. I need time to think. This…this changes everything between us.'

Sally realised she hadn't let Edward get much of a word in. She felt mortified. To have joyful, uninhibited sex on a one-night stand and then be confronted with news of pregnancy would be more than a shock.

It had been a shock for her too. She sat down on the edge of the bed, feeling drained and empty. Unable to say another word, she watched as he paced the length of the bedroom.

Finally, he turned to face her. His face was creased with concern, not anger. 'If I was simply Mr Edward Chen, I would ask you to marry me straight away.'

Sally's hand went to her heart and she stared at him, unable to find the right words to reply. Hot, handsome and *honourable*. For a moment she really wished he was just Mr Chen and that she was the marrying kind.

'That's so lovely of you to say so.' She wanted to get up and give him a hug but she was feeling too shaky to do so. Instead, she reached up and clasped his hand.

'I mean it,' he said.

He squeezed her hand, then sat down next to her on the edge of the bed as he released it. She was sitting next to a prince and she was wearing only a towel. Not that he was clad in much more: a pair of boxers and a robe tied so loosely that it fell open from the waist so she could admire his smooth, muscular chest. The bed, with rumpled sheets and clothing tossed every which way, was testament to the enjoyment they had given each other.

'I actually believe you do.' She smiled a wobbly, poor excuse for a smile. 'But…*marriage*.'

He frowned. 'You say it as if it were something not under any consideration.'

'Even if you were free to marry, it wouldn't be on the cards.'

'What do you mean?'

'We barely know each other. Our lives are on opposite sides of the world.'

'Neither is an insurmountable problem.'

'We're still speaking hypothetically, right?'

'For now.' She noted the stubborn set of his jaw. A future ruler in training for when his word became law. How little she knew about him. But she was beginning to realise he could be formidable.

'How could it ever be any different for us?'

'There could be options.'

She raised her eyebrows. 'Even so, accidentally getting pregnant isn't reason enough to marry a stranger.'

Edward didn't seem like a stranger to her—hadn't from the first—and from the ill-disguised anguish on his face she didn't think she felt like a stranger to him either. But she had to face facts. The Ice Queen hadn't got where she was by dealing in fantasies.

'Perhaps so,' he said. 'However, I come from a family—a culture—that reveres our ancestors. Your baby—*our* baby—carries the blood of a dynasty dating back many hundreds of years. He or she will be part of that unbroken line.'

Sally froze, stymied by this new information. She hadn't been pregnant long enough, or had enough knowledge of her baby's father, to even think about the immensity of such connections. What had she got herself into, albeit inadvertently?

'But on the wrong side of the blanket, as they say.'

'Which is why any possibility of marriage must be explored. The rules are strict in the Tianlipin royal family. Only legitimate offspring can be in line to the throne.'

Her baby could be in line to an ancient Asian throne? It was almost too much to take in.

'I didn't realise all the ramifications of you being royal.' She couldn't help the note of rising panic in her voice.

'How could you have, when you've only just learned my identity?'

It felt surreal to be having a conversation like this. Although she suspected the only way it could end would be with her signing legal letters from his family relinquishing any claims on him in return for a hush-hush pay-out. She would, of course, refuse any money.

'I would never make any claim on you or...or your throne.'

'No matter what, the child will be blood of my blood.' It seemed an old-fashioned term but she got exactly what he meant—and didn't miss the note of fierce possession in his voice.

She still felt too shaky to get up from the bed, but she sat up straighter to face him. 'Yesterday, when I discovered I was pregnant, all I knew of you was the name *Edward*. It might have been a false name, for all I was aware. The pregnancy blindsided me. I stared at three positive pregnancy kits over and over, shook them, waved them about, while they continued to give the same result. But I decided I would be the best sole parent I could possibly be. I'm more than capable of giving this baby a good life. I don't need you.'

Edward took a quick intake of breath at her bluntness. 'But the baby might.'

His reply seemed to hit her with equal impact. 'Yes,' she said slowly. 'A child has a right to know their father.'

'And a father to know his child.'

Sitting near him on the edge of the bed, she looked listless and as pale as the white towel tucked somewhat precariously between her breasts. Of course her breasts had felt larger. Because she was pregnant. And having a tough time of it already. He was still reeling from the impact of her news.

He was going to be a father.

'My child will grow up with me in London,' she said. 'You could play a role in their life. If not as their acknowledged father, as a…a trusted family friend or—'

Edward gave a snort somewhere between laughter and disbelief. 'One thing that will become immediately apparent after the birth is that your child's father is Asian. I might not be so easy to sweep under the carpet. There'd be questions asked about a friend who flies in from Singapore for visits.'

Sally smiled. 'If our child takes after you, he or she is sure to be beautiful. I didn't plan to get pregnant but...but I chose my baby's father well.'

'Thank you. I can say the same about you, lovely Sally.' He put his arm around her shoulders and drew her close. She snuggled against him, warm and trusting in spite of her uncertainty of what faced her. He wanted to shield and protect her. But there could be battles ahead.

'We don't find ourselves in an easy situation, do we?' he said.

'That's one way of putting it,' she said.

'Somehow I'll find a way to make it work.'

'Like royal families have been doing for ever, I should imagine,' she said. 'In the old days of our monarchy, a pregnant mistress would be married off to someone willing to give the child a name and sent off to live in the country.'

'You're not marrying anyone,' he growled in a sudden surge of possessiveness. 'And you're not my mistress. If you were, the solution would be simple. I could revive the old custom of appointing an official mistress or consort.'

She broke away from his embrace. '*What?* Are you serious?'

'In the old days of our monarchy it was common. But, to my knowledge, there hasn't been an official mistress since the nineteen-twenties.'

'Marry the Princess and have me as a mistress? You must be joking.'

'Of course I am.' He only wanted one wife. A wife to love and cherish. Besides, the King and Queen would forbid it. He almost laughed out loud at the thought of presenting the idea to his strait-laced father.

'Good,' she said. 'I don't need to be married or anyone's

mistress—official or otherwise. I can handle having the baby on my own.'

Before he had a chance to reply, his cell phone rang from where it sat on the side table. He let it ring out, but it rang again, and then again. 'I'd better answer,' he said, annoyed by the interruption. He got up. 'My sister,' he said when her ID flashed up. 'She's due back from Sydney this morning.'

He took the call, listened intently and ended it with a string of curses. He turned to Sally, gritted his teeth. 'The media have got scent of you.'

'Of *me*?'

'Of a mystery woman driven here last night.'

It was Sally's turn to utter a few choice words. 'I can't have them find out who I am. Or, heaven forbid, that I'm pregnant.'

'You don't look—'

'When I bought my dress for the gala, the sales assistant knew I was pregnant immediately. I'd only just discovered it myself. Others might have the same skill.'

'Needless to say, I don't want it known either.'

Sally cautiously got up from the bed. The towel slipped open momentarily. She really didn't look pregnant to him; perhaps at this stage only a woman in the know would twig to her condition. 'You don't want the media attention but neither do I,' she said. 'My brothers and I are relaunching the Harrington Park and the last thing we need is me getting caught up in a scandal. We're trying to restore the reputation my stepfather trashed. I don't want to give people anything else to gossip about.'

She closed her eyes tight, as if against the very thought. He realised they had spoken about his complicated family, but he knew very little about hers. Her voice hitched. 'They'll rehash my love life too.'

He had tortured himself with thoughts of her with another man. 'What do you mean?'

'I was in a relationship with a quite well-known actor and it ended badly. The press had a field day. It was more than a year ago. But I can't have them speculating I've set my sights on a soon-to-be-married prince. And it wouldn't end at that. When my baby is born, they'll count back to my time in Singapore.'

'According to my sister, they believe the woman is my mystery fiancée. They're determined to track down her identity. As I'd feared, a contingent of reporters and photographers have set up outside.'

'This is a disaster.' Sally snatched her hand to her mouth. 'How will I get out of here? I have to go back to the hotel, pack, then get out to the airport.'

'You can't. They'll follow you to the hotel. By now they might have traced my car back to the hotel. It will only take someone to identify you from the gala last night—'

'And I'm in trouble.'

'*We're* in trouble.'

'You might be in even worse trouble than I would be. Not just from your family but from your Princess's family.'

'That would be a real storm of a scandal.'

'I'm sorry,' she said.

'Why be sorry? I don't regret anything between us, do you?'

'Not at all,' she said.

'But it would be better to keep the media out of it.'

'What do we do?' He noticed the green tinge to her skin and hoped she wasn't going to be ill again.

'Take you somewhere the press can't follow.'

She gestured with her hands to encompass the world. 'Where would that be?'

Edward paused. Would it be too much of a risk? 'Tianlipin,' he said finally.

Sally stared at him. 'Surely not?'

'The foreign media can't easily access my country.'

'But wouldn't we face a new set of dangers there? Your family, I mean. Surely the last place you'd want to be seen with me would be your home country?'

'Correct. You would have to be incognito. Hide in plain sight.'

'So where could you take me?'

'Not to the capital. Not anywhere near the palace. But to my private retreat near the summer palace.'

'You have a summer palace?'

'But of course.' He sometimes forgot how others might react to the vast wealth of his kingdom.

'I still have to run my business. Does your retreat have Wi-Fi and internet?'

'Good access, high speed. I'll have to work too.'

'As long as I have that I'm okay. People are used to me being out of the country working with clients. As far as my brothers will know, I'll have extended my time in Singapore. That's what I'll tell my staff too.'

'Good,' he said.

'That still doesn't solve the problem of getting me out of here.'

'We might need help.'

Her brow furrowed. 'Who could we trust?'

'My sister.' He and Jennifer had always shared each other's secrets and had each other's backs.

'She lives downstairs, doesn't she?'

'She's on her way here now from the airport. If needs be, she would be a valid cover story for you.'

'Your sister and I are both hoteliers.' Sally narrowed her eyes as her thoughts ticked over. 'At the gala you rather cleverly established a professional connection between us.'

'Unintentionally, yes. However, now it could work to our advantage.'

'As far as the media is concerned, I could be her friend, not yours.'

'Although we don't want your identity getting out at any time if we can avoid it.'

'We most certainly don't,' she said.

He hated having to keep her a secret. He had to find a way he could acknowledge her.

'Agreed,' he said.

'How do we do this?' she said. 'I'm on a two o'clock flight to London from Changi.'

'Cancel it.'

'My stuff at the hotel?'

'Give your key card to my sister and she can organise someone to clear your room and pack for you.'

'I should do that straight away,' Sally said. 'But first, I need my handbag. I have dry crackers to nibble on. Helps with the nausea. And if I could beg a cold mineral water, please.'

'You don't want anything else to eat?'

'Not if we're travelling.' She paused. 'How are we getting to Tianlipin, by the way?'

'Our private jet,' he said.

'Of course we are,' she said drily.

'We'll take off from Seletar Airport. It's not far from the city and more private.'

'Right,' she said. 'If you can point me towards the living room, I'll retrieve my handbag.'

He put a hand on her arm to stay her. 'It might be an idea to dress in something more than the towel.'

She blushed, warm colour flooding her cheeks. 'Oh,' she said.

'Not that I don't think you look enchanting in just the towel. Or that, given other circumstances, I wouldn't be pleased to strip you of the towel and—'

To his surprise she laughed, wound her arms around his neck and kissed him firmly on the mouth. 'There's nothing I'd like better,' she said.

The towel fell off her and for a delightful few seconds he had sexy, naked Sally pressed against him. He groaned as his body responded.

'I know,' she said. 'I feel like groaning too. But we really don't want your sister to find us like this.'

'No, we don't,' he said.

Sally stepped back and immediately he felt bereft.

'How about you help me retrieve my clothes?' she said. 'After all, if you remember, you were the one who tossed them every which way.'

He remembered all right. And, despite the nerve-racking circumstances of the trip to Tianlipin, he was very glad he wouldn't be saying goodbye to Sally today.

CHAPTER EIGHT

SALLY PEERED THROUGH the window of the royal family's private jet as it prepared for landing.

Tianlipin.

Edward's country was spread below in a prosperous patchwork of green cultivated fields, rivers and lakes, natural forests, modern cityscapes, and everywhere the curved roofs of ancient temples and monuments.

'Why had I never heard of your country before?' she asked Edward's sister Jennifer, who sat opposite her on the luxurious sofa-like seating. Edward was in the cockpit in discussion with the pilot. Even their trusted staff had to believe she was Jennifer's friend and had no connection to Edward.

'It's a low-key destination,' Jennifer said. 'Mass tourism has never been encouraged. It's really only the intrepid traveller who finds us. Many want to keep it that way.' She paused. 'To be honest, I love my country but it can be a little dull for young people, which is why my brother and I both spend so much time in Singapore.'

'Won't that have to change one day?'

'You mean when Edward ascends the throne? My father is fit and healthy so we're hoping that won't be for a long time.' Sally thought she detected a note of reprimand in Jennifer's voice. There could be no doubt there was something different about those born to rule.

'Of course.'

'In the meantime, Edward's brilliant at heading the telco business and I've grown the hotel portfolio faster than anyone could have imagined.'

'Did Edward tell you I'm—?'

'A Harrington from the Harrington Park family? And sister of Hugo Harrington, boutique hotel chain owner and a competitor of mine. Not that I've ever met your brother. He's an elusive kind of guy. Clever and canny with it.'

'Yes, Hugo is all that,' Sally said with a surge of pride in Hugo that surprised her.

'I was considering a bid for the Harrington Park, but your brother beat me to it.'

Like he'd beaten her and Jay, Sally thought. Not that she'd share that kind of information outside the family. *Family.* Jennifer would be her baby's aunt. She might have to rethink her idea of family.

Sally had liked Princess Jennifer straight away. As she'd liked her brother straight away. Edward's sister— younger than him by a year—was whip-smart, forthright and incredibly efficient. She was also stunningly attractive, perfectly groomed and stylishly dressed in designer clothes from top to toe. Her black hair was pulled back from her face in an elegant high ponytail and she was perfectly made-up. That she bore a strong resemblance to her brother automatically endeared her to Sally.

Thanks to Jennifer, the escape from Edward's house had gone without a hitch. She had dressed Sally in one of her own long-sleeved, high-neck dresses, tucked her hair right up under a wide brimmed hat, applied heavy make-up and painted Sally's mouth with a shade of strong red lipstick she would never normally wear. 'I look so different,' Sally had exclaimed at her reflection in the mirror, fighting an urge to wipe off the dark lipstick.

'That's the idea,' Jennifer had said. 'If you shrink right

down in the car seat as we leave, no one should see you. If anyone does catch a glimpse, they might think you're one of my friends. But they'll be watching for Edward and his mystery woman, not for me.'

The car had driven her and Jennifer to the jet waiting for them at the airport. The women had waited nearly an hour for Edward while he made sure he wasn't followed. When he'd finally arrived the three of them had been exhilarated by their success, with much relieved laughter and high-fiving.

But that exhilaration had worn off for Sally, to be replaced by trepidation. Her life had changed so dramatically in the space of twenty-four hours and she was pedalling frantically to keep up.

'You okay?' Jennifer asked.

'A little nervous.'

'Don't be. We'll work it the same way. You and I get off the plane together and head for the bachelor house.'

'The *what*?'

'It used to be called that years and years ago by my decadent twin uncles. Heaven knows what went on there then. I dread to think.' She shuddered. 'Anyway, Edward appropriated it for himself when he was at uni as a quiet place away from everyone else for him to study. I'll stay with you there until he arrives.'

And then Sally would be alone with Edward for who knew how long. The more she was with him, the more she would want him, the more painful the inevitable parting would be.

'Thank you for your help,' she said.

'Scandal averted and that's a good result. You have brothers. I'm sure you would do all you could to help them too.'

'Yes,' Sally said.

Would she? For Jay, it went without saying. But Hugo?

Her cooperation with his plans for the hotel had been grudging at best. The problem was she didn't know her older brother any more. And what if she made the effort to get to know him again, got to love him again, and he left her again?

There'd been too much loss in her life. Not just the people—her parents, Hugo—but her life at the Harrington Park and her childhood home in the grounds of the hotel. She'd known it only as a happy place—pre Nick Wolfe, that was. Everything had changed when he'd moved in. More so when she'd got booted out to boarding school. Love led to loss. It was another reason she had to guard her heart against Edward. One part of her was singing with joy at the thought of being alone with him. The other was warning her not to let herself fall for a man who would ultimately leave her.

'Be kind to Edward,' Jennifer said, her voice lowered.

'Kind?'

'You're in a difficult situation and he's doing his best.'

'I… I didn't plan this.' She and Edward had straight away told Jennifer about her pregnancy. There had been no point in trying to hide it. Back at the house, Jennifer had brewed her fresh ginger tea, which had helped with the nausea.

'I know.' Jennifer's expression softened. 'My brother is an honourable man.'

'Yes. Yes, he is.'

'If circumstances were different, I think you'd be right for him. He looks at you in a way I've never seen him do with another woman.'

'Th…thank you,' Sally stuttered, not sure what else to say. She couldn't let herself fantasise about an ongoing relationship with Edward or she'd go bonkers.

'I've said enough,' Jennifer said briskly. 'It's up to you and Edward how you sort things out. Come on, get that lovely hair of yours back up under the hat. We're about to land at our private airstrip. There will be a driver waiting for us. Edward has one of his own cars parked there. He'll follow us in that.'

The subterfuge would continue even in his own territory. No one could be trusted with a secret of this gravity—her scandalous pregnancy.

An hour later, Sally stood facing Edward in the living room of his retreat. Princess Jennifer had left—with a warm hug and instructions on how to make ginger tea—and it was just the two of them.

'What next?' Sally asked.

Edward had his hands clasped behind his back. He was wearing a cream linen suit, much the same as he'd worn the day he'd rescued her from the pool, and a white linen shirt. He looked around him. 'Being here feels anti-climactic after the drama of our exit from Singapore.'

'How did you know I was thinking just that?'

'Because of the connection I've felt with you from the get-go?'

'Possibly,' she said.

She didn't want to go there. That kind of discussion could only lead down pathways she wasn't sure she wanted to follow.

He was to be engaged to a princess.

Instead, she looked around her. 'This is a fabulous place to hide out.'

His retreat was set on the shores of a large bay. The view was mesmerising. Limestone islands covered in tropical vegetation loomed out of a glistening emerald sea, tiny white-capped waves lapped up onto a perfectly curved white sand beach. The sky was blue with a scattering of white cloud. There wasn't another dwelling in sight.

'It's one of my favourite places to be in the world,' he

said, looking out to sea through a wall of glass doors. 'I can never get enough of that view.'

He went over and opened a set of doors that opened onto a wide covered veranda. It wasn't as hot and humid as Singapore, rather a warm sea breeze drifted through the doors, bringing with it the scent of salt and sweet tropical flowers. The breeze set off a series of musical chimes hanging from the railings of the veranda.

'Your house is none too shabby either,' she said.

His retreat—the so-called bachelor house—was no humble beach shack, but nor was it a mansion. She thought it might date from about the nineteen-fifties. The architect had given a nod to tradition in the shape of the roof and the awnings but otherwise it was a spacious two-storey house beautifully designed and recently decorated in a very contemporary style of white with highlights of blue—and no expense spared. Glass doors and walls of windows made sure the view was the focal point wherever you looked.

'As a professional, do you approve?' he asked.

'Absolutely. It's beautiful. Although there are always a few tweaks I'd like to make to any interior. You must have a good designer.'

'I leave that to Jennifer. She has a team she uses for her hotels.'

'I like your sister a lot,' she said.

'She likes you too,' he said.

'I'm glad.' For the first time, Sally felt awkward with him. As if she were scrabbling for conversation.

'I hope she might get back to see us in the next few days.'

'That would be nice.' She meant it. 'How long do you expect we'll be here?'

He shrugged. 'Time enough to let the heat die down.'

'Can you quantify that?'

'No more than a week, I should imagine.'

'A *week*!'

She began to pace the room. 'I don't know that I can be here with you for that long.'

He frowned. 'Why not?'

She turned to face him. 'I… I don't want to get too attached.'

'To the house?'

'To *you*.'

Edward saw the pain and conflict etched on her face and felt an answering ache deep in his heart. He was already too attached to *her*—that horse had bolted.

'I get that,' he said.

He could make no promises. And, even if he could, Sally had clearly stated she did not want marriage. Did not need him. But he wanted the chance to convince her otherwise. And he would have to fight for it.

Now was not the time to tell Sally he intended to petition his parents to release him from the deal with Princess Mai. Because a deal was what it was—a cold-hearted business arrangement between two rulers, with their adult offspring like pieces on a chessboard. It had nothing to do with his welfare or happiness. Or indeed the Princess's. The more he thought about it, the more he fumed it was unjust. As yet, no official documents had been signed. It might not be too late if he could win his father over.

'We could try to stay away from each other,' he suggested. 'The house is big enough to do so.'

'No,' she said immediately. 'That would be even worse.' Her shoulders slumped and she seemed very alone in the large, high-ceilinged room.

'Come here,' he said, opening his arms. After a moment's hesitation she came to him. He drew her close and she snuggled in tight. She gave a huge sigh and relaxed against him. He tightened his arms around her, dropped a kiss on the top of her head. She was just where he wanted her to be. For a moment he allowed himself the fantasy that this was how it could be for them. 'I know nothing about pregnant women. But you must be tired and hungry. You didn't eat lunch on our jet.'

'I don't think I'll ever feel hungry again,' she said. 'Although the ginger tea your sister made me definitely helped. She said she left fresh ginger and lemons in the kitchen so I could make some more.'

'You can leave that to me,' he said.

'You can make ginger tea? Is there no end to your domesticity?'

He grinned and dropped another kiss on her head. 'Ginger tea is an excellent cure for a hangover.'

'So that's how a prince learned to make it.'

'Back in my student days,' he said. 'But some skills you never forget.'

She laughed and the sound warmed his heart. She pulled back from his hug but remained in the circle of his arms, looking up at him.

'Sounds like a useful skill to me when you're sharing a house with a pregnant woman.'

'I'll make ginger tea when you need it, but it's powerful stuff so only in moderation,' he said. 'You have to be careful of everything you eat or drink when you're pregnant.'

'Did you study that in Prince School too?'

'No. I did online research while I was waiting to join you and Jennifer. On the basis of my research, plain boiled white rice is good for you when you're nauseous. Coincidentally, that's what my mother and my *amah* fed me, with sugar sprinkled on top, when I was ill as a child.'

For a long moment Sally didn't say anything. 'That's very kind of you, thank you,' she said with a hitch in her voice. 'I… I didn't expect that.'

'I'm being practical. You need to eat,' he said.

She blanched. 'Not right now, thank you. I think I'd like

to just sit down and take in that glorious view while you tell me the history of the "bachelor house". I'm more than a touch intrigued.'

He rolled his eyes. 'Trust Jen to have informed you about it.'

'Would you have told me?'

'I wouldn't want you to get the wrong idea about my retreat.'

'Now I'm even more intrigued.'

'Come out on the veranda; it's a wonderful place to look at the sea and think.'

He led her over to one of two white rattan sofas piled with blue and white cushions and placed to take full advantage of the outlook to the ocean. He settled her in the seat with the best view and sat down beside her. He thought again, as he had thought when he met her in the airport, how disconcerting it was to see her looking so different in his sister's floral dress and with so much heavy make-up.

He began. 'There was a time in the family when the heir to the throne—'

'The Crown Prince, like you?'

He nodded. 'He was given freedom to—well, basically to "sow his wild oats" as you English might say.'

'It's an old-fashioned term and not exactly in favour these days. But I get what you mean.'

'Things were very different then.'

'And the Princesses?'

'A very different story for them, believe me. They were kept closely under the eye of their mothers and grandmothers.'

'Why does that not surprise me?' she said wryly. 'So this was the Crown Prince's party house?'

'This part of the coast is where the elite of our country spend their summer vacations. Our summer palace was built here one hundred years ago as a vacation residence for the entire extended family. It's a private gated estate with our own beach. The palace is built in traditional style and is very beautiful.'

'Those were the elaborate gates we came through when I got here with Jennifer?'

'That's right. The bachelor house was built in the nineteen-fifties. The heir, and maybe his brothers or cousins, stayed here—a twenty-minute walk from the main house. Everyone turned a purposely blind eye to what they got up to.'

'Seducing women?'

'I'm sure the twin uncles took to the idea with gusto. The parties were reportedly wild. They had a habit of swapping identities to trick people.'

She wrinkled her nose. 'They must have been awful,' she said. 'The twins, I mean.'

'Never to me. They were the fun uncles who bought me and my sister outrageously expensive gifts that we loved and made a huge fuss of us when we were little. The King, in particular, must have had a good deal of personal charm to have got away with all his excesses. I could never tell my father, but I cried my ten-year-old heart out when my favourite uncle died.'

Edward had had consequent cause to loathe his uncles when he discovered the depths of the damage they had done to the country. And his arranged marriage was a direct result of their behaviour. But he couldn't forget how he'd loved them as a child.

'I guess no one's one hundred per cent bad or good. Except my stepfather, who was one hundred per cent bad.' Sally slapped her hand over her mouth. 'Sorry. Forget I said that.'

'Please tell me more. You've heard about my complicated family, but I know nothing about yours beyond what I saw on the internet.'

'I thought my family was complicated until I heard about yours. I might have to downgrade mine to a level below *complicated*.'

'I won't know how to grade them until I hear the story.'

'It isn't nearly as interesting as yours, I assure you. Seriously, how could I possibly top the drama of your uncles?'

However, her story might help him to understand her better—and the family his child would be born into. 'I doubt anyone could. But you might surprise me.'

'First, I want to ask you something more about the bachelor house.' She bit her bottom lip, couldn't meet his eye. 'Have you…have you brought a lot of women here?'

He stared at her, uncomprehending for a moment. 'You're the only woman I have ever brought here. Apart from my sister, of course.'

'Seriously?' She looked surprised but pleased in a relieved kind of way.

'My father's reign is a very different one to the monarch who preceded him. He let it be known he did not approve of their immoral ways. No bachelor houses under my father's rule.'

'So how did this one become yours?'

'When I was growing up, there was a lot of pressure on me to excel academically. Study didn't come as easily to me as sport. The sports I was permitted to play, that is.'

'There were restrictions?'

'For security and safety reasons,' he said. 'No team contact sports, for example, or dangerous pastimes like skydiving. Not for the heir to the throne of Tianlipin.'

'Sounds reasonable enough,' she said. She clenched her fists at the horrific thought of him crashing to earth in a skydive that went wrong.

'But I needed somewhere private to study, without distractions. Sometimes the timetables and rituals of the palace became too much. When I was at university I asked my father if I could use the house when I wanted to barricade myself away from everyone and hit the books. An advantage was I could swim and sail here too.'

'So it went back to being the Crown Prince's retreat?'

'But a very different kind of retreat, I assure you,' he said.

'I'm glad I'm the only woman you've brought here. It… it makes it easier.'

He kissed her on the mouth, swiftly and gently. She kissed him back, with an air of quiet desperation.

Their kisses were running out.

'There's nothing easy for us about being here,' he said. 'But I like having you to myself even…even if it's only for a limited time.'

Sally sat back against the back of the sofa. 'You did have girlfriends, right? You just didn't bring them here?'

'No one serious until the second year of my undergraduate degree at university in Singapore. It wasn't easy for me to date. There was no hiding who I was, what my destiny was. Women were either too nervous to talk to me or had expectations I wasn't able to fulfil. It could be isolating.'

'Did your family vet who you were allowed to date?'

'Always,' he said shortly, unable to keep the bitterness from his voice. 'My university girlfriend was deemed unsuitable. Her parents were paid off, she was removed from university and I never saw her again. I took care about who I dated after that.'

There had been women who had been happy to accept a discreet no-strings relationship. But there was no need to go into the details of them for Sally. Like he didn't want to know about any boyfriends who had come before him.

'Did you often go incognito, like…like you did with me?' The break in her voice belied the coolness of her question. 'You know, pretending to be someone else?'

'Never,' he said vehemently. 'What happened with you

was unexpected, spontaneous and totally without precedent. There was something so open and non-judgmental about you that my usual barriers fell away. With you I was myself. Just Edward. Not Crown Prince Edward. Not future King Edward. And you accepted me at face value for who I was. Not what I could do for you. Not for what you could get from me.'

She cleared her throat. 'You did give me a very nice dress. It fitted perfectly, by the way.' He was beginning to notice she had a habit of deflecting a conversation that got too close to any emotional truth.

'I wish I'd seen you in it.'

'After I got back to my hotel I contacted the boutique and tried to pay for it. But they refused to reverse the sale on your card.'

'Quite rightly. I wanted to help you. I told you at the time I didn't want you to pay for it.'

'I took the dress back to London. But I… I couldn't bear to wear it again. I was having so much trouble forgetting you and it brought back too many memories And yet I couldn't bring myself to throw out the dress. It's shoved to the back of my wardrobe.'

He hadn't just given her a dress that night. He'd given her a baby. And he needed to make very sure he kept both Sally and his child in his life.

In the meantime, he had to protect her—and himself—from a scandal that could be ruinous to them both if it erupted.

CHAPTER NINE

EDWARD GOT UP to get Sally a mineral water from the house and she settled back into the wonderfully comfortable rattan sofa. It was of an intricate weave pattern she hadn't seen before and she wondered if the furniture was made on the island. It would look fabulous in an English conservatory, perhaps even the conservatory that would follow in the winter wonderland space at the hotel. But she would not be doing business with furniture-makers in Tianlipin. She would want as little contact as possible with the reality of Edward married to another woman. Pain gripped her at the unbearable thought of him making love to anyone but her.

The ginger tea had settled her nausea, but she was still being cautious about what went into her mouth. She was running out of the dry crackers that had been sustaining her. Edward's plain rice might be a good place to start back onto regular food.

Who would have thought the Crown Prince would be so caring—and in such a practical way? But why should that be a surprise? She realised he had looked after her from the get-go—the *dim sum* in the hotel room, the dress, the comforting hugs. For all his powerful masculinity, his sometimes arrogant ways, there was something considerate about him, nurturing even. Perhaps that was the hallmark of a good ruler—one who looked after his people with a steady guiding hand. The people of Tianlipin were fortunate. He would be a good King.

He would be a good father.

She didn't want to entertain that thought and pushed it to the back of her mind to take up residence with all the other too-hard-to-face thoughts jostling for space. There was standing room only for recalcitrant thoughts since she'd discovered her pregnancy and Edward's true identity.

She suppressed a yawn. Not much sleep the night before and a rushed day was taking its toll. Being plucked out of Singapore just hours before she was due to fly home to London and then plonked down in this private paradise had been a shock, albeit with an element of excitement. To spend some time taking it easy might be a good thing as her body adjusted to the changes pregnancy brought with it. Next day she would get back to work. Brainstorming that elusive finishing touch to the winter garden was a priority. She also needed to fill Jay and Hugo in on her meeting with Oscar Yeo. She'd email them as she didn't want any awkward questions about why she hadn't flown home. There'd be enough awkward questions about her pregnancy to face later. She kicked off her shoes and leaned back to watch a brightly coloured traditional fishing boat tack its way across the horizon.

Edward returned with the mineral water, tall glasses filled with ice and slices of lime. 'Where does the mineral water come from?' she asked as he placed her glass on the table next to the sofa.

'The refrigerator. It's stacked with bottles.'

She laughed. 'It might have sounded like a silly question, but you tell me we're isolated here. How do we get food and supplies?'

He sat down next to her, stretching out his long legs, totally unselfconscious about his shoulders and thighs nudging hers. As if she belonged sitting next to him on his veranda. 'The summer palace is kept staffed all year around. I order what I want, and they deliver it here. Or a chef comes over and cooks for me. The housekeeping staff schedule visits to clean.'

'That's convenient,' she said. 'A different concept in take-away.'

How quickly she'd got used to the concept of him living not just in a palace but a summer palace too. And a bachelor house. Not to mention that elegant duplex in Singapore. Sally worked with some very wealthy clients, but she suspected they didn't come anywhere near the wealth of the Tianlipin royal family.

'But what happens when the staff see me here?' she said. 'How will you explain my presence?'

'They won't see you. You'll have to stay out of sight.' His tone was terser than she might have expected.

'You mean I literally have to hide myself? Like in a closet?' She couldn't keep the note of alarm from her voice. Was he serious? Her mouth went dry.

'I don't think you need to go that far. You can stay in one of the upstairs rooms behind locked doors.'

'If that's what it takes to keep the media off our backs, I guess I can find a crawl space somewhere to squeeze into.' She forced her voice to sound light-hearted, but she was appalled and more than a little angry at the idea of having to go to such lengths to conceal her presence in his home. As if she were someone to be ashamed of.

His scandalous secret.

She wanted to avoid the media discovering her identity as much as he did. But she knew it wasn't just because of the media interest she had to be hidden away while she was here. Jennifer had intimated that it would cause a royal uproar if her parents discovered he was keeping a woman in the bachelor house. Pregnant or otherwise—she would be seen as someone entirely unsuitable for their son. And risking his engagement. The thought that she might be considered inferior to him or anyone else made her feel a rising nausea of a different kind to morning sickness.

'Is it that you don't trust the summer palace staff?'

'I don't know them. The only staff I trust are mine, my security staff in particular. And the driver who picked you up from your hotel. They're my people, not my parents'—'

'Spies?'

'I wouldn't put it quite like that.' But the tone of his voice told her that was exactly what he meant.

Her heart went out to him at having to live under such restrictions. Her heart also told her that she wanted a man who would stand up for her. Mr Edward Chen might be able to do so, Crown Prince Edward perhaps not.

He put a comforting hand on her arm. 'I'll make sure you don't have to hide for long. I'll keep staff visits to a minimum. They're forbidden to come here without my say-so.'

'Perhaps you could set off a warning when they approach to give me time to scuttle around and hide,' she said, hurt putting an edge of sarcasm to her voice. 'Like the air raid sirens in London during World War Two my grandmother used to tell me about. The Harrington Park stayed open right through the Blitz.'

'Fascinating to have that as part of your history,' he said, sounding genuinely interested and possibly relieved at a change of subject.

'My brothers and I recently discovered some marvellous photos in the archives of the entertainment they used to put on. It must have been terrifying to stay in London while the city was being bombed, but the hotel escaped damage. My grandmother said they were doing their part for the war effort by keeping up morale, even though it was a financial strain.'

'Which grandmother was that?'

'My father's mother; she died when I was a teenager.

The hotel has been going for more than a hundred years and was always until recently in the hands of our family.'

He frowned. 'Tell me what happened there, how you lost your hotel. It doesn't make sense.'

Sally paused, looked at him with her head tilted to the side assessingly. 'I'm not sure I should be talking about the hotel with you. After all, your sister is a competitor and by extension so are you. My brother Hugo would be furious with me if I spilled any beans I shouldn't. He owns it now, you see.'

'Now you've really got me interested. Not in the confidential business dealings of your hotel, but in what happened to you as a family that you lost something so important to you.'

He sounded genuinely interested, which was understandable. If he used terms like 'blood of my blood' he would want to know about the family that had donated the other half of his child's genes.

She looked down at her hands where they lay in her lap. Jennifer had painted her nails for her in a similar deep red to the lipstick. Sally was proud of how good they looked, although she would normally choose a paler colour polish. She'd started biting her nails after her mother died and she'd been sent to boarding school, away from the only home she'd known. It had taken her years to get out of the habit. But she'd never got over the sense of loss and isolation that had led to the nail-biting.

'You're right; the hotel was important to us,' she said. 'More important, perhaps, than we realised until we lost it.'

She took a sip from her water to avoid his too intent gaze. 'I don't like to talk about the past. It…it makes me uncomfortable.'

'Not as uncomfortable as it was for me telling you about my wicked uncles.' He paused. 'Sometimes the past is better confronted.'

'I'm not so sure about that,' she said, as always reluctant to talk about herself and certainly not the darker episodes of her life.

Edward swivelled to come closer. 'That grandmother you told me about?'

'Yes?'

'She was our baby's great-grandmother. I have a connection. I need to hear the story.'

She couldn't help but smile. 'And the twin uncles were the baby's great-uncles.'

'Let's hope he or she doesn't inherit their wild streak,' he said.

As if he would be around to see it.

'Perhaps a touch of feistiness if it's a girl. Girls need it in this world.'

'Did you need it? Was that because of what happened with the hotel?'

Sally swirled the ice cubes in her glass, conscious it was a delaying tactic. She sensed his need to know more about her. She had never talked about how she felt about her past life to anyone but Jay. But Edward was her baby's father; perhaps he had a right to know about the family she came from. She put down her glass.

'The Harrington Park Hotel wasn't just part of our lives for my brothers and me; it *was* our life. Our house was in the grounds of the hotel and Jay and I were in and out of the hotel from when we could toddle. We weren't allowed to get in the way, but the staff always welcomed us and gave us little jobs to do while keeping an eye on us. I remember when I must have been about five, being allowed to perch on the shiny wooden reception desk and hand the big old brass door keys on heavy embossed brass tags to the guests when they checked in.'

He smiled. 'They must have been enchanted by you.'

'I don't know about that, but I do remember feeling terribly important and pleased with myself. We each felt like we were contributing, although of course we didn't really understand what that meant. But we knew we belonged. We were Harringtons. Our hotel had the same name as we did and to be a Harrington was something to be proud of. Hugo was seven years older than us and he got to do real work, like deliver special requests to guests and help the porters. The hotel was very grand—'

'I remember. Very posh, very traditionally English.'

'But it was also warm and welcoming. My family's vision was to create a home away from home for our guests. They returned year after year, generation after generation, because of the sense of being part of the Harrington family experience, children included.'

'Nice,' he said.

'Don't steal our vision for your hotels,' she warned him, with a mock wagging of her finger.

'No need to worry,' he said very seriously. 'That kind of spirit is impossible to replicate. It has to come from the heart.'

'My father, Rupert Harrington, had a huge heart. He grew up in the same house we did and had the same connection to the hotel. My grandmother used to tell me he was born with hospitality flowing in his veins. My mother, Katherine, had stayed at the hotel as a child. When as an adult she met my father at a friend's party, she remembered him being kind to her when she got separated from her parents in that big hotel and he found her, lost and crying. The way she put it, she'd fallen a little in love with him back then, at eleven years old. The hotel was special to her too.'

'That's a very appealing story.'

'It is, isn't it? I used to ask Mummy to tell it to me again and again. How did your parents meet? I suppose they had an arranged marriage?'

'Actually, they didn't. They met as the children of family

friends but never took any notice of each other. Years later, they encountered each other again at my father's graduation and fell in love.'

She looked down at her hands again. 'So they had a love-match, but you have to marry someone you don't even like. That doesn't seem quite right.'

'Yes, but my father was the third son and never expected to become King. I am the only son and Crown Prince. My marriage therefore assumes more strategic importance.'

And she wouldn't bring alliances or trade deals. Sally had to keep reminding herself of that every time she started to feel more for him than was wise.

'It's hard to imagine our parents as children, isn't it?' he said. 'It seems my father must have been born stern and strict. I think of him wearing his glasses even as a baby, but I know that wasn't so.'

'My father was jolly and generous, and I couldn't imagine him ever being any different. He particularly loved Christmas. Christmas at the Harrington Park was magical. His grandfather had started a custom of having a big Christmas tree in the lobby and inviting staff and guests to join the family in decorating the tree at a party on Christmas Eve. The way my mother put it, my father wanted to have the biggest and best Christmas tree of any hotel in London. His Christmas trees soared to the ceiling. We three children were allowed to buy a special ornament each year to hang on the tree.'

'You must have loved that. Christmas isn't a big celebration in my country, although it's getting more popular. But I'm sure you noticed it's a big deal in Singapore.'

'It was a big deal for us. My earliest memory is of my father lifting me up, safe in his arms, so I could hang my ornament high on the tree. Every year I can remember, I hung the first ornament.'

'He sounds like a generous, kind man.'

'Oh, he was. Every member of staff was given an ornament to hang. And each guest who stayed at the hotel on Christmas Eve found in their room a hand-decorated bauble with the hotel logo and their name on it. With it was an invitation to attend the party and either hang it on the tree or take it home with them. Many opted to join the party and hang their bauble on the tree, along with ours and the staff's.'

'That's a very clever marketing device,' Edward said. 'Those guests would have felt a real connection to the hotel.'

'He didn't do it with marketing in mind. According to my mother, it was instinctive and motivated purely by love and generosity.' She swallowed hard against the lump in her throat. 'I adored my father and wish I had more memories of him. But…but he died when I was six years old.'

'I'm so sorry, Sally,' Edward said, drawing her into a hug. She snuggled closer. Being close to him was like an addictive drug. Getting over the Edward habit would be way, way harder than conquering a nail-biting habit. Especially with his child in her heart as a constant reminder.

'It was a heart attack, sudden, unexpected. At six I barely understood what had happened. Just that he had left us. My mother went to pieces. And our lives changed irrevocably.'

For a long moment Edward held Sally close. She had become so important to him. He ached to comfort her. To assure her he would always be there for her. But that would be making promises he couldn't keep—*yet*.

No matter what happened with Sally, he knew he would fight against a marriage to Princess Mai, indeed any arranged marriage. He wanted to be free to offer marriage to Sally. Not because of obligation because she was pregnant, but because he was already halfway to being in love with her. She gave no indication she might be feeling the same, but who knew what might develop as they spent more time together?

He sat back against the sofa. 'So where did the one hundred per cent bad stepfather come from?' he asked.

'Nick Wolfe. I shudder at the thought of his name,' she said with an exaggerated shuddering. 'He was an American businessman, a regular at the hotel.' She paused. 'Obviously I was only a young child when Nick made his move on my mother. My knowledge is based on not just my memories but stories from both my grandmothers—each who loathed him—and my older brother Hugo. He also, as it turns out, had real reason to loathe him. But that's another story. Hugo's story.'

'I want to hear your story.'

'I know. Forgive me if you have to drag it out of me.'

He got up from the sofa and reached out his hands to her. 'We both need some fresh air. Come for a walk along the beach with me. I always think more clearly there. Something to do with the negative ions of moving water.'

She took his hands and let him help her up, not that she needed help; she just liked it. 'I'm not dressed for the beach. I'd like to change. I actually feel uncomfortable in this dress. It's because I'm a designer, I think—or maybe a control freak.' She gave a short nervous laugh. 'I can't bear to be wearing the wrong colour or shape; it makes me feel edgy. I'm so grateful to Jennifer for helping me with a disguise but I never wear florals or fussy necklines. And the dress is too short.' She put her hand to her cheek. 'Then there's this gunk on my face.'

From growing up with his sister, Edward knew he had to carefully consider his answer. It could go so very wrong. He decided to go full diplomacy. 'Whatever you think,' he said.

'What do you think?'

Was this some kind of test he couldn't study for? The truth could be his only answer.

'I like the shortness of the dress because it shows off your fabulous legs. But as for the rest of it… I agree. The dress doesn't suit you and you don't need that much make-up. That said, I think you look beautiful because you look beautiful in anything. And particularly beautiful in nothing at all.'

She laughed and gave him a swift hug. 'Thank you. So you don't mind if I pop upstairs and change? Jennifer put me in one of the guest bedrooms when we got here ahead of you.'

He wanted her sharing his bedroom.

He wanted her sharing his life.

But he wouldn't presume anything.

'Sure. Go ahead. I'm not going anywhere.' Not until he got her settled here and then made a visit to the city to present his case to his parents for release from any engagement plans to Princess Mai.

Edward barely had time to shrug off his jacket and check his phone for messages before Sally was back. She seemed to float towards him in a multicoloured silk kaftan that fell below her knees, teamed with simple strappy sandals. Her chestnut hair swung loose and the heavy make-up was gone. He caught his breath at how lovely she was. How much he wanted her.

'Now I'm ready for the beach,' she said.

It was only a few steps down from the veranda over the grass and onto the sand. Edward breathed in the salty air. Here he always felt a certain freedom, away from ever-present staff and scrutiny. The security people watching the bachelor house were hand-picked by him and trustworthy. Here he could be Edward Chen more than anywhere else. And this time here with Sally made it even better.

He walked along the edge of the sand with Sally as she also took deep breaths and exclaimed how wonderful it was. 'I love those traditional fishing boats traversing the bay,' she said. 'What are they fishing for?'

He laughed. 'I don't know what they're pretending to fish for but they're actually high-powered surveillance craft guarding the bay. There is also security posted at the top of the driveway to the house. They're my people so I don't have to hide you out of sight for fear of reports going back to the palace.'

Sally snatched her hand to her heart. 'You mean you're in danger? Are *we* in danger?'

'No immediate danger. Ongoing security is part of life for us.'

'Has anyone tried to…to assassinate anyone in your family?'

'Not in my lifetime. But there have been a few bungled break-in attempts that were diverted.'

'My heart is racing at the thought of it. Even more reason no one knows you're the father of my baby. The baby of single mum Sally Harrington is unlikely to be a target for kidnapping or…or worse.'

'Highly unlikely.'

He purposely downplayed her fears. Under the benevolent rule of his father, the elected people's advisory council, and with the high standard of living enjoyed by his subjects, there were few dissenters. But there was always the chance of some disgruntled rebel taking a stance. Sally and her baby needed to be under the official protection of the royal family, one way or the other.

'It's another thing for me to think about,' she said and went very quiet, her head down, as they walked side by side. Finally, she looked up at him. 'That really makes me all the more determined to raise my baby on my own in London with only minimal contact with you. I won't change my mind about that.'

'I won't argue with you,' he said, for the first time being

less than honest with her. He couldn't tell her of his plans, not until he got the result he wanted. But he would never let her be in danger, no matter what he had to do to secure her safety.

Could she ever love him?

They walked until the end of the beach and then turned around. 'Do you swim here?' she said in an obvious effort to change the subject.

'Every day if I can,' he said. 'I learned to swim at our other beach in front of the summer palace.' He looked down at her. 'Why didn't you learn to swim?'

'I did learn. Well, I had lessons. Not very successfully as it turned out. Shivering in a cold-water pool with a bullying teacher striding up and down the edge yelling at us didn't exactly enthuse me. Swimming was not a favoured extra-curricular activity—I'd far rather have gone to an art or craft class. Then when I became a boarder at my school—' She stopped.

'You didn't enjoy boarding?' he prompted.

'That takes me back to the one hundred per cent hateful stepfather,' she said.

CHAPTER TEN

SALLY FOUND THAT once she'd started telling Edward the history of the hotel and how the Harringtons came to lose their heritage, she felt compelled to continue. She was surprised to realise this was not so much for his sake, but for her own. Talking about what had happened for the first time with anyone other than Jay was making her see things more clearly, as if a fog was lifting from the well-worn memories.

Her actor ex had accused her of 'lacking the interpersonal skills to make emotional connections and commitments'. It had sounded like so much actor talk to her at the time and she'd coldly shut him down. He'd changed the rules and started to press for love and commitment she didn't want, *couldn't give*. But she was going to become a mother and had to be able to open her heart to love. Sometimes, in those dark hours when she wrestled with insomnia, she doubted she was even capable of love.

She'd never been outgoing like her twin, but somewhere along the line that little girl, darling of the hotel staff, focus of the love of her family, had grown into someone who had put her feelings into lockdown. Deep down, she knew her Ice Queen name was deserved, but how had she got that way? It went beyond a naturally reserved nature. Spooling through the story of her childhood was making her wonder if she had let herself be defined by loss and events out of her control.

There had been so much loss: her father, her mother, who she had loved but who had forced her to live with an emotionally abusive stepfather, her grandmothers, her older brother, her schoolfriends at a formative time, her soul-deep identity as a Harrington. No wonder she protected herself from further hurt. Locking down her emotions was something she could control.

Until now. Edward had been the first to breach her hard-set barriers. Edward, the only man to thaw the Ice Queen on that one glorious night, to get a glimpse of the real Sally Harrington. Edward, the man she was teetering on the edge of falling in love with but had to keep pulling herself back from that edge because, in his own words, a relationship with him was *impossible*.

'So tell me about this wicked stepfather,' he said. They'd reached the other end of the beach now and turned back towards the house.

'Wicked? That's another good adjective for him.'

'So far we have bad, hateful and wicked.' Edward checked them off on his fingers. 'I'm guessing there might be even more labels we can attach to him.'

'We could add greedy,' she said. 'Oh, and opportunistic.'

'Two more to add,' he said. 'I imagine the words carved onto labels like the brass key tags from your hotel you described, hanging from his neck on a chain like prisoners wear and weighing him down.'

'Great image,' she said with a grin. 'I'll only think of them like that now too.'

'I give you permission to use it,' he said.

Sally liked his unexpected whimsy. She made a mock curtsy. 'Why, thank you, Your Highness, I will.'

He caught her hand, suddenly very serious. 'Please don't call me "Your Highness". I only want to be Edward to you. Here, together, secluded, I don't want that other world to intrude on my time with you.'

She looked up into his handsome face, already so familiar. Again there was that feeling of unspoken words exchanged and acknowledged. 'Edward it is.' She reached up and kissed him on the cheek, rejoicing in her right to do so here, hidden away with him in his private retreat.

'Remember, just Edward.' He made a sweep of his hand as if he were indeed a king giving his subject permission to speak, but it was a gesture made in jest and with a smile. 'Please resume your story.'

'After my father died, my mother couldn't deal with running the hotel on her own, as well as caring for three distraught children.'

'It must have been difficult for her. The bigger the personality of a man, the bigger the gap they leave behind.'

She nodded. 'I'd never thought of it like that but you're right. There could only be one Rupert Harrington; he was larger than life. But Hugo Harrington had shadowed our father, as his natural successor. Another Harrington born with hospitality flowing in his veins. As he has since proved.'

Sally didn't want to reveal the cracks that had splintered their family, how their mother had so carelessly and inexplicably thrown away the legacy that was Hugo's birthright, how Hugo's resentment of their mother had smouldered over the years he had spent away from them. Not to a man whose sister was Hugo's competitor. But she could safely tell the surface story of the family his child would be born into.

'Surely Hugo would have been too young when your father died to play any significant role in the management of the hotel,' Edward said.

'Knowing what I know now, I reckon even at the age of thirteen he could have done a better job than my mother did, and certainly improve on Nick Wolfe's efforts. From the day that man took over, the hotel started its downward slide.'

'And you?'

'Me? Run the hotel? I never felt the calling. I loved it but I never wanted to make it my life. It was to be Hugo's.' When Nick had been declared bankrupt she had agreed with Jay they should try to buy it, but she had never seen herself as a manager.

'So when did the stepfather make his appearance?'

'Within months of my father's death he started insinuating himself into my mother's life. He appeared to be successful, charming. Maybe she thought he was someone she could lean on. But children are good at seeing people for what they are. Nick didn't fool Jay and me for long. He was attentive to us in front of our mother, but utterly indifferent when her back was turned. Hugo, being older, knew exactly what was going on. He wasn't afraid to voice it either, much to his detriment.'

In spite of the balmy air, Sally shivered. 'Nick Wolfe is not a man who should have been allowed close to children; he has a cruel streak. But just a year after our father died my mother married him.'

'Only a year? That was hasty.'

Of course Edward was shocked, as most people had been. She and her brothers had been horrified.

'I loved my mother, but I realised when I was older she was the kind of woman who couldn't exist without a man. She needed a man to lean on like a climbing plant needs a stake to cling to, losing her strength and ability to stand on her own in the process. After the wedding she wanted us to play happy families. She told us to call him Daddy. I refused. He was not my daddy and never would be. He said it was insubordinate of me to call him Nick. So I called him Mr Wolfe.'

'I imagine he wouldn't have liked that.'

'Especially when I continued to call him that for years after they were married. He saw it as a taunt, and maybe it was. I suppose it showed him up as a failure of a stepfather. Not that he had any interest in being a father to us. He wanted the hotel and he wanted my mother's inheritance from our father. Even as young children we could see that, but our mother never seemed to. Heaven knows what hold he had over her. My grandmother told me he flew into a fit of rage when he discovered our inheritances were held in trust and he couldn't get his hands on our money.'

'I'm beginning to see why you call him the one hundred per cent bad stepfather. One hundred per cent his other labels too. He sounds a very unpleasant individual.'

Sally stopped, scuffed her sandal in the sand as she figured how she could put her thoughts into words. 'The sad thing, and I find it hard to admit even after all this time, is I wanted a daddy. I was only seven years old. At the beginning he pretended to want a daughter to impress my mother, which only confused me. I wanted him to love me and for me to love him back. I… I don't know what that says about me.'

'It doesn't say anything about you except you were a little girl in need of a parent, but an awful lot about him— none of it good,' said Edward, tight-lipped. 'How did he end up owning the hotel?'

She continued to walk beside him along the sand. Edward was right. There was something about the atmosphere that gave a new clarity to her thoughts about the past. Or maybe it was simply being with him.

'He manipulated my mother into letting him run the hotel on the pretext she could have more time with her children. He then proceeded to make drastic changes and dismantle one hundred years of Harrington legacy. Everything that was dear to my father he destroyed.'

'Why? What motivated him to destroy a successful business? Was there some kind of drive for revenge there?'

She shrugged. 'I have no idea. As far as we knew, he

had no connection to our family until he ferreted his way into our mother's affections.'

'Was he using the hotel as a front for something else? Or was it just sheer incompetence? If Jen buys a successful hotel, she's careful to implement change slowly and only where it's needed. Goodwill is such an intangible but vital part of a hotel's value.'

'I don't know the answers. I was just a kid. But even a kid could notice the changes. The guests did too and voted with their feet.'

'There are many excellent hotels in London for them to choose instead.'

'Including ones your family owns?'

'Yes,' he said simply.

The relaunched Harrington Park would be competition for his sister's hotels. Could she trust him? She had to be very careful not to reveal any competitive details. Certainly not her winter wonderland.

'Over the next few years, Jay and I gradually stopped visiting the hotel. Not just because of Nick himself but because all the long-time staff who had made such a fuss of us left. He either got rid of them or they resigned because they couldn't bear to see what he was doing to the Harrington Park. One of the first things he did was cancel the traditional Christmas Eve party. That was seen as a tragedy, but he wouldn't listen to protests.'

Edward frowned. 'And your mother did nothing? Not even to protect her asset?'

'Worse than nothing. She didn't protect me; she didn't protect my brothers. The following Christmas she signed over ownership of the hotel to him. Actually gave him the deeds to the hotel that bore our name. The power balance shifted. We Harringtons became dependent on his so-called "generosity" to live in our own home. He doled out an allowance to my mother that was always laced with conditions. From her own money.'

'Not her own money if she had signed everything over to him,' Edward reminded her. 'Morally yes, legally no.'

'I think he convinced my mother he would handle the business and money side of things better than she did. She believed him; after all, my father had a brilliant business brain and she'd never had to worry. But even she must have realised it wasn't working out as she'd hoped. That's when my mother begged me to stop calling him Mr Wolfe and become more compliant, which I did very grudgingly indeed. He also managed to get rid of Hugo. We didn't see our older brother for seventeen years and our mother never told us why. She actually never saw him again—her firstborn son.'

'That really was a tragedy. I didn't know that.'

Nor should he. It was private family business. Sally cursed under her breath. 'I've said too much. After all, you're our competitor.'

Edward stopped her with a hand on her arm and turned her to face him. He cupped her chin in his hand, so she had to look up to him. 'I would never use what you're telling me for competitive advantage. You have to trust me on that.'

'Can I really trust you?' she said.

'My whole existence is based on honour. You are special to me. And you're the mother of my unborn baby. I would do nothing to harm you.'

Except break my heart.

The thought came from nowhere. Sally wouldn't admit to any truth in it. She'd known the score from the get-go. She couldn't allow her heart to get involved. The Ice Queen needed to direct her freezing breath onto inconvenient emotions that could only lead to pain when they said farewell.

'I don't trust easily,' she said. 'Perhaps you can now see why.'

'I'm getting the picture,' he said. 'The word "dysfunctional" springs to mind.'

She gave a short humourless laugh. 'An apt description. My brothers must have suffered too but they keep it to themselves. With Hugo gone, my family shrunk to my mother, Jay and me. Neither grandmother would come to the house. Nick stopped any pretence of caring for us and spent less and less time at home. Christmases were dismal, to say the least. Then…then my mother died when I was thirteen. In a car crash. She was on the way to a school function. I… I was waiting for her. Waiting and waiting. Until I got a call to the principal's office.'

Edward put his arm around her. She melted into his comforting closeness. 'What a terrible loss for you, on top of everything else.' She stayed close, letting herself believe he cared for her. But there were too many 'if only's in the way.

'It was the worst thing that had ever happened to me. Despite her sometimes inexplicable actions when it came to Nick, I loved my mother and we were very close. Her funeral was unendurable. But it was scarcely over when Nick made his next move.

'With no warning, not giving us time to grieve, he made Jay and I full boarders at our school, effectively locking us away from everything we'd known. He didn't let me take anything of my mother's, even sentimental things of no value to anyone but me.'

'I'm sorry that happened to you. It seems like inexplicable cruelty.'

'It was unnecessarily cruel. I hated being a boarder at St Mary's; I was so homesick. If it hadn't been for Jay being there too, I would have run away.' Was that when her insomnia had started? The nail-biting certainly had.

'What was your contact with your stepfather then?'

'Minimal. As much as I hated boarding, I was relieved to get away from Nick. He…he'd become borderline abusive.'

'So we add *abusive* to his list of labels.' Edward's voice was cold with anger on her behalf.

But she didn't tell him everything. As her body had matured, she'd noticed her stepfather looking at her in a way she hadn't recognised or understood. It had made her uncomfortable and frightened. She'd begged her grandmother to let her live with her during the school holidays. When she'd had no choice but to see Nick, she'd made sure Jay was with her.

'Where is your despicable stepfather now?'

Despicable. Another label to add to the list. Edward's idea of the brass labels weighing her stepfather down was strangely cathartic.

'Thank heaven he slunk off back to America for good. I need never see him again. I don't care if he's dead or alive.'

'I understand why you feel that way. But have you and your brothers made absolutely certain he, as your stepfather, can't have any claim whatsoever on you in the future?'

Fear gripped her heart with icy claws. She couldn't bear it if Mr Wolfe came back into her life in any way. 'He didn't actually legally adopt us, I know that. But thank you, I'll check into it on behalf of my brothers too.'

They were back at the middle of the beach, in front of the house. By mutual decision she and Edward turned onto the grass and followed the short path back to the house. They sat down on the marble veranda steps, warm from the sun, and faced the sand. It was so tranquil and unspoiled here on a royal family's private beach in a country she had never known existed until a few days ago.

When she spoke, she looked out to sea rather than at Edward. 'What I learned from all that turmoil was that I would never let myself be dependent on a man. I would never be like my mother. I would make the decisions that affected my life, no one else. I wanted to be my own boss, to run my own company and I'm proud of what I've achieved. I won't ever have to ask a man for money or for help. Rest assured, I will always put our baby first. I don't intend to marry and risk a step-parent for the baby and I will never let him or her be ill-treated by any person they should be able to trust.'

Would he take her words as a challenge?

'You say you're a woman who doesn't need a man.'

'That's not to say I don't want one. But not to run my life.'

He took her hand. 'I know how important your independence is and I admire you for it,' he said.

She sat holding his hand and wondered why he hadn't seen anything to challenge in her statement.

The shadows got longer and still Edward sat with Sally, holding hands on the veranda steps. Who knew the history of a hotel could hold so much angst for the family who owned it? That in all the machinations after the death of the patriarch a family had been split and a little girl left lacking in protection. Reading between the lines, he thought if it hadn't been for the support of a twin brother and caring grandmothers, Sally might not have grown into the strong, independent woman she had become. It was a credit to her character.

Possibly too independent. Her statement of intent painted her life as a woman alone and unable to accept love. Her heart was in desperate need of healing. He saw her as warm and loving, if she let herself be that woman. He wanted to be the one to help her. For her sake, for the baby's sake and for his sake. But she would have to open her heart to him first. He didn't want an arranged marriage. He wanted to be in love with the woman who became his wife—but she had to be able to love him back.

He realised she had been silent for a long time and when

he turned to her he saw her cheeks were wet with silent tears as she looked ahead to the horizon.

'Sally! What's wrong? I shouldn't have made you trawl through your unhappy memories and—'

'It isn't that.' She turned to him. 'You helped me look at those memories through a different filter. To realise how I grew too fearful to choose love and commitment in case I got hurt. But there's nothing much I can do about that. Because the only person who has ever seen my real self is Crown Prince of a country on the other side of the world who is promised in marriage to a royal princess.'

He squeezed her hand harder at a rush of answering emotion from his own guarded heart. 'I wish things could be different between us,' he said. He was determined to make that possible, but he had to be sure he was free before he said anything—and that to be with him was what she wanted. She would have to give up a lot to become his Princess.

'I wish you were just Mr Edward Chen, free to make your own choices, and that your royal responsibilities weren't so onerous. I wish we'd had that night together, then met again and discovered that we actually liked each other quite a lot beyond our incredible chemistry. That we had time to get to know each other before decisions needed to be made. I wish—'

'Why couldn't I be Mr Edward Chen for the time we're here? And simply enjoy my time with you. I meant what I said. No one has ever made me feel the way you do.'

'You mean forget all about your responsibilities and obligations?'

'For a few days? Why not? Mr Edward Chen might have to do some telco work. But the rest of his time can be spent enjoying the company of Ms Sally Harrington before he has to go back to being that…that other person.'

He stumbled on the truth of the proposed fantasy. But

he wanted her so badly he had to grab what time together he could. Time for them to get to know each other, to be sure the feelings he had for her were strong enough to carry them through a lifetime. And that she had real feelings for him.

'And Ms Sally Harrington has an interior design company to run remotely. But for the rest of the time perhaps she can suspend reality and…and enjoy the time she has with Mr Edward Chen without thinking of the *impossibility* of Crown Prince Edward.'

'Shall we do it?' She held her breath for his answer.

'I'm voting for a yes.'

'A yes from me too. Even though I fear it will make my goodbye to you when we go back to live our real lives so much more painful.'

'I'm speaking selfishly but I would rather take that pain and those memories of you into that real life than not have those memories.'

'I… I feel the same.'

'I'm a strong believer in fate,' he said. 'There is a reason we have been brought together. Some greater purpose that we've created a child.'

She frowned. 'I'm not sure I believe that. But I fell in that pool and you rescued me. Now here we are in a private paradise where we can indulge in a fantasy of togetherness. And perhaps, just perhaps, our child might be destined to do something significant for the world.'

'I like that idea,' he said.

She slid her arms around his neck. 'I'm tired of talking, Mr Chen.'

'I can think of other ways to occupy your time, Ms Harrington.'

He looked intently into her face. His breath hitched. How could it be possible that she looked lovelier every time he saw her? Sally was a beautiful woman. But now he was starting to unravel the layers of her complex personality to find the core of this wonderful woman who had fascinated him from the get-go.

He kissed her and even their kiss felt different. Less frantic. Less urgent. More a kiss without time restrictions, to be savoured, a slow fuse to a rising passion.

'Do you think your security people in that cute fishing boat that isn't exactly a fishing boat might have their sights trained on us right now?' she murmured against his mouth.

'I would hope not but I couldn't discount it.'

'We should probably—'

'Go inside so I can make you some boiled rice?'

'Ha! I have to be certain you're joking before I make a response to that.'

'I'm joking. However, if you would prefer rice to—'

'The rice can come later.' She laughed. 'But let's go inside. Should I wave goodbye to the security people?'

'Please don't,' he said as he kissed her again.

She got up from the steps, trying not to break the kiss. He got up with her, but they didn't quite succeed and stumbled. 'Call that a fail,' she said, laughing.

'No kiss with you is ever a fail,' he said.

'You do know how to say the right thing—must be that diplomacy you learned in Prince School.' She slapped her hand over her mouth. 'Oh. No. Sorry, Mr Chen, I don't know where that comment came from. I was referring to a different person altogether.'

He laughed. She tucked her hand into his arm. 'Shall we move sedately into the house, so your security people think I'm just a friend and—?'

'You could never be just a friend,' he said fiercely. 'I want you too much. I couldn't bear to have you around and not have you.'

They made it into the living room. 'Perhaps not here,'

she said. 'While there is a choice of comfortable couches on this floor, there are also a lot of windows.'

'I shall have to carry you up the stairs then,' he said. 'My bedroom or yours?'

'Whichever we get to first, Mr Chen,' she murmured.

CHAPTER ELEVEN

SALLY KNEW SHE was existing in a bubble. But it was only too easy to put reality on hold and indulge in the fantasy that her lover Edward was just a regular businessman—albeit a very wealthy one to afford to live in this luxurious retreat.

But she was greedy, drunk on the joy of living day to day with him. She wouldn't let herself look past the next walk along the beach, the next kiss, the next joyous session of lovemaking that each time reached new planes of intimacy and mutual understanding of each other's needs.

She'd given up on holding herself back, of being cautious with her emotions, even though she knew the eventual pain of losing him would be horrendous. It was impossible not to fall a little more in love with him every day. Was he feeling the same? She knew he enjoyed her company, that he desired her was beyond doubt. But could it ever be anything more?

The morning, noon and night sickness wasn't easing; at times the nausea was debilitating. Edward constantly surprised her with his thoughtfulness and, yes, his boiled rice. She experimented to find other foods she could eat without adverse reactions and he ordered meals from the palace kitchens.

She and Edward fell into a routine of each doing essential work in the mornings, working around the time zone differences between Tianlipin and London, then spending the rest of the day together.

He insisted on teaching her to swim. The sea water was warm and buoyant, and Edward was a skilled teacher. Sally surprised herself by gaining more confidence in the water with every session.

'It's all thanks to my gorgeous teacher,' she said on the day she mastered the front crawl. 'I'm never going to love swimming though, you know.'

'Well done, Ms Mermaid,' he said. 'I won't always be there to rescue you if you get into trouble in the water.' The throwaway comment gutted her, but she refused to dwell on the truth of it—that she would be without him in her life.

She became fascinated by Tianlipin and begged Edward to show her some of his country. Twice Edward took her out in a car he borrowed from his security people, on the proviso she wore a scarf that completely covered her hair and obscured her face, as well as dark sunglasses. To go into the capital would have been courting disaster. But he showed her the elegant summer palace from a distance and drove through some of the nearby villages and small towns.

It was a beautiful country, blessed with an excellent climate, prosperous and orderly. She loved the tropical plants with their exuberant foliage and exotic flowers that grew only in greenhouses back home in London.

'I wish I could see more of your country,' she said, perhaps thoughtlessly, when they got home from the second trip.

'I'd like to show it to you,' he said. But she knew it wouldn't happen.

Not only was she interested in his country for her own sake, but Tianlipin would be her child's heritage as much as Britain would be. She decided to ask him a question that had been niggling at her. 'Why do you and Jennifer have such English names? Surely you must have Tianlipinese names?'

'We have English names for the same reason my great-great-whatever grandparents changed to a Roman alphabet rather than Chinese-style characters. To be part of the greater world outside our island. It's also the reason English is taught in schools. Of course we go by our Tianlipinese names at home.'

'So tell me your real name,' she said.

'Edward is a real name, my Western name. My other name is Tian Zhi. In our language the family name comes first. So I am Chen Tian Zhi.'

She repeated it but stumbled over the pronunciation. He helped her until she got it right.

'Tianlipin means "gift from the sky"—my ancestors saw the island as a gift from the gods when they conquered it. My name means "son of the sky".'

'And Jennifer?'

'Her Tianlipinese name is Zhen Bao, which means "innocent jewel or treasure".'

'That's beautiful.'

When the time came, she would have to ask him for a Tianlipinese name for her baby.

The only blot on Sally's glorious existence was the need to lock herself in one of the unused bedrooms and keep quiet when the staff from the summer palace visited. She found it humiliating, as if she were a teenage girl caught out in her boyfriend's bedroom and forced to hide under the bed when his mother came in. Not that she'd ever been that teenage girl. She'd been a late starter in the dating stakes. And had never come anywhere near feeling for a man what she felt for Edward.

But she had a premonition that the outside world was about to intrude on their personal paradise. After a week of togetherness, Edward informed her he had to make a visit to his parents in the capital. She had a sudden irrational fear that he would never come back.

When Sally woke on the morning of his departure she found herself alone in his bed, the sheets still warm. She didn't panic; she knew he wanted to have an early swim before he left for the day.

She threw on her kaftan—so many times she'd been glad she'd packed it—and headed down to the beach. The sand felt warm under her bare feet and she revelled in the glorious view ahead of her. The early morning sunlight was dancing on the sapphire-blue water in sparkling starbursts, and she wondered how many places on earth could be this beautiful.

Edward swam back and forth along the length of the beach, his stroke graceful and powerful. He must have sensed she was there and broke his stroke to wave to her.

He swam towards shore then waded through the shallows to reach her where she stood on the sand. His black hair was sleek to his head, his body magnificent, the sunlight reflecting from the drops of water clinging to his powerful chest and shoulders. Sally caught her breath at a sudden rush of desire. She could never have enough of him.

'Is my mermaid joining me?' he called.

'Not this morning.'

As he left the water he shook himself and she was sprayed with drops of water. She jumped back and squealed. He laughed. 'You did that on purpose,' she accused.

'Of course I did,' he said. 'A mermaid shouldn't worry about a few drops of water.'

That led to Sally retaliating by running to the edge of the sand and scooping up seawater to splash him. The water fight was totally one-sided as he was already wet, and she ended up with her kaftan soaked. Laughing, she collapsed against his chest and conceded defeat.

He put his arm around her and led her back across the sand to the house. 'I need a shower, you need a shower. I suggest—'

'We shower together,' she said with a shiver of anticipation, knowing their shower would be an erotic as well as a cleansing experience.

After their shower, which was in every way as fun and satisfying as she could have imagined, Sally went with Edward down to the kitchen. With her kaftan hanging to dry, her sundress still in her suitcase as it was uncomfortably tight across her ever burgeoning bust, she wore one of Jennifer's sarongs, patterned in blue dragonflies, tied around her. Jennifer had told her she kept clothes here and to borrow whatever she wanted.

Edward was dressed in a perfectly tailored charcoal-grey business suit. He was heading off to a world in which she could never play a part. It made Sally, in her sarong, feel distanced from him. Edward Chen was slipping away from her. No matter how much she grew to care for him—okay, to *love* him—she couldn't keep him with her.

'How are you feeling this morning?' he asked, considerate as always.

'I nibbled a few rice crackers before I got out of bed. It seemed to do the trick. I'm ready for a piece of toast with avocado now. And I'll brew some ginger tea.'

But, to tell the truth, she'd probably only take a few nibbles of the toast. The morning sickness wasn't easing. Despite the relaxed lifestyle, her fatigue wasn't getting better either. Edward teased her about how much time she spent napping. She was beginning to think she needed to see a doctor, but that wasn't an option for her here, where her existence had to be kept secret.

However, she didn't say anything to Edward. It wasn't that she wanted to play down her pregnancy. Rather she didn't want to bring up the contentious issue of the role Edward would play in the baby's life. He was destined to marry a princess. Sally was still determined to maintain her independence and bring the baby up by herself in London. If Edward was able to play some role in his or her life, that would be welcomed for the child's sake. For Sally's own sake, she would have to distance herself from him. It would be too heartbreaking otherwise.

Edward downed some coffee and glanced at his watch. While he was physically still present here with her, she could see his thoughts were racing ahead to the important meeting he had scheduled for later in the morning. He was flying rather than driving the four hours to the capital, he said, to minimise time away from her. Outside, a driver waited to take him to the airport.

'I'll be back as soon as I can,' Edward said. 'While I'm away keep the doors locked and don't let anyone in.'

'Are you expecting someone?' she asked, feeling nervous in spite of his reassurances she'd be fine there on her own.

'No, but we don't—'

'Want anyone to know I'm here. I know,' she said with a downward twist to her mouth.

'I'll miss you,' he said.

'Please don't talk like that,' she said. 'We can't be allowed to miss each other, not when soon—'

'You're right,' he said hoarsely. He dropped a lingering kiss on her mouth and then picked up his briefcase and headed towards the door.

Sally held up a hand in farewell. It was like a parody of a traditional domestic situation, the guy going off to work, the pregnant woman at home, she thought. That was the life her mother had wanted so desperately to maintain she'd married the wrong man and made life hell for her kids. Fun though it might be to play housewife, it was not a real-life role to which Sally had ever aspired.

Then, with his hand on the door handle, Edward turned back. The look in his eyes echoed the feelings of despair and loss in her heart.

'Wait,' she said.

She rushed over to the door to kiss him, a brief, fierce kiss that she hoped conveyed to him how she felt. She hugged him close and he hugged her back, so tightly it almost hurt. 'Take care,' she said, her voice muffled against his shoulder. 'I'll miss you too. Terribly.'

She had a horrible fear she would end up missing him for the rest of her life.

CHAPTER TWELVE

WITHOUT EDWARD, THE bachelor house seemed very different. Sally wandered the empty rooms, admired the magazine-shoot-perfect décor, wondered what tales of decadent excess the white-painted walls could tell.

Even though she was a twin, she felt no affinity for the twin uncles and the way they had plundered the country they should have been honoured to rule. How different Edward's life could have been if his father hadn't had to step up, ill-prepared, to don a tarnished crown and restore its wealth and honour. As a result of the strict code of morality and honour the new King had imposed on the country, Edward was so duty-bound that his own needs and desires had been subsumed. But who was she to make that judgement? She'd never actually asked Edward how he felt about one day being King. The benefits of being a royal might far outweigh the strictures it brought with it. Only he knew that.

Mr Edward Chen was a fantasy and she knew she couldn't live in that bubble for much longer. Her staff were stepping up requests for a date when she'd be back. The client with the castle in Japan needed urgent advice on its restoration, and only Sally would do. Time was running out to complete the winter wonderland by Christmas Eve. But she thought she'd discovered the final elusive detail it needed—if her brothers agreed.

She settled herself on a white rattan easy chair on the veranda, in the shade of a palm tree beside a bank of potted orchids. Her conversation with Edward about her childhood at the Harrington Park had got her thinking about what she and her brothers really hoped to achieve from the relaunch. Not just in terms of furnishings and menus and the livery of the staff.

Her conversations with Edward had helped her to pinpoint it. What she believed they were seeking—consciously or not—was a spiritual healing by a return to the vision and values of the past. The hotel that bore their name and their father's name and their grandfather's name all the way back for more than a hundred years had been integral to their very being. Symbolic to that healing was the Christmas tree on which as children they'd hung their cherished ornaments in a ritual of celebration and continuity.

The focal point of her winter wonderland was a stand of fir trees, elegantly woven with fairy lights as a subtle nod to the festive season. But she realised now that it was too subtle and didn't invite any interaction with the guests. She'd let her own disdain for Christmas influence the design. Why not go all-out and put in an over-the-top tree like their father would have done? Then bring back the ornament-hanging ceremony. Include the staff. And restore the custom of the personalised baubles in the guests' rooms. Sally felt a rush of excitement. It could work. They still had time.

Hugo had employed his favourite event planner from New York, a woman named Erin, to work with him on the launch party. Perhaps Sally could liaise with Erin on the details when the planner arrived in London—if Hugo approved of the change.

Sally put together a detailed proposal for the change of emphasis and emailed it to Hugo and Jay. As she did so, she realised she hadn't actually spoken to either of her brothers since she'd left for Japan and then on to Singapore. She didn't want to give away anything of the truth of her situation with Edward. The relative anonymity of email worked fine. Jay was preoccupied with Chloe and she supposed Hugo was obsessed with the relaunch.

The morning flew as she caught up with her work. She realised she'd been neglecting her business and that the neglect had to stop. She had proudly boasted to Edward that she could support her baby by herself. But not without the very good income the business brought in. For all her ideals of independence, she had been only too happy to push everything else aside, save for the bare minimum of maintenance, just to be with him. Was that what falling in love was like? If so, she realised she had never before felt anything remotely like it. Until now.

As she made her way back to the kitchen, she heard a loud knock. Someone at the door. She froze. She couldn't be seen here. Where to hide? Dive under the kitchen table? Crawl to the broom closet? Barricade herself in the toilet? Her heart was pounding, and her mouth went dry. It sounded again. She looked around. It was just a small branch banging high on the kitchen window.

Sally slumped with the intensity of her relief. Of course no one would be knocking on the Crown Prince's door. That was what the security detail was there to stop. And yet her first reaction had been to hide in the most undignified manner. She hated the feeling it invoked in her. This went beyond avoiding media scrutiny. This was about her being subservient to the palace. She didn't like it at all.

She managed some poached chicken for lunch. It was delicious, sent over the previous evening by the summer palace staff. There again was subterfuge. Edward ordered food for one. One royal appetite requiring several courses. It was as if Sally had been blotted out of existence.

After lunch she went upstairs to 'her' room to lie down.

Of course she slept in Edward's bed every night. Waking up spooned with him was one of the great joys of this interlude away from reality. But she felt the need for distance and chose the other room. She was so exhausted from the effort of doing not very much at all that she fell asleep immediately.

Sally awoke what must have been hours later to find Edward sitting on the side of the bed. She started, then smiled drowsily at the sight of him. She stretched out her arms above her head as she struggled up through the layers of deep sleep. She was about to ask him how his meeting had gone when she noticed the glumness of his expression.

Immediately she sat up, the sarong barely covering her. 'What's wrong?' she asked. 'How did your meeting with your parents go?'

'My meeting with the King and Queen—remember they are my rulers as well as my parents—went dismally.'

'I'm so sorry to hear that,' she said, taking his hand and squeezing it in sympathy.

He sighed with a great heaving of broad masculine shoulders. 'I wasn't honest with you about the purpose of the meeting.'

She frowned. 'Not honest?'

'I let you think it was a business meeting. But it was nothing of the kind. Well, not in the straightforward business sense. I requested the meeting to lay down my case for not going forward with the engagement to Princess Mai.'

'Oh,' she said, her thoughts racing. 'Did you mention me?'

'No.'

Sally's heart plummeted. Again she had that feeling of being blotted out of his life. 'I see,' was all she could manage to get out from a constricted throat.

'I didn't want to complicate the issue by mentioning you. My argument was based on the unsuitability of Princess Mai, and that I shouldn't be forced into a marriage that might be good for the country but would not be good for me. That led to the argument that I am thirty-one years old and should be allowed to choose my own wife.'

'But...but you didn't talk about me, or tell them about the baby?'

'Would you have thanked me if I had without consulting you first?'

She shook her head. 'No. I... I would have been annoyed.'

'I've got to know you well enough by now to be aware of that.' He picked up her hand and dropped a kiss on it.

'It's actually two separate issues,' he said. 'My desire to refuse an arranged marriage to a particular princess and my desire to choose my own life partner. But the issue only came up because of you.'

'Because I'm pregnant?'

'Not because of that. Not solely. But because I've never felt about a woman the way I feel about you. How could I marry another woman? I'd rather not marry at all.' His dark eyes were warm with sincerity and conviction.

Sally felt as though all the breath had been punched out of her body. 'I... I didn't know.'

His mouth quirked. 'Don't worry. I'm not about to ask you to marry me. I know your thoughts on the subject.'

'I'm sorry. I couldn't—'

Panic seized her. To go from *impossible* to the possibility of *marriage* so quickly was too much to comprehend.

'No point anyway. They point-blank refused.'

'What? Did they hear you out?'

'They let me finish my petition—'

'You had to *petition* your parents?'

'I was asking for a change in a royal ruling. It had to be

official. I'd thought it all out, written it down. Planned what I'd say while you were lying asleep on the sofa.'

'Here?'

'Yes.'

Who knew? Was this all about her being pregnant and him wanting to do the right thing by his future child? Would he have taken his petition to his parents the King and Queen if she hadn't been pregnant?

He got up from the bed and paced up and down the room as he spoke. His fists were clenched beside him and she had never seen his face set so grim. 'They didn't allow debate. The marriage is too important in terms of diplomatic and trading relations. If we renege, the loss of face to the Princess and her father would do irreparable damage to our country. The answer was *no*. No matter how I feel about it, they decreed I have to marry Princess Mai.'

'Did you point out that your father was allowed to choose his own wife?'

'Yes, but I was shut down immediately. He was not the Crown Prince at the time. That was reason enough that I do not have the same privilege.'

Mr Edward Chen had departed the room when he'd left this morning. Crown Prince Edward had returned. They were right back to *impossible*.

Edward had never felt more frustrated or angry as he railed against the absolute rule his parents had imposed on him. He had been the dutiful Crown Prince since he was ten years old. But his desires meant nothing. He appreciated he lived a life of privilege. But how empty was the most extravagant palace without the right partner by his side? He'd accepted the need for an arranged marriage when it had been in the abstract. But that was before he had met Sally. He would not give up on this. There were further steps he could take. No matter the consequences.

Sally's face was pale with shock. Her hair was all mussed and her sarong had come loose, revealing rather more of her breasts than she might have been aware of. Not that he was complaining. She had never looked more beautiful. He had never wanted her more. But, before she opened her mouth, he knew what she was going to say.

'I have to go back home,' she said. 'It's time.'

She stood up from the bed to face him. He knew it was because she wanted to put them on a more even footing.

'I would rather keep you here with me,' he said.

'I know,' she said, her voice low and throaty with regret. 'I've loved my visit with Mr Edward Chen. But his other life is calling him, and I can't tag along.' Her voice broke. 'My life is calling me too.'

'I wish your life would be quiet,' he said in an ill-judged attempt at levity. There could be nothing light-hearted about this conversation.

She listed her reasons for that insistent call to home. 'The media has moved onto the next big thing. My business needs my attention. My brother wants my help with the hotel.' Edward could barely comprehend her words he was so caught up in his own grief at the thought of losing her. 'And I need to see a doctor.' Those words came through loud and clear and he was instantly alert.

'A doctor? Why? What's wrong?'

'Nothing is wrong. At least I don't think it is. But I'd like to be reassured that this constant fatigue and nausea is normal. All the advice online says at this stage I should check in with a doctor anyway, who'll see me through the pregnancy and birth. I need to go home.'

'There are good doctors here.'

'I'm sure there are. But not for me. Because I'm not meant to be here. I'm not meant to be part of your life in any way. I… I don't like being your secret and having to hide my existence from your family. I can't live in someone's shadow, my every move judged as how it might affect you. I've hated having to hide when your staff is here. I've found it…demeaning.'

'I'm sorry,' he said. 'I didn't know you felt that strongly. I was trying to keep you safe.'

'I know your intentions towards me have always been in my best interest. Don't ever think otherwise.'

This time alone with her had meant more to him than he could possibly articulate. He'd wanted time to know for sure she was the woman for him—and he'd been given it. But to what purpose? 'There *must* be a way we can be together.'

Sally looked up at him, grey eyes shadowed. 'I wish there could be a way. But the gate has been slammed shut. Your meeting with your King and Queen made it—*us*— even more *impossible.* I suspect they won't let you delay your engagement to the Princess any longer. Even if the post of Official Mistress was open, I would never want to fill it.'

She turned and walked away from him, only to turn back on her heel to face him again. Her face was resolute and told him Sally was of the rip-the-plaster-off-quickly school. 'I have to leave here, Edward. Now. Or tomorrow. As soon as I can get on a flight from Singapore and you can get me there to board it. I have to go back to my independent life, for my own sake and that of my baby.'

Our baby, he thought, but didn't say. He wanted to take her in his arms and tell her that he was in love with her. But how empty were declarations of love from a man who could offer her nothing but words? Until he could behave towards her with honour and make the impossible possible, he had to let her go.

Did a heart shattering into little pieces make a noise? If so, Edward would be deafened by the sound, Sally thought.

Telling him she had to leave hurt her more than she could ever have imagined. Thankfully, he didn't try to convince her to change her mind.

Over the years she'd become adept at keeping people at a distance, especially men. Even her friends were really no more than acquaintances. The only person who had any hold on her heart was Jay. They were twins, they'd been born having a hold on each other's hearts. But Edward was different. When she was in his arms he became her world.

She was in love with him.

She'd fought so hard to protect her heart but lost the battle. Although she could never tell him that. Because he, with all his talk of gaining his freedom to marry, had never said he was in love with her.

'Thank you for not making this any more difficult than it has to be,' she said. She steeled herself to sound practical because being organised, getting things done efficiently, was the only way she knew to get through this agonising wrenching away of her heart from where it ached to be.

'You book your plane home from Singapore,' he said. 'As soon as you tell me the flight details, I'll organise my jet to get you there from here.'

Their lives were spiralling apart already.

Sally had no more words. She lifted her face to kiss him. He kissed her back with a fierce desperation. She clung to him. Their time together was counting down, heartbeat by heartbeat. Soon kissing wasn't enough. Their lovemaking was thoughtful and considerate—they knew each other's needs well now. Yet the thought of separation made her reach for new heights of passion with a fierce desperation. She wanted to tell him with her body what she could never say with words.

Afterwards, as she lay in his arms, she determined that she would stay up all night. She wanted to make the most of their last night together, even if that meant simply watching his handsome, beloved face as he slept.

Of course she fell asleep, her head on his shoulder with his arms wrapped tightly around her as if he could never let her go. When she woke up, with a muffled cry of disappointment that she had wasted those hours with him in sleep, the sun was slanting bright through the shutters. Time for her to leave the bachelor house. Time for her to leave Edward.

He flew with her to Singapore on his private jet. She sat close to him, discreetly holding hands. He was as quiet as she was. All that was to be said about their impossible relationship had been said. Still being careful to avoid gossip, he stayed on his jet. She said goodbye to him with a hug that could have been a hug between friends if anyone were to witness it.

'Don't look back,' he said, his voice hoarse.

Sally was too choked to do anything but nod.

His Singapore driver was waiting to take her to the passenger terminal at Changi. There she melded into the masses taking commercial flights from one of the busiest airports in the world.

Once through to her gate, she wandered around the shops to distract herself from her thoughts, barely taking in her surroundings. She was looking for something, but she wouldn't know what it was until she saw it.

The shops were decorated for Christmas. She stopped at a boutique, mesmerised by the Christmas tree covered in glittering ornaments that filled the window. Most of the ornaments were of the type she could easily buy in London: Santas, candy canes, bells and the like.

But then she spotted an elegant tree ornament in the shape of a Merlion, the mythical creature with the head of a lion and the body of a fish that was the symbol of Singapore. It was made from white porcelain strung through with a red silk cord and tassel. She had found the ornament she would place on the Christmas tree in her winter wonderland on Christmas Eve at the relaunched Harrington Park Hotel. She had to turn her thoughts homeward.

CHAPTER THIRTEEN

SALLY STAGGERED OFF the plane at Heathrow, London. The crowds of people waiting to greet loved ones from international flights had never bothered her before. Now she had to avert her eyes from the joyful reunions going on all around her—lovers kissing, families hugging. It was too painful to endure when she had been forced to say goodbye to Edward. She had never felt more alone. The only person she had waiting for her was a driver holding up a sign with her name on it.

Icy air hit her as she left the airport to follow the driver to the car, and she huddled into her coat. It was impossible to believe that just the day before she'd wandered around a beach house filled with sunlight in only a sarong and bare feet.

She didn't tell anyone she had returned to London. Exhausted, she stayed in her flat all day. Nothing could help her emotional exhaustion. To finally find the man she knew she could love and then have to leave him through no fault of her own—or his—was an unendurable heartache. That she was pregnant with his child to love was a blessing.

But, despite her fierce protestations of independence, she knew it wouldn't be easy being a single parent. And that some kind of visitation rights would have to be negotiated if Edward wanted them. In reality, she expected instead that lawyer's letter from the Tianlipin palace asking her to sign away any claims on Edward and his family.

She did what she always did with such inconvenient thoughts—pushed them right to the back of her mind. But they wouldn't stay there; thoughts of Edward kept jostling themselves to the fore, insisting she acknowledge them and the impact he'd had on her life and on her heart.

Then he sent a text to say he hoped she had got home safely. Like a lovesick teenager, she hugged her phone to her heart, tears sliding down her cheeks. Already she missed him dreadfully. She had mourned her mother so deeply she had been ill with grief. But death was such a final farewell. This was a different kind of mourning. Edward was carrying on his life without her, about to become engaged to be married to another woman. But she knew he must be mourning her too. She had faith in what they'd had was real. Even if it couldn't last. Even if he had never actually told her he loved her.

Sally found it in her to feel a little sorry for Edward's future fiancée, especially if she became aware of how reluctant he was to go ahead with the deal. That was what he called it—a *deal*. There was nothing remotely romantic about his engagement. That wasn't to say she wasn't devastated at the thought of him with another woman.

She kept telling herself she'd get over him eventually, although the words didn't ring true even in her own mind. Life had to go on, as the tiny life inside her would grow. But, this soon in, the separation from Edward wasn't ever going to be easy.

She managed to get an appointment with her GP for two day's time. Next day, she headed into her office in South Kensington, a walk from her apartment. Her personal assistant expressed alarm at how unwell she appeared. Was it that obvious? Sally joked about food poisoning from her foreign travels and asked her to pop out to the shops and buy her dry crackers. It was disconcerting to note that no one even contemplated the thought that she might be pregnant. Not the Ice Queen who hadn't dated in forever.

Work that required her urgent attention had piled up. She should never have stayed away so long. Thankfully, her very able senior designer had stepped up to the plate, as had her business manager. As her pregnancy progressed, she would give them even more responsibility. In fact, she was considering making them partners in Sally Harrington Interiors.

Already, her idyllic time with Mr Edward Chen at the bachelor house on that glorious beach seemed a lifetime ago.

While she'd been away she'd been in constant touch with Oscar Yeo's London team about the progress of the winter wonderland. They'd sent photos daily. But she needed to eyeball the design for herself. She drove over to the hotel next morning. After all the time she had spent discussing the Harrington Park and its importance to her family with Edward, she wondered how she would feel seeing the building again—their hotel back in Harrington hands again.

Her heart lifted at the sight of the familiar façade, with its grand gates and portico. Having been away for nearly two weeks, she found the utter splendour of the building hitting her afresh. It was grandeur on an old-world scale— even with scaffolding still present on some of the external walls. The repairs and refurbishments were on a scale that she and Jay could never have afforded to do as well as Hugo with his vision and deep pockets. It was her older brother she had to thank for restoring the Harrington Park.

And yet she still felt distanced from him. Did Hugo care more about reclaiming the Harrington Park as some kind of revenge on their late mother and Nick Wolfe than he did about her and Jay? What would happen when the hotel was up and running again? Would he discard his siblings as readily as he'd done before?

Inside was a hive of industry, with tradesmen working around the clock on the renovations. The smell of fresh paint and sawn timber was familiar and exhilarating. The guest rooms were nearly complete. She inspected two and was very satisfied with the work the subcontractors had done. Seeing her design ideas come to fruition was a thrill that never got old. Hugo had set aside a makeshift office for her in an alcove in the ballroom amid the drop sheets and ladders and she placed her laptop down on the small table that acted as a desk.

Sally didn't know when she'd tell her brothers about her pregnancy, but it wasn't going to be now. She'd dressed carefully in an oversized cashmere knit top that fell to mid-thigh and stretched out leather trousers, to disguise her expanding waistline and bust. She'd breakfasted on dry crackers to fight the nausea and enable her to work. But nothing she did stopped a nagging headache she was finding hard to ignore.

Jay was in France, sorting things out with Chloe, Sally hoped. Her twin had called the heart-to-heart he'd had with her the last time she'd been in London a 'verbal slap around the head'. She was glad she'd spoken frankly with him, as she so wanted him to find the happiness that had eluded him with anyone else but his teenage love.

Jay was a one-woman man. Would Sally be doomed to be a one-man woman, forever comparing other men to Edward and finding them lacking? She honestly couldn't imagine dating another man—*ever*—after the joy she'd found with Edward.

Hugo greeted her coolly and a touch abruptly. She supposed he was annoyed she'd spent so long in Singapore. Little did he know the scandal she had averted, right at the time he wanted positive press for the relaunch of the hotel. She pasted a smile on her face. The last thing she wanted was confrontation. She didn't want to blurt out something she shouldn't have. Something that might betray Edward and the special, secret time they'd shared together.

Hugo had immediately approved her idea for the Christmas tree by return email back when she'd still been at the bachelor house. Jay had also been enthusiastic. Now, Sally found her way through the construction and down to what had been the courtyard off the foyer. And there it was—her winter wonderland, nearly complete, lake and all. She shivered, not just from the temperature-controlled chill and the snow spraying out from the artificial snow gun, but at how utterly perfect it looked.

Most importantly, the one huge fir tree—the Harrington Park Christmas tree—dominated the other fir trees. Like all the trees, it would be strung with fairy lights. But it would become the focal point of the garden when it would come to life with ornaments, tinsel and an abundance of seasonal goodwill. Somewhere there must be a store of ornaments from years gone by. She would make it her mission to find them.

The display was part of the hotel's relaunch, to what she and her brothers hoped would be a great commercial success. But the winter garden was also intensely personal to the Harrington family. Working with the contractors, she'd had the floor plan changed so there would be clear access for partygoers to hang their ornaments without slipping on the snow. She walked over, safe in her boots. The memorial plaque was in place.

In memory of the late
Rupert and Katherine Harrington
who loved Christmas.

A lump in her throat, Sally stood looking at it for a long time, remembering. The last time she'd hung an ornament on the hotel tree she had been six years old, held in her daddy's arms. Now, at twenty-seven years old, she could imagine herself on Christmas Day hanging her Singapore Merlion ornament on behalf of her unborn child. But she would be doing it alone, her baby's father far away in the country that demanded his unquestioning allegiance.

She headed back towards the upstairs ballroom, taking the grand marble staircase. The change from the freeze of the winter garden and the heating of the foyer made her feel giddy and she had to stop halfway and hold onto the handrail. Her head throbbed but she didn't want to take medication because of her pregnancy. She reached her little office and headed towards where she could see Hugo talking to a plasterer. But, as she approached him, she felt dizzy. It seemed as if the room was spinning around and around in a blur. As her knees started to collapse under her, she cried out to Hugo. She was aware of her brother catching her before she fell. And then nothing.

Sally awoke, heaven knew how many hours later, to find herself in a hospital bed in a private room. She was attached to both a drip and a monitor. Hugo sat in a chair by her bedside. 'Welcome back,' he said.

She tried to sit up, but the monitor buzzed and she lay back against the pillows. 'Wh-what happened? Why am I here?'

'You fainted. Gave me a terrible fright. I called an ambulance and they brought you here.'

'Oh. I don't remember.'

How like their mother Hugo was, she noticed, with the same chestnut hair and grey eyes. The same colouring as herself, in fact.

Then suddenly she did remember. Her hand without the monitor went straight to her tummy. 'The baby.'

'Perfectly fine. So are you. You were suffering severe

dehydration and anaemia. You're on a drip. When were you going to tell us you're pregnant?'

'How…how do you know?'

'I came in the ambulance with you. I had to kick up quite a fuss to prove I was your next of kin and entitled to talk to the doctors about your condition.'

Hugo was her next of kin. It didn't matter how many years they'd been apart, he was her older brother. Nothing could change that. They were blood kin. Like her baby would be blood kin to Edward.

'Tell me about your pregnancy.'

Sally bristled. She would have told Jay straight away. He'd told her everything about Chloe and she would tell him all about Edward. But Hugo's request sounded more like a demand. 'That's actually my business,' she said.

'You made it my business when you fainted in my arms. Hell, Sally, your eyes rolled back in your head and I thought you'd died. Can you imagine how I felt?'

At the genuine distress in his voice, she softened towards him. 'Thank you for being there for me, Hugo. I'm sorry you had to go through that.'

'There's no need to apologise. I'm your brother. I'm glad I was there to catch you.' He swore. 'When are you going to forgive me for staying away?'

'Having you back takes some getting used to,' she said stubbornly. 'But I really appreciated you helping me today.'

'Did you *know* you were pregnant?'

'Yes, I did. It…it wasn't planned and came as quite a shock.'

'The father?'

'Someone I… I care for very much. But we can't be together.'

Hugo's face set grim. 'So he's walking away from his responsibilities?'

'It's not like that at all. I'm determined to be independent.'

'Is he—?'

She put her hand up in a halt sign. 'Please don't ask me any more about him,' she said. 'But thank you so much for helping me today. I… I'm very grateful.'

A nurse came in, wanting to take Sally away for further tests. 'Don't stay, Hugo,' she said. 'I'll be in good hands here. There's so much for you still to do at the hotel, with the relaunch only just over a week away. Please. You're needed there.' He went to protest but she spoke over him. 'I'll be worried if you're not there overseeing things. Please.'

He kissed her on the cheek, which surprised her. As she watched him leave she felt immeasurably sad. First because she had grown up without the brother she'd hero-worshipped and she was having so much trouble recon-necting with him. And second because in an ideal world it wouldn't be her brother accompanying her to hospital but the father of her baby.

After the blood tests and ultrasound were done, she was returned to her room. It all felt quite surreal that she had ended up in here. Like a dream, but not a particularly happy one.

The obstetric consultant was next to see her. The con-sultant's manner was brisk but kind. She explained to Sally that she was suffering from a condition known as *hyper-emesis gravidarum*, an extreme form of morning sickness that caused excessive nausea, vomiting and fatigue during pregnancy. It was thought to be caused by excessive produc-tion of one of the hormones produced in early pregnancy, known as human chorionic gonadotropin.

Sally clutched a corner of the sheet so hard her knuck-les showed. 'What causes that? Is…is something wrong with my baby?'

She smiled. 'Your babies appear perfectly normal.'

'Babies?' Sally stared at the doctor.

'You're pregnant with twins. And a multiple birth can be associated with that kind of excessive hormone production.'

'*Twins?* I can't believe it. Identical twins?'

'Fraternal twins.'

'I'm a fraternal twin,' she said. 'I have a twin brother.'

'Fraternal twins can be more likely to give birth to twins,' the consultant said. 'You can have two girls, two boys, or one of each. But they're genetically different.'

Sally smiled. 'My brother and I are very close. I love being a twin.'

There were twins in Edward's family too.

The doctor talked to her some more about how to manage the nausea and how important it was for her not to become dehydrated and malnourished. She also explained how her antenatal care would differ from if she was having a 'singleton', including more visits to her GP and consultant. She asked about what role Sally's partner would play in her care, but didn't question her further when Sally stated flatly that she didn't have a partner. How different the experience would be if Edward was by her side; he'd proved himself to be so caring. She'd give anything for a bowl of his white rice so lovingly prepared.

After the consultant left, Sally lay back in the bed. *Twins.* She was delighted, if a little daunted. But in their father's country twins were considered bad luck. Another black mark against her suitability to be anything other than a secret in his life.

Later that afternoon the drip had done its job and Sally was feeling much better. She was able to eat a light meal and keep it down. The doctor wanted her to stay in hospital overnight for observation. She was okay with that. There was no one at home to keep an eye on her. Although, surprisingly, she suspected Hugo would if she asked him.

She had dressed back in her clothes and was sitting in

the armchair in her room reading a magazine—she didn't feel like checking in to work and having to answer awkward questions—when a nurse popped her head around the door and asked if she felt up to having a visitor. 'Of course,' she said.

Hugo again, she was sure. Her brother was the only person who knew she was in hospital. It was sweet of him to come see her again. Maybe one day they could develop a better relationship.

She thought she was hallucinating when Edward walked into the room. She rubbed her eyes, but he was still there when she opened them. Edward, in a dark business suit and a cashmere coat, with a worried expression on his handsome face.

A great bolt of joy shot through her. 'Edward!'

She went to get up from her chair, but he was at her side in a second. 'No. Don't get up. Are you okay? I'm worried sick—'

She got up anyway. 'What are you doing here? How—?'

'I went to the Harrington Park Hotel, looking for you. I'd already been to your office. I met your brother Hugo. He was hostile. Gave me the third degree.'

Sally groaned. She could just imagine the reception Hugo had given him. Her brother could be quite formidable. 'I'm sorry about that.'

'Don't be. I would react in the same way for my sister in similar circumstances. He demanded to know if my intentions were honourable—'

She groaned again. 'Oh, no. How embarrassing.'

'He behaved as a good brother should. When I reassured him my intentions were indeed honourable, he told me where you were. Hospital. I got here as quickly as I could. Are you all right? I couldn't bear it if you weren't all right.'

He swept her into his arms and held her tight.

Back in Edward's arms.

She breathed in the familiar scent of him and almost wept with happiness. 'I'm okay,' she said.

'And the baby?'

'Okay too.'

'Thank heaven. What happened? Hugo told me you fainted.'

'I was dehydrated, apparently. And anaemic. You know how sick and fatigued I was? It's an extreme form of morning sickness. All to do with an excess of a particular pregnancy hormone.'

'But why—?'

She took a deep breath and braced herself for his reaction. 'Because I'm pregnant with twins. That's why I started to show so early.'

'*Twins!* You're having twins?'

'Yes. And I refuse to believe they're bad luck or omens of ill tidings or whatever you believe in your country.'

'I don't believe that for one moment. And I think the old superstitions were probably only revived because of my uncles. They really were bad luck for the country. But not because they were twins.'

'You don't mind?'

'Why would I mind? As long as you're not at any risk, I'm thrilled. Surely two babies are even better than one.'

'It doesn't make our situation any easier,' she said, feeling as though she should bring him back to reality.

'There is that,' he said. She wondered at the big grin on his face.

She frowned. 'Just what exactly are you doing in London? And seeking me out when we'd agreed we had no future?'

'I was utterly miserable after you left. I couldn't bear to be in the beach house without you. I went back to my apartment in the palace.'

'I… I've been miserable too,' she said in a classic understatement.

'I also got progressively angrier that my life was being determined for the sake of a political relationship with a neighbour who'd played the royal family for the last twenty years. I was furious my happiness was being sacrificed for no real gain. I demanded a meeting with my parents.'

'No petition required?'

'No.' Edward made a rather rude suggestion at what the petition could do to itself. 'I told them I refused to marry Princess Mai under any circumstances. That I would rather give up my right to the throne than spend my life with a woman I didn't love or indeed like. I might have mentioned she was an airhead.'

Sally gasped. 'How did they take it?'

'I didn't give them a chance to respond. It wasn't an empty threat. I have a private fortune; I could live very well not being Crown Prince. Then I told them all about you. My life has always been governed by honour and duty. I asked them what was the most honourable thing to do—to marry someone I didn't love and doom us both to a life of misery or to marry the mother of my child, a child who bears the blood of our ancestors.'

Even through her shock Sally noticed he didn't say he wanted to marry a woman he loved, rather the mother of his child. It made her feel somehow…diminished.

She realised she'd been holding her breath and let it out in a whoosh. 'What did they say?'

'They were too stunned to speak for a while. Then my father asked me more about you.'

'Like I had to pass an interview?'

'It wasn't like that. I told him how wonderful you are, how smart and clever and what a good family you came from.'

'Did you mention I've got an earl on my father's side and a duke on my mother's?'

'No. How could I? I had no idea.'

'It might have helped.'

'What helped, I think, was I told them how much I love you.'

She stood stock-still. 'You...you what?'

He looked down at her. 'I love you, Sally. I love you more than I could ever have imagined loving someone. I'm sorry I told them before I told you.' He paused. 'Do you think you could love me?'

Her breath caught on a sob. 'I already love you, Edward.'

'Really?' He smiled his wonderful smile. 'I knew I could love you that first day. My lovely mermaid.'

Her own smile felt wobbly around the edges. 'I didn't know how it felt to fall in love. So I didn't recognise it when it happened. Looking back, I realise I fell for you then too. But it was during our time in the bachelor house. That's when I really knew what it meant to love.'

He kissed her, a long tender kiss full of promise and love and sheer bubbling happiness. Her heart, that had shattered into so many pieces, felt whole again now Edward had a hold on it and bloomed with joy.

'So what happened with your parents?' Sally asked eventually.

'They gave me permission to marry you.'

'They did? They seriously released you from the engagement? To marry me?'

'Now you've got royal approval, I'm hoping you won't disappoint the King and Queen. More importantly, that you won't disappoint me. Will you marry me, Sally?'

She thought about how much she valued her independence. But how miserable she'd been without him. And how much she wanted to share her pregnancy and the birth of their children with him. Most of all, how deeply she loved him.

'Yes. I want to share my life with you. I'll gladly marry you, Edward.'

They shared another long, sweet kiss.

'What made your parents change their minds?'

'My original petition had made them think, they said. They married for love and have a very happy marriage. My mother said they didn't want to deny their son the same chance of happiness. I suspect she guessed there might be someone special who I wasn't mentioning.'

'So you're officially released from your agreement with Princess Mai?'

'I hadn't actually got engaged. But yes.'

'That's just wonderful. I—'

He put up his hand. 'Wait. There's more.'

'More conditions, more—?'

'After I thanked them and they'd thanked me for all my service to the Crown and how they wouldn't dream of letting me step down from my royal role and of course I must do the honourable thing by you, they told me that Princess Mai had refused to marry me.'

'What?' Sally laughed. *'No.'*

'Yes. Apparently, she said I was too old for her and she refused to be forced into marriage.'

'Thank you, Mai. I wonder if she's met someone else.'

'Good luck to her if she has. My parents are pleased because they have gained significant bargaining power. They reluctantly agreed to say that the arrangement was broken by mutual consent and not by the Princess defying her father, so as to save face for Mai's father, the King.'

'That must surely mean he becomes indebted to your parents.'

'And my parents will save face when I soon marry such a smart, beautiful woman as you.'

'So we're political pawns anyway. Whichever way we look at it.'

'That's the way it is and it's unlikely to change. Do you mind?'

'I'll have to learn to get used to it. But no, I don't mind. All I want is for us to be together, and to bring up our children together.'

'We won't have to live in my country the whole time. I need to spend time in Singapore. And we have a magnificent apartment in Mayfair.'

'And the bachelor house. I love it there.'

'Of course, the bachelor house. Can we marry as soon as possible?' he said.

'Yes, please. I can't wait to be your wife.' She laughed. 'Besides, we'll need to walk down the aisle before I start to show too much. These twins are growing by the second.'

'Actually, in our culture it's not such a terrible thing for a bride to be visibly pregnant on her wedding day. It proves she's fertile.'

'I've got a lot to learn about your culture and what's expected of me as a Tianlipinese,' she said.

'And as Crown Princess.'

She gasped. 'I'll be a *princess*. I… I hadn't thought any further than being Mrs Edward Chen.'

'You'll be her too. As well as Sally, Crown Princess of Tianlipin.'

'Wow! That's a lot to assimilate. I need a crash course in being a royal. And I'll have to start learning the language immediately. I want to be the best wife I can. And best princess too, I guess. Not to mention mother.'

'I'll be only too happy to help guide you. My family will love you. Jennifer already does. But no one could love you as much as I do.'

They kissed again, a long sweet kiss.

'May I ask one thing of you?' she said.

'Anything,' he said.

'Can we be here in London together for our Christmas Eve launch party at the Harrington Park? It's a big deal for me and my brothers.'

'Of course. I know how much it means to you.'

'I want you to be by my side when I hang my ornament on the tree for the first time since I was a little girl.'

'I will always be by your side,' he said. 'As the husband who adores you.'

EPILOGUE

London, Christmas Eve, one year later

SALLY STOOD VERY close to Edward, looking up at the splendidly decorated Harrington Park Hotel Christmas tree. It was the same tree, just a little taller, that had starred in the winter wonderland she'd designed for the previous year. The relaunch party had been such a success the garden had been replicated for this year—and would be every Christmas, her brother Hugo had declared.

Last year she and Edward had stood in front of the tree, newly engaged, ecstatic to be together but not quite certain what the new year would bring. She had placed her white Merlion ornament—which had been much admired—on the tree on behalf of her unborn twins and wondered what her new life would bring.

This year Sally—now Crown Princess Sally of Tianlipin—held their baby son Harry in her arms, while Edward held their daughter Kate, named after Sally's mother. The adorable black-haired twins were only five months old, so they needed a little help in hanging their ornaments on the tree. Just like baby Sally had needed help from her father.

The exquisite hand-blown glass ornaments had been especially produced in Tianlipin to Sally's design. They were inspired by traditional silk lanterns and finished with red silk tassels. There was a yellow one for Kate and a red one for Harry—both auspicious colours. She wanted to bring a touch of Tianlipin, where she was so happy, into the rejuvenated Harrington Park, her childhood home.

As the twins lifted their little arms up to the tree—their parents with a firm grip on both babies and ornaments—there were oohs and aahs from an audience of party-goers that included Hugo and Jay, hotel guests and the staff—including some of the original staff who had known Sally as a child.

'Happy?' Edward asked. Her beloved husband Edward, who she loved more each day they were together. They often mused together how very fortunate it was that she had fallen into that pool.

'Very happy,' she said. 'It's good to be back in London for Christmas.'

'We can come back here every Christmas for you to spend it with your brothers at the hotel,' he said.

'I'd like that very much.'

She realised she'd allowed her odious stepfather to kill Christmas for her but now, celebrating the season with her beloved husband, children and brothers brought her a renewed sense of joy and wonder. There was gratitude too, for her new life. The Christmas spirit filled her heart.

She'd had some trepidation about marrying into the royal family but, as Edward had predicted, they had welcomed her. She wasn't the first English spouse in their history, her father-in-law the King had commented. He'd praised her for her efforts to learn the language and study the culture and history of her adopted country. Her mother-in-law had been reserved at first but had come into her own when the twins were born, supporting and helping Sally as much as she could. The Queen was a doting grandmother and helped ease some of Sally's sadness that her own mother wasn't there to see her grandbabies. Jennifer had become a true friend; Sally could envisage working with her when the twins got older. She'd sold her company to her business partners when she'd got married.

The twins' ornaments successfully attached to the tree, Edward swept her into a loving hug that encompassed his wife and both their children, who squealed their delight. 'Happy Christmas, my darling mermaid,' he said. 'I'm glad you're happy to be home.'

'If you mean home is wherever you and our babies are, yes, I couldn't be happier,' she said, kissing him.

* * * * *

HIS CHRISTMAS CINDERELLA

CHRISTY JEFFRIES

To Lydia Duarte Bustos. You were a strong and talented woman who could do it all and yet you never had a hair out of place. Nobody loved a party or family gathering as much as you. You were the biggest supporter of my mom's writing career, and I'm so sad that you never got to see me follow in her footsteps. I miss you, Tia!

Chapter One

In Jordan Taylor's experience, any party boasting this much wealth and this many business connections in one place—even if it was for a good cause—guaranteed that there would be plenty of beautiful women in attendance, as well. And the Denim and Diamonds gala his father and most recent stepmother were currently hosting promised all of the above.

Despite the theme, though, there were way more diamonds on display tonight than denim. Earlier today, a crew of workers had erected an enormous tent on the Taylor family's ranch for the occasion. Florists hauled in loads of arrangements and caterers set up food stations featuring only the finest cuts of Taylor beef while professional musicians tuned their instruments on the temporary stage above the dance floor. Judging by all the laughing, dancing and free-flowing champagne surrounding Jordan, Brittany Brandt Dubois, the professional party planner his father had hired, had more than earned her fees this evening.

Their friends and neighbors in Bronco Heights, Montana, might think the Taylors were simply raising money for programs to aid the families in need in nearby Bronco Valley. However, Jordan knew the truth. Cornelius Taylor III never missed an opportunity to showcase himself, his business, his ranch or his family. In that exact order.

Having dug his classic-cut tuxedo out of the back of his closet for the occasion, Jordan leaned against one of the tall blue-linen-draped cocktail tables. He lifted his glass of single malt Scotch in a mock toast to Cornelius and the much younger Jessica holding court in the center of the black tie crowd, then drained the smooth amber liquid and surveyed his options for some female companionship to otherwise distract him this evening.

Let's see. Who was here tonight?

Despite what the society columns and social media posts dubbed him, Jordan had *some* standards about who he dated. His gaze quickly passed from one young socialite to the next as he found reasons why they wouldn't interest him. Too young. Too old. Too boring. *Too married*. Too much drama.

Unfortunately, he usually had to leave Bronco if he wanted to meet someone he didn't already know. Or, rather, someone who didn't know *him*. Hell, he'd have to leave Montana for that.

Jordan glanced at the entrance just in time to see his sister, Daphne, hesitate before entering the party. Snagging two champagne flutes from a passing server, he cut a direct path toward her before she could change her mind and make a run for it.

"The prodigal daughter returns." He kissed Daphne on the cheek before handing her a crystal stem filled with liquid courage.

"Don't go killing the fatted calf on my behalf." Daphne quickly downed the first glass of bubbly, and Jordan handed her the second one. "You know I can't stand that sort of thing."

His chest expanded with defiance and he grinned. "That's why I spoke to the party planner ahead of time and arranged for a salad bar and a vegetarian station, right over there."

When a much younger Daphne first announced to her cattle ranching family that she was a vegetarian, Cornelius Taylor had rolled his eyes and suggested that his youngest daughter was simply going through a stage. When she opened her animal sanctuary instead of going to work in the family business, their father had accused Daphne of turning her back on her Taylor heritage and rejecting everything their ancestors stood for. Having three other uncles and a host of cousins who also took the family legacy seriously, his little sister had truly set herself up against a formidable wall of disapproval. Which made Jordan admire her courage all the more.

"Thanks." She offered a weak smile. "But I'm too nervous to eat anything. What did Dad say when you told him I was coming?"

Jordan knew better than to tell her what Cornelius had actually said. Even though their father was usually all bark and no bite, his harsh words would've only deepened the family rift. Their old man showed no signs of budging from his position of being the wronged party—at least in private. That was why Jordan had arranged for Daphne to attend the gala with so many people in attendance. "You know how Dad is with these public events. He'll be forced to lighten up. Or at least be polite so it doesn't cause a scene and bring shame to his upstanding position in the community."

"God forbid anyone think that the Taylors are anything less than perfect." Daphne lifted a corner of her mouth in a near smirk. "Luckily, Dad has the Crown Prince of Bronco Heights here tonight as his shining heir apparent."

Jordan playfully narrowed his eyes. "Keep it up and I'll take back that champagne I gave you."

Daphne finished off the second glass before wiggling her brows at him. "It's not like you didn't earn all those cutesy nicknames. What did that society blogger call you last week? 'He Who Will Not Be Tamed'?"

"So I like women." He crossed his arms on his chest. The narrow cut of the tailored tuxedo jacket uncomfortably bit into his biceps, the ridiculous formal garment proving to be just as restrictive as his family name. "Why is that such a newsworthy topic?"

"Because you like wo*men*. Plural, Jordan. It's never just one woman. I mean, it is for a week or two, but then you quickly move on to the next one before we even get a chance to learn her name. You know what you are? A serial dater."

"You say that like it's a bad thing. How do you expect me to settle down with the right lady if I haven't met her yet?"

"No need to settle down too soon, son." Their father clapped a beefy hand on Jordan's shoulder as he interrupted them. "I wish I would've sown my wild oats a little longer before I met your mother. Would've saved me a ton in alimony and attorney fees."

Jordan clenched his jaw to keep from outwardly cringing. Cornelius almost never mentioned his first wife. Or his second, for that matter. His doing so now wasn't likely due to any sentiment or nostalgia, though. Their father was trying to demonstrate a common bond between him and his oldest child, which would, in turn, imply how much Daphne *wasn't* like him. Luckily, his sister didn't rise to the bait.

"Daphne!" Jessica, their stepmother, rushed in and looped her arm through his sister's. "I'm so glad you could make it. There's someone I've been dying for you to meet."

As the two women walked away, Cornelius made a grumbling sound. "Did she ask you for a loan?"

"Who? Daphne?" Jordan felt a tic forming in his right temple. "No. Why would she need a loan?"

"For her Hippie Hearts save-the-animals place."

"Dad, you know damn right it's called Happy Hearts. And no, she is doing just fine financially."

"Well, you let me know if she's not. I may not approve of her most recent life choices, but us Taylors still need to always watch out for each other. How do we know her feed supplier or her hired hands aren't taking advantage of her goody goody nature?"

And so it began.

Jordan desperately needed another drink and a serious distraction from the lecture he knew his old man was about to deliver.

"Could you please get me another Macallan?" Jordan slipped a fifty-dollar bill to a passing server. "In fact, bring me the whole bottle," he added before his overprotective father started throwing around words like *exploitation*, *gold diggers*, and *access to family wealth*.

Jordan's eyes were about to glaze over from the familiar warnings when a vision in gold suddenly commanded his pupils to attention. A brunette in a shimmery sheath of sequins smiled at the person next to her. It might've been the deep V-cut of her dress that first caught Jordan's eye. However, it was those full red lips and dazzling smile that kicked Jordan right in the gut.

Her hair was slicked back into a long, dark ponytail, and her warm, golden skin was as smooth as polished topaz. Her big brown eyes sparkled as she laughed at whatever the person beside her said. Jordan felt a sudden pull to be the one who made her laugh like that.

"Who is that woman over there?" He interrupted his father's long-winded sermon.

"The one in the gold dress?" Cornelius

squinted, too vain to wear the glasses his op-
tometrist had prescribed. Clearly, though, the
old man still knew how to spot the most beautiful woman in the crowd. "That's Jose Balthazar's
daughter. I met her at that international cattle association event in Rio de Janeiro last year. Can't
think of her name off the top of my head, but
I had Jessica send an invitation to their North
American headquarters."

Now Jordan's interest was truly piqued. Beautiful, wealthy in her own right, and likely a smart
businesswoman if she took after her father. As
long as she was single, the lady in gold was
surely just what he needed to get his mind off
his own family drama. The server had impeccable timing, reappearing before the Taylor men
with the requested bottle and two crystal glasses
balanced perfectly on a silver tray.

"If you'll excuse me, I should probably go introduce myself to Miss Balthazar," Jordan told
his father. The empty glasses made a clinking
sound as he scooped them up in one hand and
grabbed the neck of the bottle in the other. "Keep
up with our foreign market interests and all that."

"Make sure she has a good time tonight." His
dad couldn't help but add some unsolicited advice before Jordan could make his getaway. "We
need the Balthazars and their shipping partners

to open a local office if we want to keep our exporting costs down."

The last thing on Jordan's mind right that second, though, was business.

According to the storybooks, Cinderella had gone to the ball purely out of curiosity. To see how the other half lived. Camilla Sanchez, on the other hand, was at this particular ball tonight for one purpose only. To network with potential investors for the restaurant she'd been carefully planning for the past six years.

Not that the Denim and Diamonds gala was an actual ball. It was a fundraiser. Albeit a very lavish fundraiser with very wealthy guests who were often considered the royalty of Montana. Camilla certainly wasn't anyone's idea of royalty.

The city of Bronco was made up of two areas. There was Bronco Heights, where the wealthy cattle barons and affluent landowners rubbed elbows at parties like this, displaying their vast riches and sitting on their powerful thrones.

Then there was Bronco Valley, where Camilla lived.

As excited as she'd been when her boss and his wife first invited her to attend with them tonight and sit at their table, it had taken less than an hour for Camilla to feel out of place and overwhelmed. Of course, it didn't help that the bouncer at the entrance had radioed something to one of the other security guards right as he was checking her invitation. Any second now, she expected to get ousted as some sort of imposter who wasn't actually there to write a hefty donation check or bid on the fancy silent auction items that she couldn't possibly afford. She was the denim compared to everyone else's diamonds.

Smiling politely at Melanie Driscoll, her former manager, Camilla checked the time only to see a row of faux gold bangle bracelets where her watch normally sat. Ugh. Had Cinderella ever wanted to dash out of her ball a few hours early?

While Camilla's borrowed ball gown wouldn't vanish at the stroke of midnight, it was way pricier than what she could afford on her waitress salary. It was also way more revealing than anything she was accustomed to wearing. Looking down, Camilla sucked in a breath and subtly tried to adjust the plunging neckline of her dress. Before she could exhale and lift her head, she noticed the black satin lapels of a tuxedo jacket directly before her.

"Let me welcome you to the Taylor Ranch." The very smooth and very masculine voice made her gulp before she could even lift her gaze.

Jordan Taylor needed no introduction. Not

only had she gone to the same high school as him—she'd been several years behind the legendary homecoming king and star wide receiver who still held the school record for most touchdown receptions—Camilla often saw his name and picture in social media posts and local newspaper articles. In fact, anyone who'd lived in Montana the past six months knew who the illustrious Taylors were. Jordan's most newsworthy nicknames were The Crown Prince of Bronco Heights, Bronco Heights' Most Eligible Rancher, and He Who Will Not Be Tamed.

And he was welcoming her to his home and pouring her a glass of…Scotch? Did she even drink Scotch? Well, if she wanted to impress him with her restaurant and possibly bar knowledge, she might as well start now. She accepted one of the two glasses he'd so deftly balanced in his hands as he'd poured straight from a bottle she recognized as very expensive top-shelf liquor.

Should she introduce herself? That might be weird since he hadn't offered his own name. Not that he needed to. Smiling to calm her fluttering nerves, she nodded at his bottle service skills. "Clearly, you have experience pouring drinks."

His deep grin revealed a wealth of charm and matching dimples in each cheek. A rich boy who was used to getting whatever he wanted. "I did my share of bartending back in college."

"Oh, really?" Camilla took a small sip of the amber liquid in an effort to hide her curiosity. She was here to meet potential investors, after all. If he had experience in the service industry, he might be interested in her ideas about opening her restaurant. "Was it at a chain restaurant or a dive bar or—"

His soft chuckle cut her off. "No, not professionally or anything like that. I usually only manned the bar at our fraternity parties. I can mix a mean sangria, though."

Of course the heir to the Taylor fortune hadn't actually had to work for a living in college. Camilla took another sip and felt both the alcohol and the disappointment burn down her throat. Yet she'd had enough experience in the service industry that she knew how to paste on her own charming smile. "I'm sure all those sorority sisters loved your sangria."

"Just between me and you…" He leaned in closer, and Camilla felt a heat spread through her. It must be the Scotch. "Being the bartender was actually my trick to *avoid* the sorority girls. Or at least avoiding them on the dance floor."

The band's lead singer directed everyone to go check out the silent auction items before launching into the appropriately titled Pink Floyd classic "Money."

As partygoers wandered away from the dance

floor to hopefully spend their cash on things they didn't need, Jordan surprised her by asking, "How's your father?"

"My father?" How did Jordan Taylor know Camilla's father? Aaron Sanchez had worked at the only post office in Bronco for the past thirty or so years. But Jordan didn't look like the type of guy who trekked into town every day to pick up his own mail. He probably had a slew of employees who did that for him. "He's fine?"

"I heard he had surgery last month," he said, and Camilla tried not to stare at the tan column of his neck as he tilted his head back and swallowed the contents of his glass. "My assistant sent something. A wine basket, I believe."

"A wine basket?" Camilla repeated, then shook her head to clear it. A few neighbors had dropped off casseroles, but she was pretty sure she would've remembered if her dad had gotten a wine basket after his bunion surgery. Especially one from the Taylors.

"Speaking of fathers," Jordan continued. "I believe my dad mentioned something about you and your family expanding your business ventures to Bronco Heights."

Camilla's hand flew to her chest. How did he already know that? Did they vet all the guests ahead of time? And expanding their business ventures was a lofty way to put it. Her mom managed a somewhat upscale beauty salon, but that was pretty much the extent of the Sanchezes' global enterprises. She cleared her throat. "Well, the restaurant I'm planning to open is more of *my* venture than my family's. I mean, obviously, they'll support me in any way they can, but I'm actually looking for outside investors."

As soon as she said the words *outside investors*, Jordan's eyes veered away from her as though he'd caught a glance of something more interesting. Great. She was already boring him. At least he was polite enough to ask, "What kind of restaurant?"

"Well, Mexican food primarily, but not Tex Mex. I've got a ton of my grandmother's old recipes, although I'm not actually a trained chef. I'd have to hire someone to run the kitchen, but I have a ton of experience with running everything else in a restaurant." Camilla had practiced the sales pitch several times in the mirror before coming tonight. However, now that she was standing in front of one of the wealthiest—and best-looking—men in Montana, she was getting it all wrong.

She exhaled. It wasn't as though Jordan was particularly paying attention to her right that second anyhow. His gaze seemed to be focused on a very pretty and very pregnant woman on the other side of the dance floor.

"Did you need to go talk to her?" Camilla offered the same pleasant smile she would use when asking a customer if she could bring him the check.

"Uh, no." Jordan's head whipped back in Camilla's direction. "Erica is friends with my sister and I was just thinking that Daphne would be happy to see a familiar face."

"Oh, so she's a family friend?" Camilla asked, knowing that it really wasn't any of her business if he was staring at every single woman at the gala. A guy like Jordan Taylor didn't get a nickname like Rancher Most Wanted because he could focus all his attention on only one female. He oozed charm and even if she wasn't already familiar with his reputation, Camilla had dated enough good-looking guys to know a player when she met one.

"Well, our families go way back," he replied. Then he surprised her by admitting, "Erica and I actually went out on a few dates one summer when I was home from college, mostly to appease our parents. She moved back to Bronco recently, and even though I've seen her a handful of times since then, it's still weird seeing kids I grew up with come back to town as grown-up adults with these totally different lives."

His sentimental words settled deep into Camilla's chest, and something about Jordan's eyes made her momentarily doubt all the rumors she'd ever heard about him. But only momentarily.

"I get that." She nodded. "Every time one of my friends gets married or has a baby, I feel as though I'm standing still while everyone else is moving ahead."

"Exactly!" Jordan lifted the bottle of Scotch as though in a mock salute. "If you're not settled down and starting a family by age thirty, society begins to think there's something wrong with you."

Her eyes traced down his broad shoulders and lean waist in that custom-made tuxedo.

"I seriously doubt that anybody thinks there is something wrong with you." As soon as the words left her mouth, Camilla sucked in a breath and prayed he hadn't heard her over the opening strains of the band's next song.

Unfortunately, his knowing smile told her otherwise. "Coming from the most beautiful woman in the room tonight, I'll defer to your judgment on the subject."

A flush of heat stole up her neck and face. Her mother had insisted on doing Camilla's hair and makeup before the party, and now she hoped the pricey bronzer on her cheeks hid her embarrassment. "Oh, I don't know if it's *my* expertise that you'd want. I'm afraid I'm in the same boat as you when it comes to settling down. It seems like there's so much to do before I can even think about going along that same path as everyone else."

He lifted his dark eyebrows and Camilla was about to artfully bring the conversation back to her restaurant. But before she could bring up potential investors again, he asked her a question. "You know this song?"

Camilla was surprised the band had moved on from 1980s hits and was now covering a Bruno Mars song, yet her hips naturally moved along to the thrumming hip-hop beat. "It's one of my favorites."

"Mine, too." He downed the rest of his drink before gesturing toward the parquet floor that must've cost thousands of dollars to rent in order to cover the expanse of grass inside the heated tent. "Let's go out there and show everyone that we've got a lot of living left to do before we settle down."

The fast-paced song meant that no touching was required, but that didn't stop Camilla's body from reacting to the way Jordan moved. Or to the way he watched her as she threw back her shoulders, dipped her knees and rolled her hips to the beat. It was as though someone had tied a string around both of their waists, connecting them by a thin thread that they couldn't break.

A second song started, this one by Beyoncé,

and even more people poured onto the dance floor. The chemistry between her and Jordan must've been obvious to everyone else, because even with the crowd jockeying for position around them, the other partygoers gave them their space. The heart-pounding music threatened to take over her body and her judgment, and Camilla had to keep dancing just to keep from drowning in his chocolate-brown eyes. The very same eyes that made her feel as if she were the only woman here with him.

Despite knowing his reputation, by the third song, she finally succumbed to the thrill that Bronco Heights' most eligible bachelor had chosen *her* as his dance partner. At some point, Jordan had shrugged out of his jacket and Camilla had to make a concerted effort to keep her focus above his chest. Speaking of chests, she needed to be sure that the double-sided tape keeping her plunging neckline in place didn't slip and cause a wardrobe malfunction.

Earlier in the day, she'd expressed that same concern to her sister Sofia, a stylist at a fashionable boutique in Bronco Heights who had loaned her the ball gown. Sofia had assured her that everyone at the gala would be standing around networking and complimenting each other on their substantial donations to charity. Nobody would be hopping around on the dance floor like a bunch of teenagers at their high school prom. Camilla couldn't wait to tell her little sister how wrong she'd been.

She attempted a casual dance move that simultaneously allowed her to adjust the narrow strips of sequined fabric covering her breasts, yet she only succeeded in drawing Jordan's eyes to that exact spot. When the tempo quickly changed to a slow song, it seemed only natural for him to pull her into his arms.

The warm fabric of his starched white dress shirt pressed against Camilla's flushed skin and she slid her own arms around his neck, her face turning toward the sleekly knotted black tie at his throat. Lord help her, she thought as she inhaled the musky scent of cedar wood and damp skin. The man smelled even better than he danced.

Her heart pulsed behind her rib cage as Jordan's fingers carelessly traced circles along her lower spine. Or maybe his fingers weren't careless at all, but very, *very* methodical. *Don't think about how perfectly you fit against him*, she commanded herself. *Just enjoy the moment.* When was the last time she'd been out dancing? Her cousin Bianca's wedding, maybe? Surely, way before she'd picked up those extra waitressing shifts. Usually, her already exhausted feet were much too tired to do more than hold her up-right in a steamy shower at the end of a long day.

"Hey, Camilla!" DJ Traub, the owner of DJ's Deluxe, interrupted her romantic thoughts. Her boss had maneuvered his wife beside them on the dance floor. "Have you mentioned your restaurant idea to Jordan yet?"

The man's reminder was as subtle as a dropped tray of dishes. She was here to find investors, not to be seduced by the town's most infamous bachelor.

Jordan pulled back, but only slightly, keeping his gaze locked on her as he spoke to the other man. "Camilla and I spoke briefly about it. Although we haven't negotiated whether Taylor Beef will be one of her main suppliers." He looked into her upturned face. "Maybe we should go sample some of the product?"

A ripple of anticipation zipped through her. Was he serious? She was still in the early stages of finding investors, yet Jordan was already miles ahead of her, talking about food suppliers. Sure, he might be a savvy businessman and probably easily navigated his way through many deals. But would he really be laying on this much charm to negotiate a deal if he didn't believe in her restaurant?

Trying to get her head back in the game, Camilla allowed him to lead her to one of the food stations, where they were serving bite-sized beef Wellington pastries and prime rib sliders. The scent of the garlicky horseradish sauce helped clear her sinuses and her mind.

"Sounds like you're not going to have any problem getting your restaurant up and running if you've already got DJ Traub talking about it." Jordan handed her a small appetizer plate and his fingers brushed against hers.

That anticipatory thrill shot through Camilla again, but this time it wasn't just because of Jordan's nearness. DJ wasn't only her boss, he was one of the best known restaurateurs in Montana. He'd known that by bringing Camilla to this fundraiser as his guest, he was all but assuring the public of his faith in her. Now it was time for her to do her part and seal the deal.

Camilla took a deep breath. "You know, I put together a financial proposal if you'd be interested in reviewing it."

"I'd love to review it." Jordan smiled again and Camilla's legs turned to jelly. "Just as long as we're clear that I'd be looking at it as a *friend*, not as an investor."

"Oh." Camilla tightened her spine to keep her shoulders from sagging with disappointment.

Jordan put a finger under her chin, forcing her to meet his direct stare. "Camilla, I never mix business with pleasure. If we were to work together, then we couldn't dance together like that again. And I really, *really* enjoy dancing with you."

"Thank you." One of her eyebrows lifted slightly. "I think."

"But I can introduce you to one of my uncles. His daughter did a semester abroad in Mexico City a few years ago and is still talking about the lack of good authentic food in Bronco." Jordan put two sliders on her plate, added several savory puffed pastries, then loaded them both down with skewers of tender marinated steak and a yogurt cucumber dipping sauce. "Let's grab another drink and maybe one or two more dances, and then we can go find my Uncle Thaddeus and maybe talk to a couple of my business associates."

Camilla followed him as he cut a path to one of the bars set up on the perimeter of the massive tent. Part of her had been hoping that having Jordan investing in her restaurant would be a quick and easy solution. The other part of her was trying to tell her giddy nerves that he was right and there was no way they could be business partners considering how her body reacted to his on the dance floor. Besides, she'd known that she wasn't going to hook an investor at her very first event. She was supposed to be meeting people and mingling tonight, networking and forming her own connections.

This time, instead of offering her a bottle of Scotch, Jordan stood back while she ordered a spicy jalapeno mojito from the bartender. They ate, they laughed and they tried each other's drinks. Then they ate a little more. It was almost easier being around Jordan now that Camilla didn't have to impress him—at least not in the business sense.

The only awkward moment came when Cornelius Taylor took the microphone to announce how much money they'd raised so far tonight. It was an obscene amount that none of the local community fundraisers she'd volunteered for ever brought in. She wanted to ask Jordan which local charities would be getting the proceeds from tonight, but she'd noticed the firm set of his jaw while his father was on stage and decided not to dip her toe into those tense waters.

When a country-and-Western song came on afterward, Jordan quickly pulled her onto the dance floor to teach her how to two-step. "Cha Cha Slide" came on next, and it was her turn to teach him how to do a line dance. His feet went to the left and his arms went to the right, and when it came time to hop five times, Camilla had never laughed so hard in her life.

Another slow song started and when he pulled

her close a second time, Camilla realized that she never wanted tonight to end. As soon as the thought popped into her mind, another couple bumped into them.

It was Erica Abernathy Dalton, her face completely drained of color. "I think I'm going to have a baby."

Chapter Two

Camilla felt Jordan's hand squeeze her waist before he dropped his arm. "I'm going to call an ambulance. Would you mind staying with them?"

"Of course," she replied, sliding closer to Erica and helping the pregnant woman's husband lead her off the dance floor.

Camilla had never actually witnessed a birth—not even on an online video. She prayed that tonight wasn't yet another first for her. Camilla hadn't been exaggerating when she'd told Jordan that she'd had no desire to follow in any of her friends' footsteps and get married or have kids anytime soon. This all looked way too painful and complicated.

"Should you sit down?" she asked Erica, whose mouth was in a perfect circle and puffing out short bursts of air.

"No. The contraction is easing up now." Erica whistled air through gritted teeth. Erica's husband—Camilla thought she'd heard someone call him Morgan—asked people to clear out of the way so they could get through to the tent opening.

Several other people crowded around the laboring woman, wanting to offer any help they could. The band stopped playing and more and more guests became curious about what was going on.

"The ambulance is on its way." Jordan returned with his cell phone pressed against his ear. "How far apart are the contractions?"

Erica was now seated on one of the chairs and as more bystanders arrived, Camilla was slowly edged out of the way. And really, it was just as well. She didn't know these people and she certainly didn't know a thing about delivering babies. There wasn't anything she could do but get in the way.

Jordan, though, had sprung into action, directing both the staff and the guests. First he ordered people to give Erica space. Then he told some random guy in a bright blue tuxedo to fetch a glass of water before instructing the security guards to ensure the long driveway was cleared for the ambulance's arrival. His take-charge attitude was quite the reversal of his earlier laid-back mood, and Camilla almost wanted to stay just so she could watch him in action.

Really, though, there was no point in her staying. Not only would Jordan be preoccupied for the rest of the night, it wasn't as though Camilla could walk up and introduce herself to Jordan's Uncle Thaddeus or any of the Taylor cousins to discuss her business model while one of the guests was currently in labor. Besides, Camilla had already gotten what she came for—some buzzing interest about her up-and-coming restaurant and even some tips about possible investors.

It was probably best to leave now with the success of the evening still glowing inside her. Camilla grabbed her faux fur stole and purse from her assigned table, and had just handed her ticket to the valet parking attendant when Jordan caught up with her.

"Camilla, wait!" Jordan was still in his white dress shirt, but the tie was undone and his sleeves were rolled up. "I saw you walking out and didn't want you leaving without saying goodbye."

"Oh, don't worry about it. I didn't want to be

in the way in there and figured everyone would be leaving soon anyway."

"I'd offer to drive you, but I should probably stay here until the ambulance arrives." Jordan craned his neck to look toward the paved private road leading to his family's ranch house. Lines of concern marred his forehead, his expression the exact opposite of the confident charmer she'd met earlier this evening. "I don't know why it's taking so long."

Camilla suppressed a chuckle. Of course Jordan wasn't used to waiting for anything. What he didn't realize, though, was that the Bronco City Council had approved a new fire station to be built in the wealthier area of the Heights, despite the fact that the majority of residents lived in the Valley. So the ambulances were usually called down the hill to assist with the regular folks, making the EMTs less likely to be on standby for the citizens of the Heights. But the poor guy was nervously rocking back and forth in his fancy black cowboy boots, so she didn't have the heart to get into a discussion about the disparities in their town's designation of civic resources.

"Like I said, please don't worry about it." Her smile wasn't forced when she added, "I had a lot of fun tonight."

"Good." Jordan's shoulders relaxed before he

reached out and traced a finger along her bare arm. "You have no idea how much better my evening got once I finally met you."

She wanted to tell him that she bet he said that to all the girls. But those dark brown eyes of his were so focused and seemed so entirely serious that Camilla found herself at a complete loss of words.

"Before I saw you, I was counting the minutes until I could leave." He took a step closer and Camilla felt a shiver travel down her back. His voice lowered. "As soon as I started talking to you, though, the night became almost magical."

She tilted her face to look up at him just before he lowered his lips to hers, brushing them ever so slightly against her open mouth. Camilla wasn't entirely sure the contact would count as a kiss, yet the tingling sensation spreading through her suggested it was even more intimate than anything she'd ever experienced. At least in public.

In fact, she almost lifted on tiptoe to try the kiss again, but a siren sounded in the distance. Several more partygoers spilled out of the tent, and Camilla jumped back. Jordan looked over his shoulder before he squeezed her hand. "I hope I can see you again, Miss Balthazar."

Camilla's heart immediately dropped into the pit of her stomach and the red warning lights flashing all around her weren't just from the approaching emergency responders.

Who in the world was Miss Balthazar? Had he mistaken her for someone else?

Her mind tried to race through all their earlier conversations to recall if either one of them had ever mentioned her last name. But her brain and her blood felt as though they were frozen. Luckily, the parking attendant pulled her car along the other side of the recently arrived ambulance. She needed to get out of here before he found out she wasn't who he thought she was.

"Thank you again for a lovely evening," she called out before rushing off into the night. Cinderella herself hadn't made such a dramatic exit.

At least Camilla hadn't left so much as a glass slipper behind.

Jordan sat in his office, scrolling through last night's RSVP list on his laptop.

"It'd be quicker if you just tell me what, or *who*, you're looking for and I find her myself." Mac, his personal assistant, came around to his side of the desk.

Jordan didn't lift his eyes from the digital spreadsheet. "Why are you assuming it's a female I'm looking for?"

"When are you *not* in search of a female?" Mac leaned in closer, squinting despite the fact that her smudged spectacles were perched on top of her Bronco Valley Little League ball cap. Jordan's own grandfather had hired the woman fresh out of secretarial school back in the fifties, and the older woman liked to remind Jordan that she'd been an employee of Taylor Beef longer than any of them. "Besides, you never ask me to forward you emails from Little Cornelius's public relations team. Something's up."

"You know, Mac, I think you're the only person alive who can still get away with calling my old man Little Cornelius."

"That's because I used to change his diapers just like I did yours," Mac easily replied. "It's the same reason why I can get people around this place to provide me party lists with no questions asked."

Jordan agreed. The fewer people who knew about his little extracurricular search, the better. That included Mac. "Don't you have a batting lineup or something you need to work on right now?"

"Nope." Mac tugged on the faded red jersey with Senior Swingers stitched across the front. His assistant was well past eighty years old and didn't really assist Jordan so much as act as a gatekeeper from keeping Cornelius and some of the other members of the board of directors from bugging Jordan while he worked. In exchange for her loyalty and dedication, he didn't complain about the fact that Mac used her desk outside of his office as her coaching headquarters for the two Little League and three year-round recreational softball teams she managed. "Not when my boy is planning to make some calls to the bullpen to send another rookie to the pitching mound."

"Can you please stop comparing my dating life to a sporting event?" Jordan's eye caught on the letter C on his screen, but the name beside it was Carmichael, not Camilla.

"Well, if the cleat fits…" Mac rested a bony elbow on Jordan's shoulder. She clearly wasn't leaving his office anytime soon.

"I'm trying to get a phone number for Camilla Balthazar." He released a heavy breath. "But I'm not seeing her on the RSVP list. In fact, I'm not seeing anyone named Camilla."

"There's an Alexis Balthazar." Mac pointed out the same thing Jordan's eye kept coming back to. He'd never really asked the woman her name last night, but DJ Traub had referred to her as Camilla. Maybe DJ had gotten the name wrong, but she'd been too polite to correct him. Jordan racked his brain trying to remember if he'd called her by the wrong name, as well.

"I think this number beside her name is for the North American headquarters." Jordan kept his fingers from reaching for his phone. The best way to avoid Mac's sports-announcer-type commentary was to ask her to do her actual job. "Will you see if you can track down a direct phone line for Alexis?"

"No can do, Sport." Mac stood up and made a motion as though she was swinging a bat. "You know what my training is like during the off-season. I've gotta get to the indoor cages before the Bronco Bombers get there and take all the fast pitch machines."

Jordan held back his knowing grin as the woman who was more like a grandmother to him took off for yet another practice. Then he shut his office door before dialing the number.

After being transferred to three different extensions and repeating the name "Jordan Taylor from Taylor Beef" at least five times, he finally reached Alexis Balthazar's assistant, who told him that the corporate jet was grounded last night in Brussels unexpectedly. The man added that Miss Balthazar was sorry she'd missed the Denim and Diamonds gala and would be sending a sizable donation when she returned to the States.

Jordan stared at the phone for several seconds after he hung up. He typed the name Alexis Balthazar into his internet search engine, and the image that popped up on his screen was a long-haired brunette, but the eye color and the cheekbones and the smile were all wrong. This definitely was not the same woman from last night.

Did Jose have another daughter? He scanned the company's website for a list of employees, but didn't see anyone named Camilla. Jordan tried several more internet searches before his cell phone vibrated with a text notification from Daphne.

Erica had a GIRL! They named her Josie after her Grandpa Josiah. Isn't that sweet? Mom and baby are both doing well.

Jordan made a mental note to send a card or something to the hospital when a second text bubble appeared from Daphne. Glad last night was a success for someone.

Damn. He'd been so focused on Camilla last night that he hadn't even checked in with his sister. Jordan quickly pressed the green phone icon to call Daphne, who picked up on the second ring.

"I take it things didn't go well between you and the old man last night?" he asked.

"It was a total disaster. Dad told me that it was never too late to apologize and admit that the animal sanctuary was a mistake. I told him not to hold his breath."

"Good for you."

"Yeah. Good for me. Except he walked away and pretty much froze me out for the rest of the night. It was so uncomfortable. At one point, we were standing next to each other at the bar and Daniel Dubois asked how things were going and Dad pretended like I wasn't even there."

"Sounds like something he'd do." Jordan put the phone on speaker and kept clicking on the keys on his laptop. He felt bad for Daphne, but they both knew how Cornelius was. He loved his children, even if he had the most frustrating way of expressing it. This kind of passive aggressive behavior was nothing new and eventually the old man would come around. "Dad can't stand not getting his way so he'll pretend the problem doesn't even exist. Not that you're a problem. It's just in his mind...you know?"

"Oh, I know all right." Daphne snorted. "If you're not with him, you're against him and all that. What's that clicking sound? Are you typing while you're talking to me?"

"Sort of. I'm trying to find someone who was at the party last night. Do you remember Jose Balthazar?"

"Not really. But I remember his daughter.

Alexis and I went to that all girls' camp together during our high school winter breaks."

"Did he have any other daughters? There was a woman last night at the party named Camilla and—"

"The brunette in the gold sequined gown?" Daphne interrupted.

"Yes!" His pulse sped up. "Did you talk to her?"

"Jordan, I don't think anyone besides you had a chance to talk with her. With the way you two were moving on the dance floor, I don't think anyone wanted to come between you."

"Aha! So I wasn't just imagining that we had a connection." Jordan almost pumped his fist in triumph. Instead, he settled for doing a full one-eighty spin in his custom leather desk chair.

"C'mon, Jor. Half the female population of Montana thinks they have a connection with you."

"But this was different. This time, *I* was the one feeling the connection."

Jordan could almost see Daphne rolling her eyes before she said, "Well, I can't help you. I have no idea who she was."

"Dad told me it was Jose Balthazar's daughter."

"Nope. Alexis is the only girl in that family as far as I know. Besides, you know how bad Dad's eyes are when he refuses to wear his glasses."

Crap. Jordan had forgotten about that part.

"So how do I find her?" he asked his sister.

"You don't. If a woman wants to be found, she'll find you first."

"But I'm not even sure of her real name. Maybe you could ask some of your friends…"

"You know who you sound like right now?" Daphne asked, but didn't wait for an answer. "Dad."

"That's hitting below the belt," he replied, not really joking.

"It's true. Once you get your mind set on something, you can't let it go."

Jordan felt his nostrils expand as he sucked in a calming breath. He was used to the nicknames and the teasing and the constant references to his dating history. But Jordan had worked his entire life to be the opposite of his father. To not take things so seriously or care what people thought about him. To not get too attached to anyone, especially women who might leave.

"Listen, I gotta get going," he said, wanting to end the call as politely as possible. He also didn't want his sister to realize how much her comparison had bothered him. She was already dealing with enough when it came to their family.

"So you can get back to the search for your missing Cinderella?"

"No, so that I can order something to be delivered to Erica at the hospital," he said, which wasn't a total lie. Although as soon as he placed the order online, he had every intention of resuming his search for the woman who'd fled the ball right before the stroke of midnight.

Not that his conversation with his sister had made him feel like any sort of Prince Charming. Far from it, in fact.

After Daphne said goodbye, he tried to remind himself that his sister was actually annoyed at their father, not Jordan. However, her expressing her doubt about his intentions still stung. Especially because what he'd experienced last night was different. Camilla was special.

If Camilla was, in fact, her real name.

Jordan drummed his fingers beside the computer mouse. His sister's words bounced around in his head. *If a woman wants to be found, she'll find you first.* Most of the women he'd ever dated, and even a few he hadn't dated, had always sought him out or made it more than clear that they were available if he were to ask them out. But Jordan had a feeling Camilla wasn't most women.

He returned his attention to his laptop and clicked on his stepmother's social media page to see if photos from the night before had already been uploaded. Sure enough, there were several... dozen. In the very last one, he was finally able to zoom in on a woman in a gold sequined gown sitting at a table with DJ Traub and his wife.

Jordan picked up his phone to call DJ, but had second thoughts. They were really more acquaintances than anything else. DJ's Deluxe did some business with Taylor Beef, keeping the local restaurant well stocked with their best cuts of meat, but that was his Uncle Lester's account. He couldn't just randomly call the man out of the blue and ask about the woman who'd been sitting at his table.

Instead, Jordan typed DJ's name in the search field on his social media tab and quickly found the page for the popular restaurant in Bronco Heights. Most of the images were of the food and the decor, but in the grand opening crowd, he thought he saw someone who might be Camilla.

An electrical current raced through him now that he'd found a clue about the woman from last night. Grabbing his car keys, he strode down the hall and out the building. He suddenly had an unexplainable craving for a porterhouse and another glass of Macallan.

Camilla's arm was already buckling under the weight of the tray holding several sizzling cast iron plates artfully displaying tonight's special—peppercorn-encrusted filet mignon in a mushroom and red wine reduction sauce, potatoes au gratin and steamed asparagus with an herbed lemon zest.

She was exhausted and deflated and couldn't wait to get off work and go climb into her bed. After Jordan had called her by the wrong name last night, she'd tossed and turned, thinking about how the only reason he'd even talked to her was that he'd thought she was someone else. She'd gotten maybe two hours of sleep this morning before having to be up for her Managerial Economics class at eight sharp. Thank God for online classes—at least she could watch the lecture in her pajamas with her hair in a messy bun and last night's leftover mascara still stuck to her lashes.

After finishing her paper on regression analysis in today's service industry, she'd hoped to get a little nap in before her afternoon shift at DJ's Deluxe. Instead, her sister asked her to drop off the borrowed dress at the dry cleaners. Then her dad needed a ride to his doctor's appointment because he wasn't supposed to be driving yet postsurgery, and her mom couldn't take him because Mrs. Waters had shown up at the salon after trying to do another home perm. The rest of Camilla's afternoon had been an entire blur.

But through it all, she kept moving, which kept her from having to mentally relive the embarrassing mix-up last night. Serving at a restaurant was a comforting routine to her. She delivered the plates to one table, dropped off the check at a second table, and was in the middle of taking a drink order from a third when she realized someone sitting at the bar was watching her.

Jordan Taylor.

Camilla froze with her pen hovering over the pad. Even if she'd wanted to dive for cover under the white-linen-draped table, her body refused to move. Why was he here? She hadn't even had time to think about the man since she'd awoken this morning. And that was a good thing. Or at least it had been.

"What kind of craft beers do you have on tap?" a customer asked, jarring her back to the real world. She was no longer at the Denim and Diamonds gala. She had a living to earn.

Despite the fact that Camilla had both the wine and beer lists memorized, she didn't trust herself not to stutter or lose focus. Instead, she told the customer, "I'll go get you a menu. Be right back."

Maybe that had been the wrong stall tactic, she realized, as she was now forced to walk toward the bar to retrieve the printed parchment tucked into a leather folder. Jordan's mouth split into that boyishly charming grin as she approached.

"Hey," he said, showcasing those knee-wobbling dimples in his cheeks.

"What are you doing here?" she asked.

"I thought about playing it cool and saying I came in for an after-work drink and a perfectly cooked ribeye. But the truth is that I was hoping to see you again."

"Why?"

"Because I've been trying to find you all day."

She refused to let her heart do a repeat of last night. "Were you looking for me? Or were you looking for Miss Balthazar?"

"Yeah, I'm really sorry for that mix-up. My father was the one who told me you were the daughter of one of our business associates. The old man is too vain to admit that he needs glasses and I was too mesmerized by you to even ask for confirmation." He formally stuck out his hand as though he hadn't just kissed her on the lips last night. Or sort of kissed her. "I'm Jordan Taylor, by the way."

"Yes, I know," she replied. The tray was still tucked under her arm, so she had an excuse to decline the handshake. But she didn't want to seem bitter. Or affected by his presence either way. She set the tray on the bar and took his offered hand. Ignoring the riptide of electricity that sailed through her skin, she added, "If you'll excuse me, I need to get going."

"Wait," he said before she could turn around. "Can I maybe buy you a drink? We could sit down and talk."

"Listen, I know you thought I was someone else last night. But I'm a waitress, not a socialite at one of your parties." She looked pointedly around at the almost full tables in the expensive restaurant tastefully decorated to accentuate its rustic origins. Then she gestured to her uniform of a white blouse, black slacks and a long black waist apron. "I'm at work."

"Right." He nodded. She had a feeling he wasn't used to being told no, even if it was for a good reason—such as not losing her job. "Then can I get your number so that I can call you later?"

"Here's the thing, Jordan. I had a great time last night. And I appreciate you coming in and making the attempt. I'm flattered. However, we all know how this will turn out."

"How *what* will turn out?"

"This." She gestured between the two of them. "Us. It might be a fun diversion for a few hours, or maybe even a few days. And if I wasn't working full-time *and* in the middle of my MBA program *and* trying to open my own restaurant, then maybe I wouldn't mind a little…distraction." She caught herself before she used the words *booty call*.

"You know…" He tilted his head and dropped his eyes to the name tag on her white uniform shirt. "You still haven't told me your full name."

If this guy was some sort of stalker who refused to take no for an answer, she certainly wasn't going to make it any easier for him. "Why do you need it?"

"Because I've been talking to a few people who may be interested in investing in your restaurant."

She narrowed her eyes. So maybe Jordan wasn't a full-blown stalker. Especially considering the fact that his reputation would suggest he was way more likely to be the one being stalked. Still. There was no reason to completely throw caution to the wind and let him think that she had any interest in him other than professional.

"It's Camilla Sanchez. If one of your contacts wants to get in touch with me, I would suggest they do so when it's not during the dinner rush."

"Fair enough," he said, that satisfied grin spreading across his way too handsome face.

Determined to maintain the upper hand, Camilla returned to her waiting customers, only to realize that she'd completely forgotten the beer list. It took her another hour to get back into the swing of things. By eight-thirty, most of her tables had cleared out and only the customers who couldn't book earlier reservations remained.

When she finally folded her apron and collected her tips, it was nine o'clock.

And Jordan Taylor was waiting by the hostess desk for her.

Chapter Three

"You don't give up easily, do you?" Camilla asked Jordan.

"Well you *did* say to come back when you weren't working."

"No. I said one of those potential investors you were talking about could talk to me when I wasn't working. And I specifically remember you saying last night that you had no plans to invest in my restaurant because, what was the tired cliché you used?" She tapped her chin thoughtfully as if she didn't already have it seared in her brain. "You don't mix business with pleasure."

"I still stand by that. Let me buy you a drink

and we can discuss the terms of our nonbusiness relationship." Jordan waved at Leo, the bartender, who probably had told him when Camilla would be off work.

"What?" She swallowed her panic as she looked around at the coworkers who would be staying another hour until closing. "Here?"

He lowered his head as though he was about to share a secret, and her pulse skipped a beat. "You would prefer somewhere more private?"

"No," she said, trying to ignore the way her knees buckled any time those dimpled cheeks were close enough to touch. "We can go somewhere very public and very well lit. Like the Splitting Lanes Bowling Alley, for example."

He threw back his head and laughed, causing the other servers and one of the sous chefs to look their way. Camilla wanted to sink into the floor. It was one thing to play make believe last night at a fundraising gala, but it was quite another to have her coworkers think she was seriously considering being used by the rich playboy with a reputation for breaking hearts. Or worse. That he was going to get into the restaurant business with her only in the hopes of also getting into her pants.

She grabbed his elbow and tugged him toward the door. "Come on. The Bronco Brick Oven is open for another hour and I'm starved."

The pizza place was a few buildings over in the recently gentrified district of Bronco Heights. What had once been feed mills and industrial factories and even a muffler repair shop were now upscale restaurants and boutiques made to look rustic and elegant at the same time with lots of restored wood, exposed brick, and metal-infused designs. She'd never understand rich people and their tastes.

He held open the door for her and she felt the warmth of his hand on her lower back. A shiver raced through her, making her think it was almost scary how her body reacted to his barest touch.

"This isn't a date," she reminded them both.

That didn't stop Jordan from asking the young waiter wiping down vinyl-covered menus if they could have one of the booths in the rear corner.

"So you've gotten me to sit down with you," she said when he took the bench seat across from hers. "Does that make me just another woman who can't resist the Jordan Taylor charm?"

"You shouldn't believe everything you read about me on social media." He flashed that playful grin again, and Camilla thought she should definitely believe every single word she'd read. "Can't a man meet a woman at a party and simply want to take her out and get to know her better?"

"When they meet under normal circumstances?

Yes. But the woman you met last night wasn't the real me."

"So then tell me about the real you." Jordan leaned his forearms on the table, as though he was actually interested.

"Well, for starters, I'm not the daughter of one of your dad's wealthy business associates. My parents aren't cattle barons or landowners who've been here for several generations. In fact, my parents immigrated here from Mexico thirty years ago. My dad doesn't get wine baskets after surgery, he gets a tater tot hot dish and a really bland tuna casserole that Mrs. Waters next door tried to make. I wear jeans and T-shirts when I'm not dressed for work." Camilla motioned to her standard white button-up shirt and black pants all the servers at DJ's Deluxe wore. Thankfully it was better than the misshapen brown polyester dress she'd worn when she'd worked at Waffle Station in college. "I don't wear ball gowns or high heels unless I borrow them. I'm a waitress and a student. I live in a tiny apartment above the post office in Bronco Valley. I drink beer on tap, not fifty-year-old single-malt Scotch."

The server returned at that exact minute, and Jordan asked, "Can we get a pitcher of Big Sky IPA?" Then he glanced at Camilla and added, "Beer on tap. Check. What else do I need to know?"

"That I never drink on an empty stomach," Camilla replied to him before turning to the server. "Can you also bring us the Italian chopped salad please? And an order of the garlic pesto twists?"

When the server left, Jordan leaned back in the booth, the sleeves of his dark blue shirt pushed up to his elbows. How did this guy look so casual no matter where he was or what he wore? In fact, even his appraising stare seemed casual, despite the fact that he was clearly sizing her up.

Finally, he nodded slowly. "So last night wasn't the real you?"

"Exactly."

"That would mean that the real you doesn't like dancing. Can't stand Beyoncé songs or the 'Cha Cha Slide.' The real you hates prime rib sliders—you ate six of them, by the way, so good job faking that—and you never lick your fingers when you spill au jus all over them. The real you doesn't smell like a wild field of lupines in the middle of June and doesn't have the widest and most compelling smile I've ever seen." Jordan's words had almost more of an effect on her than his silky eyes still drinking her in. "And the real you isn't at all passionate about the traditional Mexican restaurant you want to build using your grandmother's recipes and your hard-earned experience in the restaurant industry."

The pale ale arrived and Jordan poured her a

glass with the same ease he'd poured the Scotch last night. Clearly, everything came easily to him.

"Fair enough." She took the offered pint. "But Jordan, be honest. When was the last time you dated someone who didn't drive a luxury car?"

He pursed his lips and lifted his eyes to the ceiling as if he needed to think of a response.

She took back-to-back sips of the beer, slowly swallowing as she allowed him more time to come to the foregone conclusion. She exhaled and said, "Your silence speaks volumes."

"Maybe that's the problem," he replied. "I haven't been dating the right kind of women."

"According to those society columns you don't want me to believe, you've had quite a variety of ladies to choose from."

"Look, Camilla, my dating life is apparently an open book. You obviously know what you're getting into by going out with me. But I've never met anyone like you. I've certainly never dated anyone like you."

She lifted her eyebrows in doubt. "You mean someone in the working class?"

"I mean someone who seems to enjoy life as much as you do. Who has enough ambition to come to a party where she doesn't know anyone so that she can pitch her restaurant idea to strangers. Someone who kept me up all night thinking about her infectious laugh and when I could hear it again."

Her breath suspended in her rib cage. If she wanted to avoid going light-headed and weak in the knees, she either needed to get some food in her system or she needed to double down on her efforts to resist his charm. Although, it was becoming increasingly difficult to keep her guard up against this man when he said all the right things.

If only to keep herself on the defensive, she turned the conversation back to him. "How do I know you're not just some guy who enjoys slumming it with a girl from the other side of the tracks?"

Jordan's raised brow made her wonder if this guy ever took anything seriously. "First of all, Bronco Valley doesn't have any tracks. They all run north of the Heights." Then his mouth straightened and his jaw hardened. "And if anyone were to ever refer to me dating you as 'slumming it,' I'd personally kick their ass."

"Even your father?" she challenged. "I mean, obviously I don't condone violence toward anyone of an advanced age who clearly suffers from nearsightedness. But how would the wealthy Taylors feel about you dating an immigrant's daughter from Bronco Valley?"

Seeing the determination glinting in his

eyes, she suddenly wondered how she could've thought this multimillion-dollar businessman couldn't be serious when he needed to be. "I'd tell my family the same thing I tell them whenever they ask about my dating life. It's none of their business."

The chopped salad and the fragrant knots of perfectly baked dough topped with basil and parmesan arrived, and Jordan asked if she wanted to order anything else. She was starved after skipping lunch to run all those errands today, but she shook her head.

When the server left, Jordan asked, "How long did it take you to have me all figured out?"

She pointed her fork at him. "About five minutes."

"Because you knew my name and you knew my reputation based off some online articles." He slid a hot, cheesy twist into his mouth. Watching him, Camilla's stomach melted like the garlicky butter he'd just licked off his fingers.

"Also because I know guys like you. Rich boys who've never had to work hard for what they wanted." She shoved a forkful of salad in her mouth, not wanting to entice him the same way he was enticing her.

"You don't think I can work for what I want?"

"I'm sure you're a very good businessman, Jordan. I also read the financial articles about you, not just the society columns. Unfortunately, I'm not one of your business ventures or some associate who is open for negotiations."

"That's a good idea." He finished off the rest of his beer. "We should negotiate."

"I just said I wasn't open to that," she reminded him. But then her curiosity got the better of her. "What exactly do you want to negotiate?"

"Give me four weeks. Go out with me at least twice a week for four weeks and I'll prove to you that I'm not the guy you think I am."

"You're crazy." She chuckled, then realized he wasn't laughing with her. "You can't seriously think us dating is a good idea."

"Why not? Are you worried that you'll get too attached and fall in love with me?"

In love? Not a chance. But she was already recklessly attracted to him, so she did have some concerns about letting him get too close. Unfortunately, she'd inherited that Sanchez competitive gene and, like everyone else in her family, she'd never been able to back down from a challenge.

"I'll give you two weeks." She took another bite of salad, hoping she wasn't going to regret this. "Two weeks will be long enough for you to realize that we're way too different to be together."

And not so long that they risked getting their

hearts involved. Oh, who was she kidding? She was the only one at risk for that. But that didn't mean she wasn't determined to prove him wrong. Besides, if he could introduce her to some possible investors, then it would all be worth it.

"Three weeks," he countered before refilling their glasses and holding his up in a toast. "That's long enough for me to convince you that we have a chance."

"Fine. Three weeks." She clinked his glass with her own in agreement. "If you can even last that long."

Jordan checked his reflection in the rearview mirror a second time. He didn't want to look like he was trying too hard, but he also didn't want Camilla to think he didn't care. He'd been hoping for a weekend date, but Camilla insisted that Friday and Saturday were her busiest nights at work and she relied on the extra tip money.

He hadn't wanted to wait until the middle of the week to start their three-week agreement, so she suggested they jump in with both feet. Sunday night dinner with her family.

Really, it was more of a dare than a suggestion. One that Jordan had all too willingly accepted. After all, when was the last time he'd actually met the family of a woman he was dating?

Even when he already knew the parents—

like the Abernathys—he still avoided any setting that might suggest the relationship was at that sort of level. If he wanted to prove that Camilla was different from the women of his past, then he'd have to approach their relationship differently, as well.

The Sanchez family's house was in the heart of Bronco Valley. It was a modest one story in an older subdivision where many of the homes looked identical. Jordan had purposely driven one of the ranch trucks instead of his Tesla. Since his money was already an issue with Camilla, he didn't want to draw any more attention to it.

There were several vehicles crammed into the driveway and on the surrounding street, so he was forced to park three houses down. As he approached the front door, he could hear several male voices inside arguing about fouls and free throw lines. Jordan took a deep breath before lifting his hand to knock. Before he could, a slightly younger, shorter version of Camilla almost hit him with the door.

"Come on in. Camilla is in the kitchen with our mom and I'm on my way to the store to get more mangos." The woman passed by him as he stepped into the entry, then leaned around him to call out, "Even though everyone knows

CHRISTY JEFFRIES 63

you can't get a decent mango in Montana this time of year."

"Stop yelling, Sofia." An older, redheaded version of Camilla came out of the kitchen, wiping her hands on an apron printed with the words Your Opinion Wasn't in the Recipe. "Mr. Granada always keeps a couple of ripe ones for me behind his checkstand."

"Hey, Dad," a guy Jordan's age wearing a blue Bronco Fire Department T-shirt said. He was sitting on the armrest of an oversized brown corduroy sectional and didn't take his eyes off the TV. "What else is Mr. Granada keeping behind his checkstand for Mom?"

"Knock it off, Felix. And sit on my sofa like a normal person," the obvious matriarch of the Sanchez family scolded before her eyes landed on Jordan. "Oh, hello. You must be Camilla's friend. I'm her mom."

"It's a pleasure to meet you, Mrs. Sanchez," he said, then passed her the bouquet of flowers he'd gotten from a flower shop on his way over.

Her smile was just as wide and enthusiastic as Camilla's as she beamed at the flowers. "Please call me Denise. Aaron, did you see Camilla's friend is here?"

A taller man with a neatly trimmed salt-and-pepper beard had already hefted himself up from a recliner chair and used a pair of crutches to limp toward them. Jordan hurried to meet the man halfway. "I'm glad to make your acquaintance, Mr. Sanchez."

Camilla's father took Jordan's hand in his bearlike grip and, unlike his friendly, petite wife, did not insist that Jordan call him by his first name. But he did say, "Welcome to our home."

"Thank you." Jordan shifted the cellophane-wrapped wine basket in his arm. "I heard you recently had surgery, sir, and thought I'd bring a little something to ease the recovery."

Mr. Sanchez's eyes brightened when he noticed the wine basket Jordan had asked Mac to order on Friday. "That Napa cabernet certainly looks way better than the vegan lasagna my physical therapist brought over last week."

"Where did everyone go…" Camilla's voice died out when she entered the room and her gaze landed on Jordan. How did she grow more beautiful every time he saw her? Her hair was twisted into a messy ponytail on top of her head, and she was barefoot in her fitted jeans and long-sleeved white tee. She pushed a loose curl behind her ear, leaving a streak of flour on her cheek. "You actually came."

Jordan's throat tightened as he tried to make his tongue work. "You invited me, remember?"

Felix stood up. "Don't mind Cam. She's never invited a boyfriend over before and is probably just as surprised as the rest of us that you actually showed up."

"I'm not surprised," Denise said, nudging her daughter. "*Mija*, why don't you introduce your friend to the rest of the family?"

"Right." Camilla cleared her throat. "Well, the guy who likes to embarrass me is my oldest brother, Felix."

Felix offered his hand then asked, "Can I get you something to drink?"

Jordan glanced down at the empty bottle in Felix's hand. "One of those would be great."

"One beer coming right up."

"Grab me a corkscrew while you're in there," Mr. Sanchez told Felix before taking the basket from Jordan's arm and limping toward his recliner. "Gotta let the wine breathe before dinner."

"The guy in the Utah Jazz jersey…" Camilla pointed to a lanky guy sitting on the edge of a faded floral ottoman. "The one who can barely look over here because he's too busy watching the game? That's Dylan."

Dylan offered a wave. "Sorry, man, there's only a coupla seconds left."

"And the one who is supposed to be correcting third-grade spelling tests is Dante."

"How can I grade anything when the Jazz are about to lose a home game and make Dylan cry like a little baby?" Dante said, but set aside the papers he'd been ignoring and stood up to shake Jordan's hand. "What was your name again?"

"Jordan Ta—" Before he could finish, a loud buzzer sounded from the TV and a chaos of yells erupted around him as everyone but Camilla rushed back to their spots around the weathered oak coffee table. Mr. Sanchez had the wine basket balanced on one knee and Mrs. Sanchez balanced on the other.

"What'd I miss?" Felix handed Jordan a beer as he rushed by. "Did they get the three pointer?"

"We're going into overtime, baby!" Dylan pumped a fist while Dante cradled his head in his hands and groaned, "No!"

Several voices spoke over each other at once, and Camilla gestured at the scene in the cozy living room. "So this is my family. I hope you like basketball."

"I haven't played in a while." Jordan took a sip of the cold beer, recognizing the label of a local brewery. "Football was more my thing in high school and college."

"Not so loud." She put a finger to her lips. "Last year, Sofia brought home a guy who said he only played tennis and you would've thought he'd said he only enjoyed kicking puppies."

"That boy was no good for Sofia," Mr. Sanchez, who apparently had tuned out Dylan and Dante's bickering, called out.

"You say that about every boy Sofia brings home," his wife tutted before kissing his forehead.

"Oh, come on, Mom," Dante added. "The guy's name was Winston and he drove a BMW convertible. In Montana. In winter."

"Dante's right." Dylan still hadn't taken his eyes off the TV screen as he finally agreed with his brother about something. "That's what happens when you guys let her get a job at that stuck-up clothing store in the Heights. She ends up surrounded by all those trust fund dudes whose daddies have to give them jobs because they have no real-world experience."

Wow. Jordan's collar suddenly felt a lot tighter as that last comment hit a little too close to home. Maybe it was a good thing he hadn't said his last name earlier.

"For the record," Camilla said as she turned toward her family and planted her hands on her hips, "nobody *let* Sofia get a job there. This isn't the middle ages. She is a grown woman who does what she wants and is perfectly capable of making her own decisions."

"Says the girl who is also working with those snobs in the Heights," Dante said before pointing at the television and yelling, "His foot never even touched the line!"

"He was totally out of bounds!" Dylan yelled back, resuming the brotherly squabble.

Camilla shot Jordan a look as though to say, *See. I warned you.*

But Jordan's own family—especially his uncles—were equally as passionate when it came to football. So sports rivalries were nothing new to him. Besides, the Sanchezes seemed welcoming enough. As long as they got to know him before finding out who his father was, everything should be fine. After all, he wasn't here to talk about himself. He was here to spend time with Camilla.

Or at least that was what he'd thought before she returned to the kitchen with her mom, abandoning him to watch the rest of the game with her father and brothers. He swallowed a few more sips of beer, settled into an open spot on the sofa and found himself cheering for a team of players he'd never shown much interest in before now.

Sofia came through the door with the promised mangos, which started another round of teasing about Mr. Granada at the store having a crush on their mother.

When the Jazz finally won, Mrs. Sanchez turned off the television before Dante and Dylan could argue about the postgame interviews.

"Better get the grill going, Aaron. This chicken isn't going to cook itself."

It was still clear and sunny for a fall day, so the family went outside to a faded wooden deck that held a long patio table and several mismatched chairs. The yard beyond the deck was only big enough for a fenced-off vegetable garden, a tidy patch of grass and a smooth concrete slab with a regulation-height basketball hoop at the end.

In the center of the table was a tray of freshly cut vegetables coated with lime juice and chili powder, a bowl of tortilla chips, and the best mango habanera salsa he'd ever tasted. All three Sanchez sons offered to grill the seasoned chicken so that their father could sit down, but the older man refused, insisting that he needed to get accustomed to the surgical boot.

Jordan, though, had a feeling that Mr. Sanchez's insistence on maintaining command over his propane grill had more to do with a father not quite ready to hand over control to his sons. Cornelius, who never even used the professional grade oven at home, suddenly became a master griller every time the Taylor uncles came over for a barbecue. His dad would've accused his kids of trying to put him out to pasture if anyone suggested he couldn't handle something he thought was his patriarchal duty.

That certainly was *one* thing Cornelius Taylor and Aaron Sanchez had in common.

Camilla eventually made her way outside and handed Jordan one of the two beers in her hand before taking the seat beside him.

"Are you overwhelmed yet?" she asked under her breath, and he had to catch his. If he'd thought she'd been stunning at the gala, seeing her relaxed grin and total ease in this environment had him thinking thoughts he shouldn't be thinking in the company of her parents and three big brothers.

"Quite the opposite," he replied. "Don't forget that I have a big family, too, especially when you count my Taylor cousins. But we can wait a few more dates before I subject you to all of that."

Camilla's smile faltered and her eyes went round before she blinked a few times. "Let's get through one awkward moment at a time before we get ahead of ourselves."

"Good call." He clinked his bottle of beer against hers and added, "For once, I'm going to sit back and enjoy tonight before strategizing for tomorrow."

Unfortunately, just when Jordan thought he was going to finally get some time with her, Dante produced a basketball and spun it on his finger. "Who's up for some two on two?"

"I'm down." Felix stretched his arms over his head. "I'll even take Jordan on my team."

"Are you sure you want to go against us, big brother?" Dante asked before sharing a look with Dylan. "You know what happened last time."

Jordan glanced at Camilla, whose lower lip twisted in doubt. She lowered her voice and said, "You don't have to play with them. Dylan and Dante would rather play against each other anyway."

"No way," Denise Sanchez said. "They fight too much when they play against each other. They either play on the same team or not at all."

Jordan felt everyone's stares as they waited anxiously to see how far he was willing to go to impress Camilla's family.

He stood up and she tugged on his hand. The excitement of her touch, though, was short-lived by her warning. "They won't go easy on you."

Was any phrase more crushing to a man's ego than that? Or more compelling?

Unbuttoning his flannel shirt, he smiled. "Good."

The match was close at first as Jordan paced himself and got a sense of his teammate and his opponents. Felix was good, but Dylan and Dante were way better than their older brother. They also got along surprisingly well when they had the same goal in mind.

Jordan left the very playful trash talking to

Felix, who gave as good as he got when it came to insults. Several times, Sofia and both parents seemed to be doubled over with laughter at the zingers and one-liners exchanged on the court. But amid the fun, there was also some serious competition. The game heated up as more baskets were made and more elbows were thrown. Mr. Sanchez called out the personal fouls—and there were several of them—from his spot behind the grill.

Halfway through the game, Jordan found his stride and learned how to read the younger brothers' passes and how to avoid Dylan's larger frame trying to box him out. They were playing to twenty-one and Jordan and Felix won the first game by only two points.

They won the rematch by ten.

Jordan was covered in sweat—and possibly a few tears from holding back his laughter—by the time they walked back to the patio table.

He snuck a peek at Camilla, hoping she didn't object to his soggy appearance. Not that he'd ever cared before about how he looked. Her eyes were locked on his damp white undershirt, though, and his chest muscles flexed instinctively.

Before things could heat up too much, Sofia threw them each a towel and Mrs. Sanchez passed out bottles of ice-cold water. She tsked sympathetically at her younger sons. "To help you wash down your loss."

"You could've at least cheered for us, Mom," Dante told her.

"That's what you get for underestimating our guest, *mijo*." Mrs. Sanchez laughed. "Besides, your father burned the last few pieces of chicken because he was too busy calling out advice for you and Dylan. You two needed all the help you could get against Jordan."

Camilla had neither cheered nor offered any words of advice, but Jordan had felt her eyes on him the entire time. Even now, as she openly studied him, a slow smile playing on the corner of her mouth. She pulled out the chair beside her. "I thought you were more into football."

"I am. But that doesn't mean I'm not good at other sports." He took a long pull from the icy cold bottle of water. The aching muscles in his back were already starting to disagree.

She drew up one knee as she turned in her seat toward him. "I have a feeling that you're good at everything you do, Jordan."

"You have no idea," he promised, meeting her gaze.

Chapter Four

What day works best for you this week?

Camilla read Jordan's text on Monday morning as she huddled under her down comforter in her studio apartment.

Yesterday afternoon, she'd thought that she'd finally get him to admit defeat when it came to pursuing this ridiculous three-week trial dating period. She'd thought he'd take one look at her family's humble home, meet her obnoxiously competitive brothers, have dinner on her mom's favorite—and unbreakable—melamine plates, and hit the pavement.

Instead, he'd beat her brothers at their favorite sport and talked about grilling temperatures with her father and washed those same unbreakable dishes with Felix, whose turn it was to clean the kitchen. He'd even agreed to stop by their mom's salon for a haircut that he didn't need but Denise insisted on.

How had he won over her family so quickly? Probably because they had no idea he was one of *those* Taylors from Bronco Heights. At one point, she'd whispered a warning to Jordan not to bring up his name in front of the rest of the Sanchezes—unless they wanted to get teased unmercifully like Sofia and her last boyfriend.

Not that Jordan was her boyfriend. Or anything close to it. In fact, they hadn't so much as held hands yesterday at her parents' house. Still, it was best to keep him from getting any grand ideas.

She typed back, Actually, this week isn't so great. I'm working as many shifts as I can and I'm behind on my reading for my Business Ethics class. Plus, I have to find time to drive to Missoula to meet with my academic advisor before Thanksgiving break.

She saw the three dots indicating he was typing. Thinking he would give up, she held her breath. Then let it out in an unladylike snort when she saw his response. What day? I'll see if I can use the company chopper and come with you.

So much for him not getting any grand ideas. She groaned before replying. It's only a two-hour drive. I don't need you to go to the trouble of booking a helicopter to impress me.

I was going there anyway to meet with one of our distribution representatives. It'll be easy to re-schedule my meeting for whatever day you need to go.

He used the word *easy* as though distributors would shift their entire schedules just to meet with him. As though helicopter pilots had no problem just idly sitting around waiting for Jordan to change flight plans on a whim.

But...

Camilla's old Toyota *had* seen better days, and she hadn't had time to drop it off to get serviced lately. Plus, she'd never ridden in a helicopter before...

No. She slammed her phone down on the soft mattress. She was being ridiculous to even consider the possibility. There was no way she was going up in the air with that man.

At least, that was what she told herself all day Monday. But after working a double shift on Tuesday and barely being able to keep her eyes focused on her textbook on Wednesday, Camilla decided not to look a gift horse in the mouth.

"Put these on so we can hear each other during the flight," Jordan said on Thursday morning as he passed her an oversized headset that covered her ears. The Taylor Beef helicopter was dark blue like their ranch trucks, with only a discreet TB logo on the tail of the aircraft. The inside was plush with wide leather seats and a minifridge between the rear seat and the control panel. "The pilot said we should be there in about thirty minutes. I arranged for a car service to pick you up at the airfield. I didn't know which building you had to go to on campus, so you'll have to give the driver directions. They'll wait for you there and then bring you to meet me for lunch after you're done."

"What if I'm done before you?" she spoke into the microphone of her headset just before the enormous propeller whirred to life.

"You won't be," he replied before giving the pilot a thumbs-up.

Her stomach dropped as they lifted into the air, and she grabbed at the most solid surface she could find: Jordan's thigh. Before she could remove it, his warm hand covered hers and held it in place. As their altitude increased, so did Camilla's wonder and excitement. She leaned toward the window, staring down at the rolling green hills below.

"It's beautiful from up here," she said, the amazement in her voice echoing back through the headset.

Instead of looking at the view below them, though, Jordan watched her instead. Her ears felt impossibly hot and she tried to keep from squirming under his appreciative stare. She licked her lips and pointed to a range of dense green trees. "Is that Flathead National Forest?"

Finally, he shifted his gaze to follow her finger. "Yep. You should see it after the first snow of the season. White as far as you can see. Maybe we can go up again in December."

Camilla shouldn't need to remind him that their three-week agreement would be over by then. Jordan was a smart man and probably knew full well that he was suggesting the impossible. She told herself to enjoy the experience and not think about the messy emotions that would likely come later.

So that was what she did. She sat back in the luxurious leather seat and marveled at the majestic view of the purple-tinged mountains and lush green treetops below her. Without releasing her right hand, Jordan passed her an orange juice from the small fridge. She was glad it wasn't anything stronger, because she didn't want to be tipsy or over-caffeinated when she met with her academic advisor, who also happened to be the assistant dean of the business school. When they started their descent ten minutes later, Camilla was almost disappointed the ride was over so soon.

She told herself the disappointment was due to the thrill of being so high up, and not because she would have to let go of Jordan's firm, warm hand.

Just as promised, there were two luxury SUVs waiting for them at the airfield. Camilla thanked the pilot, and Jordan told him that he'd text when they were ready to head back. Jordan held the door open for her and insisted on carrying her messenger bag with her laptop and notes. When one of the hired drivers opened the back seat door for her, Jordan quickly brushed his lips against hers and said, "See you at lunch."

Despite the chill in the air, she was still fanning herself as they drove toward the campus— in the opposite direction Jordan was heading. Camilla's advisor was running late, which gave her more time to calm her nerves and collect her thoughts. This meeting was only to review how she was doing on her Integrated Project. It wasn't as though Camilla was presenting her work or being graded on anything yet.

Just like with any other teacher, though, Camilla still wanted to be at her best. To have her head in the game and absorb as much information as she could.

The problem was, all she could think about was that parting kiss, which had been just as light as the first, and whether there would be more where that came from when she saw him again at lunch.

Jordan glanced at his cell phone for the eighth time, trying to keep his eyes from glazing over as his distributor in the Missoula office discussed the innovations being made to the refrigeration trucking industry. Normally, when it came to Taylor Beef, Jordan insisted on knowing every aspect of the daily operations that affected his business. But he'd already read the reports beforehand and spoken with the truck manufacturers. He'd also toured the Billings facility just last week. Everything the distributor was saying was already well-ingrained in Jordan's head. He'd already met with the department heads and rushed through the presentations so that he'd be ready to leave the second Camilla said she was done.

When the text finally came, Jordan thanked the people sitting in the conference room for their time and their commitment to Taylor Beef and told the plant director not to bother walking him out.

His driver was already holding the back seat door open when Jordan stepped outside. "Your assistant sent me the address for your lunch reservation, sir. The other driver has already picked up Miss Sanchez and they're on their way."

When they arrived at the restaurant in downtown Missoula, Jordan looked up at the red, white and blue star-spangled sign plastered under the roofline.

"Players?" Jordan mumbled to himself as his head fell against the black leather headrest. This better be a sports bar and not a strip club. Mac had made that mistake once when Jordan had gone on a business trip to New York and one of their junior executive's social media posts had made headlines back in Bronco. He breathed a sigh of relief when he saw that this place had uniforms that actually covered the employees' torsos. Still, as he followed the hostess to something called the MVP Lounge, he renewed his vow to never let Mac make his restaurant reservations again.

"Sorry," he apologized to Camilla when he found her seated at a high-top table. "I had actually wanted to take you to someplace a little more..." He looked around at all the autographed memorabilia and the twenty big-screen TVs mounted on the walls broadcasting several different sporting events at once. "Intimate."

"I actually used to work at a sports bar just like this when I was in college. The tips were always great during playoff season."

"How long have you been a server?" he asked, pulling out one of the bar stools that were shaped like a catcher's mitt. Was he supposed to sit inside this thing and pretend he was a baseball?

Camilla giggled as he wiggled his butt uncomfortably in the weird-shaped seat. When she finally got control of her laughter, she answered, "On and off, about six years."

He did a few calculations in his head. "How old are you?"

"Twenty-seven. Isn't this all stuff we should've gone over on the first date?"

He dropped his chin and gave her his most charming smile. "I thought *this* was our first date."

"No, this is our fourth date," she corrected.

"You can't count some community fundraiser as a date."

"It's pretty telling how you refer to the fanciest gala I've ever attended as a community fundraiser—as though it was a school jog-a-thon or a church bake sale." She passed him a drink menu, which he set aside.

"Whatever you want to call it, that night doesn't count since we had barely even met."

"What about the following night when we had dinner at The Bronco Brick Oven?" she countered. "We even knew each other's real names by then."

"Still not a date." He held up his fingers to

count. "One, it wasn't planned. Two, I was still trying to convince you to go out with me."

Camilla rolled her eyes. "And I suppose dinner with my family didn't count as a date, either?"

"It was more of a date for me and Felix than it was for me and you. After all, I got to know him better than you that evening."

"Next you're going to tell me that our three-week agreement doesn't start until today, either." She leaned her forearms along the edge of the table as she studied him.

Jordan's mouth suddenly went dry, but he wasn't sure if it was from the way she was challenging him or from the way her V-neck sweater now framed the upper curve of her breasts.

"The agreement was six dates in three weeks. So if this is date number one, it also has to be week number one." Jordan tried to look as confident as he could in this ridiculous baseball glove-shaped chair as she playfully narrowed her eyes at him. "Don't blame me. I don't make the rules."

"Oh, it sounds like you make all the rules, Mr. Taylor. The rest of us have to play by them." Her words once again targeted his reputation, or his wealth, or any number of things that Jordan was slowly learning people didn't like about him. She softened the blow by adding, "At least you make the game interesting."

A server came to take their order. When Jordan asked if she wanted to split another pitcher of beer, Camilla replied, "I better not. I have to be at work by four."

After they ordered their iced tea, appetizers, and build-your-own burgers, he asked, "So, don't you want to know how old I am?"

"No, I already know how old you are. I wasn't the one who mistook you for someone else that first night."

"That's right. You know everything there is to know about me." When was he ever going to get her to see the real him, though? He hadn't even been able to be completely honest with her family about his last name, which was an unusual experience for Jordan, who normally was very proud of his family and his work at the company.

"Well, not everything," she admitted when their drinks arrived. "What exactly do you do for your dad?"

"Technically, I *do* work for my family's company, which is equally owned by my father and my uncles, by the way. But contrary to popular belief, I actually had to earn my position. My great-grandfather, the original Cornelius, started the precedent that any Taylor who wanted to be in the family business had to start at an entry-level position."

"So which entry-level position did you start at?" she asked.

"All of them." He saw her sympathetic expression and clarified, "And not because I kept messing up and having to switch departments, either. Obviously, I started in the product development department—which means I shoveled manure for the first year out at Taylor Ranch. Then my Uncle Victor promoted me to herding, which is not quite as glamorous as the old Westerns make it seem. Having a few of my cousins also working out in the pastures with me made for some fun and exciting stories, but I could only be a cowboy for so long before I had to move on to the next stage."

"You say *had to* move on." Camilla took a drink of her iced tea. "Is that another rule for the Taylor offspring?"

"Nope. We're allowed to work wherever we want as long as we start at the bottom. I liked herding, but I liked making business deals more."

"So that's when you started climbing the corporate ladder."

"Not exactly. The summer before I graduated college, I worked in the packing facility, which was my least favorite position for obvious reasons. As soon as I felt I had a good handle on how to raise and, unfortunately, get the cattle ready for distribution, I switched to the communications department. Once I got the hang of that, I moved on to accounting. Then to advertising, human resources, and I even worked with the legal team learning about contracts and negotiations."

"Wow." She blinked several times, her long lashes drawing his attention away from her full lips. "I really wasn't expecting all of that."

"Yeah, well, I guess that's because it's not the most interesting thing the social columns can write about me."

"Fair enough." She lowered her perfectly arched eyebrows. "So what exactly do you do now?"

"I'm vice president of operations. My Uncle Lester created the position for me since I'm one of the few people at Taylor Beef who has experience working in so many departments. My cousins call me the Smoother because whenever a manager or a client has a problem, I can usually get in there and smooth things out."

Camilla gave a chuckle. "Yeah, I'm sure that's not the only thing you're smooth at."

"What can I say?" Jordan shrugged. "It's a gift and a curse. But more of a gift when it comes to the business aspects of my life. So to answer your question, I still do a little of everything at the company, but now I have to go to a lot more meetings."

"Like today with the distributor?" she asked. "How did that go?"

As he answered, he was surprised he could remember everything he and Franco's team had discussed about the truck refrigeration and the updated shipping routes since he'd been distracted the entire time thinking about this upcoming lunch. When he finished, he asked, "Tell me about your meeting with your professor."

"It was the assistant dean, actually. She's my academic advisor for my Integrated Project. At first, I was just going to use the business model for my restaurant as my project, since I'd been working on the idea for years. But the more I got involved developing it, the more I realized that I could actually make this restaurant thing happen. So I was showing her what I'd developed so far."

He kept her talking about her restaurant and she lit up with enthusiasm as she told him about her vision for the location and the dining room layout and the types of food she wanted to serve. Camilla was so knowledgeable and so animated, quickly alternating between eating and talking with her hands, that he didn't see how any investor wouldn't want to throw all their cash at her.

They finished their lunch and Camilla excused herself to use the restroom. When she returned, she asked, "Are you ready to go? My shift starts in a couple of hours and I still need to stop by my apartment and change into my uniform."

"I just need to pay the check," he said, trying to get the attention of the server.

"I already took care of it," Camilla replied.

"When?"

"Before you got here." She pulled the strap of the messenger bag onto her shoulder, then pivoted and headed toward the door.

Catching up with her by the hostess stand, he cocked his head toward the server, who didn't run over to stop them from dining and ditching. "You paid the bill before you even knew what I'd want to order?"

"I guessed that you'd want a burger. The menu advertised the fact that they use Taylor Beef and you seem like a guy who takes quality control very seriously. It would obviously need to be loaded with bacon and cheese and all the toppings since I saw you fill your plate at my parents' house the other night and pile on as much stuff as you could onto such a small circle. Then I accounted for a side salad since you ate half of mine last week at the Brick Oven. I knew I'd want to try several appetizers, because the quality of the appetizers tells you a lot about a restaurant, so there was no guessing there. And you always drink whatever I'm drinking. So, even before you walked through that door, I knew it was going to be $42.83 before tax and tip."

"But why?" He followed her to the waiting car, mentally running through the calculations she'd just ticked off to realize she'd been exactly right.

"Because I work in the food industry and I've made a game out of guessing people's orders based on less information than I already had about you." She thanked the driver and slid across the back seat so Jordan could climb inside.

"No, I mean, why did you pay for the bill in advance?"

"Oh." Her lips spread into a self-satisfied smirk, lighting up her beautiful face in a way that made his rib cage tighten. "Because I also knew that you would try to pay for me, just like you paid for the car service and the helicopter, and dinner at the Brick Oven. Oh, and the wine basket for my dad, which was a nice touch, by the way."

"Well, I told you at the gala that I'd sent him one after his surgery." He shrugged, but the tightening in his chest didn't loosen.

"You mean back when you thought my father was Jose Balthazar?" Her smirk was now a full grin. He loved the way she wasn't afraid to tease him.

Contentment spread through him and he returned her smile. "I figured since you weren't going to let me forget about my mistake, I might as well follow through on that."

"Well, my dad loved it, so well played. Anyway, I didn't want you always paying for everything and I certainly didn't want to get into a standoff with you about it when the bill came. So I prepaid before you got the chance to outnegotiate me again. You're welcome."

She was right. He definitely would have insisted on paying for her lunch and she had been wise enough to cut him off before he even had the opportunity.

"I'm trying to remember the last time a woman bought me a meal," he finally said as he stared at her in amazement. "Thank you."

"It was my pleasure," she said, and his mind spent the rest of the ride thinking about all the other ways he'd like to bring her pleasure.

Once inside the helicopter for the return trip to Bronco, Camilla again reached for his hand during takeoff, but most of her attention was on the view from the window. Not only could he not remember the last time someone had paid for his restaurant bill, he also couldn't remember the last time he'd paid so much attention to the world below the propellers. Had Jordan really gotten so accustomed to luxury air travel that he'd forgotten to look away from his phone or his laptop during the flights? That he'd forgotten what it was like to sit back and simply enjoy the scenery?

Before they arrived back at the airfield, Jordan already knew that he wasn't going to be able to wait until after the weekend to see Camilla again. He said as much when he was walking her to her car.

"What are you doing tomorrow morning?" he asked, hoping he didn't sound as desperate as he felt.

"Laundry."

"Great." He opened her car door. "My last stepmother gave me this square tool that folds shirts perfectly. You should see my closet. It's an ode to organization and color-coded stacks. I'll bring it over and help you."

She sucked her lower lip between her teeth before answering. "Jordan, my studio apartment is probably the same size as your closet."

He knew she was baiting him again about the differences in their bank accounts, but he wasn't going to fall for it. "If this is your way of asking me back to your place so we can compare sizes, I'll gladly borrow a tape measure from one of the flight mechanics over there."

Lifting his eyebrows, he leaned in closer, and she playfully pushed him back. But instead of letting go, she kept her hands on his shoulders. "Don't you think it's a little too soon for you to come back to my place?"

"Nope," he said honestly, his deltoid muscles flexing impulsively under her touch. "But I would never push for an invite. You can have me over whenever you're ready."

"You know," she said, her thumbs driving him crazy with featherlight circles against his shirt, "when we negotiated our three-week deal, we never agreed to any of those terms you add in fine print at the end of the contract."

"So this thing between us is a business contract now?" Jordan tilted his head closer, careful not to lean forward too much and dislodge her mesmerizing hands.

Camilla shrugged one shoulder. "Well, I have a head for business and you have a head for business. So maybe it would keep things from getting too complicated if we set out our expectations ahead of time."

He glanced at her palms, which had strayed from his shoulders to his chest and were rising and falling with each steadying breath he took. "In that case, if you're going to distract me while we negotiate, I think it's only fair that I get the same advantage."

Matching her light pressure, Jordan placed his own hands on either side of her waist. He heard her quick intake of air, but she took a step toward him and asked, "So, we agree that this is date one out of six?"

"I'll concede that. For now." He already knew

that he'd want way more than six dates, but he still had time to convince her. "As long as you concede that the contract can always be extended upon mutual agreement."

She shook her head lightly, her hair rippling down her back as she smiled indulgently. "We'll see. Now what exactly constitutes a date? How do we define it?"

He looked up to the sky briefly before settling his gaze on her. "It should probably involve us spending time together. Alone."

"We haven't been alone today at all. We've either been in public or with drivers and pilots."

"I mean where we can have semiprivate, one-on-one conversations. And we should probably add that it needs to involve a full meal, since we both enjoy eating."

"If we're seen together in public too much, people are going to start talking."

He slid his hands behind her back, pulling her closer. "So let them talk."

Camilla let out a deep breath, as though he should already know full well all the reasons why she might not want to be seen with him. "So dates need to consist of semiprivate conversations and a meal. Anything else?"

"We should probably include some sort of physical contact, just so we can differentiate it as a date as opposed to a business meeting."

"Define physical contact." She was softly stroking the skin between his hairline and his collar, and he didn't think he could define anything if she kept touching him like that.

"Well…" He drew her even closer as he studied her turned-up face. "We should probably hold hands, maybe put our arms around each other on occasion."

"Like this?" she asked, her chest rising as it brushed against his own.

His pulse picked up speed. "Oh, we should definitely touch each other like this. And…"

"And?" Her heavy gaze slid to his lips.

"And we should obviously finish off with a goodbye kiss," he suggested.

Camilla didn't give Jordan the chance to simply get by with one of those soft, restraining kisses he'd teased her with in the past, though.

No, she rose up on her toes and pressed her mouth eagerly against his. The pressure of her firm lips opening beneath his filled him with a heady thrill that he didn't think could be matched. That was, not until she used her tongue to tentatively stroke against his as he welcomed her inside.

She settled her arms on his shoulders and cupped her hands behind his neck. His hands at her waist kept her close to him, but as he deepened the kiss, she arched against him.

Hearing her soft moan made his blood riot through his veins, but it also reminded him that they were in danger of going much further if one of them didn't stop soon. When he pulled away, he was slightly dazed and could feel his heartbeat thumping as though he'd just outridden a bull at his first rodeo.

"Like that?" she asked, her breathing coming in little pants.

"Exactly like that," he confirmed. "Although, I have a feeling that we just set the bar extremely high for our future goodbye kisses. I'll have my work cut out for me to match that level of wow on every single date. But I'm willing to keep trying until I get it right."

Her rib cage expanded above his grip as she shuddered. Then she straightened in his arms. "Like I said before, you're pretty good at everything you do. I don't think it's going to take much more practice."

His stomach tightened in anticipation at the thought of those practice sessions. There was no way he'd be happy with only six of these kisses.

He would definitely need to up their negotiations on the next date.

Chapter Five

"I don't think this counts as one of our dates," Jordan told Camilla on Saturday morning as they stood at the industrial-sized sink in the kitchen of the Bronco Valley Fire Station, washing multiple mixing bowls filled with pancake batter and a stack of syrup-covered dishes.

"Why not?" She laughed when he held a spatula the wrong way under the faucet and sent a spray of water right below his nose. "We're currently having a semiprivate conversation and there was a meal."

She hadn't taken him up on his offer to fold laundry together yesterday because no good would've come from it. At least she could tell herself that today they were actually giving back to the community.

"Serving the pancake breakfast at your brother's First Responders fundraiser doesn't count as a meal if we don't get to eat it ourselves," Jordan replied.

Ever since their goodbye kiss two days ago at the airfield, Camilla hadn't been able to stop thinking about the way his mouth had turned her completely inside out. Even now she could barely take her eyes off his lips. She used a dish towel to mop up the water sticking to the dark stubble along his jawline. "Volunteers eat *after* their shift."

"Good, because I'm starved."

Camilla tried not to drool over his biceps in that snug-fitting T-shirt, but he was up to his elbows in sudsy water and she was having a difficult time looking anywhere else. Besides his lips, which were also off-limits right now. In fact, she knew there was no way she could trust herself to actually be alone with him. That was why she'd suggested their next date be somewhere as public as possible.

Everyone from the Valley still came to the annual First Responders pancake breakfast, even when the station had moved to the new location near City Hall in Bronco Heights. Especially when they heard Jordan Taylor would be the one serving them. Actually, she didn't know for certain that word got out about Jordan being here, but when a group of young female teachers from Dante's school asked him to pose for a selfie with them, Camilla suddenly became aware of the fact that this was one of the largest turnouts she could remember in years.

She hadn't exactly accounted for any of those factors when she'd first promised Jordan that they could just eat pancakes with everyone else. Yet by the time Camilla and Jordan dried the last bowl, Felix had already turned off the griddle and there wasn't a pancake left in sight.

Jordan surveyed the spotless kitchen. "Looks like you still owe me a meal."

Working a volunteer shift with Jordan could be passed off as a charitable coincidence if people happened to spot them talking to each other. But if everyone saw them sharing breakfast at the diner next door, people in town would definitely start talking. It was already bad enough some of her friends had texted her with screenshots of the Denim and Diamonds gala Facebook page, which had posted pictures of Camilla and Jordan dancing together. The more people who suspected they were actually dating meant more people would know when Jordan eventually dumped her.

"We could grab a doughnut and a coffee at the bakery next door," she suggested.

Jordan pursed his lips playfully before slowly shaking his head. "Nope. The terms of our agreement were for a full meal. Only a five-year-old would consider an apple fritter to be a full meal."

"Fine." Camilla sighed. "My apartment is only a few minutes away. I'll cook you breakfast, but the goodbye kiss takes place outside."

"You don't trust yourself to kiss me again in private?" He slid his lower lip between his straight white teeth, and the wobbly feeling in Camilla's legs made her realize that she was perfectly justified in not trusting herself around the man in public, either. But she wouldn't admit as much.

"I'm just outlining the fine print, remember?"

"Got it. Does it say anything in there about me getting to keep this apron?" he asked.

She looked at the damp T-shirt sticking to his torso underneath. Maybe it was a better idea for him to keep as many layers on as possible. "No, but I think the fire station will give you a sweatshirt in exchange for a small donation."

She'd make the donation herself if it would stop her from staring at his broad shoulders in that thin cotton fabric.

Leaving the fire station, they only had to

drive a short distance to her apartment, a studio on the second floor of the Bronco Post Office. Many of the government agencies had been relocated to the Heights recently, but since the post office was a federal building, Aaron Sanchez had led the charge on keeping his workplace on this side of town.

As they exited their respective cars parked below her apartment, she realized that Jordan almost looked...normal. He wasn't wearing his designer tux or his tailored work shirts or his expensive hand-tooled cowboy boots. Instead, his faded jeans, sneakers and recently purchased blue hooded sweatshirt with the BFD logo proudly displayed on his chest made Jordan Taylor appear as though he actually belonged here in Bronco Valley.

It probably would have been safer for her to see him totally shirtless.

Camilla had no business thinking that someone like him would ever simply fit into her life. Something would eventually go wrong and he'd move back to his own world. The threat of impending disaster settled on her shoulders as she led him up the steps to her apartment.

Nevertheless, she persisted.

Her fingers trembled as she unlocked the door. The excitement of being this close to him made her lightheaded, thereby counteracting the emotional weight of her decision to invite him inside.

Contrary to what she'd boldly assumed at the airfield the other day, Camilla's studio apartment *was* in fact bigger than Jordan's walk-in closet back at the ranch house. But not by much, he calculated.

Jordan sat on one of the chairs at the tiny table in the corner between her kitchen and a blue upholstered love seat crammed with too many throw pillows to accommodate one full-sized human, let alone two.

"How do you pronounce it again?" he asked before shoveling another bite of well-done eggs into his mouth.

"*Chilequiles*. There's lots of variations, but this one is fried corn tortillas smothered in cheese and my dad's homemade salsa. This is one of my grandma's recipes that I'm toying with for my restaurant. It's much better when the egg on top is sunny side up, but broken yolks are my cross to bear."

"It's perfect," he insisted before taking another huge bite and letting the flavors of tomato and spices and tortilla come together in his mouth.

"Don't look so impressed." Camilla sat across from him, but the table was so narrow, their knees kept bumping underneath. "I rarely have time to grocery shop, and this particular recipe requires the fewest amount of ingredients and the least amount of skill. I don't really cook, even when it's my turn on Sunday evenings with my parents. I'm usually in charge of kitchen prep and I've picked up a few tricks when it comes to plating the food. But this is about as far as my expertise goes."

"You might not want to mention that to the future investors of your restaurant. Aren't world famous chefs the trend right now?" he asked.

"I don't want trendy. I want good service and great food. A place where people can go on a first date or on a seventeenth date. Special, but also ordinary, if that makes any sense."

Jordon shook his head. "There is nothing ordinary about you."

"That all depends on how you define it. If I were to come visit you at *your* house, I suppose that I would stick out like a sore thumb." She speared a mound of tortillas and egg on her fork. "But here in Bronco Valley, I assure you that I am very ordinary."

Like the Sanchez home, Camilla's apartment was stuffed with books—both business-related and an array of fiction paperbacks—and framed family photos that were not staged by professional photographers. Not everything matched, but it was clean and interesting and full of her personality. The main house on the Taylor Ranch was also full of history and personality, but not quite the same amount of warmth. At least not anymore. When Jordan, Brandon and Daphne were little, Cornelius had been a busy, yet doting single father who'd hung up his children's artwork on the fridge and didn't mind bicycles and footballs left on the front lawn. But then his kids got older and his wives got younger and a team of interior decorators convinced the patriarch of the family that his home should reflect his standing in the community.

Yet that didn't mean Camilla couldn't be equally as comfortable at the ranch. After all, the Taylor home was at its best when it was filled with people, like it had been the night he'd met her.

"I highly doubt you would stick out at my house." Jordan said. "In fact, you've already been there and as I recall, you fit in quite well."

She crossed her arms over her chest. "That was before you knew who I was."

"But *you* knew who you were and you seemed to be having a good time," he said.

"Going to a massive party in a tent on your property is a lot different than going inside your actual home."

"Prove it," he suggested.

"Prove it to who? I already know what will happen."

"Prove it to me. When's your next day off?"

"Tomorrow." Camilla narrowed her gaze. "Why?"

"Because I want you to come out to the ranch and let me show you around. It's actually the best time to visit because most of the employees have the day off, so it's usually just the family there. It's the perfect time to show up and just be yourself."

"Fine. But make sure the private chef leaves us something to eat so it can count as one of our dates."

"You don't think I can cook something for you?" he challenged her.

"Can you?" She lifted one brow.

"I can if it involves meat and bread and sandwich toppings."

"With that kind of promise, how do I say no?"

For the second time that day, he helped her wash the dishes, even though this kitchen was barely big enough for them to stand side by side, which he actually preferred.

Her apartment was so comfortable and so inviting, he wanted to kick back on her love seat and settle in for an afternoon nap while she studied, then later watch her get ready for her shift tonight at DJ's. But Jordan knew better than to wear out his welcome. He wanted to leave her wanting more.

"I guess I better take off so you can get to work," he said, balling up the wet dishcloth in his hand.

"I'll walk you to the door," she offered.

"Only to the door?" He lifted the corner of his mouth. So maybe he didn't want to leave her wanting *that* much more. "What about that goodbye kiss being in public?"

"It's probably not a good idea to do it where everyone can see us." Her brow was furrowed as though she was seriously contemplating it. "How about right outside my door? It overlooks the side alley and there shouldn't be too many people passing through there."

He followed her outside to the small balcony landing, where the stairs led to a parking area below with her Toyota and two postal trucks. The second she turned around, he didn't wait for her to make the first move.

This time he kissed *her*, pulling her in close as he cupped his hand around her neck, cradling her head. He'd let her lead on that kiss yesterday, using every ounce of his control to hold himself still as she explored his mouth. Now he was returning the favor.

His tongue stroked and caressed and promised that he was more than capable of filling her every need. In response, she pressed her body to his, straining against him as she let out a soft gasp followed by an even deeper moan. Hearing her sounds of desire only heightened Jordan's already growing arousal. It was obvious that if they continued, he'd soon have her against the open door frame. Blood was pounding in both his ears and his lower extremities when he finally pulled his mouth away and rested his forehead against hers.

It took several seconds of controlled breathing for him to trust himself to open his eyes and look at her. Satisfaction filled his chest as he noted her dilated pupils. It took more patience than he thought he possessed to not pull her in for another kiss. Instead, he asked, "So, we'll continue this tomorrow?"

"Maybe not *all* of this," she replied, then tentatively touched her full lips. "I've got to practice some restraint."

He put his finger under her chin, forcing her to meet his eyes. "Don't restrain yourself on my account. I like you just the way you are."

"That's what I'm afraid of," she murmured, then stepped backward and closed her front door.

Jordan's eyes took inventory of the house that resembled a five-star dude ranch rather than an actual residence where real people lived. Hell, compared to Camilla's apartment, this place felt like a damn museum.

He'd grown up here and it had always felt just like…well…home. It was all he knew. Wait. That wasn't exactly correct. The "kids wing," which contained the original bedrooms, felt like home because they were the least changed rooms in the house. It was also the area, other than the office building, where Jordan spent the most time.

When Cornelius divorced his first wife, he'd hired an architect and a general contractor to expand the floorplan. He'd said that it was high time to update their home, but Daphne had told her brothers that it felt like their dad was trying to erase his past with their mother. When he met his second wife, he'd brought in an interior decorator to showcase some cooked-up vision of a "modern Western vibe"—whatever that meant. After a second divorce, Cornelius hired a different interior decorator to redo the house, and soon a habit was formed. Every time Jordan's father suffered some sort of break-up or emotional setback, the old man added onto the house—making it grander than before—as a way of reaffirming his family's heritage and, in his mind, his value.

If Jordan wanted to convince Camilla that he was no different from her, then the formal entry was not the place to welcome her to his family home. He could invite her straight into his bedroom, the least ostentatious of all the rooms, but that might give her the impression that he was trying to seduce her. That left only one other choice.

Crossing the stately front porch, he headed across the circular gravel driveway and kept himself busy inside the stables as he waited for her arrival.

After their intense kiss yesterday, he'd gone straight to his office and buried himself in the latest reports on increasing the sustainable energy resources at all the Taylor Beef packing facilities. He'd been in need of an outlet to redirect his own energy, and going to work kept him from thinking about Camilla's lips and how they'd matched his so perfectly. The distraction had worked for the first hour. The rest of the night had been a struggle to focus on anything but her.

He was closing the paddock gate when he heard her engine shut off, and a thrill shot through him. She exited her car wearing faded jeans that perfectly hugged her curves in all the right spots, an old pair of tan cowboy boots, and a hooded sweatshirt that said University of Montana.

"You were right," she said as he walked around the fencing toward her. "This place certainly looks different without the huge party tent and all the cars. Where is everyone?"

"My dad and Jessica are at church, which is usually followed by brunch at the Association. I have no idea where my brother, Brandon, is."

"Only four of you live here?" At first she sounded amazed. Yet, there was no missing the teasing in her tone when she nodded at the house on the other side of the driveway and said, "Are you sure there's enough room for everyone?"

"Well, we also have employees who live on-site." He didn't admit that the stable hands stayed in the bunkhouse and the household staff had private quarters not attached to the main house. "But most of them have today off."

"Where are your uncles and their families? I thought all the Taylors lived on the compound."

"My dad, being the oldest, inherited the main house, and then each brother got their own corner of the ranch for their family spreads. We could spend the entire day exploring the property and still not run into any of them."

Camilla let out a small whistle. "Quite the kingdom. Is this the part where you impress me by showing me around?"

"No. I already know you won't be impressed by any of that. This is the part where I see if you can saddle your own horse. Did you borrow those boots?"

"Unlike the last time I came here, these particular shoes are actually my own." She stomped some dirt off one of the heels. "My dad grew up around horses in a small town outside of Guadalajara. He insisted that if his children were going to grow up in Montana, then they needed to know how to ride. We spent summers on my uncle's ranch in Jalisco and, during the rest of the year, all of us kids took lessons when my parents could afford it. In fact, not to toot my own horn, but I even did some barrel racing in high school and was the junior rodeo queen at the Bronco State Fair back in the day."

"Really?" He shook his head as she surprised him once again. "My family sponsors the Future Farmers of America building at that fair every year."

"I know." Her pointed look conveyed the unspoken words. Everyone knew who he was, yet he didn't have a clue who most of them were. Had he really been that out of touch with his own community?

"I've never been riding with a high school rodeo star before," he said, not regretting his decision to meet her away from the unrelatable wealth and privilege of the main house. "I better get you on a horse to prove you've still got it."

The challenge was exactly what Camilla needed to turn her attention away from the nonstop thoughts of continuing yesterday's kiss. Or of how amazing Jordan looked in that gray cow-boy hat. It was no surprise that he obviously belonged on this ranch just as much as he be-longed in the board room. It was getting harder and harder to prove that their worlds were too different when the man was like a damn chame-leon fitting in everywhere he went.

She followed him into the stables and stood on the lower rungs of a stall as he saddled the horses he'd already chosen for them to ride. "Do they have names?"

He stroked the white mare's nose just above her bridle. "This little beauty is Leia, named after the princess, obviously."

"And I'm guessing the black stallion is named Darth?" she asked. "After the guy with the mask and the red light saber?"

"Actually, it's Palpatine, after the emperor of the dark side." Jordan handed her a set of reins. "I bet your social media sources didn't tell you I was such a big *Star Wars* fan, did they?"

"Wait." She took a cautious breath while try-ing not to compare the size differences between the two animals as she walked between them. "I'm riding the big black stallion and *you're* tak-ing the smaller female horse?"

"Don't let his name fool you. Palp is a real sweetheart and will go anywhere you ask. Leia, on the other hand—" the white mare snorted at

Jordan and then pranced to the side as he tried to lead her out of the stable "—is exactly like her namesake. A real rebel, aren't you, girl?"

Camilla used the stirrup to mount the stallion easily enough despite how high off the ground she was. It took Jordan two tries and some sweet talking before Leia finally let him on her back. There was a whole stable full of animals he could ride, yet he insisted on taking the one who would give him the most trouble. Because of course he would.

As they rode their horses to the dirt trail heading east, Camilla took another glance over her shoulder at the house that didn't look any smaller from this distance. "Your parents must love the fact that you still live at home."

Jordan adjusted his hat. "It's just what we Taylors do. It's practically ingrained in us from birth. We work in the family business and live in the family home until we get married. I mean, not Daphne, of course, because she's smarter than all of us. But every other Taylor for the past several generations has done it."

"My parents are the same way. Minus the global family business part, obviously. But if they could've kept all of us at home, they would have. As you saw, though, our house is a bit more cramped than this one. By the time I finished college, I was too accustomed to living on my own and, even though it would've saved me a ton in rent money, I resisted their attempts to entice me back home. Although, it's such a small town I end up running into someone from my family pretty much every day. So it still kinda feels as though we all live together."

She watched his face beneath the brim of his hat, but he kept staring off straight ahead. "When my dad and Jessica first got married a couple of years ago, it seemed like the perfect time to move out. To give the newlyweds their space and all that. But then Daphne beat me to the punch and I didn't want Jessica to feel like we were all leaving because of her."

"So she's not the evil stepmother?" Camilla asked. Thankfully, Palpatine was docile enough that she could hold the reins loosely.

Jordan, on the other hand, kept a tighter hold on Leia, who kept sidestepping toward them, all but challenging the stallion to go faster. "Nah, she's nice enough and means well. But she tries too hard to please my dad instead of putting him in his place. It's like those signs at the campgrounds near Yellowstone Park warning people not to feed the bears because it only makes the bears more bold and more dependent on having their needs met. Jessica is the inexperienced camper who feeds the bear."

"Interesting analogy." Camilla appreciated the

fact that Jordan wasn't badmouthing the woman, even though many in his position could resent the fact that their father was married to someone so much younger. "But even more interesting is the fact that you've been to a campground."

"I'm not so pampered that I haven't been camping," he told her.

She gestured at the full trees and rolling green hills surrounding them. "No, I mean, why would you go to a campground when you have the great outdoors in your own backyard?"

Leia seemed to want to pick up speed and Camilla didn't believe in taming anyone or anything's spirit. So she nudged Palpatine faster and they cantered beside each other until they reached the crest of a hill that overlooked the house and several miles of pastures, which probably only represented half the Taylor holdings.

She was so blown away by the view that Camilla sighed. "Your ranch is truly beautiful."

He nodded, for once agreeing with her. "Obviously, I can't take credit for something I was born into. But I do love living here. Whenever my old man was going through a divorce or had a business deal fall through, being able to saddle a horse and get away on a ride was one of the few things that made living in his shadow bearable."

"If it's so frustrating living with your dad and working with him, why don't you take a page out of Daphne's book and move out? Surely Jessica would understand by now that it's not her."

"I've thought about it. Many times. In fact, lately I've been toying with the idea of getting a place in BH247—you know, that new condo complex in Bronco Heights—for no other reason than to stand in solidarity with Daph so she's not the only Taylor living off the ranch. I could even start a ranch of my own, but that would really send my father over the edge. And as overbearing as he can be, I do love him and don't want to be the one responsible for giving him high blood pressure. Besides, when I'm not at the office, I have the eastern suite of rooms to myself and a full-time cook and housekeeper to take care of everything else. If you ever meet my assistant, Mac, you will believe me when I say I hate hiring new staff."

"Gee. Only the eastern suite to yourself? How do you even manage?" she asked sarcastically with a friendly undertone. Instead of being properly chastised, though, he flashed those dimples and wiggled his dark eyebrows.

"See? You're the only person I've dated who will tell me things straight, no sugarcoating. I need that kind of honesty in my life, Camilla." Leia snorted, then whinnied, as though in agreement. "This is why you're good for me."

"Maybe so." She turned Palpatine around,

ready to let the antsy white mare beside them finally have the run she'd been itching for. As she took off racing, Camilla added to herself, "That doesn't mean you're any good for me."

Chapter Six

As they returned from the ride, Camilla saw the luxury car parked next to her older model compact sedan. Her heart rate had already been elevated from the fast pace Jordan and his mare had set. But when she saw who was sitting inside the vehicle, her pulse skipped a few beats. And not in a good way.

She caught the slight crease on Jordan's forehead before he managed to quickly wipe it away. He let out a breath, and kept his horse moving forward. "Looks like they skipped brunch, after all."

Cornelius Taylor and his much younger wife

were exiting the vehicle as they rode up, and Camilla's stomach twisted into a thousand knots. She expected Jordan to avoid the couple by cutting behind the corral and riding toward the rear of the stables. But he continued toward the driveway, giving her no choice but to follow.

Jordan dismounted first, which allowed Camilla to hear Jessica whisper to a squinting Cornelius, "I think it's one of Jordan's lady friends."

The older man apparently needed glasses more than he wanted to admit because with his wife's explanation, his face went from slightly annoyed to almost welcoming, and Camilla immediately wondered if he was about to put on an act for a visiting guest.

"Dad. Jessica." Jordan greeted each of them as Camilla dismounted by awkwardly sliding down Palpatine's very tall frame. "I don't know if you remember Camilla from the Denim and Diamonds fundraiser the other night?"

"Of course." Cornelius smiled at her, his perfectly set teeth very square and very white. "You're Jose's daughter."

"No, Dad. This is Camilla Sanchez, not Balthazar."

"I'm Aaron and Denise's daughter," Camilla felt obliged to point out to this man, who seemed to take so much stock in family legacies.

"Of course," Cornelius said with a confident

nod, although Camilla was certain he didn't have a clue who her parents were.

Nobody said anything for a few awkward moments and then Jessica, probably in an attempt to break the tension, said to Camilla, "I really loved the dress you wore to the gala. The gold one? Several people commented on a picture of it on my social media post asking who the designer was."

"Oh. Thank you. I…um…don't really remember." Which was truthful enough without admitting that she'd actually borrowed the dress.

The silence stretched between them again and Camilla pressed her lips together as she prayed that Jordan wasn't suddenly regretting inviting her to the ranch. Seeing Jordan around his family would be much more eye-opening than seeing him around hers. She hoped he wouldn't start acting like a kid who'd been caught with his hand in the cookie jar. The good news was, his face certainly didn't show a trace of shame. But then again, it never did.

"So, you're back from church early," Jordan finally said.

"Your father thought today's sermon on forgiveness was—" Jessica started, but Cornelius used his elbow to lightly nudge her arm.

"The sermon was so boring I could barely stay awake. It didn't help that Jessica kept me up half the night watching those home decorating reality shows she loves. You know how women are, son. You can give them all this—" he spread out his arms to encompass the massive house "—but still they want more."

Thankfully, Jordan didn't admit that he in fact knew how women were. Nor did he display an ounce of guilt for bringing a commoner like her to the Taylors' royal palace. His smile was polite, despite the fact that it lacked all his usual charm. "I was just about to invite Camilla inside and make her a sandwich. Would you like to join us?"

Camilla glanced down in time to see Cornelius briefly squeeze his wife's hand. She gave her husband a reassuring pat on the arm. "Actually, we should both probably have a little rest."

"Nice meeting you, Carol," Cornelius said before turning toward the front door.

"Dad, it's *Camilla*," Jordan corrected him. "Jeez."

He took off his hat to run his hand through his hair and probably didn't see Jessica mouth the word *sorry* to Camilla before following her husband.

"Well, that was awkward," Jordan offered, staring at the older man walking away. "My dad is usually way more charming. He must have really hated that sermon on forgiveness, especially since the minister's wife volunteers regularly at Daphne's animal sanctuary."

Camilla didn't want to point out that Cornelius Taylor's rift with his daughter hadn't kept him from smiling at his unexpected guest until *after* he'd found out that Camilla wasn't in fact related to the Balthazars. That was when the older man stopped any pretense of being charming. However, pointing out such a thing would only compel Jordan to attempt to prove her wrong, which would in turn bring more attention to an already awkward situation. So she just kept quiet as she walked her horse toward the stables to cool him down and give him some water.

Jordan, with Leia in tow, caught up to them. "I can understand why you wouldn't want to come inside for a sandwich now. Why don't I drive you into town and we can grab something to eat?"

Camilla stretched her back. It'd been a while since she'd ridden a horse, and she still needed to do some errands and even a bit of homework before dinner at her parents' house tonight.

"Maybe we should just call it a day."

"Sure, if you want." Jordan's agreement came a bit too readily as he tethered his mare to a post near a water trough. "But if we don't eat, then it doesn't count as a date."

So *that* was his game. She gave a snort of disbelief before picking up a currying brush. "Remind me how we came to the conclusion that our dates have to include food?"

"Because you like food?" He smiled at her.

"Do you want to rephrase that?"

"Why?" He dumped some oats into a hanging bucket for Leia, who immediately began chomping. "This old gal likes food, too. It's nothing to be ashamed of."

Camilla watched him caress the horse's silky nose as he murmured sweet words to her. A ping of envy darted through her as she thought about the way his very capable hands had similarly stroked her yesterday during their goodbye kiss.

She wasn't actually jealous of a horse, was she?

Leia, probably like many females before her, abandoned her treat to nuzzle against Jordan's hand. Well, Camilla certainly wouldn't be like the contrary mare and choose a little physical affection over a good lunch.

"That's because food is more reliable than men." She made eye contact with the horse, who continued to nuzzle against Jordan, refusing to be shamed. Camilla pointed a finger at the mare. "If you ever had the cornbread slathered in homemade honey butter they serve over at the BBQ Barn, you'd know that already."

Jordan laughed. "Looks like we're going to the BBQ Barn, then."

* * *

"So, what do you have planned after this?" Jordan asked when Camilla wiped her hands on a paper napkin from the dispenser. Instead of handing her another one, he used his thumb to wipe the tangy sauce off her cheek. He would've used his tongue if there wasn't anyone else in the restaurant.

"I'm supposed to go to my parents' house tonight. But after all those ribs, who has room for dinner?"

He looked at his watch, not quite ready to say goodbye. "I mean between now and then?"

"A nap sounds good." She pushed away from the wooden picnic-style table. "But I'm worried that if I fall asleep now, I'll end up in a food coma and won't wake up until tomorrow."

"So then it's up to me to keep you moving and alert. How about a basketball game?" he asked.

She held her still flat stomach and groaned. "Are you crazy? I *feel* like a basketball that just got slam-dunked."

"Not to play," he laughed. "To watch. My assistant is filling in as a substitute youth coach over at the rec center and she has a game today. It would mean a lot if we came out and supported her."

"You know, my dad is the ref for those basketball games. Or at least he was. He took off this season because of his bunion surgery. He's been telling our neighbors all about that wine basket, by the way. He didn't earn any points with Mrs. Waters when he told her it was way more therapeutic than her casseroles."

"I'll have to send him another one, then. Maybe one to Mrs. Waters, as well."

She rolled her eyes. He was getting used to the gesture whenever she wanted to convey that he was being over the top.

Before she could give him another excuse about being busy, he stood up and grabbed their plastic trays. "Come on. I'll drive."

She hadn't wanted to leave her car at the ranch, so he'd followed her into Bronco Valley and found a parking space a few rows away in the lot outside of the restaurant that was actually housed in an old barn. But now that they were so close to their next destination, there was no sense in taking both cars.

"Didn't there used to be a library here?" he asked as they drove by a single-story building that looked to be abandoned. "I remember having to do a report in middle school on the founders of Bronco, and my dad's secretary brought me over here to do research."

"I practically lived at that library when I was a kid." When Camilla smiled, it was contagious. "We would walk there after school and do our homework and read until my mom got off work. But then the city council voted to move all the government buildings—except the wastewater treatment plant, obviously—closer to Bronco Heights, where all the new developments were going in. They thought it made the town look more inviting. A group of us kids in the neighborhood protested, but you know the golden rule."

"What's the golden rule?" Jordan asked as he made a right turn.

"The guys with the gold make the rules." She slid her sunglasses onto her face, but not before he caught a glimpse of the defeat in her eyes. "After they moved all the books, a group of teens decided to throw a party in the abandoned building. The bonfire got out of control and did quite a bit of internal damage. It looks fine on the outside so nobody is complaining about it being an eyesore. The city council doesn't want to spend the money to make any repairs to the inside, not that anyone is offering to buy it since everyone seems to be building their businesses in the Heights now. So it's been sitting vacant for a while."

"How do I not know about this fire?" he asked, tapping his fingers on the steering wheel. "And before you say that I'm out of touch with our community, I'll have you know that I do pay attention to the news, and I think something like that would've at least made the papers."

"My brother Felix was one of the kids. He was still in high school at the time. He's thirty now, so that means you were probably away at college when it happened."

"Still. As a local businessman, I go to city council meetings a few times a year and never saw..." His surprise gave way to an underlying sense of shame as he realized what should've been obvious before now. "Hell. I can't believe I haven't noticed the town having a new library over in that complex."

They were at a four-way stop, and Camilla lifted up her sunglasses as she faced him. "Jordan, when was the last time you actually *went* to the library?"

The truck behind them honked, so Jordan was forced to return his eyes to the road. He had no idea if she was teasing him or not. "I actually went to library on my college campus once or twice to study."

"Yeah, well, the people in the Valley used this library more than once or twice. Some of them actually depended on it for after-school programs and the free tutoring and even internet access. Now if they want to go to the library, they have to find a way to get to the Heights.

The people with the most need for it now have less access to it."

Wow. His shoulders sagged and his throat felt thick and heavy. While he'd recently appreciated seeing the world through Camilla's eyes, up until now, he'd focused on the simple pleasures he took for granted. He hadn't wanted to give much thought to the necessities in life that he'd also taken for granted.

He pointed to one of the town's original buildings with weathered wood siding painted a shocking shade of bubble gum pink. "At least Cubby's is still here. We used to go there for malts and triple-decker sundaes after football games on Fridays nights."

"So did we!" Camilla smiled again, and Jordan's world suddenly righted itself. "It's still a madhouse on Friday nights. Especially when the high school has a home game. I think the Cubbison family got it approved as a historical monument, so the town has to keep it now."

They passed the market where the checker kept the extra mangos behind the register, then her mom's salon, which was one of the more modern-looking buildings in this neighborhood. He ran his hand through his hair. "Your mom didn't have time for me last week, so I had to schedule an appointment for Wednesday."

"I know. She told me all about it, probably

in the hopes I'll come help her at the shampoo bowl."

"You're a hairdresser, too?" Jordan asked, though at this point he wouldn't be shocked. He'd already found out that she was an MBA student, a restaurant entrepreneur, an amazing dancer and a rodeo queen.

"No. But when she was first starting out, she used to pay me and my brothers five bucks on Saturdays to ride our bikes over to the salon after we finished our chores so that we could help her sweep up hair and fold towels. She's built her business up a lot since then and has several stylists working for her now. But she still keeps our bikes in the garage and often reminds us that if we ever need to make a few extra dollars, we can pedal on over."

"It must've been nice to be able to ride everywhere." He pulled into the parking lot at the rec center. "Growing up, we always felt like we were stuck out on the ranch."

"Jordan, I was just on your ranch. I saw all the trails and the heated swimming pool. If the stable full of horses wasn't enough to get you from place to place, you also have ATVs." Camilla put her hand to her chest in a dramatic fashion. "Please tell me what a hardship it was to be stuck out there as a kid."

"I'm not saying it wasn't nice," Jordan corrected himself. After that conversation about the library, he knew he didn't have room for complaints. "I'm just saying we didn't have any neighbors nearby. We were kinda stuck out there unless we were at school. We couldn't just hop on a bike and go to our friends' houses. Or walk down to Cubby's to get a frozen cherry slush on a hot day. Even going to see one of my cousins was a hike. You haven't met Brandon yet, but trust me, there's only so much fun you can have on the ranch when you have to drag your little brother around with you everywhere."

Camilla laughed. "Well, I was the younger sibling getting dragged. Both my parents worked, so one of my brothers usually got stuck with me and Sofia. Instead of drawing straws, they'd shoot baskets. Felix usually lost."

"That's because Felix needs to lay off those three-pointers."

"Not when he has you rebounding them." She gave him a light kiss before getting out of the car.

The youth league game was already underway when they walked inside the stuffy gymnasium and headed toward the bleachers. Jordan didn't need to look for Mac on the opposite side of the hardwood court. Everyone could hear her since she was yelling way louder than anyone was cheering.

"Oh, no," Camilla said when they found some open seats.

"What's wrong?"

She pointed at her dad in the black-and-white-striped referee jersey using one of those wheeled knee walkers like a kid on a Razor scooter, zooming up and down the court as he weaved his way through the young players. "He promised my mom he wouldn't ref any more games until his doctor cleared him."

Mr. Sanchez stopped long enough to blow his whistle at Mac. "That's a warning, Coach. Watch the language from the sidelines. These are kids playing, not pros."

He zipped away on his knee scooter and Mac made a gesture at his back, which drew several gasps from the parents in the stands. Jordan scrubbed his hand over the lower half of his face to keep from laughing.

Camilla nodded toward the tall, thin woman on the green team's bench. The one with the blond ponytail, sporty yoga pants and sweatshirt printed with the words Team Work Makes the Dream Work. "Is that your assistant?"

Jordan closed his eyes and shook his head. "Nope."

"But I thought you said your assistant was coaching her first— Oh." Camilla giggled when her father blew his whistle again and Mac stomped onto the court arguing that her player didn't double dribble.

"Normally, she coaches baseball and softball." Jordan moved his hand up so that he could rub the left side of his temple where a tic was suddenly developing. "But her friend works for the parks department and asked her to sub today. Five bucks says they don't ask her back."

Surprisingly, Mac didn't get kicked out before halftime. After sending her players to get their water bottles, the older woman jogged over to the bleachers. "Whatcha doing here, Sport? You usually only come to my baseball games."

He tugged on his ear. "That's because the sound of you yelling at the umpires doesn't echo as much when you're on a grassy field instead of an enclosed gymnasium."

His assistant snorted. "Well, that ref is blind as a bat."

"Mac, allow me to introduce Camilla Sanchez, the blind bat's daughter."

"Pleasure to meet you." Mac stuck out her hand. "No offense about your old man."

"None taken." Camilla smiled as they shook hands. "Just between us, he actually enjoys it when coaches challenge him. Keeps him on his toes. Or at least half of his toes today."

"I like this one," Mac told Jordan. "She the one you had me put out my scouting report on?"

"Scouting report?" Camilla arched a brow. Jordan was now rubbing his entire forehead.

"Yep." Mac shoved an escaped wiry gray curl back under her ball cap. "After that fancy party, my boy here was all kinds of fired up wanting to find this mystery woman he met."

Camilla tilted her head as she studied him. "Is that so?"

"I think scouting report might be a bit of an overstatement." He lifted one shoulder, then dropped it. "I was just looking for a name and number."

Mac made a snorting sound, then leaned toward Camilla and stage-whispered, "Now I see why you have him swinging for the fences." She chuckled, then returned to her regular voice. "Gotta get back to my team and give them my words of wisdom for the second half. I'll catch you two after the game."

Camilla wiggled her eyebrows at him. "Now I can't wait to hear more."

"You know those relatives who like to bring out the baby book and say all sorts of stuff to embarrass you?" Jordan rolled his shoulders backward. "That's Mac."

Camilla glanced back and forth between him and his assistant on the opposite side of the court. "I didn't know that you're related."

"She's the closest thing I've got to a grandmother," he offered. "I guess you could say that since my mom left when I was younger, she really is the closest thing I have to a mom, too."

"How old were you when your parents divorced?" Camilla asked.

"Seven."

"Do you ever see her?"

"No. There was a pre-nup and she knew she wasn't going to get much in alimony, so she went the full custody route instead."

Camilla made a tsking sound. "You make it sound like the only reason she wanted custody was for the child support payments."

He crossed his arms in front of his chest and managed a shrug. But his jaw stayed tight.

"Jordan?" Camilla placed her hand between his shoulder blades. "Surely you don't think that your own mother didn't want you."

"It was the one time she stood up to my dad. Or rather her hired attorney stood up to him. She won custody and we lived with her for a whole month in a house my father bought. Turns out Cornelius only let her think she won because he knew what would eventually happen. He was just biding his time until he could buy her off. One weekend, she dropped us off at the ranch for a visit and didn't come back. My dad kept sending the child support checks, though, and she kept cashing them."

"I'm so sorry." Her hand made circles along his upper back. "I didn't think... I didn't know."

"It's okay." He swallowed, his throat thick with emotion. "There may be a lot of things I don't like about my father, but taking care of his children has always been his number one priority, no matter the cost."

Several minutes passed and neither one of them said a word. Which was a relief because Margaret Taylor was the last person he wanted to talk about. Camilla continued a rhythmic massaging motion until his muscles finally loosened.

"So tell me about this scouting report." She slid her hand from his back to loop through his arm and leaned into his side. "You really wanted to find me that badly, huh?"

"Mac has a big mouth. Especially for someone who wasn't that much help in my search."

He felt her vibrate with laughter, and Jordan realized there was no place else he would've rather been than sitting on a wooden bench inside a stuffy, overheated gymnasium watching a bunch of eight-year-olds he didn't know play a very unimpressive game of basketball.

When he was with Camilla, though, everything was an experience.

Camilla knew her dad had to have seen them in the stands since the gymnasium wasn't even a third of the way filled. But even after the final buzzer, he kept his back to the bleachers, probably to keep from making eye contact with her.

So she and Jordan waited for him by the exit.

"Does Mom know you're here?" she asked when her father realized he wasn't going to be able to roll by them on his knee scooter. "You didn't drive yourself, did you?"

"No, Dylan brought me and loaned me his referee jersey since your mother hid both of mine." Her dad turned to Jordan and shook his hand before adding, "And now you're both accomplices because you stayed and watched without stopping me. Let me change out of this shirt and then you guys can give me a ride back to the house."

"Hey, I'm staying out of it." Jordan put up both of his hands. "I've got an appointment with Mrs. Sanchez on Wednesday and I'm not about to lie to the woman who has the power to give me a bowl-shaped haircut."

"Don't worry. Mom's clients are a walking advertisement for her shop. She wouldn't want Jordan—" Camilla caught herself before saying his last name in front of her dad. "She wouldn't want *you* looking like you got a bad haircut."

Jordan tilted his head and lifted an eyebrow, as though he knew she was avoiding telling her father who he really was.

"Don't look now." Her dad maneuvered himself closer between Camilla and Jordan, as though he was pulling them into a huddle. "That crazy coach is heading this way."

"Dad, that crazy coach is Jordan's...friend." Camilla wasn't quite sure how to explain who Mac was. She didn't want to say "employee" or even "coworker" because clearly the woman was special to him. But she also didn't want to bring up the earlier conversation about Jordan's mother.

"Good game, Ref," Mac said when she approached the group.

"That's not what you said in the third quarter," her father challenged, but grudgingly shook the older woman's hand.

"You mean after you blew that whistle in my face and said I needed to stick to baseball and leave basketball to the real athletes?"

"Dad," Camilla scolded her father. "Sorry, Mac. My family is a little obsessed with their favorite sport."

"Nothing wrong with having a little passion for something." Jordan's assistant nudged him. "Right, sport?"

"Why do I get the feeling that you're suggesting I don't get passionate, Mac?" Jordan asked, almost daring the woman to announce the answer to everyone.

And she didn't disappoint.

"Well, you used to love football. But after college, the only thing you seem to be passionate about is not getting passionate about anything." Mac turned to Camilla and gave her a bold wink. "At least until now."

Camilla felt the heat rising from the depths of her chest to the roots of her hair. Jordan's own cheeks were a charming shade of pink, but his smile directed at Camilla seemed to say, *See. I told you that you were different.* It was almost as though he'd known exactly what Mac would say and purposely set up the question to prove his point.

"Oh, hell," her dad said, clearly oblivious to Camilla and Jordan making googly eyes at each other right there under the digital scoreboard. Instead, he was using his scooter to kneel down lower between them. "Speaking of passionate, here comes your mother. How did she find out I was here?"

"Aaron Sanchez," Denise called as she strode into the gymnasium. "Stop hiding behind our daughter and face me like a real man."

Mac made a snickering sound, but Jordan's eyes grew wide. Camilla thought about their earlier conversation about Jessica's interaction with Cornelius and the most recent revelation about his own mother so easily giving him up. She wondered when Jordan had last seen a wife stand up to her husband. Again she slipped her arm through his and whispered, "Don't worry."

"Hermosa!" Dad used the term of endearment that always got him off the hook with his wife. "Your hair looks beautiful. Is that a new color?"

Mom touched her freshly straightened mahogany bangs briefly—she was always experimenting with different styles and colors and appreciated it when people noticed—then quickly pointed an accusing finger at her husband. "Don't you *hermosa* me, Aaron. The doctor said no physical activity for six weeks. Do you want to make your foot worse?"

Dad took a dramatic breath, his mouth practically pouting beneath his beard. "But you don't know what it's like to be stuck on the couch while everyone else gets to run around the court."

"Oh, if you want to get off the couch, I'll give you something to do. You can start by cleaning out that garage like you promised. Then you can paint that back bedroom…" Mom's voice trailed off with a list of household chores as Dad rolled behind her toward the exit.

The muscles in Jordan's arm relaxed and he whispered under his breath, "Well, at least she didn't get mad at us."

Camilla's mom turned around at that exact

second and pointed the same accusing finger at them. "And don't think you guys are off the hook for not stopping him or calling me. You two are both on kitchen duty tonight, so you better stop by the market on your way over."

"Looks like I'm invited for dinner again." Jordan lifted one side of his mouth. Camilla pinched the bridge of her nose and didn't see his head dip close to hers until his lips brushed her ear. "And before you say it, it doesn't count as one of my dates if your mom invites me."

Chapter Seven

Early the following Wednesday morning, Jordan reminded himself that he was only making this uncomfortable sacrifice to impress Camilla. Then he pulled open one of etched glass double doors and cautiously entered the shop.

Inside, tranquil music played over the discreetly located speakers in the ceiling and displays of fancy beauty products and expensive candles lined the shelves along the walls. The floor-to-ceiling water feature behind the empty receptionist desk was made of teak wood and stacked river rocks, and he had to peek around it to see Mrs. Sanchez waving him over to her station.

As he approached, she whipped the black cape off the back of her padded leather chair with a dramatic flourish, smiled warmly and said, "You're the calm before the storm."

Mrs. Sanchez must have seen him pause in hesitation, because she clarified, "That means you're my first appointment of the day. In about thirty minutes, it'll be packed in here."

"Oh." He resisted the urge to tug at his collar. Jordan couldn't remember the last time he'd been in a place like this. Probably not since he was a kid and his first stepmother, Tania, took him and his half brothers to a high-priced salon in Billings.

Wow. That wasn't a memory he'd thought about in quite some time. He hadn't even seen the twins, who were a little younger than Daphne, since Cornelius's divorce from their mother. Dirk and Dustin were the only Taylor offspring in several generations to not grow up on the ranch, yet Jordan still kept in contact with them to ensure they had everything they needed. Or at least Mac did and then reported back to him.

"Where do you normally go to get your cuts?" Mrs. Sanchez interrupted his thoughts as she lifted and inspected several chunks of his hair through her sparkle-studded reading glasses. She'd asked him several times to call her Denise, but Jordan still thought of her as Mrs. Sanchez.

"Uh, actually, there's a guy who comes to my office every few weeks." He didn't say that Jenkins was his father's longtime barber who often squeezed Jordan in after Cornelius's routine cuts. "It's just easier for my schedule that way."

"Hmm" was all Mrs. Sanchez offered in response. However, her downturned lips said plenty. She was not a fan of either his barber or his classic, but rumpled hairstyle.

The stainless steel table stationed beside her looked like a surgical tray, the tools of her trade strategically laid out. She picked up an angled comb and powered on her electric clippers.

She'd only finished the left side above his ear when the shop door opened again and a heavyset older woman bustled around the reception desk with a folded newspaper under one arm and a Pomeranian under the other. "Denise, my sister-in-law over in Rust Creek Falls just sent me a copy of last week's *Gazette*, and it has the most unbelievable story."

Mrs. Sanchez pointed the comb at the newcomer. "Mrs. Waters, if the health inspector shows up and sees Peanut Pie in my salon, you're paying the fine."

Jordan immediately recognized the name. Mrs. Waters was the next-door neighbor who'd brought over the bad casserole when Mr. Sanchez had his bunion surgery. Seizing on an opportunity to gather some additional insight about Camilla, Jordan tried to smile at the approaching woman whose short, tightly curled hair was so silver it was nearly blue. But Mrs. Sanchez forced his head forward so she could keep working.

"You said the same thing on Sunday, Denise." Mrs. Waters made a tsking sound. "But poor Peanut Pie's asthma is still acting up with all that chemical smell lingering in my house and it's too cold for me to leave the windows open while I'm gone."

"If you would lay off the home perms, Mrs. Waters, then Peanut Pie—and the rest of us— would all breathe a lot easier."

"Anyway, do you want to hear my story or not?" The plump woman in a snug orange velour track suit plopped herself and Peanut Pie into the empty salon chair next to them and unfolded the newspaper.

Unfortunately, Jordan couldn't see much of what Mrs. Waters was showing them. If he so much as tilted his head, he'd risk Mrs. Sanchez nipping him with the clippers. Due to all the buzzing around his ears, he also missed several parts of the story. From what he could pick up, though, there was some secret baby put up for adoption seventy-five years ago over in Rust Creek Falls. Apparently, everyone across the entire state of Montana was following the story of this family's search because it had something to do with a famous psychic named Winona. There was a lead that the baby might've been named Beatrix but now went by the name Daisy. Or maybe it was Stacy? Now Mrs. Waters was singing a song about daisies. Yep. The name was definitely Daisy.

When Mrs. Sanchez traded out the electric clippers for a very sharp pair of scissors, Jordan quickly raised his head to the large mirror on the wall, only to find Mrs. Waters's eager eyes making direct contact with his. "Have you heard anything?"

Jordan slowly glanced around the shop to see who the woman was talking to. He could hear somebody on the other side of the receptionist desk asking about something called a seaweed hydration pedicure and another hairdresser was now at the shampoo bowl with a customer and clearly out of earshot. He lifted a brow and asked, "Heard anything about what?"

"About the secret baby. Rumor is that the Abernathys are involved and I figured you would know more since you live by them, Mr. Taylor."

Jordan jerked his head up and heard Mrs. Sanchez mutter a curse. "Keep still, *mijo*, or it's going to be lopsided."

He recognized the Spanish term of endearment, which made him hope that Camilla's mom was so focused on what she was doing, she hadn't heard Mrs. Waters's use of his last name. Forcing his shoulders to relax, he smiled wide at the Sanchezes' neighbor. "Please, call me Jordan. Mister sounds like you're talking to my father."

Mrs. Waters snorted. "As if anyone would mistake you for that flashy blowhard Cornelius Taylor."

Jordan's lungs paused midbreath right as the scissors poised above his scalp paused midclip. So much for hoping. Using the reflection of the mirror, he searched the face of Mrs. Sanchez, who was standing behind him. Instead of shooting daggers at him, she kept her eyes directed at the wet brown hair measured between her fingers and murmured, "Not that anyone could tell the difference judging by your duplicate hairstyles."

Thankfully, a third stylist had arrived and called the older woman over to the shampoo bowl right then and Mrs. Sanchez returned to her diligent cutting.

He should have been relieved she wasn't kicking Jordan out of the shop halfway through his haircut. After all, given Mrs. Waters's reference to his father being a flashy blowhard, it was perfectly clear how the citizens of Bronco Valley felt about his family. Now he understood why Camilla had warned him about telling the Sanchezes who he was.

Still.

Jordan couldn't just sit here like a coward, as though he had something to hide. When he finally caught Mrs. Sanchez's eyes in the mirror he said, "So, now you know."

She set the scissors down and ran the comb through his hair a few more times, as though she needed a moment to think of her response. Jordan's heart pounded as his mind rushed through several defenses and explanations. Yet he shouldn't have to apologize for who he was or where he was raised any more than Camilla should. He straightened his shoulders under the black stylist's cape.

Finally, she sighed and said, "I knew all along, *mijo*. Nobody in this town is better informed on all the local gossip—including your unfortunate nicknames—than I am. Not only did I help Camilla get ready for her big night at that fundraiser gala at your place, I spent the following week with most of my clients showing me the pictures of her online."

"So does everyone else know?" he asked hopefully. It would make everything so much easier if he and Camilla could just date openly.

"Let's hope not," she replied a bit too quickly,

and Jordan's optimism immediately deflated. "I saw you in the background of one of those pictures, you know. At the fundraiser. You were far enough away from her that nobody had put two and two together yet. But I saw the way you were looking at my daughter and I knew what was coming well before you showed up at our house."

Mrs. Sanchez spread some pomade on her hands before applying it to his hair, which he had to admit looked about ten times better than when his father's barber did it. Jordan wouldn't be satisfied with just a trendy hairstyle, though. He wanted Camilla's mom's blessing.

Or at least her acceptance.

"So you're okay with your daughter dating the so-called Charmed Prince of Bronco Heights?" Jordan inwardly cringed even as he continued to force out the hated words. "The Rancher Most Wanted?"

"Just don't bring it up to anyone else." Mrs. Sanchez whipped the cape off him with finality. "They might not understand what Camilla sees in you."

Jordan left the salon with, he had to admit, the best-looking haircut he'd ever had, as well as a ball of confusion cranking through his gut. Still, he told himself to focus on the positive. Namely, that Camilla did in fact see something in him and her mother clearly understood what that was. Mrs. Sanchez had even called him *mijo* a second time. He should at least be comforted by that, right?

Instead, all he could think about was the looming fact that the rest of her family might never accept him.

Jordan took Denise Sanchez's advice to heart and didn't say a word to the rest of the family about being a Taylor, which was trickier to do since he was more comfortable spending time with the Sanchezes than he was with his own family.

There were a few times when he'd wanted to proudly claim his heritage. But then there were the times when he just sat back and listened. Especially when Dante made a comment about his students in the Bronco Unified School District not having enough funding from the state because many of the wealthier citizens from the Heights were sending their children to posh private schools.

As long as the rest of the Sanchez family didn't associate him with some of his neighbors, Jordan grew more confident that their open invitation to Sunday night dinners would last indefinitely. Not only was it entertaining to watch them playfully argue and push each other's buttons, but being around them was a bonus to spending time with Camilla.

And considering the fact that Camilla was as active in her community as she was at work and school, the free time she *did* have to spend with Jordan was very limited. In fact, he soon learned that the best way to be around her—and not have it count as a date—was when he found out where she would be ahead of time and "accidentally" ran into her there. Never at work, though, since that would've just made things more awkward. He was now well aware of the social power imbalance between them, so having her wait on him as a customer at the restaurant would've made both of them uncomfortable.

Instead, by strategically fitting himself into her busy life, he could prove to her, and everyone else, that he was taking this seriously. By the middle of November, Jordan had already participated in a creek-side cleanup, a coat drive and a Cub Scout car wash (Mr. Sanchez, the troop leader, couldn't risk getting his surgery incision wet, so his daughter filled in). All of this, just so he could be around Camilla.

Hell, he'd volunteered so much lately, he would've been in danger of losing his own job if he wasn't already in line to inherit a share of the company.

A fact that Cornelius reminded him of a week later.

"You seem to be spending a lot of time away from the office lately," his father said at breakfast on Saturday morning. "I don't suppose that has anything to do with you seeing that girl."

"As a matter of fact, it does." Jordan didn't take a seat at the formal dining table because he had no intention of staying here long. "Her name is Camilla and I'm so glad you encouraged me to talk to her at the gala."

Cornelius's nostrils flared. "Don't try and turn this around on me, young man. At the time, I was under the impression she was a Balthazar."

"Well, your mistake helped me get my foot in the door with her so I'm grateful to you all the same. Things are going very well between Camilla and me, so I'd suggest you choose your next words very carefully."

Clearly, Cornelius knew by now that arguing with his oldest son was like a chess match, one he didn't want to lose. Instead of going after Camilla, his father stared at him for several moments, his silver eyebrows drawn together in an angry crease, before shifting tactics. "Is that another new shirt from one of your latest pet projects?"

Jordan glanced at the green Bronco Valley Rec Center tee. Somehow, he'd gotten roped into coaching the girls' basketball team after they'd asked Mac not to return. "It is. But don't worry, Dad. I'm still clocking in plenty of hours at Taylor Beef."

Which was true. In the evenings when Camilla was working at DJ's Deluxe, Jordan would return to his own office and catch up on reports and usually a stack of papers Mac left for him to sign.

"Speaking of beef." Cornelius waved away the fresh fruit and Greek yogurt parfait Jessica requested the private chef to make. "Is it too much for a man to get some steak and eggs around here?"

"But the doctor told you that you need to be cutting back on the red meat, and I thought this might…um…" Jessica looked at Jordan, her wide eyes silently pleading for some backup.

Everyone always turned to Jordan when they needed backup dealing with Cornelius.

Jordan hadn't been exaggerating when he'd told Camilla that his nickname at work was the Smoother. Unfortunately, he was usually called in to smooth things over with his stubborn old man. Cornelius Taylor's biggest fear in life was having someone think he was weak. The guy hadn't always been this way, especially when his kids were younger. But each time something in life didn't go his way—a divorce, a bad investment deal, a daughter who didn't want to go into the family business—Cornelius would double down on his efforts to be in control of his image. Or, at least what he thought his image should be.

Jordan sighed. "It's not going to kill you to eat a little healthier, Dad. Yogurt comes from cows, so nobody will think any less of you."

"This is how it started with your sister, you know." His father pointed a spoon at Jordan, and at first he thought he was only going to have to hear a rant about Daphne's food choices. No such luck. "Volunteering *once in a while* is fine, Jordan. But do you have to give up all your valuable time to these charities? You already have commitments at work and commitments to this family. Just do what I do and send a check."

"I'll keep that in mind." Jordan reached for an apple out of the fruit bowl in the center of the table. Now wasn't the time to disagree with his father because Cornelius was currently digging into his yogurt parfait and to start an argument would only serve as a distraction. It was better to pick his battles.

Or in this case, Jessica's battle, who mouthed the words *thank you* to Jordan before he headed into the kitchen to find the loaded breakfast burrito she'd had the chef wrap up for him.

Sure, Jordan might be burning the candle at both ends lately, eating most of his meals either in his car or in his office. In fact, he was exhausted by the time he fell into bed every night. But it was well worth it.

First, he was getting to know Camilla on her home turf, where she felt free to be herself. Although, if he was being honest, she was pretty damn authentic no matter where she was or who she was with. Even in a borrowed gown at a black tie gala or on the back of a thousand-pound Arabian stallion, her infectious laugh and zest for life stood out above all else.

Second, he was actually getting involved with the community again. He hadn't felt this connected to his hometown since he'd played football at Bronco High. Third, and most important, by fitting himself into her life, he was buying himself more time in Camilla's presence.

After all, their agreement never specified that the three weeks needed to be concurrent. It was a win-win as far as he was concerned because he still had those guaranteed dates sitting in his back pocket.

One downside to volunteering so often, though, was that no matter where he ended up, there was usually a news story or a social media post with a picture of him there. Camilla took great pains to avoid being caught anywhere near him in the photos since the comment sections were always littered with speculations about Jordan's newfound interest in community events.

The other downside was that since none of those events counted as actual dates and usually took place in public, he'd now gone a couple weeks without kissing Camilla.

Finally, on a Sunday afternoon before Thanksgiving, they had their fourth date. Albeit, it wasn't the most romantic place Jordan would've taken her.

"How much money do you think they waste on samples?" he asked Camilla as they turned down another aisle in some big box warehouse store near Billings.

"It's not really a waste if they end up selling more product because people enjoy the samples," she countered.

"But all these people are just grabbing the samples without actually putting the item in their carts. It'd be interesting to see a cost analysis report on it."

Camilla took a tiny paper cup filled with cornbread stuffing from a tray. "For the past thirty plus years, this company has been giving away free samples in thousands of stores all across the globe. I'm pretty sure they're still coming out on top."

"Are you planning on following that same business model when you open your restaurant?" Jordan took the last sample cup of stuffing from the tray before an employee set out another batch. "I don't know if potential investors will be on board with that."

"They already are." Camilla smiled at Jordan.

"Wait." He stopped in the center of the aisle, and an older woman riding in an electric scooter behind him clipped his boot heels as she swung around to avoid him. "You already found an investor?"

"Yep. We signed the contracts two days ago."

"Who is it?"

"They're a silent partner, so I'm not allowed to say." Camilla avoided eye contact with him by scanning her grocery list. "I think the canned green beans are down here."

"Are you sure your mom wants canned beans?" Jordan asked as he pushed the oversized shopping cart behind her. "I've eaten with your family several times now and everything is always fresh. Thanks to Mr. Granada." See, he was even in on the family jokes about the store clerk who had a crush on Mrs. Sanchez.

"My parents insist. When they moved here thirty years ago and celebrated their first Thanksgiving, Mrs. Waters gave them all these recipes for what she called 'traditional American dishes.'" Camilla held up two fingers on each hand to simulate air quotes. "Mom was pregnant with Dylan and on bed rest so my dad cooked everything himself, including the green bean casserole. Later on, they learned that there were much better recipes out there. But at the time it was their way of embracing the culture of their new country. Now, it's a reminder of all the challenges they've had to overcome since they became citizens. It's not Thanksgiving at our house without Mrs. Waters's recipes."

Jordan hefted a huge box of green beans into the cart. "Your brothers are big guys, but there's no way they're going to eat all of these."

"No, but there's a food pantry at the church and we usually give half to them ahead of time."

They were standing in front of crates of twenty-pound sacks of potatoes when Jordan tried again. "So how did you meet this investor?"

"I can't say." Camilla shrugged as she gazed longingly at the red fingerlings and the Yukon golds.

"You can't? Or you won't?" he asked, the disappointment of a missed opportunity threading through him. Despite how much he wanted to be her partner, he obviously couldn't continue his personal relationship with Camilla if he went into business with her. For one, he didn't ever want her to feel indebted to him. For another, those kinds of ventures never ended well when the parties decided to part socially. However, he'd actually talked to several of his associates who were interested in meeting with her and finding out more about her restaurant.

Camilla made a zipper motion in front of her lips, then pretended to lock them shut and throw away the key.

"It sounds shady," he finally said.

"What does?" She went with the standard russets and didn't even budge under the weight as she put the bag in the cart.

"This mysterious silent partner. Why do they want to keep it a secret? Do they not want people to know they're investing in you?"

"Jordan, I assure you that it's all on the up and up. And not *those* yams. We need to go back to the canned section for them. Do you think the marshmallows would be with the baking products or in the candy section?"

"I'm pretty sure I saw marshmallows on that display stand by the pie crusts." He put the smaller bag back, already feeling his insulin levels spike at the thought of what Mrs. Waters put in her sweet potato casserole. "What if this mystery investor is trying to take advantage of you?"

"Because I'm not business savvy enough to know better?" She crossed her arms in front of her chest, but a mom with three kids hanging off the sides of her shopping cart needed to maneuver by. Camilla's stance lost some of its defiance as she was forced to squeeze herself against the red onions. Yet that didn't detract from her argument. "Suppose I made a big mistake, Jordan? What would you do? Rush in to save me?"

"You know I didn't mean it that way," he said as he followed her down the next aisle.

"How do I know what you mean? I barely know you at all."

"Oh, come on, Camilla." The cart was getting surprisingly more full and harder to steer by the time they got out of the produce section. "By now you probably know me better than anyone else does. Besides maybe Daphne and Mac."

"And you should know that when it comes to you, I'm always going to protect myself." She held up one palm as though the hand gesture was enough to stop his train of thought. "Not that I think you would intentionally hurt me. But what happens after our three weeks are up? What happens after three months? Eventually you'll move on to the next shiny object."

"That's not fair." He leaned his forearms on the cart, not moving until she realized she was prematurely judging him. Again.

"Oh, yeah? What has been your longest relationship?" She put her hands on her waist, drawing his attention to the spot below, where her snug jeans hugged her hips.

His mouth went dry and he looked around

for a sample cart offering water or juice or even Scotch if they had it. "That depends on how you define relationship."

"You shouldn't have to define it, Jordan. You should know when you're in a relationship."

"In that case, this one has been the longest."

"This one?" She peered around him at the pallets of cereal as though there were another relationship lurking behind them. "The one between me and you?"

"If I'm defining what a relationship is, then I'd say this qualifies."

"Four dates isn't enough time to define anything," she replied.

"Here's how I see it. I've never done Sunday dinners with a woman's family. I've never volunteered for community service projects just to be around a woman. I've never let a woman ride one of my favorite horses. Don't tell Leia I said Palp was one of my favorites, by the way. She thinks she's my only one."

"Aha!" Camilla pointed a finger at his chest. "How many other females out there think they're your only one?"

"None! Because I've never done any of this with another woman." Jordan dashed a frustrated hand through his hair before he continued. "I *certainly* have never gone grocery shopping with one and gotten into an argument with her in the middle of the breakfast aisle. But what should be even more telling is that I've never wanted to *keep* doing those things with anyone else but you. Therefore, the fact that I want to be with you, along with the fact that you clearly want to be with me, makes this, by default, a relationship."

She studied him for several seconds, but he could see her breathing had quickened because her red puffy vest was straining against her breasts. Finally she asked, "How do you know I want to be with you?"

"Because you're not the kind of person who wastes time. You go after what you want." He took a step closer and, as though to prove his point, she didn't retreat. "If you didn't want to be with me, you never would have agreed to this three-week trial. If you weren't attracted to me, you wouldn't let me touch you like this." He reached out to trail his hand along her waist under her vest, and when her full lips parted in surprise, he lowered his head and his voice. "You most definitely wouldn't let me kiss you in the middle of a crowded store."

His mouth hovered above hers until she grabbed a fistful of his shirt and pulled him against her. Camilla's kisses were better than breathing. Jordan's lungs filled with the intoxicating scent of her lavender shampoo, and his hands filled with the intoxicating feel of her rear end as he hauled her hips against his. She moaned and...

Something else was ringing in his ears. He pulled back when he heard a second metal clang.

An aproned employee held a stainless steel spoon over her portable stove as she frowned at them. "You kids need to go do that hanky-panky stuff somewhere else. You're blocking my oatmeal samples."

Chapter Eight

For the past couple of weeks, Camilla had done her best to show Jordan how the other half lived in a fruitless attempt to prove that their lifestyles were incompatible. Surprisingly, though, the stubborn man seemed game for whatever she'd dished up. And he kept coming back for more.

He'd even gone grocery shopping yesterday at the big box store an hour out of town just so he could be with her. Other than that steamy kiss in the breakfast aisle, there was nothing romantic about their $1.50 hot dogs and sodas in the food court or those countless samples they'd filled up on.

Yet Jordan seemed to enjoy every second of whatever random errand or service project she had on her schedule, which only made Camilla question whether she'd been wrong about him all along. In fact, the more involved he got in the Bronco Valley community, the more Camilla felt her resolve slipping.

And don't even get her started on her family. They all adored him, even Dylan, who hadn't been too pleased to find out that Jordan's favorite NBA player was on the team of his sworn rivals.

Of course, none of the Sanchezes knew that he was one of *those* Taylors.

So far, the only thing Camilla had proven to anyone was that her and Jordan's physical attraction was only growing stronger. Maybe she needed to get him back in his own world to show him that *she* was the one who wouldn't be able to fit in. That would be easy enough to do with his dad and stepmother. Maybe even his siblings.

DJ's Deluxe was doing a limited menu this week due to all the Thanksgiving holiday takeout orders, which meant she wasn't working her usual shifts. Plus, she'd booked a couple of vacation days to be able to spend time cooking with her parents—and, of course, to spend time with Jordan. And since school was on break, she didn't have any online lectures or reading assignments. So when Jordan texted her that morning asking if they could have another "official date," she replied, I want to meet the rest of your family.

Camilla had anticipated a formal dinner at the Taylor estate prepared by a classically trained private chef and served by a stiff-lipped butler. Or perhaps another helicopter ride to a five-star restaurant in Jackson Hole. At this point, she wouldn't have been surprised if he'd pulled out the big guns and hired a private jet to ferry them to some romantic European city.

What she hadn't anticipated, she realized as they pulled up under the wooden sign of Happy Hearts Animal Sanctuary on Monday afternoon, was that he would take her to meet the other member of the Taylor family who didn't quite fit in, either.

"Jordan!" His sister nearly squealed as she ran over to hug her brother. "What are you doing away from the office? You never take time off from work… Oh." The pretty strawberry blonde trailed off when she caught sight of Camilla. "This is certainly a first on so many levels."

"Daph, this is Camilla Sanchez. Remember, I told you all about her?"

"I see my very determined and slightly stubborn brother finally found his mystery woman from the ball." Jordan's sister shot him a knowing smile before extending a hand to Camilla. "I'm Daphne Taylor."

"Nice to meet you," she replied. After a few more knowing looks passed between Jordan and Daphne, Camilla asked, "So does everyone in your family know the story of how Jordan and I met?"

"Only those of us who pay attention. Although I have to admit that I thought this particular quest would end up as another lost cause."

Something knotted in Camilla's throat at that admission, but she held her smile in place. Or tried to, but Daphne must've read her mind. "Not that I'm not happy to be proven wrong. It's just that I know how my brother is. Clearly, from what I've heard around town, though, you're not just a flavor of the month."

Camilla suddenly wanted to know what else Daphne had heard around town. But she turned to Jordan instead and didn't bother to hide her sarcasm. "Hmmm. Why does it always feel as though people are surprised when they find out we've had more than a couple of dates? It's almost as though they know your reputation."

Daphne chuckled. "It's hard *not* to know about his reputation, considering everyone reads about it online."

"You guys should understand by now that I'm not as bad as they make me out to be." Jordan dug his hands in the back pockets of his black slacks. He'd obviously come straight from his office to pick her up. Daphne's words about her brother never taking time off work repeated in Camilla's head. Maybe she was truly different from the other women he'd dated. "Besides, can't a man bring his favorite girl to meet his favorite sister without everyone bringing up his past?"

"You're right. My brother almost never visits his favorite sister. And certainly not with his girlfriend. Come on." Daphne moved between them and looped her arms through theirs. "Let me give you a tour of my farm."

Jordan's sister talked eagerly about each of the rescued animals at Happy Hearts, and Camilla tried to pay attention. But she couldn't stop thinking about how easily Daphne had referred to her as Jordan's girlfriend.

"As you can see," Daphne said as they got to an enclosed area near the end of the barn, "Happy Hearts is quite smaller than the Taylor Ranch and runs at a fraction of the cost—mostly raised through donations."

"Who's this big guy?" Jordan asked, making Camilla look inside the pen.

"That's Tiny Tim," Daphne replied. The pot-bellied pig was anything but tiny. "He came to live with us after his owner passed away."

The pig stuck its snout through the slats in the

fencing and sniffed Camilla's hand. She looked at Daphne for permission. "Is it okay if I pet him?"

"Sure." Daphne unlatched the gate. "You can even go inside and play with him. He's house-broken and actually knows quite a few tricks. In fact, that muddy wad of strings and patches used to be a soccer ball, and he'll kick it back to you if you roll it to him."

Camilla rolled the ball several times and the pig actually used a front hoof to kick it back. She bent over to retrieve the ball, and Tim pushed his snout into her palm. Camilla knelt in the straw to stroke the silky space between his ears and he oinked in appreciation. "Oh, he's an absolute sweetheart."

"You can say that again. In fact, he's a real charmer. All the females around here love him. Even old Agatha, the crankiest goat you'll ever meet. In fact, he's such a ladies' man, we thought about changing his name to—"

"Don't say it." Jordan shook his head at his sister.

Daphne laughed. "I was going to say Casa-nova. But now that you suggest it, Jordan Junior would've been just as appropriate."

"The ladies may love us," Jordan said to the pig, "but they certainly don't understand us."

Tim oinked in agreement.

"So what'll happen to him?" Camilla asked.

"My guess is as good as yours," Daphne replied, staring at her brother, who in turn was watching Camilla. "I've never seen him this smitten with a woman before."

"She's talking about the pig," Jordan said. "Not me."

"Oh." Daphne straightened. "We'll try to find him a good home. Otherwise, he will spend the rest of his days here at Happy Hearts, eating slop and lounging in the mud and charming all the females."

"Sounds like a pretty good life, if you ask me." Jordan knelt beside her. "I mean, except for the part about charming all the females. There's only one female I want to impress."

"I wish I could take you home, boy." Camilla continued to scratch the pig's head, refusing to acknowledge Jordan's comment for fear she'd turn as pink as Tim. "But I only have a studio apartment and absolutely no free time to speak of."

"Is she still talking about the pig?" Daphne laughed. "Because I already like any woman who can tell one of the Taylor men no."

"Then you'll love Camilla." Jordan winked at Daphne. "She has no problem telling me no."

A truck backed up close to the barn doors. Daphne sighed. "That's the second delivery of grain this week for the horses. I better help un-load it."

"I've got it, Daph," Jordan offered, easily swinging himself over the wood slatted fence. "You already do too much around here as it is."

He left the two women standing in the pig pen together, and Camilla knew what was coming before Daphne even opened her mouth. "Well, you've certainly succeeded with my brother where many others before you have failed."

"Don't get your hopes up," Camilla said more to herself than to Jordan's sister. "I'm sure it's only temporary. He'll lose interest soon enough."

"I don't know. When Jordan makes up his mind, it's pretty hard to convince him to change it."

Camilla tilted her head as she watched Jordan, clad in his business attire, hop into the back of a pickup truck to unload heavy burlap sacks. "He certainly is determined. I have a feeling that's what attracted him to me in the first place. The challenge."

"I'm the first to admit that my brother is used to getting his way." Daphne nodded. "In fact, I even accused him of being just like our father when he was trying to find you. I was so an-noyed with him, I told him I wouldn't help. I was worried that he was envisioning you as some sort of prize that he needed to win. But seeing him with you is different."

Camilla's emotions were so damn twisted and tangled. She wanted to be flattered that what they potentially had was something special. But it also made her more wary that it might get messy when the three-week trial dating was up. And the fact remained that it would be up soon. Steeling herself, she asked the question she might not want to know the answer to. "How so?"

"The way he looks at you. The way he laughs when you confront him. All of our lives, we've witnessed people bend over backward to accommodate our father. Fawning over him and telling him whatever he wanted to hear. When women started to do that to Jordan, he would get all cagey and cut them loose. We've all teased him about his dating history, but I'm starting to realize that the real reason he hasn't wanted to settle down is that he *doesn't* want to end up like Cornelius Taylor."

"If being like your dad is such a concern for him, why does Jordan still work for the family business? Why does he still live at home?" Camilla didn't have any experience with the man other than that day he called her by the wrong name. But Jordan didn't seem anything like their father.

"Because Jordan loves a challenge. And, in

a way, he also feels sorry for our father and thinks he can fix things. Jordan seems to think the reason our dad can be so controlling and overbearing with us kids is because deep down, he's afraid he's going to lose us. When I decided to move off the ranch to open my own farm, you would've thought I told our father that I was leaving the family for good. Who knows? Maybe it reminded him of when our mom left. All I knew was that the harder my dad tried to get me to stay, the more I needed to get out of there. Jordan, though, is the opposite. He thinks he can change my dad's flaws by working on things from the inside. And maybe he can someday. Did I mention that my brother is very stubborn and determined?"

Camilla sighed. "He's definitely determined to prove that we're right for each other."

"From what I've seen so far today, not to mention what I've read on social media about his sudden interest in volunteering, there's no question that you're the right woman for him."

Unfortunately, that didn't mean Jordan was the right man for her. Which meant that Camilla's conflicting emotions made her feel as though she was right back at square one.

Camilla cast several furtive looks Jordan's way on the drive home from Happy Hearts.

She'd seen him tired, wound up and even slightly defensive. But she'd yet to see the man in a bad mood, even when one of the grain sacks tore open as he was carrying it on his shoulder and spilled oat pellets all over his designer suit. She'd certainly never seen him as quiet as he was right now.

So when he'd barely said more than a few sentences by the time they were driving down the main street of Bronco Valley, Camilla knew something must be weighing heavily on his mind. Maybe one of Daphne's comments had gotten under his skin and now he was having second thoughts about finishing out their final week of dates.

An empty pit slowly formed in Camilla's stomach as she thought about Jordan changing his mind so quickly. Mentally, she'd been preparing herself for it all along, but now that it was about to happen, her body wasn't ready for it.

By the time he pulled into the side alley parking spot beneath her apartment, her elbow was braced on the leather armrest of the passenger side door, her fingers clenching the handle so she could quickly dive out of the car to get away from the inevitable awkward conversation.

"So, thanks for the ride," she started, gathering the handles of her purse in her free hand so she could bolt.

"Camilla, before we get out, I've been thinking about something the whole way here and I want to just get it out in the open now." He turned toward her, and that empty pit in her belly suddenly felt like a ton of bricks. His expression was somber without so much as a hint of a smirk or the creasing of a dimple as he continued. "I know we agreed on three weeks. But…"

Yep. Her entire insides went all achy as he looked up at the sunroof, as though he was trying to find the right words to dump her. "But…?" she prompted.

He opened his mouth and she thought, *Here it is.* "But I'm already done for."

"So you're ready to call it quits." She nodded in acceptance, swallowing her own disappointment.

"No!" His brown eyes widened as he jerked his head back in surprise. Then he reached across the center console to take her hand in his. He had to practically pry her fingers from the death grip on her purse. "I mean I don't need three weeks."

"But we haven't even slept together yet." Camilla nearly slammed her palm over her mouth. She hadn't meant to say that out loud, but she'd thought that if Jordan were going to break up with her, he'd likely wait until after he'd gotten the ultimate prize. "Not that I'm trying to get you in bed or anything. I just figured that you wouldn't give up before you, uh, sealed the deal."

"Who says I'm giving up?" he asked.

She tried to ignore the way his fingers were now interlaced with hers. The way his thumb was slowly stroking the soft pad of her palm. "But you just told me you don't need to spend any more time with me."

"No, I'm saying that I don't need another minute to know how I feel. I have totally and completely fallen for you." His admission shot a rush of adrenaline through Camilla, and her brain went all topsy-turvy. Before she could ask him if he was serious, those playful dimples returned and he brought the back of her hand up to his mouth. "Of course, I *am* more than willing to sleep together, if that's what it'll take to convince you."

When his lips caressed her knuckles like that, all she could think about was every other spot on her body she wanted him to kiss.

"It's just that it's probably too soon for us to be taking things to that level," she said. Sparks flew through her nerve endings as his teeth scraped against the inside of her wrist. She lost her train of thought as she stared at his very capable mouth.

His eyes stayed focused on what he was doing,

his lips brushing against her skin as he spoke. "It kind of feels like we're already at that level."

"There's just so much we don't know about each…aw, hell." She cupped his jaw with her free hand and lifted his face to hers for a kiss. It was cold outside, the first hints of snowfall dusting his windshield, but her skin felt as though she could melt an arctic freeze. She was hot and flushed and nearly throbbing with need as they fought against the center console to get closer to each other. When Jordan broke the kiss, she heard a whimpering sound and realized it came from her.

The windows were steamed with the fog of their heavy breathing as they stared at each other, both of them dazed from another heat-filled kiss.

Jordan was the first to break the silence. "I want to do this, Camilla. You have no idea how much I've been wanting to do this. But before we go any further, I need you to be sure."

"I…" She struggled to get command of her thoughts. "I want this, too. But I'm terrified of the fallout. I'm afraid that…" Camilla looked around the interior of the car, trying to find the words.

"You're afraid I'll hurt you." Jordan collapsed against the leather seat, still holding her hand in his own. She was surprised to realize that he hadn't let go of it this entire time.

"I'm afraid that I'll let *myself* get hurt." She slowly traced the calluses he must've earned from all those years of tightly holding on to the ropes and reins, a visual reminder of the way he maintained control at all costs. "And, as shallow as this sounds, I'm afraid that other people will find out and think less of me."

"I don't know how anyone could possibly think that."

"That's because nobody has ever doubted you, Jordan. You come from a world where you're the golden prince and nobody has ever called into question what you do or how you go about doing it. You could have your pick of any woman, yet here you are with me. People are going to want to know why and eventually they'll start speculating that I'm using you."

"God, woman, I *wish* you would use me. I've practically been at your beck and call, at your complete disposal, these past weeks. I've served pancakes and collected trash and washed cars and read to senior citizens and somehow ended up coaching an eight-year-old girls' basketball team in the hopes that you *would* use me."

She knew that he meant the words to be light-hearted, but this was a decision she didn't want to take lightly. Camilla said as much, then added,

"If we decide to get more physical, I don't want anyone knowing."

He glanced in his rearview mirror at a cluster of people walking along the sidewalk. People were getting off work right about now and anyone who passed by might see them walk up to her apartment together.

"In that case, give me until tomorrow to plan something a little more discreet. I promise I'll make it worth the wait. And nobody will have to know." He smiled with an amount of confidence only he could exude when faced with a seemingly impossible task.

Yet nothing ever seemed impossible for Jordan.

As Camilla watched him drive away, she got a sinking feeling that she was just as much a goner as he'd claimed to be.

Chapter Nine

Jordan wanted his first time with Camilla to be perfect. And in order to do that, he needed to find somewhere away from Bronco. Someplace that was neutral territory and where his name wouldn't be recognized. One of his buddies from college had a family cabin near Great Falls that overlooked the Missouri River and, as soon as Mac left the office, Jordan made a few calls.

"It's not much to look at," Jordan warned Camilla on Tuesday morning when she asked him what she should pack. "But it's away from here and pretty isolated."

As they drove to the cabin that afternoon,

both silence and anticipation crackled in the air between them. He'd created a playlist of several songs in the hopes that if things got awkward on the long drive, they could at least listen to the same music that they'd danced to at the Denim and Diamonds event. Jordan tried not speed up the mountain roads, like an impatient youth with only one thing on his mind. Yet the closer they got to their destination, the more his nerves hummed along to the beat and the heavier his foot got on the gas pedal.

The long dirt driveway was littered with leaves, indicating no other vehicles had disturbed them recently. When he turned off the engine, Camilla climbed out of the car and studied the log structure. "It actually *is* a cabin in the woods,"

"I told you it was rustic." Jordan retrieved a box of food and Camilla's overnight bag out of the back seat. Telling himself to take his time, he decided to make a second trip for the cooler he'd packed and for his own duffel bag.

"Yeah, but I've seen your family's version of rustic." She looked at the box in his arms. "So, I'm guessing there's no private chef here?" she teased. "No concierge to fetch things for us?"

"No. But if you're lucky, I might bring you room service."

She'd shed her coat in the car and was standing before him in a blue dress printed with tiny flowers and a square neckline. It quickly occurred to him that this was the first time he'd seen her in a dress since the fundraiser gala. The thin fabric cinched at her waist before softly falling to just above her knees. It wasn't snowing again, but he was still surprised to see her long golden legs were bare except for the tan cowboy boots. Her dark hair was loose and wavy and her wide smile made his knees buckle. "What's on the menu?"

"Only one of my finest specialties," he told her, holding the box higher so she couldn't peek inside.

"That sounds fancy." She lifted up on tiptoe.

"You might want to lower your expectations, then."

She arched her brows. "All of them?"

"Well, the ones about the food. And possibly the decorations inside. Hopefully, I meet all your other expectations, though."

Camilla's cheeks flooded with color. "It's kind of weird knowing that we're here for just one reason."

"Not *just* for one reason, I hope." Jordan set the box on the front porch as he searched behind an empty flower box hanging from the windowsill. "Even if we didn't do *that*, I'd still be happy just having you out here and all to myself."

He found the hidden key and unlocked the front door, sweeping one arm forward for her to go first. As she passed by him to enter the cabin, she looked back over her shoulder and asked, "Then you're perfectly fine sitting on opposite ends of the sofa, not touching, just talking?"

He groaned as he followed her inside. "It'll be tough to manage, but I can do it."

Luckily, the brown leather love seat facing the fireplace was just as small as the one in her apartment, which meant they couldn't sit *too* far from each other. He set her bag on a round pine table and went back to the porch to retrieve the box of food. When he returned, she wasn't where he'd left her, but the sliding glass door leading out to the deck was open. He put the food in the kitchen before heading out to the car to get the cooler and his own bag.

The stuffy, stale scent of the unused cabin was soon replaced with the brisk, fir-scented air making its way inside, and he took a steadying breath. *Take it slow*, Jordan reminded himself as he walked out to the deck to join Camilla, only to find that she wasn't there.

Huh. That meant there was only one place she could be.

Heading to the master bedroom with measured steps, Jordan's heart nearly stopped when he saw her standing in front of the massive windows framing the entire wall.

"This is breathtaking." She faced him with that amazing smile and her arms spread wide open. "Who knew some rustic little cabin in the woods would have the best view in the entire state of Montana?"

Jordan barely noticed the expansive curve of the flowing river on display outside the windows behind her. "You mean the *second* best view."

He walked toward her, but he didn't have to go far. She met him halfway across the room.

Camilla's nerve endings sizzled in awareness with every taste of him. Jordan's hands splayed against her back as he held her in place to explore her mouth, the hunger in his kisses matching her own.

There was something about Jordan Taylor that made Camilla feel as though she would never have anything to worry about. He would always take care of everything. And nothing proved that more than the way his capable fingers slowly worked their way down the small buttons along the back of her dress. His knuckles softly grazed her heated skin underneath, giving the briefest taste of what was to come. Jordan always held himself back in the most subtle way, which only served to arouse her into a state of delicious anticipation.

She tried to return the favor of unbuttoning his shirt, but her fingers trembled with excitement. She pushed the crisp, starched fabric off his shoulders, allowing her palms to finally make contact with the smooth, warm wall of his wide chest.

His mouth trailed light kisses along her jaw, down to her neck. She tilted her head back, not only to allow him more access, but also so that she could gasp for more air. The silky fabric of her dress tickled her tingling skin as he eased it down her body until it landed in a pile at her feet.

"I'll be right back," Jordan whispered before disappearing from the bedroom. Camilla quickly used the opportunity to yank off her boots, and was standing in front of the bed in only her bra and panties when he returned carrying a small leather toiletries bag. He grabbed one of her hands, and she eagerly followed him over to the side table, where he put down his bag before sitting on the fluffy white comforter.

Jordan shirtless was quite a sight to behold. He was six feet of lean, athletic muscles from his broad shoulders to his chiseled biceps to his narrow waist. He pulled her closer to stand between his legs, his jaw clenched tightly as she traced her hands along the sculpted planes of his torso. When she was touching him like this, looking at him like this, every rational thought went right out the window.

Which was probably why she didn't realize her bra was gone until she felt a cool breeze on her nipple right before his skilled tongue set it on fire. Her legs threatened to give out as his mouth began a tender assault on first one breast and then the other.

A whimpering sound tickled her throat, and his steadying hands encircled her waist, holding her upright. She slowly lifted each knee to the mattress until she was straddling him. His palms moved to her rear end, cupping each cheek as he easily lifted her, keeping his mouth on her breasts as he stood and switched their positions.

Now it was her turn to rain kisses down his torso as he stood in front of her.

He remained absolutely still, his only movement the slight shuddering of his muscles as her lips memorized first his toned pecs and then the ridges of his tight abdomen. When she got to his waistband, his breath was coming hard and fast, his chest rising and falling with the frantic pounding of his heart.

Camilla nearly smiled at the thrill of finally succeeding in completely unnerving Jordan Taylor. This time, her fingers didn't tremble as she confidently unbuckled his belt and then his fly.

Her earlier fluttering of anticipation was now replaced by the boldness of determination. She wanted this man and she wanted him now.

His pants were barely down his hips when he reached for his toiletries case and pulled out a packet. Camilla took the condom from him and slid it over the length of his arousal, his groan further empowering her.

Jordan's thumbs grazed along her jawline, tilting her face up to look into his. His voice was husky and low when he said, "I wanted to make our first time absolutely perfect for you, but I don't think I can wait much longer."

"It's already perfect." Maintaining eye contact, she shifted herself toward the center of the bed and smiled at him in encouragement. "Please don't hold back on my account."

Unlike every other article of her clothing he'd removed so far, there was nothing slow or methodical in the way he desperately dragged her panties over her hips and down her legs. It was rushed, and the realization that she'd made him lose control sent another thrill spiraling through her.

He settled himself between her knees and entered her swiftly, the air rushing out of her lungs as he filled her completely. Holding himself poised above her, Jordan kissed her tenderly as she adjusted to his size. Within moments, though, Camilla rocked her hips against his as her body searched for more contact, more friction, more pressure to satisfy the throbbing desire pulsing from the deepest recesses of her core. He responded at first with short strokes that soon gave way to longer thrusts as he built a steady rhythm that had Camilla writhing with need underneath him.

His warm breath fanned her cheek as his breathing became more labored, more intense every time his hips drew away from her. She gave no thought to her own intake of air, panting desperately as she arched against him. When she brought her knees up on either side of him, Jordan sank deeper inside, and all of the coiled tension from that very first kiss on that very first night suddenly unraveled into a spiral of contractions that reverberated throughout her body until she was shuddering underneath him.

Jordan called out her name before stiffening with his own release while Camilla kept her legs wrapped around him, anchoring herself to him as they both floated into the receding waves of the most electrifying storm she'd ever experienced.

"You weren't lying about your sandwich making skills," Camilla told Jordan as he set a plate in front of her. The dual-sided fireplace was open to both the kitchen and the bedroom, but they chose to spread out a picnic on the bed so they could watch the sunset through the massive windows. "They're almost as good as your bartending skills."

"I've barely even begun showing you all my skills." He deftly pulled the cork out of a bottle of red wine.

Not waiting for him to hand her a glass, she took a bite of the most unbelievable and gravity-defying creation. Crusty, mini loaves of sourdough were stacked high with slow-roasted Taylor Beef (of course), gourmet cheese, grilled red peppers, romaine lettuce and homemade horseradish mayo. Starving, she took a second bite and swallowed before asking, "Where did you learn how to make this?"

"One summer, we had this ranch hand who had a major crush on my nanny, Rosalie. He would always ask her to go riding with him in the afternoons, but my dad used to work late and she would tell him that she couldn't go anywhere without us. He told her to bring us along, but she always found some reason why she couldn't. One day, he asks and she tells him that the chef went home early and she has to make us dinner. He goes, 'No problem. I'll make us all a picnic.' This guy proceeds to get out every possible ingredient he can find in our fridge. Brandon and I were chomping at the bit because we could care less about a picnic, we just wanted to go ride the horses. But the ranch hand took his sweet time and made these sandwiches that Rosalie couldn't stop raving about."

"They must've been pretty delicious to leave such a lasting impression on you." Camilla took a sip of the wine, which paired perfectly with the roast beef.

"Oh, I couldn't even tell you what they tasted like. I was ten and remembered thinking that it would've been just as good and a heck of a lot quicker if he'd slapped some peanut butter and grape jelly on a couple of slices of bread. But every night that week, we got to go out for an evening ride because that man knew how to make a damn good sandwich. It suddenly seemed like an important life skill I needed to master. So I did."

Camilla laughed. "So what happened to Rosalie and this ranch hand? Did they live happily ever after?"

"No. It turns out that the ranch hand was also making sandwiches for the woman who cleaned the bunkhouse on Saturdays. And the cocktail waitress over at Wild Wesley's in town. And possibly Daphne's ballet teacher, but that was never confirmed."

"Oh, my gosh, Jordan." Camilla giggled then threw a pillow at him. "We're sharing this wonderful romantic dinner and that has to be about the least romantic story you could possibly tell me."

"What?" Jordan shrugged, then grinned. "It's not like *I'm* out making sandwiches for anyone else."

Camilla's face went warm and her stomach no longer felt empty. In fact, every part of her body felt blissfully full. Almost complete. "Are you saying that you're not dating anyone else but me?"

He drank his wine, while his eyes drank her in. Then he took her plate from her and set it on the nightstand. "Even if I had the time, which I don't because I'm always busy chasing you, why would I want to when I've got everything I need right here?"

Instead of debating the answer, she let him pull her back down to the sheets and within seconds she had completely forgotten about sandwiches and everything else.

Camilla took one last look at the log structure and already felt a yearning pull at her belly before they'd even left the driveway the following morning. She was going to miss everything about this perfect cabin in the woods, from the gorgeous views of the river beyond the bedroom windows to the equally gorgeous view of a very naked Jordan standing at the tiny kitchen counter as he made her a midnight snack.

She would miss the single stall shower where Jordan crowded in next to her, lathering her back with soap as he sang a Beyoncé song, just as much as she would miss the spacious rag rug in front of the fireplace where the only singing came from Camilla's cries of ecstasy as he lathered her front with his tongue.

She would miss the outside balcony—which was larger than the combined living and dining rooms—where they braved the cold for their morning coffee, just as much as she would miss the cozy cocoon of the bedcovers where they braved the intense warmth of their shared body heat just so they could sleep in each other's arms.

This idyllic cabin represented everything they could have if only their own lives back home weren't so different. Yet as Jordan steered the car toward the main road, the realities of life threatened to pop that perfect bubble they'd created for themselves out here so far away from everyone else.

In fact, that bubble popped much sooner than Camilla expected when his cellular service returned and his phone lit up and buzzed like a restaurant pager notifying a customer that his table was ready.

"Sorry," he said, glancing at the dashboard screen indicating a call coming through. "I really should take this."

At least he waited until Camilla gave him an approving nod before he tapped the phone icon and answered. "What's going on, Mac?"

"Sorry to bug you with this, sport, but we've got an issue with the Oakmont account." His assistant immediately started describing what sounded like a suspended delivery due to an unpaid invoice and Camilla tried to catch the details, but the entire time all she could think about was the fact that this was a first.

In all the times they'd spent together or near each other—even on weekdays—Jordan had never taken a work call. Sure, there was that one date when they flew in the helicopter and he had the meeting with his distributor, but when he was *with* her, he was always present. Up until now, Camilla had, for the most part, been his sole focus. Of course she had never expected him to devote all of his attention to her all of the time. He had other responsibilities and a business to run. It was just that she hadn't expected him to shift gears and return to business mode so quickly.

"I'll take care of it, Mac," Jordan said. "Can you connect me to my dad's office?"

As he waited on hold for his assistant to transfer him, Camilla felt a shiver travel down her neck. Did Mac know they'd spent the night together? She seemed to know everything else about her boss.

Would his father find out?

Did it matter if he did? She tried to scold herself for caring about it one way or the other, but all the twists and turns down the mountain road threatened her rational thoughts.

Originally, she had wanted to keep their relationship a secret. But her family knew about it, as did Daphne. Cornelius had even seen them riding together, so he must at least suspect something was going on. However, there was a big difference between casually dating and spending the night together.

The call was dropped several times because of the spotty reception and when Jordan finally got through to his father's assistant, he cursed because the man told him that Cornelius was out of the office. But of course the very determined Jordan wasn't going to simply let it go at that. She knew firsthand that he'd go after what he wanted until he got it.

Jordan disconnected and, without explanation or apology, pulled up the contact number for his father, which weirdly was listed on his phone as Cornelius Taylor III rather than the informal Dad. When Cornelius answered, his booming voice echoed on speaker in the confines of the car.

"This had better be important, Jordan," his

father said by way of greeting. "I'm about to walk into that press luncheon with the governor."

"Dad, please tell me you didn't stop delivery to Oakmont on the day before Thanksgiving." Something about the commanding tone of Jordan's voice made Camilla pause in her own thoughts of what she planned to say to him when he finished his business call. Maybe this was more serious than a past due account.

"They're over fourteen months behind on their payments, Jordan. Taylor Beef isn't a charity operation."

"I gave them a grace period." Jordan picked up Camilla's hand and softly kissed each finger almost absentmindedly as he began speaking to his father about trade agreements and financial solvency and fluctuating market prices.

Cornelius Taylor gave no indication that he knew someone else was in the car with his son, and Camilla would've felt guilty for listening in on the call if she wasn't becoming slightly aroused by both his touch and his impressive business knowledge.

Cornelius countered with arguments about other customers and disproportionate pricing and enforcing legal contracts. Halfway through his father's explanation, Jordan rolled his eyes and mouthed the word *sorry* to Camilla.

"I'm gonna stop you there, Dad," he finally

interrupted. A tingle raced up her arm and it wasn't just from the skilled way his thumb was now stroking her knuckles as he used his other hand to deftly steer the sports car along the winding road down the mountain. Jordan's response to his father was informed and well-articulated as he cited last quarter's profit and loss margins and rattled off the stock market's most recent closing numbers for shares of the biggest beef companies from the United States to Japan to Brazil.

This wasn't some rich kid working for the family business, she realized, as he continued to astonish her with his knowledge and insight. Jordan wasn't having this conversation, though, to impress her. He was simply being himself and, in doing so, providing her with a glimpse of his daily life.

"At the end of the day," Jordan finished, "the amount they owe us is a drop in the bucket and barely affects our bottom line."

"But it's the principle, son. You give somebody something for free and they'll just keep coming back and taking advantage of you. There's no place for emotion in business."

"Dad, Oakmont is a homeless shelter and this is their busiest time of the year," Jordan replied, and Camilla suddenly understood why he'd been so focused on responding to this particular problem. "It also falls under my scope as the VP of Operations for the company. You need to let me handle it."

"Fine. But between your bleeding heart and Daphne's, don't be surprised if our family ends up in the poorhouse."

"According to our estate attorneys and an ironclad trust fund, I don't have to worry about those types of surprises. Besides, Dad, your heart could do with a little bleeding."

"Nope. The last charity case who got too close to my heart nearly bled me dry," Cornelius said, then disconnected without so much as a good-bye.

"Give me one more minute," Jordan said to Camilla as he turned onto the county highway that would take them to Bronco. "I need to make two more calls."

First he called Mac and gave her instructions for reinstating the Oakmont account. Next, he called the director of Oakmont and personally apologized for the misunderstanding. "We'll have a delivery truck out to you this afternoon."

By the time he got off the phone, they were almost to Camilla's apartment, and she understood why they called him the Smoother.

When he parked his car in the alley below her front porch in the spot she was starting to think of as his, Camilla turned to him and asked,

"Was your dad referring to the Denim and Diamonds gala?"

"When?" Jordan asked.

"When he said that the last charity case nearly bled him dry. I assumed he was talking about the fundraiser he hosted."

"Oh, no. My dad thinks it's a clever play of words to refer to his ex-wives as charity cases. And to him, any time his net worth dips below nine figures, he thinks he's practically going bankrupt."

Her eyes widened at the revelation of the Taylors' financial standing before she blinked back her own insecurities. Would everyone else in his family think of *her* as one of Jordan's charity cases? She gulped and murmured, "How charming."

"Actually, if he'd known you were listening, he would've laid the charm on real thick, like he does for everyone else. But the real Cornelius Taylor isn't the best businessman. He's been burned by a few business associates that he thought were friends, and he's been targeted by scores of gold diggers in his lifetime. He always thinks everyone is out to take advantage of him."

And of his son, Camilla thought. But she didn't want to say that aloud and cast any shadows on their perfect night together.

Chapter Ten

"Jordan, where is your family today?" Dante asked as they gathered around the Sanchezes's dining table on Thursday afternoon.

"My dad and stepmom are hosting my uncles and a few of their friends at their house for Thanksgiving," he answered as he passed the bowl of stuffing to Dylan. "They invited us, but when Camilla told me how important the holiday is to your family, I didn't want her to miss all these traditional dishes."

Camilla wrinkled her nose at the lime-green gelatin-and-fruit salad molded in the shape of a ring before she shot him a questioning look. "They invited *me*?"

Well, not specifically. Cornelius had asked if he planned on bringing a "plus one" and then blew a gasket when Jordan said he wouldn't be home at all for the Thanksgiving meal. But the plus one would've been Camilla, so that counted as an invite, right?

Jordan shrugged. "I didn't bring it up before because I figured we'd be a lot more comfortable here."

Dylan pointed an accusatory turkey leg at him. "Doesn't your family like Camilla?"

"They've only met her once." Jordan twisted the cloth napkin in his lap as all the eyes at the table turned toward him. "My family can be a bit overwhelming. At least, some of them can."

"I bet your family's food is way better than Mrs. Waters's grandmother's runny creamed onions, though," Sophia said, refusing to take a spoonful of the untouched dish before shoving it at Felix, who also refused to accept it.

Jordan knew better than to answer that. He also knew better than to laugh too much at the Sanchez siblings' ongoing teasing and complaining about the so-called traditional Thanksgiving dishes, especially since this was their family's way of commemorating their first holiday in America. Yet even *he* couldn't argue with the fact that this was actually one of the least appetizing meals he'd ever experienced at their house.

On the other hand, it was also one of the most fun meals because they were now including him in their family's inside jokes. In fact, the more often he visited the Sanchezes, the more at home he felt here, as though they were truly starting to accept him.

Plus, the food wasn't really all that bad, especially not after Mr. Sanchez brought out a couple of bottles of chilled sauvignon blanc to help wash everything down. Jordan helped himself to one of the tastier items on the table and stared at it for a few seconds before asking, "So the rolls just come from the can like this?"

"Wait. You mean your fancy chef doesn't make crescent rolls up at the ranch?" Sophia giggled before realizing nobody else was joining in. In fact, the normally rambunctious table had grown extremely quiet.

"What?" Sophia held up a butter knife. "Are we all going to keep on pretending we don't know who he is?"

"Who is he?" Dante whispered across the table to Dylan, who shook his head in confusion.

Camilla squeezed Jordan's knee under the table, and he wasn't sure if it was meant as a reassuring gesture or a warning to remain quiet. She darted a glance at her sister. "You knew?"

"Obviously. I loaned you the dress to go to his party, remember? Besides, I work in a boutique in Bronco Heights. Half of my customers are socialites actively talking about him and his reputation."

Jordan gulped down his wine so quickly, he nearly choked.

Camilla pressed her lips together before shooting a nervous look toward their mother.

"You both might as well own up to it." Mrs. Sanchez dumped more salt onto some boiled butternut squash. "Mrs. Waters called him out in the salon in front of everyone."

Camilla cocked her head at him. "Why didn't you tell me my mom knew?"

Jordan pointed at his mouth, which was full of the mashed potatoes he'd purposely stuffed in there to prevent him from having to answer anything.

"Is there even anyone else to tell?" Camilla asked, scanning the people around the table.

"How could I *not* know?" Mr. Sanchez sat back in his seat at the head of the table and used a napkin to wipe his mouth. "I've been a mail carrier for the past thirty years and there's only three Jordans in this town."

"Here he goes with the mail-carrier-knows-everything bit." Sofia rolled her eyes. "Settle in, everyone."

Mr. Sanchez gave his youngest child a dismissive glance before continuing. "Like I was saying, one is a nine-year-old boy who writes a postcard to Santa Claus every year asking for a puppy. He's up to five dogs now and, according to his latest postcard in the North Pole drop box, he's asking for a sixth. Speaking of which, I need to give his parents the heads-up."

"You could've given *me* the heads-up that you already knew," Camilla muttered under her breath.

"Is this story going somewhere, Dad?" Dylan drummed his fingers on either side of his plate.

Mr. Sanchez took another sip of wine, apparently not the least bothered that everyone else at the table was now sitting on the edges of their seats as he took his time with his long-winded explanation. "The second one is the Montgomerys' daughter, who is away at Montana State right now. Her name is spelled J-O-R-D-Y-N-N, though, so I guess that doesn't count."

"Dad," Dylan interrupted. "*None* of this counts unless you tell us who the other Jordan in town is."

"Then there's the Jordan whose legal physical address is technically 408 Old Bronco Highway. However, he receives all his personal mail at the Taylor Beef headquarters." Mr. Sanchez's words hung in the air as the remaining family members pieced it together.

Jordan, though, wasn't about to be ashamed

of who he was. He sat up straighter and draped one arm across the back of Camilla's chair. This time when she put her hand on his thigh, it was not only reassuring, it was almost possessive. As though she was also claiming him in front of her family. His chest filled with pride, even as he squared himself for the onslaught of opinions that would surely follow. After all, the Sanchez family usually had plenty of opinions.

"Daaang," Dante said slowly as his brow creased into a V above his nose. "You're *that* Jordan Taylor? And nobody thought it was something to share with me and Dylan and Felix?"

Felix didn't seem upset, though. In fact, he'd found a sudden interest in the cranberry sauce that had been completely ignored until now.

"Hold up." The legs of Dylan's chair screeched against the hardwood floor as he shoved himself away from the table to jump up. He pointed an accusing finger at his oldest brother. "Felix *did* know! That's why he chose Jordan for basketball the very first night. You went to high school with him and knew he held all those athletic records. You've been keeping Jordan to yourself all this time."

At that, the entire table erupted and instead of anyone berating Jordan for keeping a secret— not that he'd technically kept it a secret—they all accused each other of knowing exactly who he was, but never discussing it.

Voices were raised and overlapped other voices, and the only thing he could make out was that everyone kept their knowledge to themselves because they were afraid of how the others would react if they'd known he was one of *those* Taylors. Except for Felix, who kept the knowledge to himself so he could keep beating his brothers on the basketball court.

Since none of the arguing was currently directed his way, Jordan used the ongoing distraction as an excuse to pull his vibrating cell phone from his back pocket. It had gone off several times during the meal, but he hadn't wanted to be rude and answer it at the table. When he saw the text from his father, though, he nearly groaned.

"What is it?" Camilla whispered and leaned toward him. He showed her the display screen.

You need to get here and deal with your sister.

"You should probably go," Camilla said. Was she saying that because she wanted him gone? Because now that her family knew who he was, she was suddenly embarrassed of him? Or maybe she wanted to protect him from the fallout—when all the Sanchezes stopped arguing among each other and decided to team up to demand that she stop dating him. Because despite their teasing and trash talk, Jordan knew without a doubt that this family would band together to protect one of their own.

Not that Camilla needed to be protected from him.

Regardless of what was transpiring with Camilla and her family, though, Jordan couldn't stay here and leave Daphne hanging.

"You're right. I really should go." He let out the breath he hadn't realized he'd been holding. "Any chance I could talk you into coming with me?"

"It sounds like a private family matter. I'm sure your father wouldn't want me there."

And just like that, the arguing at the table stopped suddenly and everyone shifted curious eyes to Camilla and Jordan.

"I've got a text from my father." Jordan held up his phone. "Something has come up and I need to go home."

"Oh, did Daddy summon you back to the ranch for pumpkin pie?" Dylan asked, but the normal teasing didn't seem so playful now that they knew who his father was.

Or maybe this rush of defensiveness pressing against Jordan's chest was due to the fact that he had, technically, just been summoned.

Either way, now wasn't the time for Jordan to show weakness or shame. All of the Sanchezes appreciated people standing up for themselves and if he truly wanted to fit in with them, he needed to give as good as he got.

So he looked Camilla's brother in the eye and said, "Don't worry, Dylan. I'll give you time to digest all that turkey and then I'll come back to demonstrate that box out reversal move on the basketball court."

Dylan snorted, but had a smile on his face. "Oh, I don't need a demonstration. In fact, I plan to show *you* a thing or two."

Someone suggested that it might snow tonight, making the court slippery. This caused another eruption of smack talk between all the brothers with Mr. Sanchez playing referee. Once again, Jordan used the distraction to talk privately with Camilla. To hopefully convince her that it would actually be more beneficial to have her with him.

"Daphne knows you, so taking you there with me will make her feel like she has more support," he told her. "Plus, my father typically causes less of a scene when there are witnesses around. I told you how he is about appearances and all that."

What he didn't tell her was that she would likely be jumping feetfirst into the Taylor family drama. His dad and sister loved each other, but they'd been butting heads for a long time now, the buildup of tension only making their battle lines more rigid. The showdown would likely be an emotional tug-of-war.

If Camilla could survive that, then he was certain she would finally realize that there was nothing else keeping them from being together.

Camilla's stomach did somersaults as they drove up the main driveway of the Taylor Ranch. While it felt good that Jordan wanted her by his side, she was certain that nobody else in the Taylor family would be happy to see her.

The first sign that something was wrong was when they pulled up to the main house and Daphne's vehicle wasn't in sight.

"She must've already left," Jordan said as he put his car in Park.

He took Camilla's hand as they walked toward the ten-feet-high custom-made oak front doors. From far away, the house had been impressive. Yet standing on the sprawling log-beamed porch, which was easily bigger than the entire cabin they'd shared in Great Falls, was downright overwhelming.

The massive entryway they passed through was larger than most hotel lobbies and way better decorated. She barely had time to take in the tasteful and obviously expensive furnishings as Jordan pulled her behind him toward a dining room with a table long enough to seat at least thirty people.

Judging by the abandoned silver place settings, china plates and crystal goblets, there had likely been at least that many people here earlier. But now only Cornelius sat at the head of the table, his pretty young wife to the right of him.

"Look who finally shows up," the silver-haired patriarch barked. Holding court in his throne-sized chair, Cornelius Taylor seemed as though he relished his role of monarch of his own royal kingdom.

"What's going on?" Jordan asked, his jaw tighter than Camilla had ever seen it.

"What's going on is that Jessica spent several weeks planning this dinner and it was totally ruined."

Jordan's fingers were rigid against hers, but he kept her hand in his. "How was it ruined?"

"The table was set with place cards and everything. Your uncles and cousins and all of our most important neighbors and friends were here. But when it was time for Gallagher to serve the meal, those two seats at the end—" Cornelius pointed to the opposite end of the table "—were still empty."

"I really didn't mind having empty seats." Jessica tentatively patted the older man's hand as it gripped the ornate wood of his armrest. Camilla wanted to tell poor Jessica that her husband clearly wasn't offended on *her* behalf. He was annoyed that his plans had been thwarted. That he hadn't gotten what he wanted.

"I apologize for the misunderstanding, Jessica." Jordan bowed his head toward his young stepmother. "But I told my father last night that we were having Thanksgiving dinner with Camilla's family."

Cornelius's frown got even deeper, if that was possible. "And *I* told her that you would come to your senses and stop chasing tail long enough to do your family duty."

Camilla gasped, tasting a bitterness in her throat. She'd been mentally prepared for the old man to suggest that she was after Jordan for his money. But she hadn't quite expected him to insinuate that Jordan was only using her for sex.

Before she could defend herself, Jordan had shifted himself in front of her. His intent might've been to block her from his father's attacks, but now all she could focus on was the tension stretching across his shoulders. His voice was cold and rock-steady when he said, "I've already told you that Camilla is much more than that, so I suggest you watch what you say."

Okay, so maybe some of the bitterness building inside her was eased when she heard Jordan readily jump to her defense. His warning to his father definitely gave her a boost of courage to step around his blocking back, resuming her place by his side. Just in time to see Cornelius roll his eyes to the monstrous crystal chandelier above.

"My apologies, miss." Cornelius gazed down his nose at Camilla, his tone sounding anything but apologetic. "I'm sure you're not just another one of my son's passing fancies, and I have no place pointing out to him how much he stands to lose by getting involved with the wrong girl."

"Just stop with the passive aggressive comments, Dad." Jordan shoved a hand through his hair. "You always go for the hidden insult when you know you can't win. This is why we didn't come tonight. I didn't want to subject Camilla to your whole dog and pony show. It's your own fault that you still set a place for us at the table after I clearly told you we wouldn't be attending."

She tapped Jordan on the back and pointed to the names written on the two place cards disposed of on the side table. Jordan Taylor and Daphne Taylor. "I don't think anyone was actually expecting me to show up."

Instead of relishing the fact that she'd been right all along, that she would never be welcomed in Jordan's world, Camilla's heart was trying not to sag like the used linen napkins carelessly discarded along the once carefully laid table.

"Do you know what it's like to have my own two children, my very own flesh and blood, turn their backs on me?" Cornelius continued on unfazed, underscoring the fact that Camilla's personal feelings—even her presence—were secondary to the real reason he'd summoned Jordan out to the ranch like a naughty child. "And on Thanksgiving, of all times, when everyone is here to witness it firsthand?"

"Where's Daph, Dad?" Jordan's biceps was a coil of tense muscle, his hand clenched beside hers. "Your text made it sound as though I needed to come out here immediately to talk with her. You made it sound like something was wrong."

"It is!" Cornelius slammed a fist on the table, rattling the crystal water goblet near him. "She refused to come to dinner unless Jessica added alternative dishes to the menu. What was that damn concoction she mentioned? Plant-based turkey? As if we'd ever serve anything so ridiculous under this roof."

"It really was no problem," Jessica murmured, patting her husband's hand again. "I could've had the chef prepare—"

"No." Cornelius put his palm up, dismissing his wife in midsentence. "This vegetarian phase of hers has gone on long enough. First she makes a mockery out of me—out of our family legacy—by running that Hippie Hearts animal shelter, whatever the hell that is. Then she wants to sit at my table, in front of all my friends, like some sort of social justice warrior lording her meatless righteousness over us. She's turning me into a complete laughingstock."

"Dad, you're really overreacting. Daphne's dietary decisions have nothing to do with you."

"We make our living by turning cattle into steaks and she wants to make her living by saving them. It goes against everything we stand for. Taylor Beef money was good enough for her growing up, but now she wants to publicly turn up her nose at us. When are you going to wake up, son? This is what women do. They take and take until they can't use you anymore." His scathing words even made his young wife's mouth drop open. "Even your sister—"

"I'm going to cut you off right there, Mr. Taylor," Camilla interrupted. The anger roiling through her had propelled her forward to stand in front of Jordan. "I don't know what kind of people you've surrounded yourself with before now, but that is *not* what women do. And if your neighbors and so-called friends allow you to talk about other women this way, then they are not your true friends. They're your minions. I've heard you make several disparaging comments about charity cases and chasing tail, and someone needs to tell you once and for all that blaming women for your unhappiness reflects more poorly on *you* and your decisions than it does on the women in your life. In fact, thinking everyone is only interested in your money doesn't make you sound powerful. It makes you sound scared."

Cornelius's face had gone a blustery shade of red and his eyes narrowed into angry slits. Yet he kept his voice measured as he said, "Thank you, Carol, for your insight into something that is absolutely none of your business. This is a family matter and you would do well to take yourself back to the Valley."

"If you know that I'm from the Valley, sir, then you also know damn well that my name is Camilla. So let's not play this game where you pretend that you haven't had a team of paid informants looking into my background the second you found out that Jordan and I were in a relationship."

"We've moved on from dating to a relationship now?" Jordan whispered out the side of his mouth. Camilla whipped her head in his direction and he twisted his lower lip. "Never mind. Keep going."

"Well, whatever you guys want to call it," Cornelius said as he wagged a finger between them. "This thing between you two won't last."

"Now, Cornelius…" Jessica tutted quietly. It wasn't really a reprimand, but her attempt to at least redirect her husband, to nearly stand up to him, energized Camilla. Even if she ruined things between Jordan and his father, at least she might have empowered another woman.

"Maybe it *will* last." Camilla let the threat hang in the air for a few seconds. "And maybe it won't. But either way, the future of our relationship won't be something you can control. Contrary to whatever bull you've been feeding yourself, Mr. Taylor, your children have their own minds and their own personalities and their own journeys. Jordan is no more like you than Daphne is, and he's a better man for it."

As soon as Camilla said the words aloud, she realized that she really believed it. Jordan was nothing like this bitter, high-handed braggart.

Cornelius stood up and tossed his napkin on the table. "I'm not going to sit in my own house and listen to some waitress tell me how I should run my family."

Camilla, though, couldn't let him storm out of the dining room without one last parting shot.

"Well, even this waitress knows that you can run a business, but you can't run a family. As soon as you make peace with that, you'll be a happier man."

Her heart was thudding in her chest when Jordan slipped his hand from hers. Had she been out of line? Had she gone too far? Instead of following his father, though, he wrapped his arm around her waist and led her to the door. "Let's get out of here."

Exactly three weeks after first feeling like a gatecrasher at one of their fancy parties, Camilla was actually being escorted off the Taylor Ranch.

Possibly for good this time.

Chapter Eleven

"I'm sorry." Camilla finally broke the tense silence when Jordan turned onto Old Bronco Highway. "I really overstepped. I never should have—"

"Are you kidding?" Jordan cut in. "You were magnificent. Hardly anyone ever stands up to my old man like that and I've never been more impressed. So please don't be sorry for telling him what very few people have the guts to say."

"Oh, I wasn't apologizing for what I said to him." The edges of Camilla's tongue were still tingling with defensiveness, though she'd lost some of her earlier sizzle. "I was expressing my condolences that you have to deal with that guy on a regular basis."

Jordan made a scratchy chuckle at first before bursting out in a full laugh. Like a cork being popped out of a champagne bottle, Camilla felt some of her own tension fizzle with his release.

He caught his breath long enough to ask, "Did you see his face when you told him he looked weak and pitiful?"

"Oh, my gosh." Camilla giggled, feeling all that earlier pressure lifting from her shoulders. "I turned to Jessica to see if she was going to start fanning him with her napkin because he looked like he was going to blow a gasket."

He erupted into another fit of laughter, which was so contagious, she couldn't help but join in. Even though it felt wrong to be laughing at his father's expense, relief washed through her, knowing that Jordan wasn't angry with her.

"But seriously," he said on a sobering breath. "Remember when I told you that I see things differently when I'm with you? I've gotten so immune to my father's blustering and his control tactics over the years that I was oblivious to how everyone else saw him. I can brush him off when he insults me, but I hated the way he spoke to you. He was completely out of line and you didn't deserve his condescension."

Thankfully, Jordan didn't make any excuses for his father, nor did he downplay the man's pointed comments. Maybe he really was starting to understand what she would have to put up with if they ended up together.

Camilla sighed as she leaned back in the leather seat, watching the flickering colors whizzing by her window. The Thanksgiving dinner leftovers were barely put away, yet people were already stringing up their Christmas lights. She never understood how folks could so easily move on from one thing to the next.

It brought to mind Cornelius Taylor's comment about Jordan chasing tail. Deep down, she knew that the older man's goal wasn't really to insult her. His goal was to get his son back under his thumb. She was just collateral damage.

But it didn't make the insult hurt any less.

When they stopped at an intersection, Jordan lifted his hand and gently stroked her cheek with the back of his fingers until she turned to look at him. "I am really sorry for putting you through that. I'm especially sorry for dragging you away from your own family's house and ruining your holiday."

"You didn't ruin my holiday, Jordan," she said, her eyes blinking back a sudden threat of dampness. Admitting otherwise would be like admitting that his father had the power to hurt her, which would be like admitting that, deep down, she wanted the Taylors to accept her the way the Sanchezes had clearly accepted Jordan.

So she forced a smile instead. "Although I'm pretty bummed that I missed out on the only good part of our Thanksgiving meal."

"The after-dinner basketball game?" he asked.

"No, the pumpkin pie. Mrs. Waters can't make a casserole to save her life, but her pie recipes are out of this world."

Jordan laughed, then drove her back to the Sanchez house. Thankfully, most of her siblings had already gone back to their own places and she was able to sneak out of her parents' kitchen with a prepacked bag of leftovers, half of a pecan pie—the pumpkin was long gone—and no questions about the drama at Taylor Ranch.

The adrenaline from her earlier encounter with Cornelius had drained just as quickly as it had spiked, leaving Camilla's body depleted and her mind emotionally exhausted. She didn't want to talk right that second or even eat. All she wanted was to spend the evening wrapped in the warmth of Jordan's arms. By the time they reached her apartment, it was pretty much a foregone conclusion that he would be coming upstairs with her. At least, for her it was. She knew he would never push for it unless she asked.

Following her, he carried the bag of leftovers up the stairs. The pie tin was balanced in one of her uplifted palms as she used her free hand to unlock the door. While she was distracted, Jordan shot an arm around her waist and turned her toward him. "I've been waiting all day for this, and I don't want to wait another minute."

He kissed her gently, slowly building the pressure of his lips and skillful tongue until Camilla couldn't have told him good-night even if she'd wanted to. So she did what any sane, red-blooded woman would do.

Still balancing the pie, she playfully slipped her hand down the front of his shirt until she got to his waistband. Then she grabbed the most accessible thing—his belt buckle—and pulled him inside her apartment so she could finish what he'd started.

Jordan stretched his arms over his head as he watched Camilla sleep curled up beside him in her bed. He could've stayed like this all morning, but the constant buzzing of his cell phone on the bedside table was becoming increasingly difficult to ignore.

Normally, he never bothered with the notifications from Taylor Beef's marketing team, but he couldn't disregard the three missed calls from Mac. Or her text message in all caps that said, CHECK OUT THE POST ON @AllThingsBronco.

Ugh. Mac knew Jordan hated those ridiculous social media accounts that were no better than the sleazy tabloids. He was about to set the phone down unanswered but another notification alert pinged on his phone, this time from Daphne. You better do something about this, Jor.

His chest rumbled with a groan, which made Camilla stir awake. She pressed her warm and very nude body closer to his before lifting her sleepy, sexy eyes to his face. He was more than tempted to toss the phone to the nearby sofa until she asked, "What's wrong?"

"I'm not sure. I'm guessing it's some sort of article or social media post about Daphne not showing up at my dad's last night for dinner. The people posting these things never have all the facts and always make a big deal out of nothing." He clicked on the link Daphne and Mac had both sent him.

When he saw the image fill his screen he groaned again. When he read the bold caption underneath, he cursed.

"Is it that bad?" Camilla sat up, taking the top sheet with her. "Poor Daphne."

"It's not about my sister."

She took the phone from him. He scrubbed his hands across the stubble on his jaw and then his eyes. Unfortunately, he couldn't unsee the bold caption under the picture of him and Camilla standing on her tiny porch last night, kissing.

Bronco's Most Eligible Bachelor in Torrid
Affair with Waitress

The angle of the photo meant it was likely shot
from the sidewalk across the street, where the
only nearby businesses were an antiques shop
and a dry cleaner, two places that would've been
closed on a Thanksgiving evening. "Someone
must've been following us last night."

"Perhaps. Your Tesla certainly stands out in
this neighborhood," Camilla said rather calmly.
With as much effort as she'd taken to keep their
relationship a secret, she certainly wasn't showing any emotion now that they'd been found out.
In fact, her tone was purely casual when she
pointed out, "The way I'm holding up the pecan
pie like a serving tray nicely underscores the fact
that I'm just a waitress."

He sat up in the bed. "Come on, Camilla, you
know you're so much more than that."

"Of course I know that, Jordan. But it still
doesn't seem to stop anyone from commenting
on my job title." She didn't have to point out
that his father had also made the same reference last night.

Jordan retrieved the phone from her and only
made it through the first few comments before
he felt steam practically expel from his eyeballs.

How could people be so absolutely mean about someone they'd never met? So absolutely crude?

It was one thing for him to ignore the haters when he was the target of their snide opinions and disparaging nicknames. It was quite another to see them so blatantly insulting Camilla. She'd done nothing to deserve any of this.

His fingers flew over the keyboard as he composed several scathing retorts before deleting them all. "You know what? These jerks don't deserve a response. Half of them can't even use proper grammar. I mean, what the hell is a 'goal digger'?"

Camilla lifted her eyebrows as though he should already know, which he did. Then she stood and grabbed the nearest article of clothing on her floor—his cashmere sweater—and slid it over her head. Without saying a word, she padded the twelve or so feet to the kitchen and switched on her coffee maker. "You think that's bad? Slide to the next picture in the post and see what some creative thinkers wrote there."

Jordan set his feet on the floor, but that didn't brace him for the next image. It was of Camilla—still holding that pecan pie—using her other hand to pull on his belt as she led him inside. The caption said:

Grabbing the bull by the horn, or in this case, the Rancher by the—

Jordan couldn't look away from some of the disgusting comments people were making on *that one*. But ultimately, the consensus was the same. They thought Camilla was an opportunist and not good enough for the Charmed Prince of Bronco Heights.

"How are you being so calm about this?" he asked as he yanked on his discarded pants.

"Because I expected this all along." She shrugged. "Any female who dates you must know that her name is going to get thrown to the wolves. When those females are wealthy socialites, the wolves might sniff around a bit before getting bored and moving on. But when it's someone like me—someone who shouldn't even be able to reach the social ladder, let alone climb it—then it's gonna be an open feast."

Guilt rocked through Jordan. She was right. She'd even tried to warn him, but he blew her off, thinking that it couldn't possibly be this bad. "So how do you think we should handle this?"

"There's nothing to handle." Again Camilla shrugged, and her indifference affected him more than anything else had. What had happened to the woman who'd fought for him last night? Jordan watched her in confusion as she took a sip of coffee then added, "Stuff like this is going to happen no matter what we say. And if people think we're together, it'll happen even more."

"They *better* think we're together," Jordan said louder than he intended. "They also better think that I'm not going to sit by while a bunch of strangers make insulting comments about you on social media."

Camilla hesitated and in that moment, he saw she wasn't completely indifferent. "I'm not sure that's such a good idea."

"Look." He reached up to trace the outline of her face and ended by sliding his fingers into her silky hair as he cupped her head. She leaned into him somewhat reluctantly. "Last night, you admitted that we were in a relationship. I know we agreed on three weeks, six official dates, before we made any final decisions. Now that we've come this far, though, there's no way either one of us is willing to throw all of that away."

"Be very careful about what you're committing to, Jordan." Her eyes searched his. "If we continue to see each other, this will be our reality. If we're going to come out and tell everyone that we're a couple, we will have to deal with the backlash."

He planted his feet apart and pulled her closer to him. "I'm up for the challenge."

Her chuckle was forced, but he wasn't kidding. This time, she drew her hands up to his jaw and cupped his face. "Come on, Jordan. Let's not kid ourselves. You've walked away from a number of relationships over a lot less than some negative publicity. The truth is, we've only known each other a few weeks. Before rushing into a full-blown relationship, maybe we should just take it slow and see how this all plays out."

"I don't want to take it slow." He stepped back and stretched his arms over his head. "Hell, Camilla, I want the whole damn world to know."

"That's easy for you to say." She braced one hand on the kitchen counter. "You're not the one they're calling a gold digger. Your business won't be affected by any of this. However, the business I'm trying to launch—the one I've been dreaming about and planning for the past six years—will depend on my reputation. I might be able to thumb my nose at these types of posts while we're together. But what happens when we break up?"

Break up? The words were a punch to his solar plexus. "You've barely admitted we're in a relationship and now you're already thinking about dumping me?"

"I'm thinking about what will happen down the road. If we break up, which is entirely possible since we barely even know each other, then I'm going to be the one who looks like the evil money grubber. The one who failed to sink her hooks into you. You'll always be the Prince Charming who made a dashing escape."

"Nobody will ever think that about you," he argued. How could anyone think Camilla Sanchez was anything less than perfect and smart and amazing?

She marched over to where he'd left his phone and tapped on the display screen. "They already do."

"Then I'll tell them that they're all wrong."

"Of course you will. Or better yet, why don't you have Cornelius Taylor issue one of his royal commands?"

After everything she'd witnessed last night between him and his old man, he was surprised by how much her words stung. "Are you comparing me to my father?"

"No. Maybe. I don't know." She rubbed her temples. "All I'm trying to say is that you can't go around telling people *how* they should feel or *what* they should believe."

He shoved his hands into his pockets and dropped his head. He'd gone from anger to desperation to shame in the blink of five minutes. The last emotion wasn't something he wanted to dwell on. He was a successful businessman who didn't back down from a challenge or a negotiation.

Jordan sucked in a deep breath through his nose, inhaling every ounce of determination he could harness. When he dragged his eyes up to

Camilla's beautiful face he said, "I'm not going to tell you how to feel. But I'm also not going to apologize to you—or to anyone else—for how *I* feel."

"Look, Jordan, it's been an intense few days and I have to go back to work tonight. Maybe it's best if we just let the dust settle a little bit before either one of us says something we might later regret."

"Fine." He snatched his shirt off the floor, not bothering to put on his boots before walking out into the cold, harsh reality of morning. He didn't even care that people might be hanging out on the street in front of her apartment, hoping for a photo of Jordan Taylor doing the walk of shame.

Frustration grew with each bare step he took. He was frustrated with the anonymous social media haters for commenting on things that were none of their business. He was frustrated with Camilla for not believing in their relationship. He was frustrated with his father because, well, because he was always frustrated with his old man and would think of the reason later.

But mostly, he was frustrated with himself and his complete lack of control over the situation.

How had it all gone wrong so fast?

That weekend, Camilla threw herself into work. And when she wasn't doing that, she threw herself into her plans for her new restaurant and putting the finishing touches on her Integrated Project for school. She'd already given her two-week notice at DJ's Deluxe and had even opened escrow on the old library building in Bronco Valley, which needed a ton of repairs.

She told herself that she was too busy to worry about Jordan and what he wanted right this second. She told herself that by not answering his calls immediately, she was giving him the chance to see that he would be fine without her. She told herself that the only way either one of them would be able to think clearly and evaluate their relationship was if there was some distance between them.

What she couldn't tell herself, though, was that not seeing him, not hearing his voice for several days, had only made her miss him more.

As Camilla drove away from a meeting with her investor—who, thankfully, hadn't withdrawn financial support for the restaurant after seeing all those negative social media comments about her—she saw Jordan's name appear on her phone screen. Her conflicted heart was already tearing at the seams, so she finally gave in and answered.

"Hey," she said as she pulled over to the side of the road.

"Fifth time is the charm," he replied, probably referring to the four other "missed" calls he'd made this past weekend. "How are you?"

"I'm doing okay. Just really, you know, busy right now. How are *you*?"

"Well, I'm going crazy over here not knowing what you're thinking or how you're feeling. I miss you, Camilla."

She squeezed her eyes shut. "I miss you, too."

"Then why won't you see me?"

"Because I think we both need to cool down, give each other some space, and take a little time to consider what we really want."

"Except I already know what I want. I want you."

Heat spread over her skin before a sudden chill set in. As much as she loved hearing him say the words, she knew that she had to be strong and hold her ground. "Then you'll have to wait until I figure out what *I* want."

"How long will that take?" he asked, and she could picture him looking at his watch.

"There's no timetable. This isn't something you can put on your schedule or a deadline you can write into a contract. I'm not going anywhere, Jordan. I'm just asking for some space."

"And I promise that I'm trying my hardest to give you that space." He really was, she knew. The Jordan she'd met a few weeks ago would've casually shown up everywhere he thought she might be in the hopes of spending time with her. So for him, this was progress. That didn't stop the negotiator in him from adding, "But I can't prove to you we're meant to be together if we're never actually together."

"I get it. It's just that I need to be sure you're ready for a real relationship with a woman who…" She paused, not wanting to use the same words others had used to describe her. Camilla knew who she was and refused to be defined by any of those haters on social media. "With a woman like me."

"You mean a beautiful and smart and capable woman who doesn't need me? I think I've already proven that I'm more than ready for that."

"But for how long, Jordan? How long will you be willing to put up with all the disapproval from your father and the rest of the world? Who's to say that you won't get tired of the turmoil and go back to women who fit into the mold of who a Taylor should date?"

"Neither one of us can answer that unless you give us a chance to find out," he countered. "It's like this restaurant you're planning to open, right? You've crunched all the numbers, you've analyzed all the data, you've studied all the business models. I can tell you until I'm blue in the face that it's going to be a success because I'm confident in the person running it. But the rest of the town won't know it's a success until after you open your doors and they can see it for themselves. There's no reward without risk."

"This isn't a business, though, Jordan. This is my—" Camilla cut herself off before she said the word *heart*. She wasn't ready to admit that to herself, let alone to him. "Look, it's taken me years to plan this restaurant. To, as you put it, open up my doors and take the risk. So, yeah, I'm going to want a little more time before I jump into another risk. Especially when all the cost analysis reports I've seen regarding your past dating history don't exactly show a high rate of return."

Camilla wished she could take back the words as soon as she said them. After all, Jordan had never asked for a spreadsheet on *her* dating history. She would've fumed in protest if any guy had wanted to hold her past relationships against her. Not that there were many serious ones, but there was a reason she'd never taken anyone home to meet her family before now.

"That's the difference between us, I guess," Jordan replied. "I don't see being with you as a risk."

Camilla let her head fall against the headrest. "That's because you don't really have as much to lose."

Chapter Twelve

Jordan leaned back in his desk chair, staring at the office ceiling in frustration after he got off the phone with Camilla. Then he stared at the papers on his desk until all the numbers and graphs blurred together.

"Can I be straight with you, sport?" Mac asked when she returned to the office after another coffee break and found him on the exact same page of the growth strategy report he'd been reading when she'd left.

"When are you ever *not* straight, Mac?"

She planted herself on the arm of the leather chair across from his desk. "You look like a batter in the bottom of the ninth, the bases are loaded and your team is down by three runs. You're itching to get that grand slam so bad, you're liable to swing at anything the pitcher throws your way."

He folded his hands to keep from tapping his fingers impatiently, thereby proving the accuracy of Mac's assessment. "Is this the part of the baseball analogy where you tell me it's okay to strike out?"

"Nope. This is the part where I tell you that sometimes you gotta take the walk and just get yourself on first base. Don't be so desperate to be the hero that you end up blowing the whole game."

"That's the same advice you gave me when you coached my softball team in fifth grade, Mac," Daphne said as she breezily swung into his office holding a pizza box from the Brick Oven and two plastic containers filled with salads.

"This is unexpected," Jordan told his sister, his nose lifting at the delicious scent of garlic and tomato sauce. "Does Dad know you're here?"

"Do you think I would've made it past security if Dad knew I was here? Or if he knew I was smuggling in a couple of veggie antipasto salads into the sacred halls of beef?"

"You brought me lunch?" he asked.

"Mac said you haven't been eating as well since Camilla stopped inviting you over for Sunday dinners. I guess the Sanchez family didn't like that social media piece on their daughter."

"Now that Daphne is here to coach you," Mac said as she sprang up from her seat, pushing up the long sleeves under her all-stars jersey, "I'm gonna head down to that new sporting goods shop in Billings and spend my upcoming Christmas bonus."

"You don't need any more sporting gear," he called out to Mac's back as she headed down the hallway. Then Jordan turned to his sister. "And I don't need a coach."

"Maybe not." Daphne settled herself into the chair across from him and opened the white cardboard box, sending his nostrils and his growling stomach into overdrive. "But I might have a few pointers anyway."

Jordan snorted. "How many times have you been in love, little sis?"

"Does Tiny Tim count?" she asked before sinking her teeth into a slice of cheese pizza. Her mouth was still full when her eyes went round. "Wait. Are you saying that you actually *love* Camilla?"

"I think so." The heaviness in Jordan's chest suddenly disappeared. Like he'd been holding in a breath and could finally exhale. It was such a relief to say it out loud to someone. Unfortunately, the relief was short-lived. "But even if I confessed as much to her, she'd probably doubt it anyway. She wants us to let things cool down until we can figure out what we actually want. For some reason, she thinks I'm going to change my mind down the road and call things off."

"Why would she think that?" The sarcasm dripped from Daphne's voice.

"Who knows?" Jordan shook his head, choosing to ignore his sister's tone. "What she *should* be thinking is that I'm a nice guy who cares about her and loves being with her."

"Okay, but to be fair, you're also a guy whose dating history reads like those old-timey gold mine maps they used to sell at the general store, all speculation with so many twists and turns and absolutely no depth."

"Those gold mine maps were for the tourists who didn't know any better. Just like all those ghost stories about the supposed haunted history of Bronco. People will believe anything if it's sensationalized enough. The reality, though, is that there's no comparison because I've never dated anyone like Camilla."

"She's also probably never dated anyone like you. Or at least anyone with a father like yours. Of course she's going to be wary."

"Ours," Jordan corrected as he picked up another slice. It was plain cheese, unfortunately, with no extra toppings. But at least there were pesto twists and a salad for some variety. "It's not fair for either one of us to be responsible for our dad's behavior or his opinions."

"Listen, Jordan." Daphne passed him a napkin. "I know you don't like to be compared to Dad and I don't blame you. The guy is overbearing and snobbish and an all around pain in the neck. But he's also determined and driven and isn't afraid to go after what he wants. You inherited that from him, which is great when it comes to business. But it's not so great when it comes to the people you love."

"So you're saying I shouldn't go after Camilla?"

"No. I'm saying that if you really love her— not *want* her, but *love* her—then you should sit back and give her the space that she needs. If you don't, you'll wind up pushing her away."

"But if I could just—"

"Uh-uh." Daphne waved a pizza crust at him in warning.

"I'm just saying that I could prove—"

"No." His sister drew back her arm, a throwback to her softball pitching days.

"Then how do I show her—"

Instead of the crust, Daphne switched hands and sent a balled-up napkin flying at him, clipping his chin with sauce and grease before it fell on the pile of boring reports. "This isn't about you, Jordan. It's about her. When you read through all those comments under that picture of the two of you kissing, were any of them negative about you?"

He sat back in his chair, the pizza weighing heavily in his stomach as he thought about some of the rude things people had said about Camilla. "You're right. She bore the brunt of it. I think there were only a handful that implied I was thinking with my—"

Daphne launched a cherry tomato at him this time to cut him off. "That's still not an insult to *you*, Jordan. It might sound like it at first, but what they're really saying is that your attraction to her can only be related to sex because she has nothing else to offer you."

"But that's not true," he all but shouted at the ceiling for what felt like the millionth time. He rolled his neck to loosen up the coiled muscles in his shoulders. "Camilla Sanchez is one of the most amazing women I've ever met. She has more to offer me than I could ever offer her."

"Then be patient and wait for her to offer it."

Daphne left after they finished eating and Jordan found himself even more restless than he'd been before. He'd never been very good at just sitting back and being patient.

He got through another few hours of paperwork before deciding to let off some steam by going for a run. Mac, being a firm believer in taking breaks from work to exercise, always insisted he keep a supply of athletic clothes and sneakers in his executive washroom.

Normally, Jordan would have run along the hilly terrain toward his ranch, but since the sun was already going down, he took off toward the more populated area of Bronco Heights.

A massive pine tree had already been erected in the park in front of City Hall and festive lights were strung up all over town. Most of the local businesses had decorated their storefronts with a combination of garlands, wreaths and themed window displays. He passed several restaurants with signs out front telling customers to "reserve your holiday meals now."

One restaurant he didn't pass, though, was DJ's Deluxe. In fact, he crossed the street as he neared the renovated building because he didn't want to be tempted with the thought of looking in the windows to catch a glimpse of Camilla.

Even the popular Bronco Ghost Tours seemed to be getting into the holiday spirit with a sandwich board sign outside its office offering special "Yuletide" programs. He wasn't even sure what a yuletide was. Jordan had never really participated in any of the historical traditions involving Christmas, unless he counted Santa Claus. And really, Santa had only come to his house depending on the stepmother at the time. Or unless one of his uncles dressed up for a charity event.

Normally, his family focused on the business aspect of the holiday because that was when their biggest orders came in. The only tradition that stayed the same was the huge company party for the Taylor Beef employees where his father passed out hefty bonuses.

Jessica had ordered personalized stockings this year, though. Including one for Daphne, which their father hadn't yet taken down from the fireplace mantle. So maybe some things would be changing this December.

As usual, someone had driven their plow to town and pushed the most recently fallen snow into a small hill at one end of the park where neighborhood kids could bring out their sleds and safely race each other down the man-made slopes.

By this time of the evening, everyone was off work and out of school and families were out in full force with colorful knitted scarves and mittens, enjoying the wintertime activities while happy couples moved in and out of the brightly lit shops. It seemed as though the entire town was already preparing for the most wonderful time of the year.

Everyone except for him.

Jordan zigzagged down several residential

blocks, yet each time he turned onto another street, he found his way back toward the center of town. He tried to focus on the short bursts of condensation in the cold wintry air as his breathing came faster and harder. Unfortunately, all he could see were decorations and lights and sleds and the excitement of the season surrounding him.

On Thanksgiving, he'd actually envisioned himself spending Christmas with the Sanchez family, but that was probably out of the question. With Camilla freezing him out and his own family so fractured and dysfunctional right now, where would Jordan even spend the holiday this year?

Mac had always welcomed him with open arms and Daphne might want to host something out at Happy Hearts, so maybe he had options. But not the one he wanted.

After a few laps around the park, Jordan returned to the street and slowed as he passed the decorated displays in the store windows. He would have to get presents for his sister and his assistant, and whoever else he ended up spending the holiday with. When he got to the window display at Playworks, he paused to watch an electric train zoom around the toys inside.

A plush pink pig that looked almost identical to Tiny Tim caught his eye. It would be a perfect gift for Camilla if he wasn't trying to get her to take him seriously. He glanced over his shoulder at the jewelry store across the street. If he really wanted to cause a stir, he'd head over there and give everyone something to talk about. But he didn't want to make things worse for Camilla.

Returning his gaze to the window display of toys, his eyes landed on a porcelain doll in a red velvet dress, which reminded him that Erica Abernathy had just had a baby and he hadn't bought the child a gift yet. Perhaps it was a sign. Or at least an excuse.

Opening the shop door and stepping foot in such an establishment went against every one of Jordan's natural instincts. But then again, so did buying a woman a stuffed pig.

When Erica answered the door, Jordan immediately noticed the smudged circles under her eyes and the impossible-to-contain smile across her face. "Hey, Jordan! Did someone from human resources send more paperwork for me to fill out?"

When Erica had moved back to Bronco a couple of months ago, she'd needed a job. She'd come to see Jordan as a last resort and it had been easy enough to find her a position at Taylor Beef where she could start after the baby was born. In the meantime, she'd met and married Morgan Dalton and was now living at his house out on Dalton's Grange. The Daltons were relatively new to Bronco, but Jordan had been to their ranch before to check out some of their livestock.

He held up the pale yellow bag. "No, I brought a gift."

"But you already sent the wine basket when I was in the hospital. I couldn't drink it because my milk was already coming in, but the nurses all loved it."

Jordan winced at his mistake. Maybe he needed to come up with a get-well gift that was a little less one-size-fits-all. "This one is for the baby, though. Is she here?"

Erica put a shushing finger to her lips before standing to the side of the door to let him inside. "Come on in. Morgan is trying to get Josie back to sleep right now."

"Oh, I don't want to bother you guys. I just wanted to drop this off." He passed the bag to her.

"You're not bothering us at all." She walked toward the living room, leaving him to follow as she pulled tissue paper out of the bag.

"The sales clerk said that it's for toddlers," Jordan explained as he took a seat on the leather sofa opposite her stuffed rocking chair. "So you might have to wait another month or so to give it to her."

"Jordan, how old do you think a toddler is supposed to be?" Erica shook her head, yet kept smiling as she studied the box containing miniature horses and cows and action figures. "Oh, it's a My First Rodeo Set. That's pretty cute considering this is probably *your* first rodeo buying a baby gift."

Jordan cleared his throat. "The past month has been a bunch of firsts for me, actually."

"So I've read online."

"Speaking of Camilla…" He squirmed slightly in his seat. "Can I ask you a question?"

"Jordan, you were the only person in town willing to hire an eight-months-pregnant lady without any references from my previous employer. And you insisted I didn't have to start until after the baby arrived. I think you've earned the right to ask me anything you want."

"What was it like for you when we dated?" he asked, then saw the tilt of her head and quickly corrected himself. "I know that sounds kind of awkward since you're happily married and your husband is in the other room. But I'm asking from a data analysis standpoint."

"No, I know what you meant. I'm just trying to figure out how to say this in the most polite way possible."

"Don't sugarcoat it." He leaned forward, putting his forearms on his knees as though he was ready to take notes.

"Well, it was over ten years ago and we only went out a handful of times. I had just graduated high school and both of our families were putting all that pressure on us despite the fact that we both knew we weren't right for each other. But..."

"But?"

Erica studied him for a few seconds before saying, "But I remember thinking that it was very sad that you would never know when you found *the one* because you never really spent any time with a woman long enough to figure it out. You always seemed to be looking over your shoulder."

He jerked his head back. "Like I was afraid of something?"

"No, like you were looking for something better to come along."

He scratched at the back of his neck, as though he could scrub away the mistakes of his past. "It might've seemed that way. But it wasn't how I meant it."

"Jordan, you literally told me not to get attached to the first guy I met when I got to college. In fact, I believe your exact words were 'There'll always be someone else around the corner, kid.'"

Okay, so maybe that wasn't the best philosophy to instill in an impressionable teenager. But in his defense, he'd been young too, and determined not to make the same mistakes in love that his father had made.

"Well, it seems like you held out for the right guy." He jerked his thumb toward the framed wedding photo of her and Morgan.

"That's the thing, though. Morgan came into my life when I least expected it." Erica's eyes went from tired to sparkling. "When I was no longer looking around any corners, so to speak. See, it doesn't matter how many other women are out there waiting for you, Jordan, if you refuse to settle down long enough to give the right woman a fair shot."

"Okay, I might've been that way ten years ago. Or even ten weeks ago. But now I've actually found the one. My problem is that I haven't been able to convince her that I'm the one *for her*."

"And you're used to convincing people into anything," Erica replied, repeating what everyone else had already been saying about him.

"What is up with people always jumping to that conclusion about me?" Jordan asked.

"Sorry to interrupt, babe." Morgan came out of the hallway cradling a little bundle wrapped in blankets. "Josie wants nothing to do with her crib. I have a feeling she recognized the voice of the man who sprang into action when her mama went into labor and cleared all those partygoers out of the way like he was culling a herd of cattle."

"Here, I'll take her." Erica held out her arms for the baby, whose eyes were round and alert.

Jordan stood up to shake Morgan's hand. "Sorry for barging in like this. I wanted to drop off a gift."

Erica pulled a pink blanket off the ottoman beside her so Morgan could take a seat. "I was just about to tell Jordan that he can't convince Camilla he is the one for her. He's going to have to wait for her to come to that conclusion on her own." She turned back to face Jordan. "If it's meant to be, you guys will find your way back to each other."

"What do you think, Josie?" Jordan asked the baby girl in Erica's arms, who was staring at him with curiosity. "Do you think I should just give up on the woman I love?"

"No!" both Erica and Morgan said loudly in unison, causing the baby to pinch her tiny face into a startled expression.

"Sorry for sounding so adamant," Erica said, then murmured reassuringly until her daughter's face softened again. "It's just that we're witnessing firsthand what happens when someone gives up on the love of their life."

Jordan glanced between Erica and Morgan,

who by all appearances seemed to be completely smitten with each other.

"No, not us," Morgan clarified. "Erica's grandfather, Josiah."

"Oh, I heard he's out at Snowy Mountain Senior Care. Do they let them have girlfriends there?"

"No, Gramps was in love with a woman named Winona seventy-five years ago. We found his journal where he talked about how they had a baby girl named Beatrix, who was given up for adoption against his wishes."

"I think I heard about this." Jordan snapped his fingers. "One of the customers at Camilla's mom's beauty shop was talking about some missing baby. She mentioned the Abernathys being involved, but I didn't realize it was your grandfather."

"Probably because you never pay attention to social media. My brother, Gabe, his fiancée, Melanie, and I have launched a nationwide search for Beatrix, who might be going by the name Daisy now. Anyway, my point is that Gramps totally regretted giving up on Winona and losing track of her and their baby. Don't be like Gramps."

"Okay, but you just told me *not* to try and convince Camilla to be with me." Jordan scrubbed his hands over his face in exasperation. "If I'm not trying, then I pretty much *am* giving up."

Erica sighed as if it should be so obvious. "She doesn't need to be convinced to be with you. Camilla will figure that out all on her own as long as she knows that you're not going to take off running at the first opportunity."

"If I was in your boots, which I was not too long ago—" Morgan smirked at him before giving a pointed nod toward the ring on Erica's finger "—I'd make sure that the woman I loved knew I was committed to being with her for the long haul."

Erica turned to her husband and kissed him warmly, making Jordan miss Camilla all the more. Baby Josie also stirred in her mother's arms, as though trying to remind her parents they weren't the only two people in the room.

"Well, I should probably get going. I hope you guys find this missing relative. And I hope *you*," Jordan said as he pointed to the sweet little face peering at him from her nest of blankets, "enjoy your first rodeo set. But apparently not until you're a little bit older."

Josie made a cooing noise as Jordan stood up to leave, and the charming sound echoed in his ears as he drove away from the Dalton ranch. The momentary pang bouncing around his chest was unexpected and different from any of the other pangs of loneliness he'd been experiencing lately. This one wasn't because of the story of Josiah's lost love or even the threat of Jordan losing his own love if Camilla decided she didn't want him.

This pang was due to that adorable bundle in Erica's arms and that sweet cooing sound and the thought that Jordan might never have a baby of his own.

Whoa.

Where had that thought come from? He'd never so much as bought a baby gift, let alone been around an actual baby. In fact, he'd never given more than a passing thought to the idea of having children, yet suddenly he was envisioning all the babies he wanted to have.

With Camilla.

Slow down, he told himself, glancing in his rearview mirror as though the baby patrol was right behind him. Having kids was still a ways down the road. But just the thought of building a relationship with Camilla—building a real future with her—made him envision the life he hadn't known he wanted. Love, partnership and eventually a family.

Unfortunately, he still wasn't any closer to convincing Camilla of their future together.

Chapter Thirteen

Camilla officially finished her last shift at DJ's Deluxe on the first Friday in December. She'd purposely chosen one of the busiest nights of the week so that her coworkers wouldn't be able to make a big deal or throw her some sort of farewell party. But then DJ had talked her into working Saturday night selling hot cocoa and beef sliders at the food booth during the annual tree lighting ceremony in the park. Since everyone in the Sanchez family usually volunteered at the various booths during community events, and since people would have made even more suspicious assumptions about Camilla if she didn't attend, she'd grudgingly agreed.

But her heart wasn't in it. In fact, her heart wasn't into anything lately.

Just as she was clocking out for the final time, one of the bussers came into the office upstairs and said, "Hey, Camilla, there's a guy waiting for you in the bar."

Her heart fluttered inside her chest and she thought, *Finally*. She'd told Jordan to give her more time, but that hadn't stopped her from expecting him to show up at the restaurant like he had after they'd first met. The man didn't give up so easily no matter what anyone said.

This past week, Camilla should've been glad that he was following her wishes. However, as each shift had gone by and he hadn't so much as made a takeout order, she'd begun to think that maybe he'd already gotten over her more quickly than they'd both expected.

But now he was downstairs in the bar. A thrill of excitement shot through her, and she stopped by the employee break room to check her appearance in the mirror and maybe run a little bit of gloss over her lips. She shuddered when she saw her reflection, though. Her hair was in a lopsided bun, her shirt was a wrinkled mess, and her red-rimmed eyes suggested she hadn't slept in days. Overall, she looked about as miserable as she felt. Probably because she'd been burning the candle at both ends, trying to stay busy so she wouldn't have to think about Jordan.

She fixed her hair, then eagerly descended the steps to the main floor, taking a deep breath and preparing herself for what she would say when she finally saw him. Yet instead of seeing Jordan waiting for her at the bar, it was her father.

"Don't look so disappointed to see me, *mija*," Aaron Sanchez said as he spread open his arms.

Camilla was wound so tightly with so many different emotions, she fell into his embrace. As he wrapped her in a bear hug, she experienced all the warm comfort of her childhood right here in the bar of the busiest restaurant in town. When she finally pulled back, she explained, "I'm not disappointed, Dad. I was just expecting it to be someone else."

"Still haven't talked to that Taylor boy, eh?" Dad patted the bar stool beside him, then asked Leo the bartender to bring them both a glass of the Chateau Montelena. This must be serious if Dad was ordering one of the most expensive chardonnays in DJ's fine wine cellars.

"He called me last week, but to be fair, I *did* tell him I needed some space."

Her father nodded. "It's good that he's respecting your wishes."

"That's what Mom told me, too. Which is weird because I thought you guys liked Jordan."

"Oh, we like him just fine. But if you don't want him, then we're not going to try and talk you into being with a man just because *we* bonded with him."

Leo placed the two chilled glasses in front of them, and Camilla had to wait forever while her dad first sampled the wine, then nodded for the bartender pour it.

"How could you have bonded with him, Dad?" She took an unladylike gulp as soon as Leo left. "You barely even know him."

"Know him? *Mija*, I've sorted and shipped and delivered all the mail in this town for how many years now? You know who knows the most about the residents?"

"The mail carrier." She recited the answer ingrained in her since childhood, and was recently reminded of during Thanksgiving. All her life, her father let it be known to his family that he delivered the most personal information to people's houses every day.

"Exactly. I know who gets letters from the IRS and who gets those magazines that come in brown wrappers. I know who belongs to which political parties and who tries to reuse the same stamps over again because they need every cent."

"Is this where you tell me all of Jordan Taylor's secrets?"

"If he had any, yes." Dad clinked his glass against hers before taking another sip and swishing it around his mouth slowly, as if he was at a leisurely wine tasting event. Camilla could've finished an entire bottle in the amount of time it took him to finally continue. "Instead, this is where I tell you that I also know all the good stuff about him."

"Like what?" Camilla asked, a regular glutton for punishment. The man had likely given up on her by now, and learning about the one she let get away was bound to only depress her more.

"Like he gets personally addressed letters from countless charities—the kind you usually only receive if you make big donations. The humane society, Girls in Science, scholarships for local kids, as well as kids all over the world. You know, all the organizations ol' Cornelius doesn't give to because it doesn't involve a flashy gala where he is the center of attention."

"Don't knock the fancy galas, Dad. I've been to one and it actually raised an obscene amount of money."

Her father continued as though he didn't hear her. "Jordan also sends his former nanny a box of her favorite chocolates and a card every year, I assume for her birthday. And she sends him one in return. He has a pen pal through the Best Buddies program *and* the Wounded Warriors

Foundation, and their letters go out and come in like clockwork. Plus, it's no secret he mails off a check every month subsidizing the owner of those batting cages over by the Bronco Little League field so that competitive assistant of his is always guaranteed her favorite fast pitch machine. Should I go on?"

Camilla's shoulders sank lower with every example her dad relayed as proof of Jordan's upstanding character. "I know he is a good man, Dad. I mean, I knew he was willing to volunteer for all those local events with me. I guess I just didn't realize he'd been doing those kinds of good deeds all along."

"Probably because you were like everyone else and stayed blinded by what they wrote about him in the society pages and on social media."

"It's not that I didn't know he was capable of it. It's just that I also wasn't looking for reasons to fall in love with him any more than I already am."

"So you *are* in love with him." Her dad let out a deep breath. "Your mother said that might be the reason why you're pushing him away."

"Who says I'm pushing anyone away?" Camilla asked, knowing full well it was exactly what she was doing. She preferred thinking of it as giving Jordan time to figure out how he felt about her. But really, she knew she was just giving him the reason he probably needed to break things off and go his own way.

"Because you did the same thing when you were in high school and that geography teacher wanted everyone to do those reports about a country. You spent days working on that report about Mexico and then you gave a presentation in class about the culture and had to bring in a food item from that region. Remember we got those recipes from your *tio* Marco and you were supposed to bring all the ingredients to class and then show everyone how to make *birria*?"

"I thought I made quesadillas for that report." Camilla swallowed her feelings with another gulp of wine.

"You did. You took in grated cheese and those store-bought tortillas and melted it together in a pan when it was your turn to present. You were afraid that if you got up in front of the class and tried to make what you really wanted, you'd mess it up and everyone would say you weren't truly Mexican. And to be honest with you, there was probably no way you could've pulled off that recipe. At least not on Mr. Watanabe's portable stovetop and that microwave he borrowed from the science teacher."

She narrowed her eyes. "I seem to recall you being a little more supportive of that presentation back in high school."

Her father threw up his hands. "Of course I told you that you could do it, even though it took you at least five times practicing at home before you finally got it right. But you were so afraid of messing up, of being laughed at, that you gave up and went the easy route."

"Is there a point to this story other than reminding me about my hopeless cooking skills?"

He took a much bigger drink of his wine this time, as though his own patience were also coming to an end. "My point is that you should've made the *birria*. Even if it wasn't perfect, it still would've been more authentic than those quesadillas. Just like you should try and make things work with Jordan. Even if the relationship ends up being a disaster, at least it would be authentic because you're being true to yourself."

Camilla set her elbows on the polished bar top as she massaged her temples. "What if it's too late to make things work with Jordan?"

"Why would you think it's too late?" her dad asked.

"Because you and Mom were right and I probably did push him away. I was afraid that if I fell for him and he ended up leaving, it would hurt too much."

"What would hurt? Your heart or your reputation?"

Camilla drew in a ragged breath. "Both."

"Maybe. But you won't know unless you give it a shot." Her dad tucked his hand under her chin and lifted her face until she was staring at the unwavering love reflected in his eyes. "Plus the poor guy is so *crazy* about you that he and Felix actually lost last weekend's basketball game to Dante and Dylan. Your brothers have no intention of letting him live it down, either."

"Wait." Camilla sat up straighter on her bar stool. She'd purposely avoided going to her parents' house because she didn't want them asking questions about what was going on with him. Had she missed something? "Jordan came over for Sunday night dinner?"

"Not for dinner because he said he was trying to respect your space. But when Felix called him to see if he could still shoot some hoops, he couldn't get there quick enough. Mom was upset that you weren't there, by the way. You never miss family dinners so she's been worried about you. She tried to ask Jordan what was going on, but he kept pretty tight-lipped."

"Good," Camilla said, though something in her heart suddenly felt much lighter. If Jordan had gone to see her family a few days ago, then he hadn't really given up on her. "You guys are all too nosy and need to learn how to mind your own business."

"You kids *are* our business." He finished the

remainder of his wine, then pulled some cash out of his wallet and left it on the bar.

It was then that Camilla noticed the knee cart wheeled up against the other side of his stool. She looked down at the soft cast on his foot as he scooted forward, then she scanned the waiting area. "Dad, did you get the okay to drive out here?"

"No, your mom drove us. She sent me in here to talk to you since I'm the family referee."

Camilla followed her father out of the restaurant, pulling on her puffy down coat as they went toward the end of the street where the employees parked. "So if you've got referee duty tonight, then what is Mom doing?"

"She's running the scouting report." Her dad held open the car door for her. "Your mom overheard Sofia talking about meeting some new guy at the Brick Oven, so she's stationed over there to check him out. I'm going to meet her there."

Apparently, Cornelius Taylor wasn't the only over-protective parent in town. Just one more thing she and Jordan had in common.

"Are you and mom going to tell the others about this potential boyfriend?" Camilla sank into the driver's seat, her aching feet tingling with relief. "Or are you going to wait until Christmas dinner for everyone to find out like you guys did with Jordan?"

"We'll see if this new one lasts that long." Her father shut the door, then gave one last wave as he scooted away.

Camilla sat in her car as the heater came to life.

The shops and restaurants of Bronco were in full holiday mode with lights and decorations and even a dusting of snow along the sidewalk. December in Bronco was the most magical time of the year and an hour ago, Camilla hadn't exactly been feeling the holiday spirit.

But finding out that Jordan was still interested in her suddenly made everything shine brighter. It certainly made her heart feel lighter. She just needed to figure out a way to make things right with him.

Maybe she should remind him that, according to their original agreement, they still had one date left.

On the first Saturday of December, all the local merchants and craft vendors came together to sponsor the Bronco Tree Lighting Ceremony at the park in front of City Hall. It was one of Camilla's favorite traditions, and nobody in her family would even consider putting up their own decorations or buying so much as a stocking stuffer until the town tree was officially lit.

Camilla also knew it would be the perfect

place to talk to Jordan. She was the one who'd been so insistent on keeping their relationship private, so it was up to her to prove that she would be willing to finally take things public. And what better place to do that than at Bronco's most public event of the year?

Working in DJ's booth on the side serving hot cocoas, Camilla had a perfect view of the enormous tree and the stage erected in the town square. First the mayor would speak and introduce all the council members, and then various dignitaries and community leaders would all stand around patting each other on the back. This year, Dante's class was the winner of the annual Christmas carol contest and would be performing on stage right before the grand tree marshal (similar to a parade grand marshal) led the countdown before flipping the switch that turned on the lights.

The white folding chairs in front of the stage were usually reserved for town VIPs, so she easily spotted Jessica and Cornelius Taylor and a couple of gentlemen who were probably Jordan's uncles. She saw several people from the Abernathy clan with them, as well as Daniel DuBois, who was sitting with his wife, Brittany, and their ten-month old, Hailey.

Amanda Jenkins was in the crowd with her fiancé, Holt Dalton, and his parents and brothers. Holt's son Robby had actually been one of the first customers when the hot cocoa stand opened.

So many wealthy ranchers and notable townspeople were in attendance tonight, it was hard to keep track.

Camilla waved at Daphne in between orders and even caught a glimpse of Daphne's brother Brandon with a couple of his Taylor cousins.

The only Taylor she hadn't seen so far this evening was Jordan.

Maybe he knew she would be there working at the booth and he was still trying to give her space. Camilla's brain wanted to be happy that he was willing to do what she wanted, but her heart was in a flurry as she searched out every dark-haired man that passed by her booth.

However, her plan to talk to him soon lost traction as she realized he might not show. As the night wore on, the speeches were made, the carol was sung, the tree was lit, and everyone in the park let out a roaring cheer. And still no Jordan.

Camilla was vacillating between frustration and regret as she continued to pass out hot cocoa, one after the next, averting her eyes from the customers—many of whom were her neighbors and friends—until she heard a very familiar voice.

"Do you have any toppings to go with the hot cocoa?" Jordan's dimples flickered in the twinkling lights, but Camilla could also see the vulnerability written all over his face.

He was here. Standing in front of her. Making her pulse race with excitement. And all she could think to say was, "Um, we've got whipped cream and chocolate syrup. We might still have some marshmallows left."

"Great. I'll take all of them."

"Of course you will," she said, unable to contain the smile spreading across her face. "You're all about the extras."

"I'm here purely as a customer," he said, and her stomach dropped.

"Oh." She paused long enough to blink back the disappointment. Then she transferred the steamed milk into the to-go cup.

"I mean, I'm here to see you, obviously. But I know you're working. I was going to wait until later, but I started getting cold and thought you wouldn't mind serving me if I was at your booth for legitimate reasons. Anyway, I just wanted you to know that I'd like to talk to you when you're done, but I understand if you'd rather do it another time."

"Leo, can you take over for me?" Camilla asked her coworker manning the cash register.

Then she handed Jordan the cup and said, "I'll be right out."

Shuddering with excitement, she didn't bother with her purse, but managed to grab a scarf before meeting Jordan outside the booth.

"Hey," he said, almost tentatively. She hated that she'd been the one to make him doubt himself around her.

"Hi," she replied.

"Maybe we should go somewhere private and talk?" he asked.

"Actually, I was hoping to get a close-up view of the tree."

"But there are people around." He glanced sideways at her.

She took his hand and pulled him forward. "Jordan, there will always be people around."

His smile returned with its full force, and her knees reminded her that she hadn't grown immune to the flooding sensation of Jordan flashing those straight white teeth at her.

As they neared the stage area, which now featured a quintet of singers dressed in Victorian costumes and singing "O Come, All Ye Faithful," she asked, "So what did you want to talk to me about?"

He cleared his throat. "I'm not sorry that I mistook you for someone else at the Denim and Diamonds gala because it led me to go searching for who you really are. And I'm definitely not sorry that I talked you into letting me take you out on those dates. But I *am* sorry that I might've come on too strong at first and I'm sorry that my father can be a pain in the ass and I'm especially sorry that I put you in the position where people questioned who you were and why we were together." Jordan paused long enough to draw in a deep breath before soldiering on. "I can't change who I am. I'm always going to be a Taylor and gossip is always going to follow me. I know that dealing with all of that is a lot to ask of you and, believe me, I wouldn't ask if I wasn't one hundred percent sure that it wouldn't be worth it for you in the end. Because I love you, Camilla Sanchez, and you're the only woman I will ever want. So whether it takes six dates or six years or six decades, I will be here waiting to prove myself to you."

Jordan had just told her he loved her. Her heart felt as though it was lifting off in that private helicopter of his, soaring in the sky above the mountains and looking down at her and the view of this amazing man in front of her who had never backed away from a challenge. Camilla didn't think she could be any happier.

Still. She had her own plan of what she wanted to say to him and just because he was surprising her by pledging his love first didn't mean that she wasn't going to tell him exactly how she felt. After all, one of the major rules in a negotiation was to always be ready with a counteroffer.

"Five," she corrected him.

Jordan scrunched his brow in confusion.

"We agreed on six, but we've only had five dates," she clarified. "You still owe me one more."

"Well, if we're going by our original dating rules," he said as he held up the cup of warm milk she'd given him before even bothering to add the cocoa mix, "I'm going to need more of a substantial meal than this."

"Done," she said, taking the cup from his hand before tossing it in the nearby trash bin.

Then she planted her hands on the front of his jacket, pulled him closer to her and said, "Right after I get my kiss."

Chapter Fourteen

Camilla was kissing him. Right here in front of the entire town, and likely their cameras. And Jordan had never been more willing or determined to be a public spectacle in his whole life.

He wrapped his arms around her waist and slid his hands underneath the hem of her coat, relishing the taste of her mouth. It had been a little over a week but he'd already missed the feel of her in his arms.

When he pulled back, he smiled down at her upturned face. "That was a hello kiss, not a good-bye one, right?"

"It was more of an 'I'm sorry' kiss," she replied. "It was unfair of me to let my own fears get in the way of us trying to make this relationship work. I love you, Jordan, and I never should have held back on my feelings."

Her words hit him with a force and his knees nearly buckled as his chest expanded. "You love me?"

"Of course I do." She held his face in her palms, but she might as well have been holding his heart. "I usually pride myself on being so passionate and forthcoming and at ease when it comes to everything else in my life. The night I met you, I was all of those things because I didn't think I had anything to lose. But as soon as I started to feel something for you, I held myself back because I got scared."

"You had every right to be wary, though. I know my track record and I know my family." He jerked his chin to where Cornelius was standing with the mayor in front of the kettle corn booth hosted by the Future Farmers of America. Jordan's father didn't look too pleased by his son's very public display of affection, but the old man better get used to it. He turned back to Camilla. "I promised not to pressure you or push you into making any decisions. And even though you just openly admitted that you loved me in front of basically the whole town, I'll still give you as much time as you need. As long as you know that I'm not giving up."

"Even if it won't be easy?" Camilla asked. Her arms were still loosely draped around his shoulders, proving that she clearly wasn't willing to give up, either.

"Few things worth having are easy. I knew I loved you after our first week together and I'm not going to stop just because things get hard. You should know by now that when things get tough, I only dig my heels in deeper."

Camilla threw back her head to laugh, the musical sound making Jordan feel a million feet tall. "Well, my family is heading over this way, so you better be sure that this is what you want."

"What I really want is to spend this Christmas with you. And every Christmas after that. If that's what *you* want."

Camilla's lips quivered and she blinked several times. "Are you asking what I think you're asking?"

"Not if it will scare you off." Jordan held up his palms. "I'm not rushing you. I'm just saying that when you're ready, I'm ready." He reached into his pocket and pulled out a small box wrapped in gold foil paper and tied with a red Christmas bow. "You don't have to open it now. It could be a Valentine's gift, or a Fourth of July gift, or even a gift for Halloween fifty years from now. Just put it under your tree and open it whenever you're ready. Or whenever you need a reminder of the night we first met. But I'll give you a hint. It's not denim."

Camilla's eyes sparkled and she twisted her bottom lip between her teeth as she stared at the box in his outstretched hand. Finally, she lifted a corner of her mouth and asked, "What if I wanted to open my Christmas gift a little bit early?"

Camilla's fingers were practically shaking as she tore off the wrapping paper. Her eyes grew damp as she saw the familiar logo of Beaumont and Rossi's Fine Jewels on the lid. Before she knew it, Jordan took the velvet box from her trembling hand and dropped down to one knee. Camilla's stomach dropped as well when she saw the sparkling diamond ring blink up at her.

Then his words made everything else drop.

"Your smile is the first thing I want to see every morning and the last thing I want to see before I fall asleep every night. You have opened my eyes to a whole new world and a whole new way of living life, and I love the person that I've become when I'm with you. You are the most incredible and refreshing and smart and authentic woman I have ever met. Camilla Sanchez, I would be honored if you chose to make me the crown prince of your heart."

Joy radiated like a spiral from the tips of Camilla's toes all the way to her cheeks, which couldn't stretch any more to contain her grin. She heard the clicking shutters of several nearby cameras, but for the first time, she truly didn't care what anyone thought.

Nodding eagerly, she pulled the leather glove off her hand so that Jordan could slide the ring over her finger. When he stood up, he lifted her with him and swung her around as his mouth claimed hers, her body now as weightless as her floating heart.

Several cheers and a few claps on her back caused them to finally break the kiss. Jordan set her back on her feet so they could meet the crowd of people who'd circled around them.

"Congratulations, *mija*!" Her mom wrapped her in a hug. Then her parents switched out and, as her dad hugged her, Denise embraced Jordan. "Welcome to the family. Officially."

"I told you she'd come around," her father said as he shook Jordan's hand.

"Did you know about this?" she asked her parents.

"Of course they did," Sofia said before congratulating them. "When Jordan came to get their blessing, I insisted on going with him to the jewelers. After all, I picked out the dress that caused him to fall in love with you. It was only right that I help him pick out the ring." Sofia lowered her voice before whispering in Camilla's ear. "I also made sure it cost a fortune so that all the gossips couldn't miss it on those social media posts."

The sound of a throat clearing rather dramatically caused the normally exuberant Sanchez family members to go suddenly quiet. However, even the disapproving expression on Cornelius Taylor's face couldn't dampen her mood.

"Hey, Dad, you remember Camilla?" Jordan lifted her hand in his so that the engagement ring reflected in the lights of the giant Christmas tree, as well as in the calculated gleam of Cornelius Taylor's eyes. "This is her family."

"Is that so?" his father asked through his clenched jaw.

"Oh, Cornelius and I go way back." Aaron Sanchez reached out his hand first. A camera flashed, causing the senior Taylor to revert into his public persona mode and at least pretend to politely return the handshake. Camilla's dad used the opportunity to pull Cornelius in closer as he lowered his voice. "I'm the mail carrier who knows about all those letters that come back to you marked Return to Sender."

Camilla's ears perked up at that revelation, but Cornelius pasted that phony smile on his face just before another camera shutter clicked.

He spoke through his gritted teeth as he said, "Jordan, I hope you know what you're doing."

"Dad, I've spent all of my life proving to you that I know exactly what I'm doing. Now, you can either add another offspring to your ever-growing list of children who refuse to speak to you or you can finally swallow your pride, congratulate me and welcome my charming fiancée to our family."

Camilla's chest flooded with pride as Jordan placed a protective arm around her shoulders.

This time when Cornelius cleared his throat, it wasn't so much for attention as it was to help him force out the words. "Congratulations, son. Miss Sanchez, I'm sure that you will make a very lovely bride."

It wasn't a hearty welcome to the family such as the one Jordan had received from the Sanchezes, but at least the older man hadn't said anything about prenuptial agreements. Yet.

"Thank you, sir." Camilla smiled with as much grace as she could muster. She used a little less grace when she purposely lifted her left hand to waggle her fingers in a wave at Jordan's stepmother as she approached the group. "Hey, Jessica."

"Is that from Beaumont and Rossi?" Jessica gave an excited little clap. "Let me see."

This brought another round of oohs and ahhs

from several women who gathered around. When one of the city council members came over to see what was going on, Cornelius puffed out his chest and spoke as though he were on the stage behind them. "Obviously, we'll have the reception out at the ranch. We'll use Brittany Brandt Dubois again for the wedding planning since she did such a great job with the gala—"

"Dad." Jordan held up his palm like a stop sign. "Just a word of warning in case you haven't already noticed. Camilla prefers to make her own decisions and you probably shouldn't try to force her into—"

"I'd be honored to have the reception at the ranch," Camilla interrupted. "After all, that's where Jordan and I first met. As long as you don't have a problem with my new restaurant catering the event."

Cornelius raised a slick silver eyebrow, and for the first time ever, Camilla saw the hint of an authentic smirk that was very similar to Jordan's. "Will this new restaurant of yours be using Taylor Beef exclusively?"

"If we can negotiate a fair price, I will be," Camilla challenged, and Jordan laughed.

"Mr. Taylor, I'm Denise Sanchez, Camilla's mother." Mom suddenly linked her arm through Cornelius's, making him do a double take at the petite mahogany-haired woman who'd suddenly appeared. "I'm noticing that your hair is in desperate need of some updating. Come into my salon next week and I'll give you the family discount."

"That would be great," Jessica interjected quickly, for once oblivious to her husband's sudden frown. She looped her arm through Cornelius's free one and, along with Camilla's mom, steered him away, saying, "I've been trying to get him to change it up a bit."

Camilla stifled a giggle, and Jordan's eyes shone with amazement. "See? A little change is exactly what my family needed."

She snuggled in closer under his arm. "And you, Jordan Taylor, are exactly what I need."

Instead of having him to herself, though, Camilla got her first experience of what it would be like as the wife of one of the most powerful and well-known businessmen in town. She could barely remember half of the names of the people who introduced themselves and offered their congratulations.

The one person, though, who didn't make their way over to wish them well was Jordan's sister, Daphne.

After shaking hands and being slapped on the back by almost everyone in town, Jordan finally turned to Camilla and asked, "Do you think the hot cocoa booth is closed yet? I never got all my toppings."

"Come on." His new fiancée's smile lit up brighter than the Christmas tree in the middle of the park. "I'll buy you one."

As they were arguing over who would pay for his drink, Daphne walked up to them. "Hey, guys, I heard the news, but didn't want to come over while Dad was around and risk causing a scene."

"You guys still haven't talked, huh?" he asked his sister, whose smile didn't quite meet her eyes.

"Nope. But don't worry about it. Tonight is all about you guys. I'm so happy my big brother is finally settling down with a woman who will keep him in check." There was a hint of sadness in her eyes before her gaze shifted to the snow flurries coming from the sky. Daphne shivered. "Anyway, you guys are very lucky to have found each other. Not everyone gets that."

"Don't worry, sis. I'm sure you'll meet some-one special soon."

"I don't know if you've noticed, Jordan, but most of the ranchers around here aren't going to fall for the vegetarian of the notorious Tay-lor family. It doesn't matter, though." Daphne shrugged, her tone practically resigned. "I've got my animals and they've got me. Speaking of which, I have to go home for the evening feed-ings. Congratulations, guys."

They both gave Daphne a hug. After she left, Jordan was about to ask Camilla if she thought his sister seemed a little off, but he didn't get the chance because they were next in line.

"Have you told him the big secret?" Mac asked Camilla before handing Jordan a hot cocoa with all the toppings. Apparently, there were now two women in this world who knew what he wanted before he even asked.

"What big secret?" he asked cautiously. "And why are you working at the DJ's Deluxe booth, Mac?"

"I wanted to get some experience in the food industry before our grand opening," his assistant said.

Jordan took too big of a gulp and scalded his tongue. He hissed as his mouth drew in a few pants of cold air. "What grand opening?"

Camilla squeezed his hand. "Mac is my silent partner."

"What?" Jordan looked between the two women, unsure if he could handle any more surprises today. "When did this happen?"

"When I ran into Camilla over at the U of Montana. One of my players is being scouted by a club team over there and we got to talking about the college campus. You know," Mac said as she leaned against the table, ignoring the line of people behind them, "if U of M woulda had a softball team back in my day, I'd have gone to a real school instead of Miss Grossmont's Academy of Secretarial Arts in Missoula."

Jordan scratched his head. "I'm still waiting for the part where you tell me how you became Camilla's silent partner."

Mac straightened to her full height of five feet. "I may have started out as a secretary with a pretty face, sport, but I've learned a little bit about how businesses work while I've been with Taylor Beef. Got a bonus every year, including those years during the recession when Cornelius the Second had to make massive cuts. He gave me stock in the company and it turns out I'm pretty good at knowing a great investment when I see it."

"Well, Camilla is certainly the best investment around." Jordan smiled at his new fiancée. Man, he wouldn't get tired of calling her that. Actually, he couldn't wait to start calling her his wife.

"My assistant dean asked me to come speak in one of her intro classes the week after you and I were there. When Mac saw me on campus with my Integrated Project proposal, she seemed really interested. I told her how I'd gone to the Denim and Diamonds gala hoping to meet a few potential investors. She suggested that was a waste of my time."

"Not a complete waste, I hope." Jordan smirked. "After all, that's where you met me."

Mac chuckled. "I believe my exact words were, why go after prince charming when everyone knows it's the fairy godmothers who get things done?"

Jordan leaned over the counter to wrap the older woman in a tight hug. "Mac, I should've known. I couldn't imagine a better fairy godmother than you."

The older woman wiped something from below her eye before she straightened her ball cap. "Speaking of getting things done, sport, you need to move along and let me go back to work before this hot cocoa line gets out of control."

Jordan grabbed his drink off the table, winked at a clearly flustered Mac, then threw his arm across Camilla's shoulders as they walked along the park.

"So, you don't mind that Mac and I will be working together?" Camilla asked as she looked up at him, her knit cap causing her brown hair to burst out in a riot of curls around her face.

"Are you kidding? Mac is barely in the office as it is. It'll be good for her to have a whole other reason to sneak out of work for something that isn't baseball related."

"Well, she'll still be getting her sports fix.

One of her conditions was that I agree to have big-screen TVs in the bar area."

Jordan slapped his hand to his forehead right as Camilla leaned into him, throwing them both off balance. He recovered quickly, but not before he bumped into a man staring down at his smart phone.

"Sorry about that," he told the man, but the guy seemed to be lost in whatever he was reading on his screen.

As they continued through the park, more people offered their congratulations. Every time Camilla smiled or waved at someone, Jordan's heart stretched and his chest filled with pride. When she paused in front of the giant Christmas tree to stare at the bright star on top, he stood behind her, wrapping his arms around her waist and drawing her against him. She sighed and leaned the back of her head against his shoulder.

He kissed her temple. "It's only the beginning of December, and so far this Christmas is promising to be the best one yet."

She turned in his arms. "But I haven't even given you your gift yet."

"You said yes," he told her. "That's the only gift I need."

Epilogue

Desperately Seeking Daisy

Desperately seeking a woman named Daisy who was born in 1945 to teenage parents and placed for adoption somewhere in Montana. Your birth family would like to meet you! Please contact the Abernathy family at the Ambling A Ranch, Bronco Heights, Montana. Time is of the essence!

The man's eyes widened as he read the social media notice on his phone.

He looked around, as if to make sure no one

had seen his reaction to the post. The couple who'd bumped into him a few seconds ago only had eyes for each other. Most of the other revelers were either in lines for food or still gathered around the newly lit Christmas tree in front of Bronco City Hall. Between all the noise from the carolers singing up on the stage and the kids racing by to take their sleds to the plowed slope behind his vendor booth, the man was surrounded by yuletide overload.

Bah humbug! he thought. There was no way he would've attended the small town's annual event if his local business didn't require it.

He certainly wouldn't have been scrolling through his phone if he wasn't completely bored by all the festivities. Which meant he never would have seen the online notice. It probably was just a coincidence.

There was no reason for him to worry. No sense in stirring up trouble.

* * * * *

MILLS & BOON

Coming next month

AWAKENING HIS SHY CINDERELLA
Sophie Pembroke

"Trust me," Damon said, with feeling, "it's drawing exactly the right amount of attention to your figure. You look incredible." And he really had to stop looking at his big sister's best friend that way. Not least because she'd never given him even the slightest hint that she wanted him to.

There was that one night, his brain reminded him. That one night when you could have kissed her, if you'd wanted to.

But he hadn't. Because she was Celeste's best friend. Because she wasn't the sort of girl you messed around with, and he hadn't known how to do anything else.

Because she'd seen deeper than he liked, and it had scared him.

Her smile turned shy and she went back to studying the creatures on her dress, thankfully oblivious to his thoughts. "It is like my windows, isn't it?"

Somewhere someone clapped their hands again, and bellowed for them to take their places.

"Come on. We're starting." Damon took her arm and led her towards the bar. He needed another drink, and she hadn't even had one yet. "Let's grab a glass of something bubbly, and you can tell me more about your windows and your work until it's time to shout out the countdown, or whatever we need to do."

"You really want to know more about the windows?" She sounded astonished at the prospect.

"As it happens, I really, really do." And not just because of the way she lit up when she spoke about the things that mattered to her. Or because it would give him a chance to listen to her melodious voice. Those things weren't important to him. Or shouldn't be, anyway.

No, he wanted to know more because he had the inklings of an idea that could help both of them get what they needed in life. If he could persuade her to take a chance on him.

It was just business. That was all.

He just needed to keep reminding himself of that.

Continue reading
AWAKENING HIS SHY CINDERELLA
Sophie Pembroke

Available next month
www.millsandboon.co.uk

COMING SOON!

We really hope you enjoyed reading this book.
If you're looking for more romance, be sure to
head to the shops when new books are
available on

Thursday 12th November

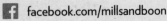

JOIN US ON SOCIAL MEDIA!

Stay up to date with our latest releases, author
news and gossip, special offers and discounts, and
all the behind-the-scenes action
from Mills & Boon...

 millsandboon

 millsandboonuk

 millsandboon

It might just be true love...

  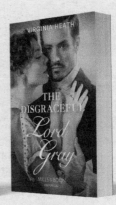

MILLS & BOON
MEDICAL
Pulse-Racing Passion

Set your pulse racing with dedicated, delectable doctors in the high-pressure world of medicine, where emotions run high and passion, comfort and love are the best medicine.